The Prison of Perspective

RUDOLPH BADER was born in Zurich, Switzerland, in 1948. At university he read English and German literatures and linguistics as well as Islamic studies and near eastern languages. He has lived and worked as a researcher and university professor in many countries including Germany, Switzerland, Canada and Australia. Under his German name he published widely in the field of postcolonial literatures, he translated Shakespeare, worked as a book reviewer and a theatre director, and he has always been very active in teacher training and in various intercultural projects.

The Prison of Perspective is Rudolph Bader's first novel. He is already busy writing his second novel. Today, he lives in Sussex and in Switzerland.

Praise for

The Prison of Perspective

The story moves effortlessly from character to character, place to place and past to present. A well-chosen selection of historical events relates the protagonists' careers to what happened in the world from the 1950s to our current decade.

With ease the novel radiates an in-depth awareness of the modern lifestyle as it has developed during the last few decades.

PROFESSOR DR NORBERT PLATZ
UNIVERSITY OF TRIER

An incisive first novel rich in incident whose constant twists of plot and skilful shifts of perspective require – and reward – a second reading.

The intricately woven plot, the shifting perspectives of the characters and the unpredictable impact of violent events and emotional involvement make this original novel a challenge and a pleasure to read.

PROFESSOR DR GEOFFREY V DAVIS
CHAIR – ASSOCIATION FOR COMMONWEALTH
LITERATURE AND LANGUAGE STUDIES
CO-EDITOR – CROSS/CULTURES: READINGS IN THE
POST/COLONIAL LITERATURES IN ENGLISH

Published in paperback by SilverWood Books 2010

www.silverwoodbooks.co.uk

ISBN 978-1-906236-20-5

British Library Cataloguing in Publication Data
A CIP catalogue record for this book is available from the British Library

Set in Stempel Garamond by SilverWood Books
Printed in England on FSC paper by The Cromwell Press Group

RUDOLPH BADER

The Prison of Perspective

SilverWood

PART ONE

Ivan

ONE

As he is driving past this tall church in South London he sees a group of three veiled women walking in the opposite direction. Their black robes blow lightly in the wind, creating an impression of three limping blackbirds. "How odd," he thinks, "two world religions in such proximity." But immediately he checks himself. One must not think such things. And yet, his mind cannot abandon the thought of two interpretations of the world confronting each other and causing so much uncertainty. So many people would welcome less confrontation and more harmony, more mutual understanding, especially here in London. But then, would they?

He is on his way to East Grinstead, a small town some twenty miles south of London. He has to meet a business partner from Korea who is staying at the Old Felbridge Hotel. His driving style is brisk. His black Audi with its snarling radiator grille and tinted windows gives him priority in the heavy traffic due to its aggressive appearance, an aspect that has never occurred to him but is obvious to other motorists, to cyclists and pedestrians. To him it is part of the order of nature that he manages to edge forward more swiftly than most of the other cars around him. He accepts the fact that he always leaves half a dozen cars behind him between two sets of traffic-lights as a matter of course. Embedded in the red leather interior he lives in a world with its own rules. He only allows certain carefully filtered impressions from the outside world to enter this sphere of peaceful certainty inside his car, like the shutter mechanism of an ancient box-camera opening for fractions of a second and allowing a view of the world to enter and to be frozen for eternity.

His name is Ivan MacGregor. He is forty-nine years old and he has a good job. Financially and professionally he has no worries, at least he is not aware of any problems or dangers. His nature is generally more exploitative than altruistic. He knows he is brilliant, and he believes that others must see him in the same light. He sees himself as a dynamic man who moves with the flow of his times. If there are any things that sometimes cause him to stop and worry they seem of minor importance, such as his name, which he never really liked. There is simply no discernible Scottish connection in spite of his family name. It must have been several generations back that his ancestors came down from Scotland.

Equally absurd and unconnected is his Russian first name. He cannot understand how his parents could have chosen such an unsuitable name. He believes it was his mother's idea, some silly protest at the height of the Cold War. According to his father, she was an idealist who honestly believed that the Soviet system had found a nearly perfect way of distributing wealth equally among its people. In the wake of the Cuba Crisis in the early sixties, however, a journalist friend of hers – how close they were Ivan never learnt – took her along on his trip of political conversion, which involved weekend stays in the New Forest. One day they just did not come back from the New Forest and their bodies were found in the oily waters of Lymington harbour a few days later.

His father never explained the details surrounding his mother's death, and Ivan never asked. Ivan always meant to take it up with his father when the mood was right...but the mood never was right. His father died taking the secret to his grave, and all that was left to Ivan of his mother was his Russian name. Over the years he has grown accustomed to it, but he has never learnt to like it. Sometimes he hesitates when he has to introduce himself in more informal settings; he feels he is some fake person using such a name, so he lets that fraction of a second elapse before admitting to his own name.

Abruptly he slams on the brake. "Can't that stupid idiot see where he's going?"

As he sees it, the world is not a very complex matter at all. He thinks he understands all its aspects quite naturally. He is not particularly impressed by people who make a big fuss about everything. Why make problems where there are no problems? Although he never admits it to himself, he is really convinced of his own personal superiority. He knows he is a winner. So far, his happiness has never been disturbed by failures or major worries. If things threaten to turn into unpleasant anxieties there is always the simple solution of alcohol. Always in moderation, though. But why worry about things when life can be so carefree? The only real danger, he is convinced, comes from women.

He adores women, their beauty, their sing-song voices, their whole aura. He has had his share of female companionship through the past two decades. Affairs, friendships, flirtations. But he has never allowed any of the women to get too close, to disturb his peace of mind. He has always kept a certain healthy distance. Well, yes, women can become a nuisance, a real bore, especially when they want to take possession of a man. He has never allowed that to happen. The greatest danger for a man, he believes, is to lose his head over a beautiful female body. Being intimate with a woman, kissing her, stroking her smooth skin and taking in her scent can carry a man off into an alien realm of stupidity.

There was a woman who nearly got him there. That was many years ago. He can still remember the intoxicating scent of her fine skin after more than twenty years. He wonders what has become of her. Is she still alive? He forces himself to dismiss the memory from his mind. After all, it was only one night. Better to forget it. He has to dismiss such thoughts if he doesn't want his driving style to become more aggressive.

He concentrates on the traffic. As he checks the mirror for the cars behind he shifts in his seat and catches a glimpse of his own face in the mirror. His slick dark hair, the golden rim of his stylish glasses. He lifts his right hand, strokes his hair, his well-shaved cheek and his firm chin. He is perfectly satisfied with his good looks. He knows that most women would call him handsome.

Traffic is getting thicker. Again and again Ivan has to let other cars squeeze into his lane right in front of him. Twice between Norbury and Croydon he has to slam on his brakes at traffic-lights, not daring to rush ahead with the amber on the verge of changing over to red. He is not quite sure about all the police enforcement cameras along this stretch although he uses it at least two or three times a month.

Waiting at the second of these traffic-lights he presses the button on the radio and Classic FM immediately envelops him with Tchaikovsky's string serenade. It is the third movement, the Elegy, a typical evergreen with Classic FM, and the effect of the music on Ivan is overwhelming. "Not that," he says and sweeps the back of his right hand across his forehead.

The music carries him off in his mind, and he drives the next few miles without realising what he is doing or where he is going. The fact that he neither loses his way nor causes an accident proves that he knows this stretch of road quite well in spite of his relative ignorance about the positions of police cameras. For Ivan, this piece of music is inexorably connected with sexual pleasure, and still now – after how many years? Twenty-five or more? – he finds it difficult to suppress a hardening of his sexual organ, at this moment rather an uncomfortable effect since he likes to have the steering-wheel in the lowest possible position. He has not had this experience for years, and he is surprised at this sudden onslaught of memory triggered off by Tchaikovsky.

* * *

His company had sent him to Australia for a few months, more than twenty-five years ago. He was a promising young man, full of optimism and extremely self-centred. Unmarried, with no close family ties in those days, he did not really mind where in the world his suave career, of which he was as certain as one can be of anything, was going to take him, in purely geographical terms. He was based in the company's Australian headquarters in North Sydney. He had been there for over two months when one of his business friends, a real Aussie with broad drawling diphthongs and low-keyed sing-song invited him to spend a week's holiday at his beach house on Bribie Island, just north of Brisbane. Ivan could easily get two weeks off, so he thought he could accept the invitation and get to know the leisurely life in the Great Australian Outdoors – with bronze bodies flexing their muscles on the beach, the famous life-savers, the thundering surf of the Pacific and, who knew, perhaps some hot Aussie girls.

Arrangements were made in the easy-going Australian way, with Ivan deciding to hire a car and drive up the Pacific Highway to see something of the landscape and then take the plane back. Time between their arrangement and the actual date flew, and before he knew it he faced the thousand kilometre drive from Sydney to Brisbane and beyond.

The landscape for the first two hundred kilometres was Mediterranean-like, full of forests, small lakes and hidden inlets. Conifer forests of the type that suggested a predominantly hot climate. To his disappointment, however, the Pacific could never be seen, just guessed in the distance from time to time. His rented Holden Commodore – dark-yellow with black velour seats and good air-conditioning – pulled along with a satisfying purring sound coming from its smooth six-cylinder engine. North of Newcastle the landscape became dull; the Pacific Highway just a narrow two-lane road full of bends like some secondary country road in the English Peak District, not at all the grand American-style highway Ivan had expected. So by the time he reached Nambucca Heads, the legendary half-way post between Sydney and Brisbane, he was not only tired from the long drive but also dazed by the vacancy in his visual mind caused by the utter boredom of the landscape he had travelled through.

Nambucca Heads probably owed its existence to its position exactly between the two state capitals, a position which guaranteed its array of hotels a steady influx of overnight guests. Ivan did not see the town itself, if there was a town at all, he was content with the row of hotels just off the Pacific Highway. He chose a large hotel that boasted a restaurant as well. It was half brick, half timber and sported those quaint frilly curtains behind its fake-homely windows, reminding him of a chalet in Bavaria or Austria. He checked in and booked a room for the night. He threw his overnight-bag on the bed, took a shower and went down to the restaurant intending to make this an early night. He asked the waitress if he could sit opposite the counter with its old-fashioned copper-coloured cash-register, near the front door. In this position he would be in no danger of being talked to and dragged into a one-sided conversation by a talkative Australian travelling businessman with an overdose of XXXX or Foster's inside him, an experience he knew all too well and for which he just wasn't in the mood. Also, the proximity of the door would make an early retirement easy. Though, on second thought, who should mind whether he went to bed early or not?

His steak was as he had expected: the meat of excellent quality but burnt to a sad shadow of its potential by the Aussie chef. All in all, however, it was a decent meal, considering the relative wilderness he believed himself to be in. He was lost in thought, chewing on his last rubbery bit of steak, when a young woman stormed into the room, posted herself in front of the counter opposite and demanded to see the manager. The cocky expression of the middle-aged man behind the counter turned into a slight sneer, and the woman had to repeat her request twice before the man complied with it, grumbling something under his breath that sounded like an outlandish swearword. While he was invisible somewhere in the back-rooms of the place, the young woman tapped her right foot on the floor and slowly turned round, obviously inviting the rest of the universe to sympathize with her complaint. Her glance swept over the heads of the numerous diners in the restaurant seeking some eye-contact for sympathy. Having just cleared his plate of the last morsel, Ivan happened to look up just at the moment her glance fell in his direction. He felt like a small fishing-trawler on its quiet way back to the safety of the harbour suddenly caught in the bright glare of a lighthouse beam sweeping by.

She took a step in his direction, gesturing towards the door through which the sneering man had disappeared. "You'd think a hotel of this category should be interested in complaints like that, wouldn't you?"

Ivan felt at a loss. "Well, yes."

She shook her head and turned her eyes up towards the ceiling. "I should have taken my friend Paula's advice. She warned me. They can get away with anything in this place, since it's the obvious overnight-stop."

Ivan thought that was the end of their short conversation, but she took another step in his direction. She said something about more advice she had received from her friend about travelling the Pacific Highway, but he was not really listening. It was just words, words, words, and he was getting tired. Instead of listening to what she was saying he began to study her face. He was struck by the gripping beauty of her face, in particular her brown eyes.

Just then the sneering man came back with the manageress of the place. The young woman turned to the counter and began the story of her complaint. Ivan caught something about two huge cockroaches in the bathtub, but the rest of the altercation between the two women was lost to him. He was beginning to plan the itinerary for the following day, and he had just unfolded the primitive roadmap on the table when the young woman approached again.

"Well, it was nice talking to you." She had obviously completed her business and was about to leave.

"Why don't you sit down and have a drink with me?" The words slipped out, surprising him. "You know, just a night-cap."

He was intrigued when the woman accepted immediately. Why didn't she hesitate or find some excuse, as most women would have done in this situation?

"The name's Cathy," she said with a quick smile, and sat down on his right. "Yes, I think I deserve a good drink now."

This was the beginning of a conversation which became very lively, despite his former fatigue, and which also became more and more exciting as it developed into the night. She told him she was a visiting student on a special travelling scholarship, and she was affiliated with the University of Queensland. She was fascinated by the colourful beauty of the campus at St. Lucia. Even though Ivan found it hard to imagine colourful natural beauty after driving from Sydney to Nambucca Heads he believed her, she was so convincing in every way, particularly when he looked into the dark brown of her eyes. Ivan felt drawn to her, and before another hour had elapsed he thought her the most fascinating woman he had ever known. He was intoxicated. And when the time came to retire for the night it was the most natural thing for him to follow her to her room.

Cathy switched on the bedside lamps and busied herself with a small cassette tape-recorder she had obviously brought along because, as she had already told him down in the restaurant, she thought she could not live without music. This statement had seemed a little exaggerated to him, but he had accepted it for what it was: an admission of a great love for music. The little machine click-clacked with a cheap plastic resonance when she inserted a cassette. She disappeared in the bathroom – checking on the cockroaches, as she said – while he drew in the first bars of a piece of music that was so unbelievably beautiful that he just sat down on the bedside and let the harmonies carry him off, along with the sweet presentiment of physical pleasures to come. He didn't know how long he had been lost to the music when Cathy came back from the bathroom and her beauty became one with the beauty of the music.

"What's this piece of music?" he asked with a hoarse voice, regretting his banal question immediately because it clashed with the magic of the moment.

"That's one of my favourites, Tchaikovsky's string serenade." Her voice exonerated him from his blunder, and the magic of the moment was restored as if it was the most natural thing in the world.

It was seven o'clock in the morning, the sun was sending its first rays through the frilly lace curtains, everything was still quiet in the hotel. Ivan woke up with an extremely good feeling about the world at large, about the freshness of the new day, about his own body – especially about his own body – and about the smell of Cathy's naked skin. She was lying next to him, still asleep, breathing quietly and with a peaceful rhythm. He lay still for another half-hour merely enjoying the bliss of the moment and the cosy warmth of a truly satisfied awakening. What an extraordinary woman she was. And what extraordinarily good luck for him to have run across her, here, in the middle of nowhere, amidst all this Australian ugliness…

Cathy stirred. Ivan shifted closer to her. A small moan came from her. He stroked her hair and kissed the nape of her neck. Immediately he was caught again by an overwhelming desire.

When, later, he looked at his watch on the bedside table he saw that another hour had elapsed. Cathy cleared her throat and said good morning with a mock-sing-song voice. He looked into her eyes, and she smiled.

"Do you sometimes think of things you don't want to think about?" she asked while she pulled the bed-sheet over the lower part of her body with one hand.

Her gesture drew attention to the physical proximity of her nakedness, and he couldn't help looking with great satisfaction at the smoothness of her pale skin, the unbelievable softness of her breasts, the tender pink circles of her large nipples lying very flat now.

"What do you mean?" he managed to ask, tearing his eyes away from her body and looking into her smiling face again.

"It's when you are made to think, not when you want to think."

"You mean now, for example? No need to think, just enjoy the beauty of the moment?"

"Yes, perhaps. But I mean more than this. Sometimes you want to think beautiful thoughts and your mind is constantly pushed into ugly thoughts." She pulled a wisp of dark-brown hair from her forehead and then stretched her arm up into the air.

"Are you thinking ugly things now?" he asked.

"Well, it just occurred to me, you know."

But he wanted to know for sure. "What were you thinking just now when you first asked?"

"I thought of what my brother would be doing now if he was still alive."

"You had a brother who died?" His concern for her possible grief overshadowed his initial disappointment over her negative thoughts in a moment of perfect sexual bliss with him.

"Over three years ago," she said. "He died in an accident."

"Do you want to talk about it?"

"I don't know."

"Was it a car accident?"

"No, he was a pilot. He crashed with another plane in mid-air somewhere over the hills. The investigations proved it was his fault. We all felt awful towards the family of the other pilot. We saw them at the inquest…they even came to my brother's funeral."

"Do you often think of him?"

"Yes. Even though it's over three years I still can't believe he's dead. He's no longer there. He just doesn't exist any more. Sometimes when I see something that I know would interest him my first impulse is, oh I must tell Stephen, and only then it occurs to me I can't because he's dead."

Ivan felt he could not enter this compartment of Cathy's life, but he held her hand as she talked. They went on talking about her brother for a while, then they decided to get up and see if the hotel could manage a decent breakfast or not.

Three hours later, Ivan was on the road again. The Holden Commodore and its smooth six-cylinder burr gradually sobered him. The more kilometres he managed to put between himself and Nambucca Heads the clearer his mind became. It was like waking up from a beautiful dream induced by some intoxicating drug. He began to place his thoughts and feelings in some sort of order. What had happened to him was so wonderful, and yet it had been so unexpected. Had it changed him? Was Cathy thinking of him now? Was this what people called falling in love, or was it just a one-night fling? They had taken a small breakfast, after which they had gone back to her room and made love again before getting ready for their separate departures. They had exchanged addresses and telephone numbers, and walked down to the car-park holding hands. After a long last kiss they had climbed into their separate cars – hers a somewhat dilapidated Toyota Corolla of indefinite colour between green and blue – and driven off in opposite directions. She said she was on her way to Newcastle.

He ought to have asked her for a picture, perhaps a passport photograph, something that would last, a milestone of his personal history.

He was suddenly urged to stop at a small rest area by some strange physical need to re-live the moment when he had been drawn in by her charm. He switched off the engine and put his hands in his lap, open palms facing up, and he almost talked to the skin of his palms. These hands had actually touched her skin only a few hours earlier. And as he was savouring the memory of their physical contact he heard the Tchaikovsky piece in his mind. He swept the back of his right hand across his forehead. This piece of music became inseparable from the intoxicating attraction that Cathy still held for him.

Ivan was ripped out of his ruminations by the thunder and the hurricane-like onslaught of air caused by a passing truck of immense size. He shook his head in disbelief over his own sentimentality and started the engine again. But as he continued driving for the next few hours the Tchaikovsky kept coming back to him and gradually allowed him to make his peace with his urge to think of her.

A bluish-white light flashes from nowhere. Oh God, caught by a speed-camera! And this happens as he is already on the Croydon by-pass. How did he manage to handle that difficult roundabout about a mile-and-a-half back without really driving with his mind? The Tchaikovsky string serenade must have hi-jacked him into that dreamland. Strange how the mind of a driver works! I could have caused an accident, he thinks and begins to accuse himself. He decides to concentrate on his driving from now on. He switches off the radio and is glad to continue his journey in silence.

But he cannot take his thoughts off Cathy. What could have become of her? Is she still in Australia? Is she still alive? He should have made contact with her again. Or shouldn't he? Looking back now it seems wrong and illogical that he never saw her again. But these things happen. One is so busy in one's job, so full of other things, so caught up in all sorts of social gatherings, meetings, discussions, new activities, old duties and routines, and before one is aware of it the time to contact a woman one has met just once no longer seems right. Well, he had tried to contact her from Bribie Island, he called her number in St. Lucia, but there was no answer. But after that he was too occupied with other things.

Around him, the afternoon traffic has become lighter. The open stretch of road between Croydon and Purley tempts him to accelerate, but this impulse is immediately curbed by the very recent shock of the flashing speed camera. As the car descends along the bends leading down into Purley he has to apply the foot-brake several times. At the bottom of the hill the traffic lights are on green, so he pushes the accelerator, takes the right lane and turns right, facing the Tesco supermarket. He is about to turn the wheel to the left in the direction of the A23 when he realizes he has taken the wrong way, he has to go round the one-way system, pass through the same traffic lights at the bottom of the hill again and then drive straight ahead in order to follow the A22, which will take him in the direction of East Grinstead. He is disappointed at himself, normally his driving is more disciplined, if perhaps a little more pushy. He decides to concentrate better on the road, on the traffic.

Soon he has left Greater London behind. He drives round the big roundabout with the M25 interchange and heads for Godstone. He has regained his former relaxed mood. In a way, he feels a little embarrassed about his sentimental lapse back there. How could he let himself go like that over a piece of music? People meet other people all the time, they get together and they part again, sometimes they even get together in a very intimate way and then part. It's the way of the world. So why get carried away by nostalgic thoughts? Ivan decides that it's a sign of weakness.

It is in the roundabout near the Mormon Temple that the accident happens. Ivan doesn't really know how exactly, and even later he cannot make a fully consistent statement to the police. All he remembers is that his Audi somehow got caught between a lorry tearing round the roundabout from the right and another car – a small red Nissan – joining the roundabout from the left. He must have stepped on his brakes to avoid being squeezed between the other two vehicles, and the lorry then crossed his path and pushed the nose of his car into the Nissan.

Silence.

Ivan breathes out. The interior of his car is full of glass. He feels no pain. A strong smell of burnt rubber. But no fire, no smoke. On the right is a dirty piece of grey metal, a part of the lorry. On the left, a mess of red metal, broken glass and, yes, blood. Ivan finds himself asking aloud, "Are you all right?" before he realizes nobody can hear him, of course. He is alone in his car. Then blackness overwhelms him.

TWO

The voice pushes through a cloud. Ivan tries to find out who is talking. As his senses return he finds a nurse talking to him. "No, don't try to touch your face. The doctor will be with you soon."

Where is he? What has happened?

Gradually, his memory comes back. He was driving to East Grinstead. What did he do when he arrived there? Did he meet the Korean businessman? What was his name? No. He distinctly remembers driving over the North Downs, past the M25, but he simply can't remember what happened then.

He loses consciousness again, and when he next opens his eyes the light in the room is different. The lamp to his left is now switched off. A doctor is bending over him.

"You are a lucky man, Mr. MacGregor. No broken bones. No internal injuries."

Ivan tries to speak, but he finds it a bit strange. What have they put in his mouth? And what have they done to his nose? He cannot breathe through his nose. Still, he manages to ask the doctor what has happened. His voice sounds odd, deeper, croaking. "What's happened?"

"You've been involved in a serious accident." Somewhere in the room a pager goes off and with this the doctor's face disappears from Ivan's field of vision.

The nurse appears again. "I'm afraid the doctor's been called away to an emergency. Would you like something to drink? You can try a sip of water if it doesn't hurt too much."

"What I'd like to know first," Ivan croaks, "is what happened.

Where am I? What accident was the doctor talking about?"

"You were involved in a car accident," the nurse explains. "You're in the Royal Victoria Hospital in East Grinstead. But you seem to have no serious injuries. Your face was cut – probably by broken glass. You've got some sutures to your eyelids, nose and lips. You've been unconscious for quite some time so the doctors would like to keep you here for observation for a day or two."

"What do you know about the accident? I can't remember anything."

"I don't know too many details. The police will probably want to talk to you later, when you feel a bit better."

"Were other people involved?"

"There's a young woman who was in the same accident, and she wasn't as lucky as you, she's in surgery now."

"A young woman? What's the matter with her? Who is she?"

"You shouldn't worry about things like that right now. Just try to relax and take a rest. Shall we try a sip of water? "

Ivan feels a wave of irritation. If there is anything that he hates about being a patient in a hospital it's the nurses' use of the first person plural. Well, at least this nurse's tone has nothing condescending about it. No motherese or baby-talk.

He gives in. He manages to swallow some water, then the nurse leaves. He feels exhausted, as if he had completed a tough physical piece of work like felling a tree, splitting firewood for a whole army or running the New York Marathon. He allows himself to drop off to sleep.

When he wakes up for the third time it is almost dark in the room. Ivan marshalls his thoughts. He should contact the Korean businessman – what was his name? And then he should touch base with his office, John is sure to be puzzled if not furious. John is his boss and occasional friend. Ivan never quite knows if he can call him his friend or not. They go to the pub together, they have the occasional game of tennis and sometimes share a heart-to-heart talk about relationships. He feels a sudden desperate need to contact John.

"Are you feeling better now?" the nurse asks when she answers his call. She is still on duty. Either they must have very long shifts, or he hasn't slept for very long.

"Yes." Ivan answers with what he believes to be a voice of some authority. "I have to make some important business calls. Can you tell me how to operate this telephone? Do I have to dial 9 or 0 first to get an outside line? Or can you get my mobile from my jacket pocket?"

The nurse lifts the handset on the hospital phone and passes it to him. "I'm afraid you won't be able to use a mobile phone on hospital premises," she explains. "But you can use the bedside phone. All you have to do is lift the receiver and the switchboard will connect you. Who did you want to call?"

What business is it of hers? Stupid nurse! "I have to call my boss," he mutters.

"I'm not sure if you'll be able to call your business numbers at this hour. It's half-past nine in the evening."

Ivan suddenly feels very lonely. Now that he is virtually cut off from the world he realizes how dependent on constant company, on the feeling of being connected at all times and on being in charge he has become. What will he do all night long? And how can he get back into his normal life again? Here he is, inside the bowels of this monster of a hospital, utterly and completely at the mercy of this nurse. She is not even good-looking. On an impulse he remembers the silly male fantasies about nurses' sex appeal which he has seen on saucy picture postcards and in girlie magazines. While she busies herself with some gadgets and medical boxes on his bedside-table he tries to look at this nurse with that cliché in mind. The thought disgusts him. He tries to analyze this disgust. For one thing, he finds that there is hardly anything further from his mind at this moment than sex, and then he finds it really difficult to imagine this nurse as an ordinary woman in normal clothes. She must have been born with this stiff uniform. Perhaps that is why he has not bothered to read her name on the small badge on her front.

Her voice pulls him out of his thoughts. "Now I'll say good night and good-bye. This is the end of my shift. The night nurse will take over. Have a good sleep, and I'm sure we'll be all right again in no time at all."

"Who do you mean – we?" Ivan demands. But she has already reached the door, and within two seconds he finds himself alone again.

So this is it. He decides to let his mind roam about and take him into whatever realm it pleases, trying to relax as effectively as possible at the same time. He expects to be led into attractive and innovative ideas about how he can get round to the Korean businessman and close the deal even more advantageously than John ever expected. He just has to let himself drift and the good ideas are sure to float by.

For a certain time this seems to work, but soon enough he arrives at the former disappointment, the emptiness and utter loneliness. Somehow, the Korean deal is completely irrelevant. His entire job is irrelevant. What remains to him is this dark-blue waterhole of isolation. It pulls him down. As he begins to fling his arms about trying to keep afloat it occurs to him that he would feel less lonely if he was not alone.

He suddenly senses that there is another person in the same waterhole struggling as desperately as he is. It is the young woman the nurse told him about. In their struggle to keep from drowning their waves unite. He tries to swim closer to her. He tries to call out to her, but to no avail. He tries to identify her face. It is a blank. This can't be. There are no people without faces. This is like the Dali sequence in Hitchcock's film *Spellbound*, that old Freudian parody from the 1940s in which there were people with blank faces…

"Am I dreaming?" he asks out aloud.

He finds his hospital-gown drenched in sweat. His breath

comes fast, his heart-beat gallops.

After a few minutes, in which he manages to calm down, his curiosity about the young woman returns. Aren't they connected by their common involvement in the accident? He feels an irresistible urge to find out more about her. The night nurse should be able to help him. He reaches for the call-button.

He hardly hears the opening of the door. All at once a figure in a light-blue nurse's uniform stands next to his left elbow bending over him and asks in a warm, soft voice if there is anything she can do for him.

"Perhaps. I am so worried about the other persons involved in the accident." Why is he using the plural now? He couldn't care less about the lorry driver – he is only interested to learn more about the young woman. "As far as I know there is only one other person, and she is in the intensive care unit. A young woman…"

"I wouldn't worry about her now, Mr. MacGregor. I don't think there is anything either you or I can do for her at this point."

"But I need to know if she's alright."

The nurse looks sympathetic. "I can try and find out her name, if you like," she says. "But I won't be able to give you much more information than that. There are rules about patient confidentiality, you see."

Immediately, Ivan likes the night nurse. "What's your name? It's too dark, I can't read your name badge."

"I'm Nurse Campbell-Jones. But just call me Wendy."

"Thank you, Wendy."

Wendy. What an old-fashioned name! Probably short for Gwendolyn. Perhaps her parents were fond of Oscar Wilde's Gwendolyn Fairfax? He wants to ask her, but she has already left the room. Thank God they are not all of them like yesterday's day nurse!

* * *

29

The pale morning light shines through the windows and Ivan is content to note the swaying tree-tops outside when Wendy appears with her bits of information.

"The young woman's name is Emma Richardson. She's in a critical condition in Intensive Care. I can't tell you any more."

With that Wendy leaves. Her voice is still in the room after she has left. It bounces off the walls and envelops him with sharp-edged concern. Ivan turns her words round and round in his mind. He arrives at the conviction that now, with such serious injuries, Emma Richardson and he are even more definitely connected. He does not know why he feels like this, but deep down he is convinced of a new bond between the young woman and himself. He does not question this conviction. It is a plain fact. He will have to wait, but soon he will find out more about her. He will get to know her when she is well again...if she is ever well again.

The morning passes in quiet hospital routine. Some time in the afternoon, a man appears and introduces himself as a policeman although he has no uniform. He questions Ivan about the accident. But all Ivan can remember is his driving out of South London into the country along the A22, passing the M25, then a big blank. This does not seem to surprise the policeman. He says this often happens, this amnesia about the few moments just before an accident and about the accident itself. Memory might return. But even if it doesn't they have enough witnesses to reconstruct the facts and establish the situation. Ivan wants to ask if he can be blamed for the accident. It's an aspect he has not thought about before, but now it suddenly seems to become very important. What if he has caused such a terrible accident?

He takes all his courage and asks the policeman: "What about the blame, the guilt question. Or however you put it?"

"It's probably too early to establish blame, but from what the witnesses in the vehicle following you said, it appears that you entered the roundabout at considerable speed." The policeman interrupts himself, probably realising he has already said more than he intended to say. He looks at his watch, stands up, places the visitor's chair in the corner and reaches for his crumpled raincoat. "Your memory might come back, sir. When it does, would you please contact me and tell me everything you can remember? Here's my card. Well then, I hope you will be up and about soon. Good afternoon, sir."

As the policeman walks to the door he reminds Ivan of Inspector Columbo, from the TV series he used to watch when he was a student. It must be the crumpled raincoat. But then, real policemen are not at all like the ones in films, or are they? Ivan is not sure. He thinks of Laurence Olivier and Michael Caine in *Sleuth*, trying to fool each other with different games of humiliation, Olivier thinking he knows what real policemen are like. Ivan comes to the conclusion that it is less a question of fact or fiction, but more likely one of perspective. Probably it all depends on where you stand. A policeman may appear in a very different light if you are a criminal.

Ivan pulls himself out of his ruminations. He decides to find out more about the accident and about that young woman, Emma Richardson. As soon as he remembers what the nurse told him about the woman he feels sick. His stomach contracts, and he wipes across his forehead with the back of his hand.

"It's my fault, I am sure it is."

The words have hardly escaped him when he begins to feel better. The act of pronouncing these words has made the admission more real, more true, has converted what began as a fearful question into a certainty, a fact.

He gets up from his bed and puts on his dressing-gown, a light beige dressing-gown with the name of the hospital in small brown letters on its front.

"Are you doing your walking exercise, Mr. MacGregor?" Wendy asks from down the corridor while he closes the door behind him.

"Yes."

"And a good thing, too. You remember what the doctor said. You shouldn't lie in bed for too long, it's better for your system if you go for regular walks. After all, you want to be discharged before the weekend." And she gives him a big smile.

Ivan smiles back and makes his way along the corridor. Should he ask the person at the front desk? Or can he find the intensive care unit on his own? He decides to approach the front desk.

"Excuse me, please. I wonder if you can help me. I am the patient from room 216, and I have to find out more about the accident that got me in here."

"I don't see how we can help you there. You just have to wait for more information from the police." Her badge says 'Mrs. Waterstone'. She gives Ivan a friendly smile. All the women seem to smile at him today, he thinks. He must have regained some of his old charm.

"But I have to know more now."

"Why?"

"It's…well…my boss…he called, he needs to know, I think for insurance purposes…" This is a complete lie. When he talked to John on the telephone that morning they only talked about the failed Korean deal and about the general fact that Ivan would be out of action for a few days, perhaps for a week or two.

Mrs. Waterstone pulls a funny face and leans forward. "I can tell you something I heard about your accident, but only if you're a good boy."

"What do I have to do to qualify as a good boy?" He winks at her.

"We'll see about that. Well, I heard that it was a pretty bad accident. Something that hardly ever happens, three cars crashing sideways inside a roundabout. But they say the lorry-driver wasn't hurt at all."

Ivan decides to break off this conversation. Somehow, the

woman's way of talking about the accident upsets him. He finds it offensive. He mumbles a quick 'thank you' and walks off into another wing of the hospital. As he walks along unknown corridors he thinks how unfair the world can be. Is it true that he was driving dangerously? Was he lost in his day-dreaming? If the accident was definitely his fault he will have to make it up to the young woman, Emma Richardson. Being young, she has probably had very little driving experience. She is more vulnerable in the aggressive world of today's traffic. Whereas he, with his long experience and his acute sense for dynamic thinking, well, he carries a heavier burden of responsibility *a priori*. The thought of what he has done to this young woman nearly makes him sick. He will have to apologize to her, face to face. There is no other way.

He sees a friendly face coming towards him.

"Can you tell me where I can find the intensive care unit?" he asks.

"Just keep going and you'll see it on your right."

And so it is. Ivan finds the glass door, pushes it open and steps inside. Here, the corridor widens and it is flanked by walls with large windows that allow a good view of the intensive care rooms on the other side. He walks past the windows of several rooms. A young nurse is standing in front of one of the rooms, leafing through a brochure or manual. Ivan takes a deep breath and asks her:

"Can you tell me in which room I can find Emma Richardson?"

"She's right in there," the nurse points at the big window across the corridor. "Are you a relation?"

"No."

"Then I can't allow you in. But you can have a look at her through the window if you like."

Ivan steps up to the window. He has never seen an intensive care room in reality, only in films. The amount of complicated machinery and of different types of wires connected to the bed in the middle of the room takes him by surprise. All he can see of the patient is her pale nose with tubes coming out of her nostrils, her mouth with yet another tube, and her closed eyes, her eyelids sporting a blue-black hue. No movement at all. Suddenly he fears she could be dead already.

"Is she alive?" he asks the young nurse.

She looks up from her brochure and nods her head with a confident smile that dispels all his doubts. He sees that there is nothing more that he can do at this stage, so he thanks the nurse and makes his way back to the other part of the hospital. Back in his room, he sits down on the visitor's chair and tries to sort out the situation. He wants to find out where he stands now, what his next steps are going to be, and how the present situation might develop over the next few days. Is there anything he should not forget? What are the priorities he must think of when he gets out of hospital?

His job is no problem. John was very understanding on the phone. He can take enough time off to recover. John will certainly not press him. So it is probably a good idea to take a week or two off. He could go down to Brighton and relax by the sea for a while. But then, that would take him away from Emma. He is convinced he must stay near her. He wants to be with her when she wakes up from her coma. He will find out if she has any family, and he will contact them and explain. Yes, this is his duty.

When an Indian-looking hospital-helper enters with his evening meal, Ivan has already put together an action plan for the next few days. He feels better.

As he is trying to sip the hot soup from the spoon, the cuts in and around his mouth hurt him very badly. The pain makes him put the spoon down and forget his preoccupations for the time being. Though, in the course of his second attempt, as he is blowing on the smaller amount of soup in the spoon, suddenly the principal tune from the Elegy of Tchaikovsky's string serenade enters his mind again. This takes him by surprise, but it brings back the memory of driving along the Croydon by-pass before the accident. How long before the accident?

After the evening meal, Ivan feels extremely tired. He decides to take action in the morning, but first he has to get enough sleep. He settles comfortably in his bed and is already falling asleep when yet another night-nurse appears to give him his medication.

The morning brings good news. After the consultant has seen him for one brief minute, Ivan is told he can leave the hospital today. He takes a shower, gets dressed, walks over to Intensive Care to find there is no change there, says good-bye to Wendy in the corridor, and settles the paper-work with Mrs. Waterstone at the front desk. Finally he walks through the glass doors and hails a cab.

"Take me to Gatwick," he tells the driver.

Hearing his own voice gives him confidence. He will get his life back on track again. He will be in charge of his destiny again. Things will turn out fine.

From the South Terminal he takes the Gatwick Express train to Victoria. The taxi from Victoria to Bloomsbury makes very slow progress through the heavy traffic and Ivan thinks that the congestion charge is a good thing, after all, if only it could solve the problem once and for all.

When he enters the sleek atmosphere of glass and aluminium in his flat the total silence hits him like a hammer. Why is that? He has never allowed such silence, certainly never for very long, so he has never really experienced it. His usual form of existence in his own flat is always wrapped up in noise and activity. Television, DVDs, or CDs playing almost without interruption, even when he is busy writing up a report or studying paperwork for his job. He is practically incapable of serious concentration, he cannot even read the newspaper, without the cocoon of sound.

This does not mean that he ever really listens to any of his CDs or really watches any of the television programmes or DVD films. They are just part of his environment.

Now, however, he suddenly becomes aware of a complete and utter silence.

He goes to the small kitchen, fetches a can of Worthington's and settles down on the sleek white designer-settee in the lounge. He takes a few sips of beer and looks at the wall with the LCD flat-screen. He ought to put something on that wall. It's too bare, too cold. Should he go for a small bookcase or rather a poster or a painting? A Klimt, perhaps? No, that wouldn't go with the flat-screen.

He reaches for the phone and dials John's number.

"Hi, John. I'm out. Can we meet?" This is the curt style they both love, especially in situations that could become emotional.

"Fine. That fits. Shakespeare's Head, in an hour?"

" Okay. See you."

Shakespeare's Head is a traditional pub in Soho, north of Shaftesbury Avenue. Ivan does not really like the place, it is too touristy for his taste. But he knows John likes to meet there, it's half-way between their apartments, more or less.

Looking round the pub and taking note of an irregularity in the wooden wall panel, Ivan steps up to the bar and gets an orange juice – he cannot handle another beer on top of the medication from the hospital – and sits down in a corner under one of the stained-glass windows. He overhears a conversation between two older men who are having a cup of tea – Ivan has never seen anybody having tea at this pub – at the table to his right. They complain about the foreigners who come here just to take advantage of the social benefits. They agree that the country is going far too soft on all the illegal immigrants who are taking away the jobs, causing nothing but trouble...

Ivan has heard it all before. He hates that kind of talk. He is not a very political person, his job doesn't leave him a lot of spare time to follow up all the details in current affairs, but he is convinced that there is no logical connection between immigration and unemployment in Britain. Also, he knows that this country will only survive if it accepts the multicultural nature of its population. He feels that it owes this to the rest of the world, given the heavy burden of guilt from its colonial history. His thoughts have just reached this point when he spots the small white cube on one of the men's saucers. Two cubes of sugar wrapped in white paper that says 'Tate & Lyle'.

Ivan grunts with satisfaction. "That fits," he murmurs to himself. "They should read George Lamming. Racism, colonialism and the sugar industry..."

He is pulled out of his thoughts by John's arrival.

"My, you look pretty shaken, old boy!" he booms.

"Charming welcome, John. Good to see you." Ivan gets up to fetch a drink for his boss.

But John is already at the bar. "I'll take this. Another juice for you?"

"No, thanks."

The two men sit down and sip from their glasses for a few silent moments. Then John questions Ivan about the accident, about his present state of health. When they switch over to business, John is very generous and allows him to take off as long as he likes.

"I need you in top shape. So take your time."

"Thanks. I think I'll nip down to Brighton for a week or two. Relax. Breathe in the sea air. Recharge my batteries, as they say. But of course I'll have to contact the police first. Make my statement. I wonder if I can get away with a fine or if they're going to take it to court. In any case, this is going to put up my insurance. The premium will rocket sky-high."

For a brief moment, Ivan wonders if he ought to tell John about the young woman, Emma, and his need to get in touch with her. He decides to keep this newly acquired urge to himself.

Probably, John would not understand anyway.

They talk for another half-hour, then they say good-bye and walk away in different directions. Ivan turns south-east and strolls through Chinatown to Charing Cross Road, down to Trafalgar Square, the Embankment, across the river, and he finds it very refreshing just to walk along the south bank of the river, past street musicians and various tourist attractions. He likes the view of the river from here, the City in the background.

Tchaikovsky's Elegy blends in with his feeling of unrest.

THREE

He leaves the Indian restaurant in Preston Street and walks down to the sea-front. He crosses the busy street, reaches the railing facing the sea and looks left. Brighton Pier has just been lit up although there is still some pleasant evening light in the air. He feels satisfied, if a little heavy. He tends to eat too much in Indian restaurants, the curries are so tasty. They make him happy, especially the chicken pathia with sag aloo and mushroom pillau. The only trouble is the over-full stomach afterwards.

Still no news. When he called the hospital this morning they couldn't give him any information because he is not related to her. What should he do now? What can he do now?

Ivan turns round and begins to walk west. Now he has the sea on his left and the street on his right. A black Audi passes him, it is travelling considerably faster than thirty miles an hour, he can see that. It reminds him of his own driving style. That driver could be himself, speeding, speeding, speeding not only along Brighton's sea-front but also speeding through life. It occurs to him that he still has no car, he has come here by train, and what really strikes him now, he has not bothered to think about his car after the accident. How can this be? He who normally makes sure he is always up-to-date on cars, who keeps his car spick-and-span, who never misses the motoring news? Now he cannot even remember the name of the *Top Gear* presenter. Jeremy something? He reviews the situation. His Audi can be repaired. But does he want that? His cherished car would be tainted for ever after this, it would never be the same. The logical conclusion is that he will get himself a new car. Under normal circumstances, this prospect would make him very happy. No time like car-buying time! Selecting the right make and model, studying car brochures and test reports, visiting car showrooms and browsing through the lists of cars available, chatting with the salesmen, exchanging information on horsepower, torque, wheelbase, standard equipment and options, checking boot capacities, sitting behind the wheels of different models – even models one could never afford – and taking in the blissful atmosphere evoked by the smell and the shiny newness of the cars on display and by the prospect of acquiring a new car: all that is like waiting for Christmas as a boy, or even better! But not now.

He dismisses these thoughts about cars and looks out over the silvery surface of the English Channel. His eyes follow a yacht out there, a fine sloop with brilliant white sails full of the fair sea-breeze. His mind trails off into nothingness. It is drawn into the distance beyond the horizon.

A sudden pang in his heart stops him in his walk. He knows what to do. He walks on at a brisk pace for a mile or so, crosses the street and checks the name of the side-street turning away from the sea-front. It must be somewhere along here. He remembers the address of the private investigator who was so efficient in the case of one of his friends. His offices are somewhere up this side-street, practically between Brighton and Worthing. After a few turns, he finds the front door with the little metal plate that bears the inscription: *Oscar N. Dixon, Private Investigations, Second Floor.*

Ivan rings the bell and is immediately admitted to the offices of Mr. Dixon, who welcomes him with a hearty hand-shake.

"Now, what is it I can do for you, Mr. MacGregor?"

"It's not the usual story, Mr. Dixon," Ivan hesitates. How can he make himself clear to this detective?

"There is no such thing. No case can be called 'the usual story' in my line of business. Every case is different. So, Mr.

MacGregor, you see, you can be quite frank with me. Nothing that is being said in this office ever gets out of here. It's all confidential."

"Yes, I can see that. But my case is perhaps a bit more delicate."

Ivan realizes that he has to trust this man a hundred per cent or not at all. This makes him see his mistake. It hits him like a heavy blow that this is all wrong. He cannot spy on Emma like this. He will have to wait until he can talk to her. He is only entitled to such information about her as she is prepared to share with him.

"I'm sorry. I've changed my mind." Ivan gives Mr. Dixon a wry smile.

He walks back to the sea-front and heads east. Soon he reaches the small hotel where he has set up his headquarters for the time being. It was very good of John to suggest he should relax by the sea for a week or two.

Stepping into his hotel room, Ivan takes off his jacket and flings it on the large double bed. He enters the bathroom and looks at himself in the mirror. He is quite a good-looking fellow, after all. His straight dark hair is fresh and suggests a dependable if unpredictable character. If you look at it from the right angle his face resembles that of some romantic film star in the 1930s, a young Olivier or such. His deep-set, dark eyes corroborate this impression. Yet, there is nothing devilish about him. In a way, he looks terribly ordinary. He is clean-shaven – for a moment he remembers the relief he felt when he shaved off his stubbly beard three months ago – and his cheeks still sport the smoothness of a man twenty years his junior. He feels no vanity about his good looks, he is merely conscious of it. He knows that he is the type that inspires confidence, especially with women his own age, and they are the most interesting.

He leans closer to the mirror and flexes his facial muscles, pouts his lips for a second, then raises his eyebrows. Yes, he is satisfied. His injuries are healing nicely, and his handsome face will be restored to him in a short while. He does not worry about the blue and yellowish stains on his forehead or the swollen shape of his nose. Even the purple line across his chin, the line caused by the stitches from the hospital, seems incapable of damaging his looks in the long run.

His normal routine of looking at himself in a mirror includes taking off his shirt and inspecting the athletic shape of his torso. But right now he does not feel up to it. Is it that he is afraid of detecting a slight weakness, a flabby stomach or a softening of his breast muscles? No, he just doesn't want to look at his torso right now. No fears, no hidden agenda, just that. He is satisfied with himself as he sees himself now, in his tailored shirt and with his tie on.

He walks back to the bedroom and sits down on the easy-chair by the window. He picks up the newspaper from the bedside table and tries to relax. The paper is *The Times* in the old format, not the tabloid version. It is full of reports from the Middle East, Iraq, Palestine, and Ivan is drawn into the world of international affairs. While he is reading the various articles on world politics he is beginning to connect them with the developments of the new markets that his company is trying to open in the Far East. Only three weeks ago, John said Ivan might have to go to China for a consultation with some potential business partners over there. But now that the deal with Korea has fallen through?

Gradually, Ivan's mind is absorbed by professional considerations, professional perspectives and professional views of the world. By the time he reaches the personal columns he has already concocted a few new ideas that he can discuss with John on Thursday. His mind is still strutting across the stage of business opportunities when it is arrested by a single word in bold print in the personal columns: 'Emma.'

It is an item about some other Emma, certainly not 'his' Emma. Obviously an older person. He is surprised to catch himself thinking of Ms. Richardson as 'his' Emma. He must be going crazy. What is that woman to him? She was seriously injured by his negligence. So they have been connected by fate. Pure coincidence. It could have been a different person in the other car. He could have stopped for petrol in Croydon, then he would not have been in that roundabout at that time, and the red Nissan and the lorry would probably have got past each other without any difficulties. Yes. But he didn't stop for petrol, and he was there at the exact moment to cause that accident with the red Nissan and the lorry. And it was her in the Nissan. And that connected him with her, his life with hers.

It never occurs to him to wonder about the lorry driver. It is only Emma that catches his attention. Emma and her fate absolutely envelop him, she becomes part of his daily existence.

After reading the paper Ivan takes a nap on his bed. He sleeps for an hour, and when he wakes up he knows he had a dream about Emma again, but he cannot recapture it. He realizes that his own obsession about Emma does not make him depressed, but rather happy, elated. And he knows that this elation is not the same that he used to feel when he managed to make the acquaintance of a new woman and got her into bed. No. This is different. There is no erotic component in his interest in Emma. Her name leaves his male ego utterly unmoved. The thought of her does not include a vision of her naked body. He thinks of her as a person of indeterminate sex, a fellow human being, yes, a wonderful, valuable, important, unique person. This is a new experience for him. Of course, he does not know what she really looks like, but he is sure she must be beautiful, and he is convinced she has deserved her beauty. It is not a superficial prettiness but a deep-rooted beauty, a beauty from her inside. She is a human entity that has been violated by the coincidental contact with him, the traffic accident connecting them both.

He pulls himself out of his thoughts and gets ready for a walk along the sea-front. The weather has turned cool and quite breezy, so he puts on a thin anorak over his jacket. Once on his way along the sea-front he wonders if it was such a good idea to take this walk. He spots the cinema across the street. He wonders what films are on today. He crosses the street at the traffic lights and begins to study the colourful posters mounted along the side wall of the cinema. He can hardly make up his mind, and in the end he decides to watch a film with Rhys Ifans, one of his favourite actors. It is *Enduring Love*, a film released about three years ago, based on a novel by one of the contemporary British novelists he has read about but whose name he can't recall at the moment.

Leaving the cinema after the film, Ivan is utterly dazzled. He cannot take his mind off the intensity of Rhys Ifans's acting. What obsession! The author must have gone through a similar experience to his. Really and truly, the film proves that he is right, an accident does connect the people involved. There is no getting away from that. However, contrary to the situation in the film, Ivan does not want to harass Emma. All he knows – and of that he is absolutely convinced – is that he wants to know who she is, apologize to her face to face and then look after her welfare. He will then see what to do next.

In the evening, watching a commercial on TV in his hotel room, he remembers that he has to decide the question of his car. It is suddenly clear to him that he will get a new one. The commercial is about Audi cars: *Vorsprung durch Technik* pronounced wrongly by an English speaker. Ivan's German is not perfect, but he realizes how badly the speaker pronounces *Vorsprung* and the soft *ch* sound in *Technik*. Should he go for an Audi again? He is not convinced. Yes, they are certainly good cars, but he wants a change. Perhaps a BMW? No, a BMW is too much like an Audi. He switches off his TV and leaves the hotel for the near-by convenience store, where he buys a copy of a magazine called *Which Car?* He has to find out tonight. What's his next car going to be?

Back in his hotel room, he makes himself a cup of tea and unwraps one of the biscuits provided on the tea tray by the hotel management. He settles in the easy-chair and slowly turns the pages of the car magazine. For a brief moment he interrupts his movements and asks himself: "Is this right? While Emma is probably still in a critical condition, perhaps her life in danger, what am I doing? Studying a car magazine and thinking of adding yet another luxury to the enormous heap of luxuries my life is surrounded by, walled in, as it were? Is this ethical?" He checks himself. "It is right. Like this, my mind is taken off her for a certain time. Besides, I have to be mobile again if I want to be of any use to her when she comes out of hospital, haven't I?"

But after this brief conversation with himself it is clear that he must go for a less luxurious car. He turns the pages until he reaches the section with the Japanese cars. Or should he try a Korean one? No, not after the fiasco with the Korean businessman. Eventually, after spending more than two hours considering and reconsidering, he bangs his right palm on the little tea-table and almost shouts: "That's it. A Toyota Avensis Estate! That's cheap, practical and unpretentious." And with this decision he calls it a day and prepares to go to bed. It is half-past twelve.

He is woken up by the telephone on the bed-side table. It is exactly eight-thirty.

"Hi, old man. It's John. How are things?"

"Bloody early for a social chat, I'd say."

"Come on, old man. I've been up and about for over an hour. You know, business hours in Soeul, and with the time difference..."

"Are you telling me we're back in the driving seat with the Koreans?"

"How slow you are!" John says this with the sing-song of an American teen-age actress in some cheap soap.

"No need to become all sissy on me. What's the news?"

"You know, old man. I shouldn't really be letting you in on this. You're on sick leave and need your peace and quiet."

"That's why you call me so bloody early in the morning. Out of consideration for my terrible state of health, practically on the brink of death."

"You got it," he laughs and clears his throat. "Korea is back on the map. That's the news. I just thought you might want to be the first chap to be told, it might make you feel better about missing Mr. Yi the other day."

"Well, that's good news. Thanks."

"Yes, I think I deserve a fair amount of gratitude from you. I spent hours on this. But we'll go into that when we happen to hit the next pub together, won't we? So what's your news? Health improving? Sea air doing you any good?"

"Thanks for asking. I'll tell you on Thursday."

"Okay, see you."

"See you." Ivan hangs up and climbs out of bed. Two more days here in Brighton, and he will be back to normal, he thinks. He decides to devote these two days to the purchase of his new car, which ought to take his mind off Emma. Of course, he will ring the hospital again, just to see if anyone can give him any reliable information.

After breakfast he walks to the sea-front. He intends to take a morning walk to summon his energies. He is just walking opposite the cinema where he saw the film last night when his attention is caught by a man with a dog. The man is very slim, with a furrowed face and ginger-grey hair and a stubble all over his chin and jaws. His back is slightly bent. Together with his gaunt appearance, his large nose and his croaking voice, this gives him the air of a vulture. Ivan stops and watches as the vulture-man bends lower and croons to his dog, some unidentifiable mongrel with a shabby fur. Man and dog are obviously the best of friends, and the man now gets worked up, his excitement rising from moment to moment. From what Ivan gathers it appears that he is sad about the death of a common friend. Whether the deceased individual is a man or a dog, he cannot find out from the mumbling and crooning. The man's tears are clearly genuine, and the dog seems to understand. The cries of the seagulls accompany the woeful scene. Ivan has never seen an old man cry before, so this scene touches him. He knows he will always remember it, he will always think of it as the vulture-man crying with his dog. And the scene will always keep its enigmatic significance for him.

After some ten minutes, the man walks off in the direction of the car parks on the other side of the street. The mongrel follows at his heels. It is ten o'clock in the morning.

FOUR

When Ivan leaves the car-park at Gatwick on Thursday afternoon he is very excited. He has just had an extremely pleasant
working lunch with John. He is now on his way to the Toyota
dealer in Crawley. He has decided to order his new car there
rather than in London. For the time being, however, he has to
make do with a rented car. He wonders how long he will have to
wait for the delivery of the new car, probably not quite as long
as he had to wait for his Audi. He is still thinking of the delivery delay when he reaches the Toyota dealer. He gets out of his
rented car – a plain grey Vauxhall Vectra – and starts to walk up
to the main entrance when his mobile phone rings.

"Mr. MacGregor?"

"Speaking."

"This is Detective Inspector Melville. From what you said in
the course of our last interview I understand that you would like
to speak to Ms. Richardson personally."

"Yes, indeed, Inspector."

"Well, I am authorised to inform you that Ms. Richardson's
condition now allows her to receive visitors. I spoke to her this
morning and informed her of your intention. She has consented
to an interview with you."

"So I can see her right now?"

"Yes, sir. You are free to do that. However, I should like to
warn you, Ms. Richardson may not be exactly overjoyed to make
your acquaintance at this point in time."

"Of course, Inspector. I understand. Thank you."

He orders his new car in Crawley, then he drives over to

East Grinstead. At the hospital, Mrs. Waterstone at the front desk beams at him. "And a very good morning to you, Mr. MacGregor. Come to see young Ms. Richardson?"

He swaggers along the corridors that he remembers from his recent indoor walks. He enters the intensive care unit. He is given a hospital coat which he has to put on before they enter Emma's room. Suddenly he finds himself standing at her hospital bed and looking at her contorted and frowning face. Parts of her face are swollen and sport a variety of hues, but for a short moment he is truly taken aback by her beauty. A strange feeling takes hold of him all of a sudden, a feeling he has never known before. He has looked at many good-looking women with the eyes of a man, which means that female beauty has always been connected with his biological self. His judgement of a woman's beauty was congruent with his evaluation of her physical attraction, or even with her erotic potential. But this is different, this is a dimension of beauty he has never experienced before. This is a new category of beauty, a pure sort of beauty which is not limited to the woman's sexual attraction. The radiance of her eyes, the features around her relatively thin lips – though swollen at the moment – speak an aesthetic language that he has yet to learn in order to understand. He knows with absolute certainty that his interest in this young woman is different from any previous attraction he felt for the numerous women he loved or liked. It is a non-erotic interest, a case of *caritas*, not of *eros*.

"So you're my shadow?" Emma asks. "Or should I say my violator, my evil spirit, or my stalker?"

He smiles down at her and politely introduces himself. Then he faces the difficult task of apologizing to her.

"I have come to tell you how sorry I am for what happened. You see, it was all my fault. I was driving quite recklessly, and I wasn't paying attention when I entered the roundabout. I wrecked your car, and I caused you endless pain. For this, I am truly sorry."

She looks at him without a word for a few moments. The frown on her face softens. After a moment of hesitation she slowly lifts her right hand and gestures in the direction of the soft chair next to her bed. "Why don't you take a seat?"

Ivan remains standing. He feels he has to stand. A sign of respect, like in church or so. He would like to smile down at her, but he finds his facial muscles will not obey him. His expression remains serious. "I felt I had to see you."

"So they tell me. I'm sorry I can't help you if you want to discuss the accident. I fully depend on what they tell me about it. Yes, and they told me it was primarily your fault. You did this to me. But let's change the subject. What makes you take an interest in my case? Are you a doctor or a policeman?"

"I am neither. To tell you the truth, I don't exactly know why I wanted to see you, apart from apologizing to you. Our cars crashed and so we are connected by fate. I feel responsible. Now that you ask me such a simple question it suddenly dawns on me that it doesn't make sense. Not in a rational way, anyway. Do I sound silly?"

"No, not at all. I'm glad that you care."

"It just seems to me we have to stick together in this."

"What do you mean?"

"I happened to enter that roundabout from one direction and you happened to arrive at the same spot from another direction, our cars crashed…isn't that fate?"

"Or reckless driving."

"Yes, of course, I admit that, and as I said I am really sorry. But quite apart from all that, I also see it as an act of fate. I could have gone a bit faster and I would've passed that roundabout minutes before you arrived. But I didn't. Or you could have hesitated somewhere on your route before you reached that roundabout and you would've passed it minutes later. You know what I mean?"

"Yes. But one can speculate like that in almost every situation.

That's how things happen. They just happen."

"I am sorry," the nurse interrupts. "This is enough. The patient needs rest."

"Just one more word, nurse, please," Ivan begs. "Can I visit you again; Emma. I may call you Emma?"

She gives him a faint nod and closes her eyes. The nurse ushers him out of the room. In the corridor Ivan takes his leave from the doctor and walks back to the car-park. He knows that now that he has actually met her he will remain connected with her. He is surprised at his own surprise. Why should he find it so unusual to make the acquaintance of a beautiful young woman without the emerging desire to approach her sexually? There must be a new dimension hitherto unknown to him, a dimension of love – yes, he admits to himself, I must call it love – which may exist even between a highly attractive woman and a man, but without the erotic component. So far he has known such pure love only between men, although he never called it love for fear of associating himself with the sheer idea of homosexuality. But now he discovers that love need not necessarily be tied to sexuality. There is a bond between Emma and him that he cannot define yet. But it is there.

He drives back to London. On his way through the outskirts of the great metropolis he has to take a detour because the police have blocked off a section of the road. The great number of policemen in signal-green anoraks and the sound of distant sirens remind him of another large police action some years ago. He is thrown into a day-dream…

It was a pale grey day, back in 1996. Ivan was in top form, and he was thoroughly enjoying his high-flying life-style. He had recently adopted a new hair-style with its required amount of hair-gel and he had changed to black clothing, like most of his circle. It was the fashion, and if you wanted to be accepted you had to go with the flow. Although he drew a good salary he found himself in a dry spot. His bank account was not overdrawn, but only just. He had lost his car by his own reckless driving. It had all been his fault. Too many pints, a wet road at night, high speed on a narrow country lane. He had really dismissed the experience from his memory. No use crying over spilt milk. But now he needed a car and had hardly any ready money. He told himself that any old car would do for a few months as long as it came with an MOT and was safe enough. Given the amount of his disposable income – lovely term, that, wasn't it, 'disposable income' – he should be back in the driving seat of a decent motor again before too long. He would only have to cut down on his expenses on new outfits, posh restaurants and lavish invitations for women that he wanted to win over. He asked some of his acquaintances if they knew of any old banger going for under three hundred pounds. His friend and former fellow-student Stout, who was now a university lecturer, had come up with a bit of information relating to this quest during one of Ivan's visits to his old *alma mater*. Stout was not his real name, but they all called him Stout because his real name was Guinness. Whenever he was introduced as Stout and the explanation was added, he made a special effort to point out the fact that he did not like this association, he preferred to be associated with Sir Alec, the great actor.

Stout seemed to know about a possible bargain for Ivan. "If you're looking for cheap wheels I happen to know of an old Ford Sierra going for two-fifty. You interested?"

Ivan looked into Stout's pale Irish face with the red stubble. "Yeah, tell me more about it. Here in Cambridge?"

"No, you'd have to go down to London for a bargain like that. My cousin's pal knows of this Sierra for sale, somewhere off Finchley Road. We could run down in my wreck if you like."

Ivan was interested and Stout made the necessary phone calls. On the following day they drove down to London in Stout's old Peugeot. They took the M11, then the M25 for a few sections, and approached the Finchley Road area via the A1.

Ivan had the *A–Z* on his lap and tried to give his friend directions, which was a difficult business because Stout interrupted him all the time, making Ivan's explanations the results of complicated negotiations between them. Several times they took a wrong turning. When they arrived at last, the man with the Sierra was already waiting for them. The car was dark brown, had 120,000 miles on the clock and had black leather seats that looked shamelessly tired. But the engine had a healthy sound, so Ivan decided it would do. They came to a quick agreement. The man insisted on cash, so Ivan walked back to the Barclays branch he had spotted in Finchley Road on their way there.

He had just filled in the withdrawal form and was about to join the queue for the cashier counters when the world around him collapsed.

Suddenly there were loud noises and a great deal of commotion, screeching human voices, an alarm going off, everybody moving but not knowing where, shots being fired. Then smoke, police sirens, more shots, and finally he was practically run over by several policemen. He lay on the floor, dazed for a few minutes, and he heard more loud noises all round. He heard his own heart-beat and realized that he had wet trousers. His legs were shaking. He did not know what was happening to him.

When he managed to sit up after a while that seemed like eternity he saw other people sitting or lying on the floor. The entire hall was full of policemen in signal-green anoraks. His legs were still shaking. A man sitting about two yards to his right had a bleeding wound on his forehead. Their eyes met and Ivan gave him his handkerchief, which the man gratefully accepted and began to wipe the blood off his face.

"What happened?" somebody asked.

"I think it's a bank robbery," someone else said.

Loud voices were heard. "Stand back, please!"

The police were doing their job. Gradually the situation became clearer. A group of paramedics were rushing around, three of them bending over a woman who was lying near where Ivan and the bleeding man were sitting. Ivan looked at the man and shook his head. The man pulled a sad face and shook his head, too.

"I think the poor woman got shot," he said with a slight accent. Ivan speculated if it was a Dutch accent. Or perhaps South African?

Ivan looked around. He was suddenly interested in the woman, who was receiving first aid treatment. He could not really see her face, but her hair looked familiar, its colour and the way it fell down in gentle waves.

"Hey, what are you doing to her?" he shouted at one of the paramedics.

"We're dealing with this, sir," was the curt answer.

Then a policeman took hold of his shoulders, lifted him to his feet and led him out of the hall. Outside the building they had cordoned off a section of the pavement to keep out any onlookers. They placed the people that they got out of the bank on some benches which they had erected there for this purpose. Ivan found himself next to the man with his handkerchief. Somebody came and handed them a warm cup of tea. A paramedic came and asked everyone if they were hurt. The man with the handkerchief said he was all right and they proceeded to the next person sitting there.

"But don't you want them to have a look at your head?" Ivan asked.

"It's nothing," he answered with a shrug. "There are other people who need their aid more urgently."

Then the police came and asked them a lot of questions. One of them was a plain-clothes officer who introduced himself as Detective Inspector Johnstone. He took a few notes of their answers and asked them for their names and addresses. He told them they might be asked to come to his office on one of the following days in order to give more detailed evidence if they could.

How quickly one could be plunged into a tragedy, Ivan thought. All these people being drawn into it. They all had their normal lives and *bang*! All of a sudden we are all connected by fate. This could not have been foreseen. He was standing in the queue, everything appeared normal, no bank robbers visible, and then this sudden chaos. Who could possibly have seen anything? And who was hurt? What about that woman with the beautiful auburn hair? Was she dead?

When they were allowed to leave, Ivan still had shaky knees. He felt he could do with a drink before going back to where Stout was waiting for him. The other man took the handkerchief from his forehead and offered to give it back to him.

"I don't think I need that back," Ivan smiled, "but you may want to join me for a drink. There's a pub over there. What do you say?"

"A splendid idea, thanks," the man answered with a sigh and proffered his right hand. "Hoffmann. Peter Hoffmann."

"Ivan MacGregor. Pleased to meet you, although I'd have preferred a more pleasant occasion to meet new people."

They went and had a drink at the pub. Over their drinks they speculated about what had happened at the bank. They wondered how many persons were injured or even killed.

"It'll probably be on the news tonight," Ivan suggested.

After two pints each they shook hands and parted. Only when he left the pub and saw a clock on the building opposite did Ivan realize that Stout must have given up and left for Cambridge. Crossing Finchley Road he thought he would never forget this day, the noise, the cries, the gun shots, the policemen with their signal-green anoraks.

Now, looking back in his mind after all these years, Ivan thinks that the two big catastrophes in his life, the bank robbery of the mid-90s and now this car accident could be placed alongside each other in his memory bank. Both were events that were unforeseen, they brought together people who had had no connection previously, and they made one realize the limitations of life. Also, they were probably experienced and interpreted quite differently by the different people involved. He could still see the woman who was shot in the bank robbery. She was dead. She was killed by a gun-shot fired by one of the robbers, it was reported later. Ivan had never seen a dying person before. The image of that head of auburn hair has been engraved in his mind all these years and is still with him today.

He wishes he could interpret what he feels through a better medium than the language of his thoughts. Artists can do that. And some great artists have tried to transcend the limitations of their own medium. Just think of Moussorgsky's piano cycle *Pictures at an Exhibition*, in which the composer tries to convey with music what could otherwise be conveyed by the drawings of Viktor Hartmann. Or take Olivier Messiaen and the different colours connected with his *Préludes*. Patrick White tries to paint pictures with language in *The Vivisector*. Then there is Vikram Seth with his attempt to approach the magic workings of music through the medium of literary discourse in his novel about the violinist in that string quartet and in his unhappy love for a pianist facing deafness. Have they all failed? Ivan wishes he had only half the talent of one of them.

The police direct the traffic through a series of back streets. Of course, this means an entire hour of tedious stop-and-go, seemingly endless waiting periods behind the wheel. Ivan has a lot of time to think. His mind returns to the time of that bank robbery. He concludes that his subsequent life-style was definitely influenced by that experience. When you are only in your thirties and already confronted with death as a fact, death as an unalterable destination, what must the logical conclusion be? Make the most of your life as long as you can, *carpe diem*, or make hay while the sun shines? Yes, there was that chap Williams in that film about posh kids in an elitist boarding school in the States who taught them to enjoy their lives to the full while studying Shakespeare's *A Midsummer Night's Dream* and trying to write their own poetry. Wasn't he right? Somewhere deep down in his mind he knows there are different interpretations of what constitutes 'making the best of one's life'. But the top layer of his mental arrangement of his world is convinced it could only mean one thing. Enjoy! Ivan has to think of the way the waitresses in American restaurants shove your totally laden plate in front of you and chirp their stereotypical 'Enjoy!' in such a way that makes you want to run out of the place and forget about the intake of food for the rest of your life. But at the time of that sobering encounter with the certainty of death, the complete and unconditional enjoyment of his life had become his motto.

FIVE

When Ivan came back to the man with the Sierra he found that Stout had already left for Cambridge. He met him again about three weeks later. Stout had some business in town and the two friends met for lunch at a small Italian restaurant in Soho.

"How's the new luxury vehicle? You must be getting a lot of envious looks!" Stout pronounced in a pompous voice with a straight face. That was pure Stout. He could tell the funniest jokes or pull your leg with a stupid story and keep a perfectly earnest face.

"All the good-looking women of London want a ride in it."

"Good on you, mate," was Stout's answer, and he slapped him on his shoulder. Both of them had spent some time in Australia, though at different periods, but they had absorbed enough of the Australian way of life to be fond of some typical phrases from Down Under. "Good on you, mate" was their favourite.

"I say, I didn't quite get it why you were so long getting back to that place. On the phone you told me something about a robbery. But you sounded so confused."

"Yes, it was a bank robbery. And I was caught up in it."

"That must've been good fun. Real Hollywood, was it?"

"I'd prefer to call it real hell. Scared the shit out of me, it did."

"Come on," Stout crooned and handed him the menu. "Forget it. What are you having?"

"Just a Pizza Margherita and a glass of Chianti."

Stout called the waiter and gave him their orders. He was about to begin a chatty talk about a new student of his who had obviously made a lasting impression on him right the first time she'd come to his seminar, when Ivan interrupted him. "You know, the woman actually died right there and then."

"What?" Stout took a moment to realize his friend was still stuck in the previous topic. "Oh, you mean the bank robbery?"

"Yes, and I tell you, it's something I can't get off my mind just like that."

"Who died?"

"There was this woman. Just one of the people in the bank, a customer, I think. She was shot dead. She died there, right on the floor, only two or three feet away from where I was. She died."

"Did you know her?"

"No, of course not, though – "

"Then why all the fuss? Okay, it's a sad thing, a terrible thing when someone is shot like that, I give you that. But it happens all the time. Only because you happened to be there it doesn't make it special or different from all the other accidents that happen. You see?"

"How cynical can you get? I just can't forget her. She had something about her. I liked the colour of her hair. It seemed familiar, somehow."

"Look here," Stout accepted the two glasses of wine from the waiter and handed one of them to Ivan. "Have a drink. This will make you feel better. Forget the woman's hair."

The wine helped. Ivan gradually drifted into the other topics that Stout wanted to discuss with him. Apart from Stout's new book project, their topics included cars, football and women. Stout was eager to paint his erotic visions about his new student. The last time he had taken advantage of a student he had told him every detail and afterwards regretted his openness, particularly when the story had become hot because it almost cost him his job.

"You shouldn't be telling me these things, you know," Ivan remarked. "You remember that time with…what was her name? You thought her the hottest bird you'd ever laid eyes on, and from what I remember you laid quite a bit more of yourself on her, and it nearly turned sour."

"Oh, you mean Jennifer Young. That was a different case. She turned into a real bitch and tried to ruin me." Stout sighed.

"You see what I mean. I'm just trying to warn you." Ivan raised his eyebrows and pointed at his friend's face with his right index finger.

"I appreciate your concern. Really, I do. But this is different. I know Rachel O'Connell would never turn against me. She's Irish."

"You are hopeless. I give up on you."

The two friends continued discussing the ups and downs of a clandestine relationship. While they were talking and exchanging their views on various flaws in the female character, Ivan found himself losing interest. He felt he could no longer participate in such conversations with the usual pleasure. Stout's colourful descriptions of a good-looking student used to have the power to make him imagine the girl in question very vividly and sometimes even to arouse him. But not so now. He even found it a little tedious to listen to the same old ravings about some unknown woman's physical attractions. Boring.

Over the following months in the full swing of London's night attractions, Ivan gradually found that his life-style had become schizophrenic. His reckless life, his speed in everything, the risks he took, the one-night stands he eagerly sought on most Saturdays and abandoned with equal zeal on the following Sundays, his way of drifting into and out of superficial activities: All his actions lacked coherence and authenticity. There was no congruence between his actions and his feelings. His day-to-day energies were spent in ways that were contrary to his emerging philosophy.

It took him a long time to admit this to himself. Though he felt more and more uncomfortable about his life he could not clearly identify the problem. For over two years he just dismissed any critical questions he was tempted to ask himself. Until he was confronted with a spectacular natural phenomenon, which threw him back on his own self.

It began from within the context of his swinging social life in London. One weekend, about three years after his crucial experience in Finchley Road, Ivan and a group of people that included Stout were drinking heavily in a pub somewhere near Finsbury Park. Apart from the usual hedonistic topics that were discussed, some of the women in the group brought up the topic of the solar eclipse that was going to take place in two or three weeks and that everybody was talking about.

"I read that it's going to be a one-off in a lifetime," Jackie said.

"Yes," Pauline added, "and they say it's going to plunge parts of France and Germany into absolute pitch-darkness. Wouldn't that be something?"

"Why don't you go to France then?" Stout asked and hiccupped. "Girls like to nip over to naughty Frogland anyway. Here's a good reason."

"I wouldn't take you with me, you dirty old beast, that's for sure," Pauline sneered. She wouldn't leave out any opportunity to get back at Stout whenever she could. She had a grudge against him. None of the others in the group knew about it, but Stout had taken her to bed a few weeks ago and it had turned out a real fiasco for both of them. They had simply been too drunk and Stout failed to perform, and afterwards they blamed each other.

"You go with the girls, and the boys will form their own party. I say, Ivan old man, what about popping over to where the action is in France?"

The result of this was that they all went together in two cars. It was in the middle of August, and it was a very hot day. They left London in the evening, travelled through the Channel Tunnel and booked into a small hotel in St. Omer. Jackie was very disappointed that they were too late for a nice French evening meal, and she couldn't quite make her peace with the fact that they were going for a drinking spree instead. Pauline comforted her with the prospect of a really expensive bottle of French champagne. She did not know a great deal about French champagne or good wine, the only thing that counted in her eyes was the stiff price. Jackie relented a little. Their proposed pub-crawl in St Omer turned into a long session in one single establishment, all the other bars within walking distance already having closed down for the night. The women had several bottles of Laurent-Perrier. The men stuck to Kronenbourg beer. In the morning they made an early start. They drove down the A26 to Reims, then they followed the A4 in the eastern direction. Already en route they noticed the unusual density of the traffic. There were many cars with British number plates, all going in the same direction. Obviously other people must have had the same idea.

The motorway rest area near Verdun was packed with cars, but they found a good spot to park their cars and get out their picnic chairs. Stout had brought special sunglasses for all of them. They settled down and waited for what was going to happen.

"It's a shame having to watch this in a crowd like this. Couldn't we have stopped somewhere along the motorway?" Pauline complained.

"You silly woman," Stout said. "Didn't you read the pamphlet they handed to all the motorists back there at the toll-gates?"

"It said there was absolutely no stopping on the emergency lane just to watch the solar eclipse," Jackie explained. "The police are going to be very strict about this."

Ivan walked away from the group. He wanted to be alone. He was fed up with each and everyone of the group. Their talk had become so superficial. But then, was his talk less superficial? Did what he had to say make any better sense? Was there more depth in his own contributions to the conversation?

He managed to step over the fence at the back of the rest area and walked into the corn field beyond. The others did not notice his absence. They were all looking up into the sky with their special glasses on their noses and munching sandwiches. From time to time Stout would lecture them about the astronomical constellation that made it possible for them to see this eclipse, but nobody listened to him. They looked like children from the distance.

The corn field exuded dry warmth. The world was yellow. Blue from above contrasted sharply with it. The intoxicating smell of summer enveloped him. Bird-twitter seemed far away. Where had the birds left their hearts?

Then the world changed. The black disc shifting itself in front of the sun created an eerie atmosphere. Everybody stopped talking. In weird silence, hundreds of people in and around the rest area stared at the sky through their glasses, some of them in utter disbelief. Gradually, the light began to fade.

Suddenly it was pitch-dark. You couldn't even see your own hand in front of your face. There was absolute silence.

Ivan felt how the magic of this darkness lifted him up. It pulled him up and up until he merged with the sky. He had become darkness. The world would never be the same after this, he knew. It is not light that gives us knowledge, he realized, it is darkness. The same light will never return.

The spectacle was over with the same suddenness as it had begun two or three minutes earlier. People began to talk, shout, laugh, cry. Some rushed back to their cars and started their engines. They were in a hurry to continue their journeys. The world seemed to return to a degree of normality.

Ivan rejoined the group. They were all very excited. They had never witnessed anything like that, and they knew they would never witness anything like it again in their lives. This gave the whole experience a phenomenal importance.

"I was so surprised it was all so silent," Pauline said. "I know it's stupid, but somehow I expected there to be a sort of noise."

"I felt the same when I was in an earthquake in Guatemala last year," Jackie added. "I had expected a noise, too. And it was as mysteriously silent as this thing here." But nobody was interested in Guatemala.

At last they calmed down and got into their cars. On the way back they had to fight the same heavy traffic as on their way out in the morning. Ivan was driving one of the cars. He remained silent almost all the way, but nobody took any notice. An invisible wall emerged between him and the other occupants of the car.

After their return to London Ivan thought he would never see the others again. He buried himself in his flat in Bloomsbury and put on a CD of John Coltrane. He turned up the volume of his sound system and lay down on his white leather sofa with a bottle of Château Margaux next to him of the coffee table. He intended to drift into limbo hoping to get some answers to the questions that had been nagging him ever since that darkness in that corn field. What could it all mean? What would make him want to continue living?

What if there was no meaning? He might as well fall back into his hedonistic life-style. Had any of the others ever asked themselves such questions? Or were they sleep-walking? Stout claimed he had all the answers, but the man was a fool.

Ivan poured a glass of wine and took a sip. He moved his tongue around his mouth giving every corner of his palate the welcome opportunity to taste the valuable nectar and swallowed the richly textured flavour of the cherished dark-red liquid.

Wine. Rich red wine. The drink that was believed to turn into the blood of Christ. Did it have the power to make people see things? To understand things?

"I may have associated myself with the wrong people, after all," he spoke aloud, and he was shocked to hear his own voice. It was like a voice from somewhere above.

* * *

Now, more than seven years later, he sees a clear connection between the darkness falling over the French corn field and the two great moments of crisis in his life – the dying woman in Finchley Road and the accident with Emma – although he cannot understand or explain this connection.

One thing is clear. After that eclipse, Ivan's quest for meaning in his life has become more pronounced. His schizophrenic life during this period has become more manageable. He has learnt to cope with the two conflicting poles. He has learnt to socialise with his friends and colleagues, being jolly and reasonably happy in his daily luxuries, and at the same time to look out for signs of higher significance.

This is such a moment of insight. He knows and yet he does not know. He sees and he cannot see.

His second interview with Emma takes place on Saturday. This time he finds her in a different room, still by herself, but no longer in the intensive care unit. Her face is freed from all the tubes, but there is still an infusion on her left arm.

"They put me here because they needed the space in Intensive Care," she explains.

"That can't be the reason," Ivan answers. "They wouldn't have released you from there unless you're out of danger."

"Do you think so?"

"Of course. And I am glad. Really, I am. How do you feel? Still in pain?"

"Well, the cuts in my face are still quite irritating and from time to time my back gives me hell, but they keep me on a variety of drugs, so it's not too bad, after all. What brings you here? Why are you visiting me again?"

"Well, I –" he hesitates. " I thought I'd come and see how you are today. Oh yes, and I brought you these." He produces a bunch of flowers which he has mechanically kept hidden behind his back. He holds them up so she can see them.

"Oh, thank you. These are lovely." Emma tries to smile, but

the attempt fades quickly. She turns her face in his direction and gives him a critical stare. "What's your game? You don't know me, and I don't know you. And here you come to my bedside and bring me flowers."

"I don't want to impose, but as I said on my first visit, I feel responsible, I want to apologize…"

"You've done that. What more do you want?"

"I'm sorry, I must seem awkward. But the truth is I don't know how to go on from here. I just want to be of use to you. I have no hidden agenda, I don't want to influence you about your evidence in connection with the accident."

His awkwardness and particularly his clumsiness with the bunch of flowers seem to make him human in her eyes. Her expression softens. "Well, I must say, you've made a good beginning. You know: the flowers. Now won't you take a seat this time?"

Ivan pulls the soft chair to a position that allows him to sit down and still be within her field of vision. He places the flowers on top of the bedside table. "I hope a nurse will look after these," he mumbles. "I can see it must seem a bit fresh to accept flowers from a stranger." Then he looks about the room. "No other flowers?"

"Who else should bring me flowers? The policeman who questioned me?"

"Of course not. I mean, what about your family? Your friends?"

"I've got no family left. My parents are both dead, and I have no brothers or sisters. I had a guardian when I was under age, his name is Peter, he is very good to me, and in fact I still get on very well with him, but I don't want to burden him with my accident yet, he would fuss too much, can you understand? I'll contact him later. He is very busy with his real estate business. As to friends, well, how would they know about my accident? I must have lost my address-booklet and my mobile phone in the accident, so I can't contact them. And my best friend Peggy happens to be on holiday in Spain with her boyfriend."

Ivan hesitates before he reacts to this prompt. "What about your boyfriend?"

"I don't know why I'm telling you this, but the fact is I broke off with him only three weeks ago. We had some really big quarrels, so it was the right thing to put an end to it. We were not getting on about a lot of things." She sighs. "But that's history."

"I'm sorry."

"That seems to be your favourite phrase. Please, Mr. MacGregor – "

"Call me Ivan."

"All right then, Ivan. Do please stop feeling sorry for me. Stop being so gloomy. Why don't you tell me about yourself?"

Ivan welcomes this change of atmosphere. It is like a door opening onto a beautiful landscape, the sun just emerging from behind the clouds and brightening up the green fields. He clears his throat and begins in a friendly tone. Giving her the basic facts about himself, he punctuates item by item with a slight wave of his right hand as if he were ticking off a list.

"I'm forty-nine years old, I'm still single, I live in London, I work as a sales executive for a London-based company dealing in various kinds of security systems, my parents are also dead, I have an elder brother who lives in Canada…"

"Canada, that's where my father lived when he died."

"Oh, I see. Well, I have very little contact with my brother. Yes, apart from that there's not much more about my family. What else would you like to know?"

"What makes you get up in the morning? I mean, not your job, I mean what makes you tick? What are your interests, your ambitions?"

"I don't know if I can answer this question just like that. I have my usual things, things that men like, you know, nice cars, football…I really think my life is in transition at the moment. I feel I no longer have the same priorities as I had a few years ago. I don't know why, but somehow I seem to be looking for more sense in things. You know, reasons and explanations behind things..."

"But that's certainly a good sort of transition, I think. Don't you think so?"

"Yes, probably it is. But it leaves me with a deeper sense of unrest, a less stable confidence in my own self. Whereas only a few years ago I believed I had all the answers I am confronted by more and more questions these days."

They remain silent for a few minutes. Both of them are grateful for this silence. Then Ivan ventures: "And what about you?"

Later, when he leaves the hospital he feels strangely elated. He knows he has made a good beginning with Emma. Her initial distrust was dispelled, it turned into a wariness, and eventually it ended in a careful neutrality. "She may learn to trust me," he says to himself as he walks back to the car-park.

In the weeks and months following his first personal progress with Emma, he works out how he can be of any help for her. He wants to do good things for her. He does not intend to become a hero in her eyes. He just wants to help her. She has deserved it. Through his car insurance he gets the information that her insurance company is not going to pay for a new car for her; they're only going to pay her a small sum towards it. He does not know if she will be able to afford a new car. "So here is something I can do for her," he tells himself with a degree of satisfaction.

While such material concerns merely require the necessary financial means, the emotional progress between Ivan and Emma remains a more delicate matter. On his third visit to her bedside he offers to contact all her friends and make a whole lot of other arrangements for her. He calls at her work-place – she works as a fashion-journalist for a small magazine in Richmond

– and brings her all the paperwork that has accumulated on her desk. This opens the gate of trust for her. She cannot detect any double meaning in his actions, and his voice inspires her with confidence. He seems to be saying the right things, and they appear to share the same sense of humour.

On the day he can take delivery of his own new car he drops off his hired Vauxhall and steps into the salesroom of the Toyota garage. The suave salesman with his dark pin-stripe suit and his loud necktie who has sold him his car approaches him with an outstretched hand and a beaming face. "Your car is ready, Mr. MacGregor."

"Thank you. That's great."

"Will you come this way, sir?" The salesman leads the way to a more comfortable section of the salesroom. That's probably where they take customers they want to impress or those who have earned the right to take a seat in there because they have been caught unaware and bought a car they don't really want, Ivan thinks.

"Just a moment," he stops the eager salesman. "Can I get another car?"

"What?" The man is clearly taken aback. "You don't want the car you've ordered?"

"I don't mean it like that." Ivan laughs. "I mean: Can I order another car, a second car, an additional car, now that I'm here?"

"Oh, of course, absolutely!" The man is truly relieved and gives him a big smile that he normally reserves for really big customers. "What were you thinking of, sir?"

"It's not for me. It's for a young woman."

"Girlfriend or daughter?"

"Well, neither, really. I just want to buy a car for a woman I know. Is that not possible?"

"No problem. Selling cars is our business."

"All right." Ivan glances around the showroom. "What about a Prius? That would save her some money on her petrol bill, wouldn't it?"

"Yes, it certainly would. But unfortunately, there's a bit of a wait for a Prius. We can't deliver as fast as the orders are coming in. If time is an important factor I'd recommend a Yaris. This model is available within a couple of days, in almost every engine size and colour scheme."

Ivan thinks for a moment. "Yes, I think we'll go for a Yaris then." He tells the salesman what engine size he wants and selects the optional equipment and the colour. He chooses red. After all, Emma's old car was also red. When the salesman has completed the contract Ivan signs it. Then they proceed to the other part of the building where he takes delivery of his new Avensis. It is not black like his previous car, but blue.

Driving back to London, Ivan is very satisfied. The fact that he has just bought a new car for her gives him a great deal of confidence. He will see her again soon. She is scheduled to leave the hospital in a few days from now. He has already arranged to meet her and give her a lift back to her home. This will be a great moment indeed, he thinks.

On the day of her release from hospital he has everything arranged. He arrives at the hospital at ten in the morning. He waits in the waiting area for more than half an hour. Then she comes, carrying a sport bag containing the few things he had to get for her.

Ivan remembers what he said when the nurse asked him if he knew of any friends or relatives because the patient needed a few personal items from her own home. "I know for certain that she has no near relations, and I don't know any of her friends, but I can get the few things for her if you like."

"But you couldn't get into her flat. We wouldn't let you have her keys."

"I understand. But I can go out and buy the stuff she needs. What does she need? Nightgown, toothbrush, toothpaste, hair brush, an array of cosmetics? What else does a young woman need?"

"That's very kind of you. If that's what Emma wants, I'll help her to draw up a list for you."

Even though Emma has learnt to trust him over the past few weeks, she has never let him have the keys to her flat; so everything Emma carries in her bag at the moment has been bought by him. He feels very proud when he sees her walking slowly towards him in the reception area of the hospital. Her face looks perfect. She must have covered up the remaining scars in her face with some assistance from the cosmetic industry. Her elastic walk despite a slight limp and particularly the strangely ludicrous way she moves her arms and turns her head suddenly hit him. Something in these idiosyncrasies reminds him of something in his past. They are inexplicably familiar. But hardly has he recognized this before he dismisses it from his mind. "It's impossible. I can't have met her before. She's far too young." With this, he pulls himself back into the present.

She hesitates. Her first words come out in an uncertain tone. "I still don't know why I should trust you."

"Never mind," he answers. "It only shows your knowledge of people. Your trusting me is proof of your good judgement. But come, let me carry your bag. You shouldn't exert yourself too much." And he leads the way to the car-park. When they are both seated in his car and he is about to turn on the ignition, she says, "Wait!"

"What is it?"

"I do trust you, yes. But before we set off, let me just ask you a few questions."

"Please, feel free to ask anything you like. What do you want to know?"

"I know you feel responsible in a way which you explained to me when we first talked together in the hospital. And I know all the other things about you that you told me on your visits over the past few weeks. I honestly appreciate your concern and your support in everything. What I want to know is where this is going to lead us."

"I can't answer this question. I don't know the answer myself. All I know is this is not going to turn into an affair."

"I should hope not," she says a little too quickly but immediately apologizes. "Oh, I didn't mean to offend you."

"I know what you mean, and it's all right. I find you a very attractive young woman, but not in the way that…that…besides, there's the age difference."

"That's exactly how I feel. I couldn't handle another relationship so soon after my last one was shattered."

"So that's settled then. Next question?"

"Where are you taking me?"

"I told you. To your flat in Dorking. That is, if you've got your keys."

"I do," she says and searches through her jacket pocket. "Yes, here they are."

"Any more questions?"

"What will happen then?"

"You mean, when are you going to see me again?"

"Not exactly, but something like that."

"Well, let me take you to your flat first. Then we'll take it from there. Would you want to do some shopping on the way? You must need a few things, you know, milk, bread…"

"If you're sure you've got time." She smiles at him. "There's a big Tesco supermarket the other side of Gatwick, just about a mile or two from the North Terminal, you know, after that roundabout with the traffic lights. Let's go there if possible."

Ivan nods and starts the engine. They drive out of East Grinstead. When they pass the Old Felbridge Hotel on their right he waves his hand in that direction. "I was heading for this hotel when our cars collided."

"Were you? Did you stay there?"

"No, I was just going to meet a potential customer."

They continue in silence. Traffic is not too bad. When they

join the M23 for one section he accelerates the car. He thinks he can feel her stiffen a little. "Are you scared?"

"It's nothing," she answers. "It's only, you know, the accident. It's my first time in a car after my accident. I have to get over it."

He tries to drive with extra care, avoiding any sudden movements. They reach the supermarket, where he helps her select her food items. When they reach the drinks section she smiles at him. "I think we should celebrate. Don't you agree? Have you got time for a drink at my place tonight?"

"I'd be delighted. But let me get the booze. This is a man's job."

"How old-fashioned you are!"

"Please, it would give me pleasure." He takes two bottles of Veuve Cliquot from the shelf and places them in their trolley.

It is twelve o'clock when they reach the street of her flat. He finds a parking space opposite her building. He can see the brand-new red Toyota Yaris standing on the visitor's car-park near her front door. The red paintwork shines in the midday sun and comforts him. He puts his hand in his pocket and touches the keys of the Yaris. "She doesn't know," he thinks, "I'll tell her when the right moment comes." He hasn't got a plan of how he is going to present her with her new car. "I'll find a way," he thinks.

They enter her flat. He helps her with the shopping bags. She opens some of the windows to let in some fresh air. They put the shopping away, milk, vegetables and meat in the fridge, everything else in its proper place. He realizes that she is very methodical and painstaking in every detail. He likes this.

"You know," he ventures, "they say you shouldn't keep potatoes in the fridge. It's not good for them. Keep them in a cool spot, but not in the fridge."

"Is that a fact?"

"I read it in a paper some time ago," he explains and walks into the lounge. "A very pleasant place you've got yourself here,

I must say."

"What about a nice cup of tea?" she suggests.

They have their tea in the kitchen. Ivan looks at her as she goes about the routine jobs in the kitchen. Her movements are elegant and harmonious despite her limp. She is a very able woman, he notes. She is both intelligent and street-wise. Her language betrays a higher level of education.

They spend the afternoon in conversation. He helps her with some of the paperwork she has to go through in connection with the accident. She tells him that she will not have to go back to work for another month at least. She has time to recover. Ivan begins to tell her some of the less shameful episodes from his life. By the end of the afternoon they both feel more comfortable with each other in this environment. Whereas she learnt to trust him from her hospital-bed, to trust him in the intimate surroundings of her own flat is a different challenge.

At half past five she says: "Time for our little celebration. I'm allowed to drink alcohol in moderation."

Ivan fetches the champagne from the fridge in the kitchen while she gets the glasses and a packet of peanuts. They sit down at the coffee table. He opens the bottle, carefully avoiding the shock of a big bang like a true connoisseur, and he pours the sparkling liquid that always suggests boundless possibilities. The rising bubbles seem to address him with an encouraging prologue. He takes his glass in his right hand and stands up, which makes her smile. She finds this funny. But she accepts the fact that he is about to make a speech.

"Dear Emma!" he begins in his best speech-making mode. "I know you hardly know me. In effect we are really two strangers, even opponents in a car accident which happened a few weeks ago. So we shouldn't really be talking to each other, certainly not in a friendly way. However, I find that this accident has connected us. Among the millions of people rushing about on the face of the earth, fate has selected the two of us and brought us together in this accident." He pauses in order to compose an adequate continuation of his speech in his mind.

"Well then," he continues, "since this is as it is, let me make it quite clear to you that I feel in duty bound to make every effort to…to…well, to make sure you are well and happy and things don't go against you. I have no hidden designs. I am not a dirty old man trying to trap a beautiful young woman. All I can say is I feel responsible. But there are absolutely no obligations on your part. You are as free as you have always been. And now, to mark this responsibility and to celebrate your marvellous recovery from your bad injuries – "

"I'm still not all there," she interrupts.

"Yes, I know, but we have a lot to be grateful for, haven't we?"

"So I am told by the doctors."

"Indeed. Now, to celebrate all this and to underline my feeling of responsibility for you, here's to my young protégée Emma!"

She stands up, too, and they clink their glasses. He drinks with relish, while she only sips a small amount.

"Years ago I was my guardian's protégée, now you call me yours. I seem to be in repeated need of male protection," she laughs.

"And now," he announces with a certain degree of self-importance, "to complete this little ceremony, I'd like you to step outside. I've got a surprise for you."

In front of the building he hands her the new car keys and waves his hand in the direction of the shining red Toyota Yaris. "Voilà, madame! You need new wheels."

At first she does not understand what he means. But when the penny drops she cries out, "This is too much! You can't mean this!"

"Oh yes, I can and I mean to."

"But I can't pay for a new car, not until the money from the insurance comes through. If ever."

"It's a present," he says simply. "A present for you from me. Don't you like it?"

"I'll have to sleep on this," she says and turns round. She walks back into her flat. He follows, sensing that something is wrong. He follows her. Her back looks very stiff and upright. There is determination in her shoulders.

"Don't you want to have a good look at your new car first?" he carefully asks.

She looks him up and down. "What sort of a man are you? What do you want?"

He is speechless for a moment.

"I think it's better if you leave now," she says in a flat voice. "I need to be alone. I have to lie down. Please go."

Ivan obeys. As he drives away he asks himself if the gift of the new car was really such a splendid idea. Could it be interpreted as a selfish idea? he wonders. He tells himself he must be more careful with her, otherwise she might misinterpret his generosity.

On the following morning he finds a text message on his mobile phone: *Please just disappear from my life. E.*

He lacks the courage to act against her wishes. So he does not try to contact her for the first few days. He does not see her again for almost two weeks. Either he is too busy – he has to rush over to New York for three days on business – or when, eventually, he does try to reach her she is not in. Then, suddenly she calls him on the telephone while he is in a meeting in Edinburgh, so she speaks to the electronic answering service. "It's me, Emma. I've thought about lots of things. I'd like to apologize. I've been ungrateful. Please, call me when you have time."

He is extremely happy when he hears this message. He calls her back from the George Hotel in Edinburgh. Her phone rings several times before she answers it.

"Hello," she says in an uncertain tone.

"Emma, it's me, Ivan. I was so glad to get your message. Are you all right?"

"Yes, I'm all right. I had a few bad days with headaches but I'm a lot better now."

"That's better."

"Listen, Ivan. I'm sorry I was so rude. I thought about it. You see, when a man makes such expensive presents he always wants to get the woman into bed. So I was shocked at first. I was disappointed because I thought our relationship wasn't going to be like that and then you did that. What was I to do? How could I understand your generosity? I decided to send the car back to you and to dismiss you from my life."

"Yes, I can see that now. I'm sorry. I was so clumsy."

"Don't be sorry. It was my prejudice. I spoke to my old friend Peggy, and she asked me a few questions about you."

"Is that your friend who was in Spain when you were in hospital?"

"Yes, I really missed Peggy when I was in hospital."

"So you told her about me?"

"Yes, she was back from her holiday on the evening I sent you away. I contacted her and told her everything. She came round immediately and made quite a fuss. She was worried to death about me and my accident. Well, there was so much we had to catch up on that she stayed the night. We talked and talked. Of course I told her about you, your unusual interest in me and your generosity."

"And was her verdict the same as yours?"

"At first, yes. But when we talked about you again a few days later we both began to see the positive side of the situation. It was her who said that the way I talked about you indicated that you couldn't be such a bad guy after all. She reminded me of the fact that I had always got on well with older men. You know, first my step-father then my guardian, Peter. And she's right. I seem to find it easier to trust older men than the boys of my own age-group. So she made me see you in a better light. Eventually I was ready to forgive you. But then it took me quite a while to build up the courage to call you."

"I'm very glad you've called. I'll be back in London tomorrow evening. Can I come round?"

"I'd prefer to meet in a restaurant."

He agrees and they arrange to meet in a quaint country pub about ten miles from her flat. He realizes that she prefers to re-build their relationship in a neutral environment, not in the intimacy of her flat.

When they meet they have their open talk about their relationship. It is an unusual relationship. They both have to admit that. But they both accept it as it is. Emma accepts Ivan as her benefactor and unofficial guardian, an older friend to whom she has no obligations. Ivan accepts the rules Emma sets before him. He will not interfere with her decisions about herself and her private life. He will always get her consent before visiting her. He will not let his life be influenced by anything she says or does, at least he says he won't.

"One thing I have to confess, though," he adds.

"What is that?"

"You have already influenced my private life. I can't go back to the situation before our accident in one respect."

"And what would that be?"

He hesitates. "You know, my private life has been a bit complicated, I mean with women. A bit...what do they call it...? A bit promiscuous. What I mean is, I've been with quite a few women. But ever since I've met you and thought about your side of things, I mean all these past weeks, well, I've not become involved with anyone, and the most important aspect of how I feel is that I've come to see younger women – say, your age-group – in a new light. I could no longer draw a woman young enough to be my own daughter into an erotic adventure. It just wouldn't wash."

Emma looks at him in silence.
Then she agrees to accept the red Yaris.

PART TWO

Peter

SIX

Back then, in the early nineteen-fifties, it was the spirit of mediocrity which reigned supreme. Mediocrity in taste, mediocrity in judgement, mediocrity in one's ambitions. His parents represented the epitome of mediocrity, they were mediocrity personified. From a very early age he learnt to keep his wildest dreams and his keenest wishes to himself. He had made the mistake of mentioning an extraordinary idea to his mother once, back in the dim days of his early childhood, but that turned out to be a serious blunder.

It was on a Sunday evening in late summer, one of those Sunday evenings so full of frustration, towards the bottom end of a long day of best behaviour because there had been visitors. Not that his parents had visitors very often in those days, but on this particular Sunday it seemed to him that Uncle Charles and Aunt Ellen came to spoil all his Sundays.

Uncle Charles with his supreme knowledge on all matters of the world, his unquestioned political judgement, his unchallenged mastery in all sports, his wealth of jokes and stories that always proved him right. Aunt Ellen who simply knew everything in domestic matters, from the right way to bring up children to the best shops for women's underwear. It was truly amazing how his parents admired their old friends Charles and Ellen. They were the law-givers, they were always right and when they came to visit the entire household, the entire structure of the day – usually a Sunday – revolved around them, their presence threw a golden blanket of merry imprisonment over the family. Charles was very tall, with a daring moustache, Ellen was round and fat with a jolly double-chin, and both their voices were a lot louder than his parents'. So they filled up the house even physically. They were stern but cheerful. And most important: they had a car.

Was it evening or late afternoon? The sun was low, but it was still quite warm, the view down the street, beyond the bit that was covered with macadam on to the dusty road that had just swallowed their car, was drenched in pure gold. They were all standing in the middle of the street, turning around from waving good-bye to Charles and Ellen, starting to walk back to the house, when he asked his mother: "Why can't we have a car?"

"Now, Peter, you know your father hasn't got the money."

"But if we really saved up," he suggested, "I mean, couldn't we all make an effort so that we could afford a car?"

"How many times have a told you silly boys that only rich people have cars?" She shook her head, and Peter asked himself if the exaggerated loudness of her voice was an expression of her anger at his stupidity or rather of her own disappointment. She always put on this front of resilience as a woman of fortitude in the face of poverty, but he doubted her complete sincerity in this pattern. Didn't she have her own secret ambitions and desires?

"Couldn't we at least try? Fred says his friend Robert's parents are saving for a car, and the whole family makes a contribution."

"Then why don't you go and live in Robert's family?"

"I just think it would be something to look forward to, an aim, something…"

"You silly boy. Do you think money grows on trees? And besides, I don't want to see the day when a police officer stands on my doorstep to tell me that my husband has been killed in a car accident."

That was that. Peter had found that his mother always had plenty of sound arguments to defeat any of his ideas that went beyond the mediocre. That golden Sunday afternoon had taught him the important lesson to keep his best ideas to himself. What was the point of telling your parents about your really great ideas if these ideas were so cruelly crushed by a broad phalanx of sound, decent, intelligent, superior arguments from the adult world? Peter found that there was a tacit understanding with his brother Fred about this.

The brothers developed a regular habit of meeting in one of their bedrooms in order to discuss whatever was on their minds. This habit developed into what they called their board meetings. They had heard from Uncle Charles how the big companies were governed by board meetings, how all the great new ideas came out of these board meetings, and how such meetings were at the source of business transactions and money-making. Once the idea of the board meetings was born the two brothers experienced a new sense of purpose, a new confidence in their future and a new bond between them. Peter would wait in eager anticipation for Fred to come home from school. All through the long day he would store up his good ideas to be laid before his big brother at their board meeting. They found two old leather briefcases in the attic. The briefcases were a bit tatty and even torn in places, but they represented some sort of continuity, they had probably belonged to one of their grandfathers or to Uncle Eugene, who was a wild adventurer, so they radiated possibilities. Fred suggested they take these briefcases into their board meetings just like real company directors.

In what they felt to be their first board meeting, which took place in Fred's rather dark bedroom, they sat down on either side of the raw school-desk and set down the rules for all their future meetings.

"First of all," Fred said, licking his lips, "we have to decide on our factory. Board meetings are in charge of big factories."

"Yes, but Mother and Father mustn't know. They're too stupid to understand."

"Of course. Let's say this is our important meeting. This is where we take decisions. We're in charge."

"Great. Now what about our factory?"

"I'd say we produce many things. Our factory must include all sorts of possibilities."

"So why not call it the All Sorts Factory?"

"That's a brilliant idea. Sounds great."

So the regular board meetings of the All Sorts Factory became part of a vital rhythm in Peter's life. He enjoyed sitting on the low stool in the corner of Fred's bedroom and listening to his brother's explanations of all the important features of the world's relevant phenomena. While listening to Fred he would look past his brother's bushy head of dark brown hair, through the small window, and his glance would brush the top branches of the old plum tree across the field near the edge of the wood in the distance. Sometimes he managed to get his brother really interested in one of his own problems, such as his puzzlement over Susie and her strange behaviour. She lived only a few houses down the street, and he often wondered about the odd things she would say to him when they played in the street. He already knew that girls were strangely alluring but unfathomable creatures, but Susie presented a case that often occupied his mind. Clearly a topic for serious discussion at the board meetings. He never knew if the meetings had the same significance for his elder brother, but for him they were nothing short of a life-line, an umbilical cord which connected him with the really important things in life. Everything that really mattered was discussed in the board meetings. The wealth of ideas negotiated during the meetings was the fuel that carried him through the tediousness of the grey mornings and the boredom of those endless afternoons when Mother and Grandmother were talking, talking, commenting on their neighbours, often setting down the laws that ought to govern the behaviour of the male half of the population. At times, Peter even got the impression that they considered all men inferior, especially when they agreed that there was only one thing that men wanted. He never found out what that one thing was, but from the tone and looks that Mother and Grandmother adopted on these occasions he assumed it must be some really dirty thing. One day he even wondered if that black and dirty flaw in men's characters also applied to Father. Why then had they both got married to men? And how was it compatible with the image of Father – an image of perfection – that Mother constantly taught the boys? Also, if Mother was so worried about Father getting killed in a car accident if they ever got a car, that must mean that she was fond of him and wanted to keep him.

The 'car' discussion with his mother produced another result in Peter's imagination. The image of the police officer on the doorstep grew into an absolute certainty about people with cars. Whenever Peter saw a policeman walking up to a house – which was not very often, but nevertheless very effective – it was clear that the terrible news of a fatal car accident was about to be broken to a family, an unsuspecting widow and a small bunch of unsuspecting orphans. Whoever acquired a car was certain to meet his fate in such a way sooner or later. Mother made things even worse one day when Father mentioned the remote possibility of car ownership in the more distant future, rather in the mood in which one might refer to the possibility of winning the lottery one day. This time she didn't conjure up the image of the police officer on the doorstep, but angrily grumbled, "I'd be terrified to think of you coming home with your head under your arm." Peter's imagination painted the image of his father turned into some headless bloody monster with his head under his left arm, squeezed between his elbow and ribcage.

It was about a year earlier when Mother and Father had been taking the two boys on a cycling excursion to a beautiful spot under some huge fir-trees by the river where they had spent the afternoon playing ball and building a dam. Fred rode in the bike's baby seat with Father, Peter travelled with Mother. Whereas the baby seat on Father's bike was mounted on the crossbar between the handlebar and the saddle, allowing Fred to watch the road ahead with all its excitements, Mother's bike had the baby seat at the back, mounted over the rear wheel, so Peter had to be satisfied with the view of his mother's round backside shifting rhythmically from side to side. The only good thing about this was that he could smell Mother's summer dress, which gave him a warm sense of security and well-being.

On their way home they rode past a bad car accident. There were two black cars. One of them was an Austin with a pot-bellied boot-lid. Although there was not very much to be seen on account of the small crowd of onlookers, Peter spotted a bloodstained hole in the windscreen of the Austin. What did the man look like whose head must have hit that windscreen? Was he still alive? Had they taken him away because he was dead? Would a policeman have to go to the doorstep of the man's wife and give her the bad news?

Two images merged into one. Peter knew what happened to people who had cars. One day, inevitably, a bad accident would happen, there would be a bloody hole in the windscreen, and a police officer would appear on the family's doorstep. Even though this recurring image faded over the years, it was the first thing that sprang to his mind when his parents did buy their first car about five years later. But by then, many things were different anyway.

As was to be expected, some of the most imaginative decisions that came out of the board meetings were brutally opposed by parental mediocrity. The implementation of some decisions was indeed doomed to fail in the face of hard negotiations with Mother, usually with Mother, who, whenever further arguments failed her, invoked Father's authority: "Besides, your father is also opposed to this stupid boys' scheme. He wouldn't have it." Only in very serious cases did Father get involved himself, in cases that couldn't be dealt with by Mother alone with mere reference to his alleged opinion. Among the hardest cases fought over, Peter would always remember those of their projects that included some building component.

A truly brilliant idea was the board meeting's decision to cut a big hole for a door between Fred's and Peter's rooms. This project, which would have improved the house and would have made it possible to call board meetings at any time even during the night, was bitterly opposed by both Mother and Father. Equally doomed was the plan to dig a tunnel from the boys' sand pit in the corner of the garden to the unused room in the cellar. This project was only abandoned when Father himself sat down with the boys and gently blackmailed them. "If you only so much as start to dig a big hole in your sandpit we will cancel the family holidays that we have planned for next spring." That was hard, since it was the first family holiday planned ever. And during this holiday in spring, which they spent in a primitive but adventurous hut in the mountains, a hut full of the smell of burnt wood and warm fresh milk, Peter often asked himself if they really owed it to their abandonment of the tunnel project. Over the months, Fred and he came to the conclusion that none of their building projects would ever become reality. One day in late May, they had a special board meeting to discuss their limits. The final decision reached was that parents obviously saw it as their main task to oppose all their children's good ideas. In the course of the following two years, the board meetings continued – although the All Sorts Factory never managed to take up production – and remained Peter's life-line until they gradually faded out when he started school.

After they moved to a different suburb around the time he started school, life took on a new dimension. Forgotten were the old building projects, and even the vision of the serious police officer or the headless monster on the doorstep faded. What suddenly opened up new possibilities was the circle of children in the new suburb. Everything was new. For the rest of his life Peter's nose would remember the carbolic smell of the brand new wooden fences along the gardens in their street, especially mixed with the smell of the wet macadam after a fresh summer shower.

For him this smell stood for all the new possibilities. Anything might happen here, anything could be achieved, there seemed to be no limits.

"I'm sure you don't know what a naked girl looks like," a small boy with a smeared face taunted him one afternoon. This came as such a shock that he thought it better to avoid this boy, at least for the time being. However, before he even found out that the boy's name was Thomas he regretted his first reaction. After all, the idea of a naked girl had never occurred to him, but now, all of a sudden it surfaced as an overwhelmingly important if somehow frightening image. Peter had never ever seen a girl without her clothes on, the fact that they must exist as naked bodies underneath their skirts, blouses and jumpers dawned on him as a revelation which proved to him that the future was full of possibilities and discoveries. But what did they look like?

Without letting on to Thomas, Peter began to be aware of the girls in the street. Even though most of them still seemed rather stupid creatures to him, reminding him of Susie in the old place, they appeared to have a special aura about them. The way they looked at you when you stood in front of them trying to teach them a new game with a ball, this could really unsettle you. Why did they have to look at you in this way? And what was it that made them laugh without cause, out of the blue, as if they lived in a different reality? He attributed such strange behaviour to their basic stupidity, and yet there remained a certain fascinating enigma whenever you had anything to do with them.

It was Thomas who drew him into the circle of the boys in the street. It was almost like some secret club, they had code words and secret names for certain activities, people and places. It felt good to belong, to be part of their league. The other boys seemed older and more daring, except for Thomas, who was definitely younger. As if to compensate for his younger years, he was the sauciest member of the group and he often came up with the wildest suggestions and the most cheeky ways of attempting forbidden pranks. Peter reserved his judgement and held back his trust.

"I know that Daniel's mother is a thief," Thomas revealed to his astonished listeners one afternoon. Peter and two other boys constituted his audience on this particular occasion. They were all sitting in the tall grass on the further side of the local wood. It was a great spot. Since the wood was situated on a hill slope the boys could sit at the top end and peep round the few corner trees, and this gave them a fantastic view over the entire suburb which everybody still called a village. Behind them lay open countryside. And if they wanted to meet in a secret spot where nobody could find them and they still wanted to be near the look-out at the corner of the wood, what better place was there than just a short distance into the tall grass of the field beyond?

"She can't be. You're nuts."

"You needn't believe me, but I know."

"How?"

"I just happen to know. That's why Daniel is always so nervous, and he doesn't join us sometimes. Look here, she goes round to other people's places when they're not in, and then she's got these flashy dresses. My dad says he's seen her come out of his old chum Rob's house, and she had nothing to do there."

Though the three boys were not convinced, the image of Daniel's mother as a thief stayed in Peter's mind for a long time. Even years later in his adult life, whenever a female criminal was mentioned or reading a report about a petty theft in the paper, the haggard face of Daniel's mother would flash up in his mind. She was a very thin woman with shiny black hair and deep-set, sad eyes. She was often seen smoking a cigarette in the street, and she always seemed to be in a hurry. In Peter's world, she was the exact opposite of Aunt Ellen, in looks, in temperament and in the ideas she provoked in his mind.

Thomas also claimed to know the colour of Daniel's mother's underwear, an item of knowledge that didn't strike

Peter as particularly relevant but impressed him nevertheless. Especially when, one morning on their way to school, Thomas came running up to him and whispered in his ear: "She's got herself a new set of underwear, and it's the colour of leopard skin." Later on the same day, Peter found out that all the other boys knew. The effect that this revelation had was threefold. First of all, it somehow gave the stories of Daniel's mother as a thief a higher degree of credibility. Secondly, she became the only adult woman the boys took an interest in, she took the position of 'the woman' and you could always count on an attentive audience when you invented a crazy story about her. And last but not least it gave cheeky little Thomas a more important standing among the boys. Despite his years he became the first authority on all matters related to women, girls and other slimy things.

Peter, though very happy to be accepted by all the boys, remained more on the quiet side when he was with them. True, he was fascinated by their superior knowledge of so many things in the world, and somehow he admired all of them. But there was also a strange feeling of being drawn out of his depth into treacherous waters that left him insecure. Sometimes he simply couldn't figure out what they were talking about, they seemed to know so much more about what was good for you or about things that adults seemed to be interested in. The girls puzzled him even more, especially scrawny, red-haired Heidi, whose parents had the corner store, and Rose from the other side of the big main road, he had a feeling of certainty that deep down he could trust them, that they were somehow more reliable than the boys. There were about half a dozen girls that he knew in this neighbourhood, they all talked to him and it didn't make him as tense as when he was with the boys. And by the late summer of 1956, which suddenly brought so many changes to the village, he realized that one of the girls gave him a particularly relaxed feeling. She seemed to understand him better than anybody else. Her name was Vita and she lived in the quaint little house opposite, the one with the steep roof and the decorated front door. Since Mother had become friendly with her mother they often met, chatting about their children or helping each other with an egg, an onion or some good advice. Like this, he was often thrown together with Vita.

She was an extraordinary girl. Her skin was soft and very pale, her hair dark but not quite black, and the colour of her eyes seemed to hover somewhere between blue and green. She had a voice that had a resonance that belied her youthful age, it was almost a man's voice, and she had a smile that sometimes gripped him in his stomach. What could it be about her?

"Let's go up to my room. Our mothers will be a while over their coffee," she suggested, a cheerful and open smile on her face. "Come, let's sit down here." She motioned to a low green pillow-seat. "Would you like to see my postcards?"

"Yes, that'd be great."

She fetched a shoe box from a shelf above her bed. As she did this, he looked around the room. So this was a girl's room. He was disappointed, he had imagined a girl's room to be a lot more mysterious, sweet-smelling and frilly, well, just more girlish. This was not at all like that. Vita's room struck him as banal, ordinary, normal, not any different from a boy's room. Until he discovered the doll at the top end of her bed-cover. So there was a difference.

"Look here, I've ranged them all in this box," she blurted out as she threw herself down next to him again. The jolt of her landing on the pillow-seat tore him out of his thoughts, and he immediately liked her companionship. It was only after getting back to his own room later that he would fully realize he had been sitting next to Vita, who was a girl after all. This was a first. He had never before been so near a girl, so close to her that he could see the faint freckles on the side of her nose. And he believed he could even detect some soapy smell about her. Or did he only imagine this later?

"I also think postcards are great," he said. "You can see other places, other countries, you know, big cities, monuments, waterfalls and such things. Fred even got a postcard from his godfather with the Eiffel Tower on it. That's in Paris. I'd like to go to Paris when I'm grown up. Would you like to go to other places, too?"

"Of course. My favourite place is Buenos Aires – "

"That's the capital of Argentina. I know because Fred and I sometimes play capital cities and country games, you see, who knows the most countries or capital cities. Do you know the capital of Mongolia?"

"Is it Bangkok?"

"No, it's Ulan Bator. Bangkok is the capital of Thailand, where the Siamese cats come from. We could play this game, too – "

"No way. You'd win all the time. But you know, my mother's family come from Argentina. I'd like to go there one day." She grabbed a postcard out of the pile in the box. "See, this is the government building in Buenos Aires. See the blue sky?"

"Yes, but they always do that. They always make the sky blue on picture postcards."

"Why not? I like to imagine fine sunny weather all the time in Buenos Aires." Her eyes glowed and adopted that mysteriously distant look. "Wouldn't it be great to have sunny weather all the time? My mother said they never planned for bad weather when she was a girl, they just went on picnics whenever they liked."

"What's a picnic?"

"It's when you go to places in the country and you sit on a blanket somewhere in the grass and you have sandwiches and tomatoes and apples, and you laugh and you have a good time. The whole family, sometimes with lots of friends."

"Have you done it? Going on a picnic?"

"Yes, more than once. But now with Mum not being in very good health, Dad says we shouldn't go on any more picnics. It was always Uncle Alfonso who took us. He had a car. But that was a while ago."

"Oh, you have been in a car? My, you have done some things. The only time I was in a car was with Uncle Charles. It was a dark blue Ford with that thing in the middle of its front which looked like a nose or a third eye. An American car. Uncle Charles said it could go very fast. Wouldn't you like your parents to get a car?"

"I don't know. It never occurred to me."

"Well I would."

They looked at more postcards, and it was only when Mother called to tell him they were leaving that he realized he had been with Vita all this time. Mother and he took their leave and walked back across the street. Back in his room, he regretted the slimness of his own postcard collection. Vita's family must have lots of friends that she managed to get all those cards from so many places around the world. His family received very few cards. He looked up at the ceiling for a long time thinking of Vita and her superior experience.

Throughout the following months he saw her regularly. They would spend at least two entire afternoons per week in each other's company. This did not strike any of the boys in the crowd as odd. After all, the boys did not meet so often during the winter months. There were fewer things they could do. Besides, the boys were more concerned about the new Hungarian family who had moved into the rear apartment of Daniel's mother's house and who had two boys called Miklos and Laszlo. Also, the boys had endless discussions about the danger of all motor traffic becoming illegal, that absence of cars on the roads on a Sunday due to what was called the Suez Crisis had been such a shock to all of them. So he was free to see Vita more often and he grew accustomed to her company. While he was with her she was a companion, a playmate, and it was only from time to time, alone in his own room, when he thought about her, that he reminded himself that she was a girl. A girl who was a real person. A girl who had absolutely no connection with the image of girls conjured up by sleazy Thomas and his gang. In fact, Peter never ever connected the juicy details about girls which were traded in low voices by Thomas and the others with his own experience of Vita. For example, when Thomas described in detail how girls went to the toilet, a procedure which appeared incredibly complicated and yet fascinating, Peter simply could not imagine Vita doing anything like it. But then, Thomas ought to know, he had an older sister. So, because the two worlds were utterly incompatible Peter stored them in two different compartments of his mind. He did not arrive at this solution by logical reasoning, but it just happened to him. Things just fell into place like this. Whenever Thomas or one of the other boys came up with new bits of information about girls' intimate activities or girls' bodies he imagined these things to be true about other girls; girls that he would never get close to, girls he would never be able to understand, especially all those girls who giggled all the time.

This world order carried Peter peacefully through the winter season. It was a winter season that proved to be one of the most carefree phases in his life. Everything had its place; Mother and Father remained mediocre but provided an atmosphere of reliable if somewhat boring stability, Grandmother hovered in the grey background and mostly endeavoured to make her favourite grandson Fred happy. Fred continued to be his best friend and most valuable companion although the brothers were more and more drawn into their respective circles of friends at school, and then there was Vita across the street. It was good to know she was there.

SEVEN

In the spring of 1957, the season began with an abundance of bright days with hard-edged sunshine. Promises were in the air, and the hill-slope to the north looked particularly gentle and well-meaning as if it wanted to invite one to a world beyond. He knew that the new greenness of the grass had something to do with him, it spoke to him, but he was as yet unable to comprehend its message.

While things at home and at school dragged along in their well-trodden grooves, Peter's imagination undertook more frequent, longer and more extended journeys. It seemed to him that he no longer enjoyed the other boys' company as much as he used to. Somehow he felt more detached from them. One of the novelties in his life was his gradually growing interest in stories that the teacher told them in class. His parents had never taken a great interest in stories, though they always seemed to listen with fascination to any of Uncle Charles's stories, but those were stories that were not really free and detached, they merely served to show up Uncle Charles's superior knowledge of things or his cunning in tricky situations, so Peter saw them as stories that were tied down, stories in captivity. Also the stories contained in his Uncle Eugene's letters, sent from distant shores, were fascinating and captivating in their exotic oddities. But they could not satisfy him because in essence they did not reach beyond Uncle Eugene's cynical world-view. In contrast, the stories he heard from the teacher at school were unbound, they had wings. Anything could happen in them. They were not focused on the person who was telling them. One of the stories that made him aware of the true freedom that stories brought with them was a story the teacher told them out of a handsome book with a grey and orange cover. It was about a wooden toy-donkey. From this story he learnt that in the old days river boats used to be pulled along by donkeys on tow-paths. This idea set off a series of colourful images in his mind, and he saw himself travel down a big river on a comfortable river boat. He would daydream about all the wonderful places he was going to visit on his journeys down the river. Sometimes the views of riverside-towns merged with images from Vita's postcards.

Somewhere in a story which the teacher managed to tell them with particular relish there appeared some Italian place names. The names that impressed Peter the most were the names of Piombino and Portoferraio. Somehow these two towns appeared to him like two brothers, a connection which was underscored by fact that their names began with the same letter. Though he had soon forgotten the exact context in which these names had first appeared in the story – he could only remember that one of them was on an island and they were both connected with each other by a ferry service – he treasured the music of these names and along with it his vivid image of colourful sea-ports with palm trees and boys with curly black hair. And the big ships that passed by on the open sea carried him off to a wealth of new worlds.

The most important lesson he learnt from the stories was the fact that people in stories could do a lot more things than all the ordinary people he knew. Mothers in stories were a lot more adventurous and understanding than his own mother, and fathers owned fantastic things or if they didn't they were ready to go along with all sorts of interesting projects such as unexpected trips or meeting new people, or else they received unexpected letters and telegrams from people they didn't know, which started them on new adventures. Also, people in stories always seemed to know how to do difficult things, they knew how to walk up to strangers and ask them things, they could book trips on railways and boats, they could influence important persons and they could move hard-boiled crooks to pity.

His new pleasure was private. He sensed that the other boys did not share his interest in stories. Also, he did not dare to let the teacher know that her stories were the absolute highlights of the tedious school week. What else was there to rival or challenge the stories' radiance? Most of the things taught in class were banal anyway, he could not see why such a fuss was made out of reading and writing letters and words or out of playing around with numbers. Why go to all the trouble and do all sorts of exercises and play all sorts of games when you could just take up a story and read it or just write down what you felt like telling the world? And numbers were a funny game anyway, you could never really take them seriously. Peter took in all the numbers he could see – in shops, on car registration plates, in telephone directories and all kinds of lists – and turned them over in his mind, trying out combinations, parallels, relationships. By the time the teacher announced that they would now be learning numbers beyond 100, Peter had already fathomed the mathematical possibilities of all the car numbers, phone numbers and birthday dates that he knew in his street. He had realized, for example, that you could add up the phone numbers of three of their neighbours and just knock off the two noughts at the end and you would get Daniel's mother's car registration number exactly. Or he had figured out a system by which you could add up the same number several times much more easily by memorising all the results. It was only two years later that they came to learn this at school, and Peter was surprised to learn that the method invented by himself had actually existed before and it even had a name, multiplication. How unfair that the teachers had never told him before!

Stories and numbers were it. They made life worth living, though in different dimensions. They complemented each other. While the numbers gave you a huge playing area full of criss-cross paths that gave you a very vivid but somehow superficial and fleeting pleasure, the stories opened up a less limited and much more serious sort of pleasure, a pleasure that was open towards the light, a pleasure that made you feel that the further into the unknown outer spheres you ventured the more new possibilities and unexpected vistas would allure you even beyond.

Getting up in the morning, you could look forward to new discoveries. You might get to know new exotic places or strangely fascinating new people in stories, or you might find out a new game with numbers, for example you might try out, just as you found 'multiplication' by repeated adding up, if you could find yet another level of number games by repeated multiplication, and then repeat that process again and again, there may be endless possibilities…Numbers were fun, but not really serious. Stories, however, encapsulated what life was all about. Stories were the most important and the most serious thing.

Peter was sitting with Vita on her pillow-seat. They still enjoyed looking at picture postcards together and they still told each other stories that they had heard from their families, from their parents, uncles and aunts, but over the past few weeks their conversations had become more and more personal. One day he discovered that he could actually exchange opinions on their real-life situations and on their social environment with her.

"What do you think of Thomas?" he dared to probe her.

"What an awful horror! I never talk to him. Sometimes when I see him on my way home from school I go down a different street to avoid meeting him."

"But he seems to get everybody else organised."

"Yes, his sister told me. But I just get goose-pimples when I get near him. I don't trust him." Vita stood up and walked over to the window.

"I don't like him either. He says some awful things sometimes, but somehow I can't help listening to him when he brags about things." And Peter immediately regretted admitting such an intimate conflict to her. The mixed feelings he had about Thomas were something very personal, and his confession now made her an accomplice, it established a new bond between them.

It was in April and the days were quite mild already. Peter had heard some rumours about a really daring scheme some of the boys were involved in. He gathered that it was something really naughty, something absolutely forbidden, but something that promised to take them all onto a new level of experience. At first, he dismissed it and tried to remain detached, but gradually its fascination caught up with him. On a Monday afternoon, as he was sitting with Vita, he suddenly got the impression that she also knew about it, but when he asked her she evaded him and led their conversation in another direction.

"Have you heard of that secret place some of the boys seem to be talking about?" was the most direct question he asked her.

"Stupid boys often seem to have secrets. They need them to feel important," she answered and changed the subject. He felt like asking her about girls' needs for secrets, but he decided against it. Nevertheless, the fact that she changed the subject so quickly confirmed his impression that she knew more about it than he did. And it was this realization that somehow marked the beginning of this strangely attractive but frightening episode which was to become one of the most haunting experiences of his boyhood years.

Remembering this episode later in life, Peter never quite knew how he came to be involved, too. Also, he could never determine whether it was really Thomas who had been in charge or whether the affair had sprung out of several children's secret desires and curiosities. Much later in life, he came to the conclusion that it could not have been brought about by Thomas alone, it must have grown out of the restricted upbringing of his generation and the mendacity of their parents' generation in the nineteen-fifties.

Some distance to the north of the main road leading past

the housing estate that was the home of Peter, Thomas, Daniel and the others, there rose the gentle slope that dominated the distant view. All the way up the slope you could climb along the edge of the forest that stretched east, from the top of which you had that fantastic view over the entire village. It was half-way up along the forest edge where, just inside the woods, there was a platform of more even ground than the general slope warranted, a platform overhung by several large oaks with hollows under their partly-bared knobbly roots. The effect was that of a large room of a raw wooden cabin, with an open space of considerable size right in front of it like a balcony or terrace, the entire area being shielded all round by thick foliage, which gave the place a secluded atmosphere. It was the perfect location for forbidden activities.

Not long after he had touched the subject with Vita, probably something like ten days or so later, Thomas half-whispered something he couldn't understand at first.

"Are you coming to the pissing-tree?"

"What do you mean?" They were on their way back from school. "Now?"

"Yes, just meet me at five, I'll take you there."

Peter still didn't know what the pissing-tree was, but it certainly sounded exciting. Or was it just an exaggerated name for a boys' meeting place? Well, he would soon find out if he agreed to join Thomas at five.

"All right, I'll come."

When Thomas met him at ten past five he had that strange smirk on his face, a thoroughly objectionable expression which Peter hated because it made him wonder how much Thomas really knew and if he was not secretly looking down on you. They walked north across the large field and began their ascent up the slope along the edge of the forest. Soon they reached the secluded space in front of the oak-tree. After following Thomas through the thick foliage, Peter saw that there were about twelve or fifteen other children gathered there, boys and girls, sitting or standing, playing with twigs or shifting their feet from side to side on the ground, chatting and laughing. Nothing extraordinary. Except for the strange atmosphere of secrecy somehow magically created by the charm of the location.

Peter was immediately drawn into the dream-like atmosphere and the daring mood. He was still wondering and looking around to see who was there – recognizing about half of the other children, but not really caring if he had ever met them before – when Thomas announced that Oscar was giving the orders today. Oscar was a boy about five years older than Peter, he only knew him slightly because he did not really see him as a boy, rather something between a boy and a man.

Oscar stepped round the oak-tree taking an elevated position. He looked down on all the children gathered below and he slowly took a pack of cigarettes from his right trouser pocket. With practised ease he pushed a cigarette from the pack and flung it between his lips with a sort of flourish. He quickly lit the cigarette, inhaled the smoke and blowing it out of his nose and mouth at the same time, announced:

"Boys go first today."

Eagerly, but without haste, all the boys climbed the distance to where Oscar stood and he made room for them on top of the large tree-root extending along the ledge. Peter clambered after Thomas, and it never occurred to him to stay behind, it was the most natural thing to do as all the other boys did. Later in life he sometimes wondered if they had all been afraid of Oscar, but he always came to the conclusion that this was not the case.

The boys placed themselves in a row standing on the ledge, looking down on the girls waiting below, their heads about level with the boys' feet. Some boys were talking or whispering, but the mood was very relaxed and quite natural. When Oscar smiled and nodded twice the boys grabbed their trousers, some of them had shorts, and they all lowered them and stepped out of them.

Peter followed their example and took off his trousers. Then they all pulled down their underpants and threw them on the ground. The slowest boy was still struggling with his balance on one leg as he was tearing at his underpants when the fastest boy – Peter saw it was Thomas – took his penis between the fingers of his right hand and began to piss right into the open space in the direction of the girls below. The girls seemed to be familiar with the procedure and knew how to avoid the liquid arch and yet to step as near as possible to watch, and in no time at all the boys were all pissing. Everybody laughed, boys and girls, some of the girls clapped their hands, some gave encouraging shouts.

Peter just did as the others did, and he thoroughly enjoyed the mood of merry companionship. He did not feel embarrassed one bit. If he had been asked in a different context if he would ever stand naked from the waist down in front of a girl the mere thought would have made him sick with embarrassment. But this was a different matter. He was carried along by the general wave of merriment, and the girls below were not individuals but just a crowd of smiling faces. He could not identify a single face. They were just eyes and mouths.

It was soon over. The liquid arches collapsed, the boys gathered up their underpants and began to dress again. The general noise did not subside but continued in mixed chatter and giggles from the girls, while the boys grew silent as they finished dressing. Peter felt like stepping into a different room. Although the general mood did not change, his own perception of himself in the world shifted. The boys jumped or slid down the slope onto the platform where the girls stood. He heard Thomas bragging to some girls, "Now, whose was the biggest?" Peter could not make sense of this question. Why should anything be the biggest? Wasn't it all about showing the girls something the boys could do that they couldn't do? Peter was still absorbed in his dream-like mood when Oscar's voice commanded:

"Now the girls, but one by one."

The girls giggled even more, and then one of them – Peter thought he recognized Marianne, one of Daniel's sisters – climbed up, positioned herself so that all the others could see very well from below, pulled her red tartan skirt over her head and then, very swiftly and with a short laugh, stepped out of her white knickers. Peter felt a strange knot in his throat as she placed her legs well apart, bent her knees slightly and began to urinate down at them.

He would never forget this sight as long as he lived. So this is what girls look like between their legs! He forgot everything around him, he could only stare at such strange beauty and such an extraordinarily shaped part of a human body, and this pale nothingness with its small slit seemed so very naked, somehow more naked than naked and so very vulnerable to him. He could not take his eyes off such a miraculous sight. He was so elated and yet so sad. This was not for him. He was an intruder, a trespasser. This was not right. This privacy belonged to this girl, not to him, not to all the other boys, not even to the other girls. Why was Marianne doing this?

Suddenly it was over. She put her knickers back on, with a laugh arranged her clothes and climbed back down. But it was not over. The next girl – Peter did not even get round to looking at her face, so he could not identify her – had already positioned herself on the ledge and was pulling at her skirt. Again, he could only look at the ambiguous emptiness between her legs. He wanted to look away, but it allured him and disgusted him with such irresistible force that he had to glare at the new nakedness this second girl was offering them. This time he registered a significant difference in shape and skin texture, and he became aware of the squirting piss from the tiny slit, something he had not registered with the first girl. Some time during the second girl's performance – for a performance it certainly was – Peter's vision became blurred, and he lived through the remaining parade of half a dozen girls' private parts in a trance-like state.

The last of the girls was just about to expose herself when he realized from her movements that she was more reluctant than the others, and when he heard her embarrassed giggle he was sure she did not really want to be doing this. This realization connected her with him, it made him suddenly tear his eyes away from her intimate nakedness and look into her eyes. A pang shot through him – it was Vita!

Peter could not remember the remaining time they spent there. He could not remember what happened after the girls had done their part, he could not remember what anybody said, how they got away from that place, or how he got back to his parents' house and to his room. The film was torn the moment he had looked Vita in her eyes.

In the days and weeks following this episode Thomas often tried to persuade him to come and join them again at the pissing-tree. Initially he refused, finding some excuse about duties at home, but eventually he found his way back one more time, only to be disappointed. The daring atmosphere of novelty was gone, gone was the mixture between fascination and disgust. All that remained was an atmosphere of something between embarrassment and utter ridicule. He decided he would not go to the pissing-tree again. Whereas he had hardly been aware of the girls' identities that first time, this second time he took in all their faces, and they seemed blank and uninteresting to him. With quiet satisfaction he noted that Vita was not among them the second time. Had she had similar feelings that one time? After a break of a fortnight he found himself with her again, up in her room. Neither of them mentioned the embarrassing episode, and hesitantly they resumed their former friendship. But Peter knew that they could never return to their former intimacy. That unmentioned and unmentionable episode stood between them.

Much later, when Peter was a grown man, he sometimes remembered that youthful folly of the pissing-tree, and the older he grew the more convinced he became that all children must go through some strange experiences of that kind, experiences that officially could not exist in the adult view of childhood. At one point, about thirty years later, he even spoke about it when a woman he got intimate with was curious enough to question him about his discovery of sexuality. It cost him quite an effort to report every detail as honestly and as accurately as he could remember it. Her reaction was unexpected. She stiffened, her eyes took on an aggressive insistence and she flatly refused to believe him. "That's typical! Pure male fantasy, how could you expect me to believe you? But then it's clear, that's what all men have on their minds. It's about time for you to grow up." Insulting as her remarks could have been for him, he did not really mind because he knew better.

After some consideration he arrived at the conclusion that the woman must have had very similar experiences or even the very same memories. The more he thought about it the more convinced he was that she was ashamed of realities from her childhood which simply must not be true in view of public adult morality. But why should he be ashamed of his own memories? He knew that that experience was part of his personal biography. And the embarrassing eye-contact with Vita remained part of the experience, it was one of the most vivid memories he kept of her, even long after she was dead.

The first discovery of the true nature of girls' bodies came to be linked, not so much with Vita and the change in their relationship, but much more clearly with the developments at home. Peter was still struggling to come to terms with the enormity of the episode in the woods and with what he had witnessed there – a phase which kept him preoccupied and made him more taciturn when he was in the company of other boys – when his mother took him and Fred aside after their evening meal.

"Tomorrow's going to be a big day."

"Why? What's going to happen?" Fred prompted her.

"It's a secret, so don't tell anyone, not even your best friends. We're going to take delivery of a new acquisition."

"But what is it?" Fred urged, while Peter thought how typical of her to use this stilted phrasing. She just couldn't be straightforward, she always spoilt the best moments. If this was going to be such an important 'acquisition' why couldn't she just tell them they were buying such and such?

"You will see. Don't be late coming home from school."

When Peter came home the next day he had quite forgotten Mother's announcement of the previous evening, he was too preoccupied in his thoughts and he was going through his memory of the pale skin on the inside of Vita's legs when he saw a grey van standing in the street in front of their house. He didn't bother to investigate the van more closely but stepped through the front door. It was only in their living-room that he realized that this was what Mother had meant. Two men in grey aprons were fiddling with wires while Mother was rearranging the furniture. Then he saw the new piece of furniture in the left corner. What was this new object, a chest of some kind? a new type of radio? a drinks cabinet?

Mother was beaming and biting her lower lip. Father came in from the hall, put his briefcase down and gave Mother a long hug. "I managed to get home a bit earlier today. I didn't want to miss this."

One of the two men in grey aprons seemed to be the boss. He was older and he gave the orders while the younger one had to kneel down behind the settee, fetch things from outside – from the van in the street? – and go upstairs to do whatever his boss shouted after him. Gradually Peter realized that they were installing some kind of machine. There were electric wires, and it all had an air of extreme importance. He knew electricity was dangerous, so he was confirmed in his assumptions when he saw how carefully the men handled their wires, connected things and plugged and unplugged something at the rear of the chest.

Then suddenly the older man opened the door at the front of the chest and a dark grey shining glass screen was revealed.

"Now, Mr. and Mrs. Hoffmann, this is the great moment." The man showed his stained teeth, his smile was so big it seemed unreal to Peter.

He pressed a button. At first there was just that little click and nothing else happened, but after about fifteen seconds a dim grey light appeared on the glass screen. It was only a small spotlight in the centre, and after another fifteen seconds it spread all over the screen. Peter could not understand what it was supposed to be, or what the whole new gadget was supposed to do. The final picture was a symmetrical array of different geometrical lines and shapes in different shades of grey.

"This is the test picture," the man said. Then he fiddled with the knobs under the screen. After a few attempts, the men managed to get the central shape into a perfect circle and the various bars into straight oblongs. Eventually, they declared everything ready.

"Now we only have to wait till six o'clock," the younger man said.

"No, there's nothing at six today. It's half past seven. Yes," the boss said, checking something on a small piece of paper in his hands, "there's a documentary at half past seven, and then there's the news at eight. So, we can switch it off now. What you have to do at half past seven, Mr. Hoffmann, is simply press this button. Don't touch these, and also leave the channel button alone, since we've only got the one channel with the type of aerial you've got. So, as I said, switch it on and wait for the picture to come on, then check the quality of the picture. If you're not happy with it – say it's not clear enough, or it won't stay in place – one of you can go up to the attic and shift the aerial while the others stay down here and shout when the picture's fine. I'm sure you'll be happy with this set. Yes, that's it, I think. Let me thank you for choosing our long-established business. We have to be off now."

The men collected their array of tools, bits of wire and mysterious gauges, and they took their leave, shaking hands with Mother and Father. As they were driving off in their van Fred came home. He ran to the living-room and immediately began to go over the array of buttons at the front of the set. Mother ran after him, shouting, "Fred, don't touch anything! It's always the same story with you naughty boys, here we bought ourselves a television-set, and what do you do? Before we have even used it to watch a programme you must damage it!"

So now Peter knew what this chest was: a television-set. He wondered why Fred had known about it. And how did he dare to touch those buttons? Nobody could know what they were all for, there were so many. But he had seen Fred going at other machines or technical gadgets before. That's what Fred was like, he just couldn't keep his hands off when he saw a machine or an electric appliance. As for Peter, he was never tempted to unscrew the back of an alarm-clock and take it to pieces or, as Fred had done only three weeks ago, dismantle the electric plug of the living-room lamp. From Mother's frequent warnings he was sufficiently aware of the dangers involved, particularly when it came to electricity. On the other hand, electricity had a fascination all of its own. Part of the fascination came from what it could do. Also from its mysterious invisibility. Peter was convinced it had its own smell. At least he was aware of the smell whenever Fred was fiddling with electric wires, and now the same smell emerged from the television set, especially from its back. Pungent, esoteric and yet homely, metallic and rubbery all at the same time.

At twenty past seven the whole family gathered in the living-room again. Even Grandmother had come down for the occasion. Such was the significance of this historic moment, the first television viewing in the family. Father was arguing with Fred whether it was a good idea or not to switch it on before half past.

"The man said at half past," Father emphasized with a certain degree of authority, although his voice betrayed a trace of uncertainty.

"But if we switch it on before half past, and it takes a while to warm up, it should be ready for the programme to come on. Otherwise we're going to miss the beginning of the programme."

At last they agreed to start the process at twenty-seven minutes past seven. Father and Fred both checked their wrist-watches. Peter did not own one in those days. At last it was time. Father was about to stride up to the set and press the button with an air of ceremony when Fred overtook him, rushed forward and pressed the button first. Intoxicating silence. Everybody's eyes were glued to the dark grey glass screen. Grandmother stood up from her easy-chair and coughed. The spot came on, the test picture came on, and to everyone's delight there was even a sound of light music. After a few moments, the music stopped, the test picture disappeared, there were some irregular light flashes on the screen accompanied by a crackling noise. Then the sound of a gong, and suddenly the face of a young woman, all in different shades of grey like a picture in a newspaper, smiled at them from the screen. She said good evening and announced the programmes which were about to follow. Peter did not listen to what she was saying, he was too fascinated to see the face of the woman move, just like the cinema. They had been to the cinema with Mother and Grandmother a few months before, they had seen Charles Chaplin in a gold-rush story, and Peter remembered a scene with a house hanging over the edge of a precipice. But this was not in the cinema, this was at home. Peter wondered if they would now be able to watch such a Chaplin film at home.

The documentary started. It was something about shipbuilding. About three minutes into the programme, however, the picture suddenly ran down the screen very quickly. Father and Fred immediately tried to set things straight. But the process proved to be a lot more complicated. There was angry shouting, there were accusations like "This is all your fault," or "You shouldn't have touched that button," or "Now you destroyed the family evening." Fred was sent up to the attic, Father shouted directions, more accusations, more frustration. In the end, everybody was disappointed. They did get the picture back for a few moments, but it was never right, either too blurred behind a screen of what looked like sand-grains, or running down the screen. Mother went to the kitchen and Grandmother set the table in the small dining-room. Peter just watched what was going on. He felt he shouldn't interfere with the frantic endeavours to get the television-set back on track, that was all Father's and Fred's domain.

They sat down to a quiet evening meal at a quarter to nine.

"We'll have to call that television shop first thing tomorrow morning," Father said. No one answered. Peter noted that the atmosphere was so tense that it was best just to eat his soup in silence.

They did get the television-set running a few days later. While it was indeed a historic addition to the household, the boys had to accept the fact that it was primarily a source of entertainment for the adults, the programmes normally beginning at half past seven or even eight in the evening. On Tuesdays there were no programmes, as Father explained, because even the television people had to have a day off. Only on Thursdays there was a children's programme between half past five and six. Fred and Peter watched it at first, but soon they found it too childish, more for smaller children. And since they were only allowed to join their parents in front of the television screen on Saturday evening in order to watch some comedy or a more or less educational quiz show, sometimes a mixed show of popular music that was more in Grandmother's line, the attraction of the television-set for the boys gradually dwindled away. Except as a field of exploration and technical experimentation for Fred, of course. But in terms of the programmes one could watch, the boys came to consider them rather silly.

"We got the television-set mainly for Grandmother," Mother explained. "You know, boys, she's not in very good health and finds it hard to go out, so your father and I decided to get this as a source of entertainment for her."

As it turned out, Grandmother's health was indeed getting worse. In early June she fainted while she was peeling potatoes in the kitchen. The doctor came to examine her. He called an ambulance and they carried her off on a stretcher. Peter ran after the men carrying the stretcher to the rear door of the ambulance. He grabbed Grandmother's right hand, and she responded with a slight pressure of her hand and with a faint smile on her pale grey lips. "Don't worry, I'll be all right, old iron will not rot," she breathed as they were shoving her stretcher into the ambulance.

Three weeks later Grandmother was dead.

The evening before, Mother and Father had rushed out of the house after an unexpected phone call from the hospital. The whole night Fred and Peter were alone in the house, a state of affairs they had never experienced before. Mother had told them nervously that they didn't know when they'd be back, but Peter began to worry when he woke up at two in the morning and they were still out. He sat up and listened to the dark silence in the house. He wondered if their unusually prolonged absence was a good sign or not. He wondered what Grandmother was doing at the moment, but he soon gave up and fell asleep again.

When he woke up in the morning he heard a loud wailing sound from downstairs. It had a frightening intensity which scared him. He had never heard such a woeful sound before. After some hesitation he got up and went downstairs. There was Mother, crying like a small child, sobbing and wailing aloud, her face flushed and covered in tears. She was sitting at the dining-table while Father was standing behind her, gently stroking the back of her head and her shoulders. After a while Mother saw

Peter. Through her tears she looked at him with a distorted face.

"You must be very brave, my boys. You have lost your dear grandmother."

She stood up and walked over to him. She took him in her arms and hugged him for a long time. He could feel the spasms of her whole body as she continued to cry. It occurred to him that something was very wrong in this situation. Though he couldn't have explained it then it was his first taste of irony. If Grandmother was no more that was no reason to be crying. It was rather something to be glad about. She would no longer tell him off with her stern voice, and she would never again treat Fred with demonstrative preference when she came home from shopping in town. All those little humiliations would be a thing of the past. And here was Mother doing her best to comfort him. It was not he who needed comforting. He should be comforting her.

Grandmother's death changed the family routine for a long time. Peter began to observe every event and every new arrangement with a certain detachment. More and more over the following months he became an outside observer in his own family. He found himself watching his parents' activities and listening to their conversations with the air of a visitor to the zoo watching the animals' behaviour. All the fuss at the funeral! Even Uncle Eugene came from far away, probably from some exotic place in Asia, just to be with them for two days. And then the strange way of talking everyone adopted.

Soon after the funeral things were changed in the house. Grandmother's old room was rearranged. Ever since they had been living in this house – unlike the house in the old suburb – Fred and Peter had had to share a room between them. Now, they were told they no longer needed to share a room, they could choose who wanted to move into Grandmother's old room. Since their formerly common bedroom was larger, Fred said he would stay there. He was the older boy, he said, and Peter had to do what he said. So Peter accepted the smaller room. At first it seemed odd. He was not sure if there was still Grandmother's smell in the wardrobe, and he wondered if it would change now that she was dead, become more deadly. But he soon forgot about Grandmother and enjoyed the new freedom he had gained. He could do as he pleased in his own room! Apart from Mother's weekly cleaning invasions he now had a world of his own.

So, all in all, Peter's first experience of a death in the family turned out to be a factual improvement and rather a happy affair. It took him a very long time in his life to learn about the other faces of death.

EIGHT

Both novelties – Grandmother's death and the new television-set – opened up a new phase in Peter's life. It was 1957. Peter was nine years old. He felt that everything around him had some meaning. The trees stood there because they were meant to, the houses stood where they were meant to stand, every man had to be the way he was, every woman had to be the way she was, only about himself he was not too sure. Was he meant to be who he was? Could he have a say? Could he influence parts of his own life? Why was he in this family? Why was Fred his elder brother?

For the next few years, questions like these often dominated his thoughts from time to time. He would find himself sitting down on a park bench, on the river bank or in an easy-chair at home, lost in thought. Sometimes his mind would go blank after a while, but he did not mind. He enjoyed these moments of nothingness, time seemed to be held in limbo for a while, his whole world was kept on hold, it was like those moments on television when suddenly all motion stopped and the picture stood like a photograph for a brief moment. He knew that it was not supposed to do that, it was a faulty moment. So he came to think of his own periods of thinking nothing as faulty moments.

In addition to his faulty moments, he developed another type of special moments that took him out of his physical existence for a few seconds. These were his photographic moments. It happened the first time during a fishing excursion with Father and Uncle Charles. They travelled in Uncle Charles's blue Ford. They drove to a lake about three quarters of an hour away. The men had unpacked their fishing gear and all the paraphernalia they used to take along and Peter had just settled down quite comfortably on a tuft of grass from which he could overlook the surface of the water and lose himself in pleasant day-dreaming, when Father threw one of their boxes on the ground and began to swear. They had forgotten to take the tin full of worms that they used as bait. Uncle Charles calmed him down.

"No problem. Don't worry! I'll drive to the nearest village and get some."

This was a reasonable proposition. Peter saw his chance of getting another trip in the Ford. "Can I come along with you, Uncle Charles, please?"

"Of course, hop in."

They drove only a short distance to the nearest village. It was a small farming community on the left of the main road. Uncle Charles commanded:

"You get out here. Walk down to one of those farmhouses, they're bound to have a manure heap in their yards. Here, take the tin, you'll find lots of worms in the manure." He opened the side door and motioned Peter to get out.

What a horror! Not only to be practically thrown out of the Ford, but to be expected to walk up to a strange farmhouse – possibly with a fierce dog – and to dig for worms with one's hands! Before Peter could recover Uncle Charles had banged the door shut and driven off. He had said something about finding a good spot. What had he meant? Within seconds the Ford had disappeared from the landscape. The world was silent. Time stood still.

What was to be done? Peter walked a short distance in the direction of the nearest farmhouse. There was no manure heap but there was a sleeping dog on a long leash. The dog was huge. Peter passed the danger zone in a wide circle and checked the yard of the next farmhouse. Again, no manure heap! He tried two more farmhouses, then he gave up. He decided to tell them he couldn't find any worms because there weren't any manure heaps. Let them do their fishing without worms. What a cruel idea anyway, to send him to pick up yacky worms with his bare hands! If they didn't believe him he would just stick with the same version and not budge: there were no worms.

Then it occurred to him that Uncle Charles had driven off. Had he abandoned him? Was this one of his special tricks, part of an adventure he would brag about afterwards? Whatever it was, Peter realized he was alone in this grotty little farming village. How would he ever get out of this? How would he ever get home again?

He sat down on a low brick-wall and heaved a deep sigh. He would not cry, he knew he would not. He was a tough boy. Perhaps not tough in the sense of some of the other boys, not tough like Daniel or Thomas, but he had mental resilience. He would draw his strength from within. He saw himself sitting on this low brick-wall, all alone in the middle of this farming village far from home, abandoned by his parents. He took in every detail surrounding his position and took a mental photograph of the entire scene, himself at the centre. He imagined the camera position up there on the left, about a man's height from the ground, and he pictured the photograph in his mind. This was one of his memorable photographic moments.

The main features of such a photographic moment were all there: He found himself in a desperate or otherwise spectacularly intensive situation from which he did not know how to escape, he had no idea of the direction his life would take from here. Where would he be in a day from now, a month from now? Would he be wandering through the countryside begging for food? Or would he, through some miracle as yet unimaginable, be restored to his home and his family? This was the first such moment, and much later in life he knew he was collecting such moments, each single moment preserved in a mental photograph and equipped with a caption asking a question that did not greatly vary. It was usually something like "How will I ever get out of this?" Sometimes the caption was a statement: "This is such a special moment, I have to take a mental photograph of it."

When he was a young man in his late twenties he tried to come to terms with this experience, with his view of personal experience through the medium of mental photographs. His critical reviewing of his own method was triggered by his reading of Proust's *A la recherche du temps perdu*, Snow's *Strangers and Brothers*, and Powell's *A Dance to the Music of Time*, all of which made him think about the nature of experience, the passage of time as such, and the process of living through the dimension of time. He was particularly impressed by Powell, who, in one instance, talks of the ageing process as an almost unbearable accumulation of experiences. Smiling at his own naiveté he thought: "Well, what a good thing I haven't accumulated too many mental photographs."

The episode with Uncle Charles and the unsuccessful quest for worms was solved in an anticlimax. After about half an hour on the brick-wall Peter decided to take things in his own hands and he walked back to the road. No cars in sight. So he just started to walk back in the direction they had come from. It would take him a very long time to get back to his father on the lake-shore, but he had to try. He had been walking for only about five minutes when he suddenly heard a car approaching from behind. He turned round and saw the blue Ford, its brakes screeching. Uncle Charles threw the passenger-door open and looked at him with a reproachful face.

"Where were you? I got bloody scared. Thought the worst had happened."

"I was looking for worms, but there weren't any. There weren't any manure heaps either. So I kept looking and looking."

"But why in hell didn't you come back to where I had told you?"

"You didn't tell me anything. You just drove off!"

Uncle Charles fell silent. Peter realized that there must have been a terrible misunderstanding between them. When they got back to the lake Uncle Charles dropped him off and drove away again. When his father asked, Peter only said that they hadn't found any worms. After a while Uncle Charles returned with a tin full of worms. Soon, the men silently held on to their fishing rods and looked out over the surface of the water. Peter wondered why Uncle Charles did not say anything to his father about their embarrassing episode. In fact, the episode was not mentioned at all for years. Only when Peter visited him as an old man in a care home Uncle Charles came out with a cryptic remark. "You gave me the shock of my life." At first Peter did not understand what the old man was referring to, but when Uncle Charles added, "You know, that time with the worms," Peter knew at once. It made him truly sorry for the old man. Had he really given him such a fright? Of course, from an adult point of view, it must have been awful for him, fearing he might have lost the boy of his best friend while he was in his care. Uncle Charles must have gone through hell for about half an hour back then. Strange that he never ever mentioned it in all these years!

The year which marked the beginning of Peter's faulty moments and his photographic moments – at least in his memory – was the year in which everybody talked of the first satellite in space. It was called Sputnik. Peter considered that a charming name. It could be the name of a circus clown. When his parents discussed it they became very serious. They said it was not good for the West. Peter asked Fred about the satellite. His brother explained what it was and what it was for. As it appeared, it was an iron ball with long spikes sticking out from it. It flew round the earth at enormous speed, higher up than any aeroplane could ever fly. It was for science, Fred said. In spite of Fred's complicated explanations, Peter wondered what exactly it was doing up there in the night sky and why it could be bad for the West.

The West. Adults often used this word. He knew the

directions, north and south, east and west, he could even point them out. West was over the top of the tree to the right of Vita's house. How could that Sputnik thing in the sky be bad for things beyond that tree? Or did they mean the whole of the west? Half the earth? The west ended on the back side of the earth-ball, in the middle of the Pacific Ocean. Did they mean all that?

The subject came up at school. The teacher told them more about the new satellite. Not everything she said was compatible with the information he had from Fred, but he learnt a lot more about the reasons behind it. The teacher told them that the Russians had shot the satellite up there in order to spy on the West because they wanted to know everything about the West. This was the moment Peter had been waiting for.

"Please, Miss. I wonder if you could tell us a little more about the West. What area of the earth-ball is it that the Russians want to spy on?"

"Of course, Peter. This is all very important. And it is good for you children to know about these things. The Russians want to attack all the countries in the West, especially all of Europe and North America," she said in her even voice that Peter liked, and walked to her desk. She took a wooden globe from her desk and held it up for all the children to see. She pointed with her finger.

"Look here, children. All this is Russia, all this green area. And all this," shifting the globe round and holding it higher up for emphasis, "all this is Europe and this is America." Peter noted that she included Canada. He knew better, but he did not mind because here at last somebody explained the political situation to them, the situation the adults were only furtively referring to when they spoke about "the West".

"Now the Russians are trying to take all this," she circled her finger over an area covering not only Europe and North America but also the Atlantic Ocean and parts of western Africa. "And they are a very treacherous people. They cannot be trusted."

"But, Miss, aren't there any normal people, too? I mean, people like us, or do all the people in Russia want to take the West?"

"Those who don't agree with this plan are trying to get out of Russia. Like Miklos and Laszlo, whose family preferred to come here."

"But, Miss, they come from Hungary, not from Russia," Peter blurted out.

"Don't correct me, Peter. Hungary belongs to Russia these days, I'm afraid."

Their lesson on the teacher's version of the Cold War continued for over twenty minutes, and in the end all the children walked home with a strange feeling of unease. When would the Russians come here with their tanks and rockets?

The Sputnik affair made everybody more interested in the daily news. In Peter's home, this meant absolute silence during the midday meal because Mother and Father were listening to the radio news. In the evening, the television-set was switched on in time for the news on that medium. Neighbours began to talk more openly about the Russians, about what Eisenhower was going to do and about the general danger of the times. Since no other family in the street had a television-set it became quite common for neighbours to come round and ask if they could watch television with Mother and Father. The arrival of such neighbours usually marked the end of the day for Fred and Peter. While the adult people settled comfortably in the living-room the boys were sent up to bed.

Among the television visitors, Thomas's father put in by far the most frequent appearances, sometimes with his little mouse of a wife, sometimes on his own. One day they even came with their children, but when they were told that children were not allowed to watch television in the evening they drew long faces trying to hide their disappointment, and they sent their children home. Even though they smoothed over the momentary embarrassment with over-friendly smiles Peter registered that Thomas's pale mother was offended and perhaps even quite angry. From then on, she rarely came along, but her husband kept up his routine, he even seemed to come more often than before.

One morning, Peter saw that his parents were in a very strange mood. They hardly talked during breakfast and the atmosphere was thick with unspoken words. There was puzzlement and an inability to cope with a difficult situation. Peter knew that no questions could be asked at this stage, but he was confident that Mother would tell him something over their afternoon tea. Of late it had become a regular custom for him and his mother to have a cup of tea between four and five in the afternoon, and this became a time of intimacy between them. Mother would often explain things more clearly or he would tell her about unsolved mysteries among his friends at school. Sometimes they planned imaginary trips together. So he knew she would talk about whatever had worried them in the morning.

"I don't want you to play with Thomas," she began.

"Don't worry, Mother. I don't really like him. He's dirty and I don't think he can be trusted. He's cheeky, slimy, cunning."

"That fits. No wonder, with such a pig of a father," she almost spat when she said this. Peter was shocked by the strong language. She had never called anyone a pig before.

"You see, my darling, you will grow up to be a man one day. I only hope neither of my sons are ever going to be such pigs. So it's perhaps a good thing for you to know what happened last night. That man came to watch the quiz programme on television. You know your father was out teaching evening class, so it was just the fat man and me. We were watching the programme on television when he suddenly shifted and sat down beside me, touching me and trying to kiss me. I jumped up and managed to escape from his dirty fingers. I made quite a scene and threw him out. As he crept out he mumbled something, he tried to justify himself, he had only been trying to have some fun with me, why couldn't I be his sweetheart and so on. The man is married, for God's sake!"

Her fury boiled up while she stopped for breath, and Peter knew that it must have been an awful experience for her. He did not ask any questions.

"You see," she moaned and shook her head, "deep down, all men have a dirty spot. You listen. I never want you to do dirty things to a girl. As a man, you have to keep the animal inside you under control. I know it will be hard for you, because all men are the same. All they really want is to do dirty things to women…"

Peter was impressed. On one hand, he felt honoured, Mother had told him about an experience which must have been very difficult for her, an adult experience. On the other hand, he had an uneasy feeling about the warning she had given him. He had heard her say similar things about men before, only in less violent terms, talking in the kitchen when Grandmother had been alive. So there must be something really dangerous about being a boy, a man, a male. If it was such a dangerous thing – an animal inside oneself? – he would have to be very careful. Of course, it was a dirty thing if Thomas's dad tried to touch and kiss Mother, with him being a married man, married to his own wife whom he could touch and kiss as much as he liked – Peter found it hard to imagine Thomas's parents hugging and kissing, with him being such a big, fat man with a beer-belly and her being such a humble slip of a pale young woman always seeming to apologize for something – but was it dirty if you wished to touch a girl? He admitted to himself that he had wanted to touch Vita, but he had never dared.

With all the complications that human intercourse appeared to entail, Peter found it comforting to spend more time at home than with other children in the street. He liked to read stories, to draw pictures, to build little houses from scraps of cardboard, sometimes to attempt to write a story. With these occupations he never missed the company of any of the other boys, he was fulfilled, his world was clearly mapped out in his mind. Coming home from school he began to look forward to the peace and quiet in his own room, which was only interrupted by tea-time with Mother. All in all, this life-style made him a very content and indeed a very happy boy by the time he reached his tenth birthday.

Then there was the great moment when he was allowed to watch the first film on television. It was quite a festive affair. Mother announced over breakfast that there would be a big surprise for them in the evening, on condition that they were going to be good boys throughout the day. Of course, Fred wanted to know what the big surprise would be, he tried to worm it out of Mother, but without success. Walking to school together Peter and Fred speculated and came up with various solutions. Fred's predictions were more pessimistic than Peter's. While Peter was hoping for a new toy, perhaps a dinky toy car or something to go with their electric train set, Fred said it was more likely to be some silly but useful present, knowing their mother all too well he put his money on a new pair of socks knitted by Grandmother and found among her things by Mother last night.

Peter made sure to be home in good time after school. He had tea with Mother, Fred joined them, Dad came home, but still nothing was explained until they were all sitting round the dinner table having their potato mash and sausages.

"Your mother and I decided to give you a very special treat tonight," Father began as he was folding his napkin – a thing he often did during the meal, only to open it and spread it across his lap again. This was a true sign, it indicated that he was having difficulties saying things that had a heavy emotional component and he hoped for his wife to take the direction of the conversation in her hands.

"Well, boys," Mother continued, beaming at her patient boys. "It is as your father says. Tonight we are all going to watch a film on television. Now you know that films are only for grown-ups because children often have nightmares from bad things in films, but we trust that in this case we will be quite safe. It's a film I saw with Ellen two years ago when it was in the cinemas, so I know it's not going to do you any harm. They're showing it on television tonight, so we're all going to watch it together."

Mother went on and on about the qualities of the film, her favourite actors in it, the moral aspects of the plot and the general atmosphere she was so fond of. Peter didn't listen to her speech, he was so excited. He was going to see an entire story on television. What a treat! He could hardly wait until half past eight.

The boys helped to carry the dishes to the kitchen and to wash and dry them there. While they were working through these chores, Peter heard Fred mumble something like, "I knew this was going to be a flop!" This was unfair, Peter thought. They were in for a really nice treat. But obviously Fred was disappointed.

"Aren't you pleased?" he asked him when Mother was not listening.

"What's so special about watching a stupid old film on TV?" Fred snarled.

"I like it. I'm looking forward to it. I'm terribly excited."

"You would be, little snapper, wouldn't you?"

"I thought you liked television?"

"But not that sort of thing! Why on earth would I want to watch a film that Mother found gorgeous when she watched it two years ago? It's bound to be some old people's stuff, boring, full of moralizing acidity and old world charm."

Although Peter was impressed with 'moralizing acidity' – a term which he had not the slightest idea about, but he was not going to ask – he suddenly realized that Fred and he would always look at things from two different angles. It dawned on him that Fred was not really interested in stories. What fascinated him about television was not its capacity for the life of story-telling but only its physical existence as a machine, a technical gadget, a dead object. This came as a small shock. Peter had just experienced the fact that two people could look at one and the same thing but really see two quite different things. He was sure this was going to shape his understanding in so many ways in his future years. For the moment, however, it was not something to brood over. Joy and anticipation were the words now.

They had all settled comfortably in the living-room, Mother and Father both with their cups of coffee on the low table in front of the settee. Their faces beamed with pleasure. Peter cast a sidelong glance at Fred and he saw that his big brother could either hide his sad disappointment very well or he was caught up in the general mood and decided to go along with a good sense of humour, because Fred was beaming like everybody else.

The film began, and immediately Peter was lost to the outside world. It was just wonderful, it seemed to last for ever and ever. The family of the village policeman was caught up in all sorts of complications, the girl was oh so lovely, and the crafty businessman who turned out to be a gangster in the end had such a funny way of stroking his hair back, it was all like real life. What a lucky fellow was the shy young man who managed to win the girl's love, and they went for a drive in an open sports car together. And then the girl's brother! He was called Peter, – what a coincidence! – he wanted to be an artist, but his father – the stern old village policeman – would have none of it, he wanted his son to become an accountant. Peter liked the bit best where the policeman's soft heart prevailed and he allowed his boy to work for an artist. That moment was brought out in its full emotional force by the music that accompanied the scene, the violins swelling up and making one understand the extreme effort it cost the man to shed his hard shell and listen to the voice of his good heart.

When *The End* came up on the screen and the violins again went all over the house of harmonies, Peter saw that Mother had tears in her eyes, and he knew they were tears of joy.

It was not until about three or four days later that he could talk to Fred about the film. Of course, their opinions were as far apart as anything.

A new chapter in Peter's life was opened in the year 1958. His father took driving lessons and bought a car. They were the fourth family in their street to own a car. Of course, when the car was delivered it was the same story as when they got their television-set. Fred knew all about it, he wanted to open the bonnet and look at the engine, he said they should all practise changing the spark plugs and the wheels, but he was checked by Mother and Father, who were afraid he might damage something. The usual row followed, and in the end Fred managed to get Father to let him have the car keys after they had all gone back inside the house. So Fred carried out his technical investigations with the car outside while Mother and Father were busy reading the papers in the living-room.

There was one drawback, however. They could not go for a drive immediately because Father was still learning to drive. On the following Wednesday he had his next driving lesson. Peter thought this a wonderful opportunity.

"Can't I come along?" he begged.

"We're not allowed to take passengers along," was Father's reply. But when the dark blue Volkswagen of the driving instructor arrived at their garden gate Peter ran after his father and the instructor beamed with good-natured contentment.

"Want to come along with your father?" he asked before either of them could say anything.

So Peter came to accompany his father on most of his trips with the instructor. It was different from what he remembered about Uncle Charles's driving style. Father was going a lot more slowly and the instructor's car was a lot smaller. But Peter enjoyed every moment of it. They usually travelled through the countryside, and Peter was pleased to watch the green meadows, the leafy trees and the massive, brown-grey farmhouses pass in front of his side window. This routine was changed when Father had mastered the art of changing gears. Then they drove through more urban areas.

"The old man's really not very gifted, is he?" Fred remarked one evening when the boys were sitting on Peter's bed exchanging their views on their parents. "I mean the ages it takes him to pass the driving test."

"But changing gears is really difficult. It takes a while to learn it."

"Nonsense. Every child can do it, I'll show you." Fred fetched their piano stool from the living-room. It was a stool with a round seating top you could turn to adjust the height, and the boys had used it to play car or bus, sitting on a chair and turning the stool top as their steering wheel.

"Look, this is how it's done," Fred proudly declared. "This is your right foot, which you use to press down the gas pedal, like this." He pressed down his right foot in the air, leaning back on the edge of the bed.

"Now, watch this! I have revved up my engine to over 4000 rpm, so now I have to change gears, to shift from first to second gear. And what do I do?" He lifted his right foot and pressed down his left foot, fiddled around in the air with his right hand and then reversed the process with his feet.

"See? It's dead easy. All you have to do is disconnect the gearbox from the engine, which you do with your clutch pedal. That's your left foot."

"And what were you doing when you waved your right hand?"

"I didn't wave, I changed gears. I moved the gear-stick from first to second."

Although not everything was quite clear to Peter, he understood that changing gears was the real test when you learned to drive a car. He decided to start practising this art for his own driving career soon. He was very fortunate to have such a clever elder brother who could explain everything.

Meanwhile, Father's driving made good progress. When Uncle Charles and Aunt Ellen came to visit the next time, Uncle Charles offered to go on a practice drive with him. Peter went along. They drove through the city, through several suburbs, then out into the open country. Father said he was getting tired, but Uncle Charles overruled him.

"This is only the beginning. Now you have to practise manoeuvring and reversing."

He planted a few sticks in the forest ground at the roadside, announced that these marked the edges of other cars parked along the street, and he forced Father to park his car between the sticks, again and again and again for more than a whole hour. Peter noticed the drops of sweat on his forehead. But there was more to come. Poor Father was forced to drive backwards along a narrow country road, between hedges, up a hill and down into a valley and up again, for another full hour. The sun burned down relentlessly and heated up the interior of the car. They had all the windows open, even the rooftop, but it did not help much. Father kept complaining that he'd had enough, but Uncle Charles would have none of it, he really flogged his pupil to the utmost limits.

"Why on earth did I agree to go on a practice drive with such a maniac as you?" Father moaned as they reached home.

"But you've made tremendous progress, you'll see, you'll pass your driving test very soon now. You'll be grateful to me."

And Uncle Charles was right. Within two weeks after that terrible drive Father passed his test. Everybody was happy, and Father called his flogging master on the telephone on the same evening.

The big announcement that came with the newly acquired freedom concerned the plans for the family holiday in July. They would drive to the seaside. They would see Uncle Eugene, who had settled in a small seaside resort. They would stay with him and his family for four weeks. All this was possible because they now had a car and Father could drive. It was fantastic. The new possibilities that opened up because of the car. The world was theirs now. There were no limits. Peter felt elated.

It was a hot day in July. They had made a very early start and they were all in a festive mood, Mother, Father, Fred and Peter. They were driving through France. Peter kept his face glued to the window. This was pure bliss: to glide through unknown territory, to see fields and forests one had never seen before, to be carried through space by the secret hands of some invisible god, to hear the pleasant and confidence-inspiring purr of the car engine, to watch the shadows of trees, houses and bill-boards as they flitted by at a speed which was just right. The bill-boards of France, a fascinating new experience! *Kléber-Colombes, Dubonnet, Panhard*...truly amazing, the sheer size of some of the boards. Peter found it particularly thrilling to discover the goods and services that were awaiting the travellers in the next town, as became clear from the increase of bill-boards on each approach. He learned which car makes had agencies in the different towns, all complete with the addresses and telephone numbers of the garages. He counted the number of hotels and restaurants announced on each approach, the advertisements for washing-machines, aperitifs, car tyres and shoe factories. The only features that could compete with the bill-boards in terms of connections with new worlds were the signposts, particularly the distances in kilometres indicated on them. And wherever they were, there was always a signpost for Paris: *Paris 354, Paris 271, Paris 168, Paris 99*. Peter fell in love with the style of the black letters on the white signposts. They were black and white birds pulling him towards all those destinations.

On the summit of a small hill he discovered a bill-board carrying an advertisement for a bottle with the word *Rémy-Martin* written on its label, and near this board stood a signpost with *Paris 229* on it. This scenery presented such a perfect picture of exotic beauty that Peter experienced one of his most memorable photographic moments. He would remember the soft glow of the afternoon sun and the warm colours surrounding the board and the signpost, together with the dark green trees in the distance, as one of the outstanding pictures in the film of his life.

The trip through France taught him that their car was relatively small and slow. They were overtaken by hundreds of bigger and faster cars. He thought the people in the cars overtaking them were probably laughing at them, looking down on them. Were they really such a poor family? Why had his parents bought such a little car? It lacked not only size and speed but also style and social prestige, a word he did not know at the time but a concept he clearly understood because he could read it on the children's faces pressed to the side windows of the passing cars.

But all in all it was a good holiday trip. It was an experience that mattered.

NINE

The early 1960s constituted an ambiguous period for Peter. On the one hand, it was a time of sleep-walking through life. On the other hand, it was full of important experiences – experiences that would assume a significance much later in his life. Some of the most outstanding moments he would store visually. They formed the continually growing collection of his photographic memories.

It was a time of personal and social upheaval for him. It was also an era of disappointments and regrets. When he turned fourteen he began to realize for the first time that the strange urges he felt from time to time were not some hidden disease that would kill him within a short time but had something to do with girls. He felt extremely uncomfortable and yet at the same time elated when he looked at some of the girls in his neighbourhood in a certain way.

One day, it became almost unbearable when he saw one of the older girls from further up in the same street – she was already sixteen – riding her bicycle and moving her body in a way that immediately gripped his chest. He nearly stopped breathing. This experience was more than a photographic moment, it was more dynamic, it was rather a film sequence that he was sure he would remember till his dying day: the lithe young body writhing rhythmically from side to side on the saddle, accompanied by the girl's carefree tinkling laughter.

In his class there were only boys. He could handle those. There were the bullies like ginger-haired Bruno, there were the slimy sneaks like dark-haired Tony and there were the naïve milksops like fair-haired Alfred. He could almost predict their actions and they held no secrets for him. But when it came to girls he was lost. More and more over the years, they became alien creatures. They would laugh at you from the distance, or at least that was what he believed. They would always stick together in groups, especially when they went to the toilet. He found it irritating that the girls never went to the toilet alone, they usually went in pairs. Boys would never do that. What on earth were the girls doing on the toilet together? He often wondered.

He also found girls evasive. They would never approach the boys and talk normally, from one person to another. But he had to admit to himself that neither could he. He couldn't imagine stepping up to a girl and asking her a simple question or telling her a piece of news that he would tell a boy, for example. He was far too scared of being laughed at. He was convinced that he was an extremely ugly and ungainly person. Boys that were admired by girls looked different. He could never measure up with them. To make things worse, his voice was the first to break in the whole class, and he felt ashamed of the deeper resonance in his voice. In music lessons he had to sit apart from the others because the teacher told him not to join in the singing, otherwise his voice would spoil the pleasure for everyone else. He had to be considerate. As it turned out, 'considerate' also became one of his parents' favourite words. All of a sudden it became very important not to stand out, not to be different, but rather to blend in, to be like everyone else, to be more considerate.

He often wondered how the other boys were getting on in these difficult times. What especially intrigued him was the question of how boys with sisters felt about the whole girl situation. One of his classmates, René, often talked to him about this question. René had no sister either, but he said he knew everything about girls, as indeed he claimed to know everything about women in general.

"You know, Pete, when you have a question about the

womenfolk just come to me. I can tell you anything you may want to know."

He sounded very convincing. So convincing, in fact, that Peter never even thought of questioning his authority on the subject. It just never occurred to him to ask René why he knew all those things that he claimed to know. At first he did not know that he had no sister, and when he was enlightened on this fact by Robert it still did not diminish René's aura of authority. He had something very worldly about him. When he explained certain facts about women that Peter had not heard about before, he assumed a tone of voice that reminded Peter of heavy-weight politicians or important businessmen in wood-panelled clubrooms, cigar in one hand and whisky tumbler in the other. The air was full of smoke.

"What do men of the world do when they want to know things about women?" René lectured one afternoon as they were standing on the street corner where they normally parted because their homes lay in different directions from here. "They look it up in a magazine."

"What magazine?"

"Come along, I'll show you." René led the way across the busy street.

"I haven't got a lot of time. My Mother is expecting me home."

"This won't take very long. You see that newsagent's over there?"

"That's the place where Fred used to get *Mickey Mouse* when he still read those. We've still got them."

"Well, chum, this is going to be very much like *Mickey Mouse*, I can tell you, only for older boys, if you know what I mean." He sniggered.

"You mean I should go and buy a magazine? I haven't got the money for that."

"Not buy. Come along and do what I tell you. It won't cost

you a thing."

He walked into the newsagent's. Peter followed. They stood at the counter for a few seconds before the woman saw them. She was an older woman, Peter guessed at least forty, with a pleasant smile and a mole on her left cheek. She looked down at the two boys and asked them in a friendly sing-song voice what she could do for them.

"Can I have the latest *National Geographic Magazine*?" René asked in a polite voice full of self-confidence.

"Just a moment," she said and turned around, "I'll have to get it from out the back, but it won't take more than a moment."

This was the moment René had been waiting for.

"Quick," he hissed. "Pull out that magazine with the blue cover from under that other one with the face of Fidel Castro on it. But be quick."

Peter obeyed. He took hold of the magazine with the blue cover.

"Now, put it in your schoolbag before she comes back," he urged, looking left and right. Nobody could see them.

Peter did as he was told. The woman came back just as he had finished closing his schoolbag. She held a new issue of the *National Geographic Magazine* in her hands and wanted to hand it to René.

"Oh, I'm sorry," René said to the woman in what seemed to Peter a very theatrical manner. "I've got the wrong purse. I haven't got enough money to pay for the magazine. I'm really sorry."

"No need to be sorry, my dear. You come back for it when you have the money."

The boys turned round and walked away. René led the way to his place. It took them about five minutes, but they didn't speak a word all the way. They stepped through the front door, and René shouted to his mother that he was bringing a friend to do their homework for school. They climbed the stairs to his room, still not speaking a word. At last they closed the door and René turned the key.

Peter whispered, "That was stealing."

"Oh, come on. She won't notice. She's got such a lot of magazines and papers, she won't know if one of them's gone missing."

"I have never committed a crime before."

"That's not a crime. We're only helping ourselves because they'd never sell this to boys our age. Now, come and open your bag. Let's look at it."

Peter took the stolen magazine from his bag. It was quite a fat magazine, very glossy and expensive-looking. It had a forbidden air about it. It was called *Playboy*. René took hold of it and opened it in the middle. The centre pages folded out and revealed a picture of a naked woman. She had very blonde long hair and lay on a heap of straw in a barn. She was smiling at the camera in a provocative way. She had not a stitch on her body. Peter gasped. He had never seen anything like it. He was reminded of the experience of the pissing-tree many years ago.

René showed him more pictures of naked or half-dressed women in the magazine, but the boys had to turn back to the big fold-out picture in the middle again and again. For them, this picture was an absolute masterpiece. Peter believed it was the most beautiful photograph he had ever seen. And the most beautiful woman.

When Peter left, René wanted him to take the magazine with him, but Peter refused.

"I wouldn't know where to hide it. Mother would most certainly find it."

So René agreed to keep it at his place for the time being. But he made him promise that he would take it over after a week or so. They both did not like the idea of such hot stuff in their homes for their mothers to find.

When Peter walked home he could not take his mind off the

picture of the blonde woman, and that night he saw her in his mind very clearly. She made him feel very strange but extremely happy as he was drifting off into a sleep full of new dreams.

At school the next day, René only winked at him from time to time. Peter knew what that meant: "We both know something that the others don't. We have seen the blonde woman naked." But of course, he did not let any other boy suspect that anything could be out of the ordinary. He wondered how they would react if they saw such a picture. Would they all be as impressed as he was? He was sure they had never seen anything like it. They couldn't, or they wouldn't look so ordinary. But then he also did his best to look normal. He realized that most people had secrets that others couldn't guess just by looking at them. He wondered whether everyone had a parallel existence apart from their public face.

At the end of the school day, the teacher asked Peter to help him put away some materials, so he was the last boy to return to his own desk to collect his stuff and to pack his bag. When he opened his desk to get his history book he discovered the issue of *Playboy* on top of his schoolbooks. He nearly cried out. René must have put it there, passing on the hot potato. Peter waited for a few seconds for the teacher to turn his back and then quickly slid the magazine into his schoolbag.

On his way home, he saw René standing by the bicycle-shed with a group of other boys from their class.

"Hey, Peter, a lot of homework today, don't you reckon?" he shouted across.

"No problem for me," was all Peter managed to answer.

"Well, I'd say some of the homework should be especially interesting for you tonight, shouldn't it?" René grinned and then beamed at the other boys.

"As I said, no problem for me. I'm good at history."

"Yes, history," René laughed, and one of the other boys said something about the boredom of history.

Peter kept on walking. At home in his own room he tried out several different hiding places for the forbidden magazine and finally decided to slip it in between some older books at the bottom of his wardrobe. He was confident that his mother would never look in there, so the magazine would be quite safe. He was relieved when he had stowed it away, but throughout the evening he was aware of the blonde woman in his wardrobe. He realized that having her there meant a heavy burden and an awful responsibility, but on the other hand it also meant that he could look at her whenever he wanted to. But only when it was safe to get her out.

He knew he had to tell Fred. So, a few days after billeting the blonde beauty in his wardrobe he grasped his opportunity. He got Fred to come to his room after their evening meal, while their parents were watching television.

"Look here. This is what I got from René." He did not dare to tell Fred that he had actually stolen it himself. As he saw it, he was only an accomplice because he had acted under René's orders.

"Yes, that's *Playboy* all right," Fred smiled. "I'm glad for you."

"You mean you know the blonde woman already? You've seen her?"

"What blonde woman?"

"The one in the magazine."

"So they got a blonde one in this issue? You should have seen the hot bird they had as last month's playmate. She was really a knock-out."

Peter was impressed. Fred knew a lot more about this magazine; he even knew about previous issues. And he was obviously familiar with the right jargon. From this day on, the two brothers often talked about their discoveries concerning girls, women, even sex. Fred moved in circles where some of the boys claimed to have real sexual experience, and some with sisters instructed the others about some physical details they were not so sure about. All in all, this all-important topic connected the two brothers in a more permanent way. It was a bond of confidence, a safe haven. It was wonderful to have such a knowledgeable elder brother.

In the months after they had tightened their relationship and formed their new bond, Peter and Fred gradually got to know each other's friends, or at least some of them. There were two of Fred's friends who had already left school and who went to work. Their opinions were much more important than all the other boys' and more reliable than many of the stories that their parents told them. And for Peter, they were certainly more reliable than René. As René gradually drifted out of Peter's orbit, it was his classmate Robert who became more friendly with him. Over the months, Peter and Robert formed a quiet and reliable relationship that had all the qualities indicating that it would last for years to come.

Peter's intellectual development was equally influenced by what they did at school and by what he discussed with Fred. One of the most memorable moments at school was when, after the summer holidays one year, the Latin teacher gave them the first test translation. The first sentence they had to translate ran thus: "Through the old capital of Germania they have recently built a wall; it separates slavery from freedom." Apart from the fact that this was a very easy sentence for Peter to translate, it made the boys aware of the fact that world history was being made even in their days. History was not only about the ancient Greeks and Romans, it happened here and now. This also became evident when, several months later, Fred told him that there was a great danger of the Third World War breaking out any day now, unless President Kennedy did the right thing. Everybody was talking about this danger, the teachers at school, Fred and his friends, their parents, and everybody seemed to know what 'the right thing' was.

On television they showed aerial pictures of ships which were said to carry deadly rockets. Peter found it hard to identify the tube-shaped things and the huge boxes on the decks of those ships as rockets, but the news-readers put on such grave faces that it had to be true. People believed they had seen the rockets that were going to wipe out the human race from the face of the earth, they had actually seen them with their own eyes. When, at last, President Kennedy appeared on television, facing the camera with his drooping eyelids and moving his small mouth very quickly, everybody heaved a sigh of relief. He had done the right thing and the world was saved.

There were other pictures from television that contributed to Peter's intellectual development in that period. For example, there was Krushchev, the fat and ugly Russian with a bald head and a large mole on his cheek, who took off one of his shoes and banged on the rostrum in front of the assembled leaders of the world in New York. Peter cut out the picture from the newspaper and stuck it in his album. Since he had discovered that world history was being made, he collected some of the memorable pictures from the paper and kept them. He had no clear idea why he was collecting them, he just thought it would be good for later. So the picture of the ungainly Russian leader holding his shoe in the air above his head and pulling a threatening grimace was added to the collection. It already contained about three dozen pictures, and it was still growing.

About three years after he had started the collection he was surprised to find that it contained a great number of pictures of politicians, many of them of President Kennedy, but there were also others, for example of soldiers building the wall between freedom and slavery, of a young man dying at the foot of the same wall, of an African leader getting out of a golden Cadillac, of students running through the streets shouting and burning parked cars: the collection also contained a great deal of pain and suffering.

Another source of information about the world was Peter's collection of pen-friends. It was not only useful for his intellectual development, it was also very fulfilling in terms of his emotional development. It had started when their language teacher had drawn the class's attention to some centre in Finland through which they could acquire pen-friends from all over the world for a small fee. Peter begged as much money as he could from his parents and ordered fifteen addresses. On the form, he had to tick his age, his sex and the countries he wished to get pen-friends from. He had to fill in the boxes that listed his hobbies and his languages. For a period of at least seven years, letter-writing was his primary occupation when he was free from school and later on, after he had moved on from school to university. On most week-days he would write two or three letters in the evening, sometimes more. And his letters were long, at least three pages, sometimes eight or ten pages. Two thirds of his pen-friends were girls. He liked that very much. Like this, he had an excellent opportunity to get to know the female psyche and to compensate the deficit he had from his school experience. He learned a great deal from both his male and his female pen-friends.

One evening, he was busy writing a letter to his pen-friend in Malaysia. It was November and quite dark outside. He had already written five pages and he was just explaining his plans for a great trip to Singapore in a few years hence when he heard his parents cry out in front of the television-set. He rushed out of his room and wondered what could have happened. As it turned out, President Kennedy, the saviour of the free world and everyone's hero, had been shot. The television pictures showed him standing in his open car and suddenly collapsing. They showed this sequence again and again. Then everything went crazy. The announcement of Kennedy's death, the capture of a man called Oswald, the pistol shot from some night-club boss, the allegations and commentaries, the new President with the long face and the large ears, the funeral with the two children standing there in their overcoats, the veiled face of the widow.

Looking back at this period later, Peter felt that all these things had happened on the same day. Of course he knew they had not, but it just felt as if they had. As it turned out, his Malaysian pen-friend was busy writing a letter to him at the very same hour when the news from Dallas travelled round the world, and they exchanged their sadness and their shock at what had just happened in their letters to each other. Peter soon began to consider his letter-writing an important contribution not only to his emotional balance but also to his personal interpretation of world history as it unfolded.

Many of the lessons he drew from present world history were at odds with what his parents or his teachers had taught him. For example, there was the question of truth and authenticity. He was taught that you had to speak the truth, at least to the best of your knowledge, and you had to be authentic. Being authentic meant several things. First of all, it was an honest connection between your actions and your words. Secondly, it was a logical connection between what people asked you and what you answered them. One evening he saw the tall French leader who had such a big nose that he often appeared in the political caricatures in the papers, Charles de Gaulle, giving an interview on television. He was asked by a journalist what would happen when, one day, he would no longer be President. In other words, who would be his successor. His answer, delivered slowly, very deliberately and with the customary rhetorical pauses in between, was so much more than just diplomatic that Peter would remember it for the rest of his life: "Il est bien possible que – un jour – moi aussi je vais mourir. Mais, messieurs, je peux vous assurer que, juste à présent, je ne me sens pas mal." What an answer! And what arrogance! Peter was fascinated. So it was actually possible – even acceptable, as it appeared – to answer a public question by saying something altogether different, something that had only an indirect logical connection to the question, something that actually criticized the very question, even though the question was perfectly appropriate and justified. This experience made him like the French President; he saw him as a man of character.

In spite of all these important experiences, life also had a certain unreal quality. Peter sensed that there were things going on around him of which he had no idea. He felt like a happy sleep-walker. He satisfied himself by admitting that he couldn't keep abreast of everything that went on in the world. He knew he had to make his own choices. Some things he was meant to understand, to participate, to acknowledge. Other things were destined to pass him by unheeded.

One area in which this principle of selective participation became evident to him was the world of art. While being very interested in modern painting and modern literature, he had absolutely no understanding and no patience for modern popular music. When he and his friend Robert visited London for the first time in the summer of 1964, everybody was crazy about a popular band of young men with long hair who called themselves the Beatles, and indeed they appeared to have been in fashion for quite some time already, for one of the cinemas near Piccadilly Circus was showing a film about them called *A Hard Day's Night*. Both Robert and Peter wondered what made people want to watch a film about a band from Liverpool that made music which meant nothing to them. It was impossible to escape from the songs of that band in London at that time, their screeching voices were blaring out of every loudspeaker, it seemed. In shops, in cheap eating places, on the radio. But that type of music just did not agree with Peter's aesthetics, nor with Robert's. In fact, it was not even music for them. It was merely badly organised noise. And when, later, they became aware that there were more and more noisy groups of young men with even longer hair and usually dressed in rags or otherwise styled as tramps, they gave up the mere attempt to understand the ugly sound produced by those groups. In the following years there were often pictures of such groups on television, and then there came the crazy crowds surrounding the tramps that produced the noise they called music, and most people in the crowds looked even dirtier. Sometimes Peter thought he could smell their dirt and their sweat when they appeared on television. One of the most disgusting events they reported about was an open-air festival of this slovenly subculture of ugliness somewhere in America, in a place called Woodstock.

Peter and Robert lived in a world that was miles away from such dirt and ugliness. Probably the main reason for their complete rejection of pop music and pop culture stemmed from the fact that they were both going through an extremely intensive period of discovery in a different music department. They had both been taking piano lessons for several years and reached a mediocre ability on the instrument when they were given the opportunity by their piano teacher to accompany her to a concert. They had no idea what they were going to listen to, because they both came from totally unmusical families. Their parents had simply paid for their piano lessons because both households happened to have a piano standing in their living-rooms that nobody could play. When Peter and Robert became good friends they only gradually admitted to each other that they were having lessons. They went to the same teacher, Mrs. Sartorius, for their lessons. Through their piano careers they had heard the names of certain composers, but these did not mean anything to them. Peter had one record that his godfather had given him for his twelfth birthday. It was in a green cardboard envelope and was called *Eine kleine Nachtmusik*, composed by the Austrian composer Mozart. He liked it well enough, but he never got it out after listening to it a few times in the first weeks after he had got it. Robert said his parents had two or three records, but he could never remember their titles. One of them contained a piece that they called *The Children's Symphony*, but he had never listened to it or any of the others.

So they were totally unprepared for what was going to happen to them that evening at the concert to which Mrs. Sartorius had invited them. The programme consisted of Symphony No. 94 by Joseph Haydn, Beethoven's Piano Concerto No. 4 and Brahms's Festival Overture. The soloist in the Beethoven concerto was an elderly woman called Lili Kraus.

In the interval, Mrs. Sartorius explained many interesting points to the boys, and after the concert she asked them what they thought of the music they had heard.

Robert said, "It was very beautiful."

Peter did not know what to say at first, but then he managed to mumble, "It must have taken her a long time to learn to play that concerto so well."

Back at home, when Peter lay in bed, he could hardly go to sleep. He told himself he was such a fool. What he had said was so insignificant in the face of such true greatness they had witnessed that evening.

The day after that memorable concert they talked about it in the morning break, and they admitted to each other that it would be wonderful to be able to play such great music. After school, Peter went to the music shop in town and bought the pocket edition of the full orchestral score of the concerto they had heard. He rushed home and sat down at the piano. He marked the piano part with a red pencil all the way through and then spent the rest of the afternoon practising the short introduction of the first movement, which consisted of one line only. His mother came and stood behind him at one point and asked him why he was playing the same notes again and again.

"You don't understand, Mother. This happens to be really great stuff, I tell you."

"As long as you don't forget your homework for school."

"Don't worry, just let me try to get this passage right." He pressed the keys again.

His mother shrugged her shoulders and walked away.

The next day at school, Peter asked Robert to come to one of the music rooms. They found one that was not occupied by a pupil practising an instrument or having personal tuition. Peter took his yellow pocket score out of his bag and placed it on the piano. He sat down and played the introduction. Robert was full of praise and enthusiasm. He asked if he could have the score for a day or two, he wanted to try the beginning of the slow movement. Peter considered it an act of true friendship that he let him have it. "But only till Thursday," he pleaded.

The following week, Robert bought the record. They went to his home and listened to the entire concerto. While they were listening, both boys were tapping the coffee table in front of them with their fingers in such a manner that gave them the illusion that they were playing the piano part themselves.

Over the following weeks, one discovery chased another. They were in a real delirium about Beethoven and his music, especially about his five piano concertos. They told each other everything that they had read or heard about them. For example, it came as a shock to them when Peter read in a musical encyclopaedia that Beethoven's fourth concerto in G Major was first rejected by the audience because of that very short introduction played by the piano, they would have expected it to set out with the customary orchestral exposition. How ignorant the people must have been at that time!

Because the two boys were in this intensive phase of discovery at the time, it was obvious that they could not participate in the general trend when the world around them embraced the Beatles and their new pop music style. And when Peter realized after two or three years that he and Robert constituted a minority it was too late. The world of classical music had completely and utterly engulfed them and there was simply no room for pop music. The rich variety of emotions, linked to intellectual fascination, leading to the highest peaks of beauty which the music of the classical composers could convey became one of the most important treasures that life held for Peter.

The following years passed very quickly, at least so it appeared to Peter when he looked back at this period later. Peter and Robert remained the best of friends. They not only played the piano and went to concerts, they also made their first trips together without their parents. They went on bicycle tours that took them to various European capitals and allowed them to get to know something of the world on a very cheap budget. Then they left school and started their university careers, after which their paths separated. But the connection they had found in the world of classical music remained the most important source of lasting happiness, and they stored a great many common experiences, which meant they always remembered and valued their early friendship.

In 1968, the year after Peter had started his university career, he spent his summer holidays in Greece. There were four of them, all fellow-students on the same course, and one of them got his mother's car for the trip. On their trip back through Yugoslavia, all the way from the Greek border to the northern end of Slovenia, it struck them how many tourists from Czechoslovakia were on the roads. The four friends discussed this phenomenon at length. They also talked to some of the Czech tourists when they stopped for petrol. What they learnt was that the Dubcek government had taken a more liberal course, which meant that the people could travel abroad more easily. This was quite a revelation. Peter had become accustomed to the fact that the Eastern European countries were shut off from the world and their people lived very much as they had lived before the Second World War. It was surprising that one country could suddenly afford to open up like that. Peter heard that everyone referred to it as 'the Spring of Prague', and he wondered how the country's oppressor, the Soviet Union, was going to take it.

Only a few days after their return from their holidays, the four friends were shaken by the news that Russian tanks had invaded the city of Prague and were enforcing Soviet supremacy over the country. For weeks the news programmes and the newspapers were full of reports about the Czech people attempting to resist the Russian take-over, and soon the first Czech refugees appeared in their neighbourhood and at university. All of a sudden, there were Czech fellow-students, and everybody liked them. Peter had vague memories of a similar influx of people from Hungary twelve years earlier, and he admired the courage of these people and their willingness to integrate into their new host society. It was truly marvellous.

By the end of the nineteen-sixties, Fred and Peter were still close although their careers were taking them into different directions. Peter's studies took him into the realm of history, while Fred had reached his dream-job as an engineer before the end of the decade. They often visited each other. Fred had a modern apartment in a high-rise building in one of the newer quarters. Peter lived in a cheap one-bedroom flat near the university. Usually twice a week they met for a simple dinner and a long chat, sometimes in Peter's flat, but more often in Fred's more comfortable apartment. On one of these evenings Fred, who up to then had never had a girlfriend because he had always been too busy with his machines and his mechanical constructions that he just hadn't had time for such things, surprised his younger brother with the good news that he had started to go out with a girl.

"Fred, that's great! I'm so happy for you. Who is she?" Peter was honestly glad to see his brother in this new state.

"Her name's Elizabeth," Fred said. "She works for social services. She's rather a quiet girl. I'm sure you'll like her."

"How long have you known her?"

"We met two weeks ago, at a party."

The two brothers were silent for a few minutes. Fred was re-living the happy moments when he had fallen in love with Elizabeth. Peter was thinking of his own situation in the love department. He'd had several girlfriends over the past two or three years, but never anything really serious. "Actually," he said to himself, "I would be ready for another relationship now." He was a person who could be very entertaining and he always made lots of friends, but when it came to a more intimate desire for a girl he was usually tongue-tied and did not know what to do. Only about two months ago he had met a very attractive girl with red hair. She had been sitting next to him in the lecture hall, and he had asked her to join him for a cup of coffee afterwards. Not only had she come with him, she had actually given him to understand with her body-language – at least so he thought afterwards – that she liked him a great deal. But when it came to the point where he should have made a move he shied back. Suddenly he remembered his mother, who had told him so many times that the things men wanted from women were basically naughty, dirty and rotten. Now, on the point of making the decisive move and speaking the decisive words he was checked by the memory of those words of his mother's. He did not want to appear dirty and rotten to this girl. She was too beautiful. She was obviously too good for him. So they never met again.

"What about you?" Fred asked in his quiet voice.

"Me? Well, things are on the move," Peter said, not ready to share his awkwardness with his brother.

Fred smiled. 'That's good," he said.

TEN

Peter bought his first car in 1975. It was a red Renault 12, which he managed to get second-hand at a very cheap price. It was already a few years old. When he walked around the car it seemed to him that it looked quite a different type of car depending from which angle you looked at it. Whereas from the rear the concave slope of the line from the rear window on to the boot-lid gave it an almost daring and ultra-modern appearance, the front struck you as a homely, traditional, even banal piece of technology. When he took his position behind the wheel and switched on the engine he remembered his childhood ideas about car-ownership and its dangers. He laughed aloud. The man from the garage who had just sold the car to him came up to the window and asked if there was anything wrong.

"No," Peter laughed through the window. "Everything's fine."

"That's ok then, sir. I always say laughing's a lot better than crying."

"You bet it is," shouted Peter and drove off. It felt good to have his own car at last. He decided to drive around a little, just to get the feel of it, then go over to Fred's place. Fred had recommended the garage, so Peter thought he should see the car before anyone else.

He parked the car on the huge open space in front of Fred's apartment block and rang the bell. Fred came down, and the two brothers had a good look at the car from every angle, in the engine bay, in the boot and of course they sat in it and discussed its positive and negative points.

Peter got his camera out. "Can you take a picture of me with the car?" he asked.

"Of course, which side do you want? And where do you want to position yourself?"

It took them more than ten minutes to get the photographs the way Peter wished them. This was a historic moment for him, so he wanted to make sure it was marked accordingly, which meant it had to be captured for later.

When Peter was satisfied they went up to Fred's apartment. Fred brewed a cup of strong coffee. As Peter was taking his first sip he asked, "What about your flying?"

"I got all the licences and certificates I wanted. I'll take you up in the air some time. So you can see how wonderful it is. It's just one of these things that make life worth living, to be up there and to look down at the landscape, to see villages and towns, fields and roads, lakes and rivers, all from up there!"

"I'd love to come with you one day if you'll have me. Has Elizabeth been in the air with you? She must like it."

"Yes, she has, in fact several times. She likes it well enough although…" his voice trailed off. "It's a bit of an awkward situation. She has some fixed ideas about flying. It's not that she didn't like it, but she doesn't want me to take it up more seriously."

"What do you mean?"

"The thing is, she sees my flying hobby with mixed feelings. It boils down to the fact that she's jealous. She'd prefer me to spend more time with her rather than up there. Also, she has these irrational fears."

"You mean, she's afraid of flying?"

"No, not really. She's more concerned about me."

"What are you going to do? Give it up?"

"I don't think so. But it's going to be difficult with her. She said it's either her or my flying. It's sheer blackmail."

"Perhaps if you can make her see what it means to you …"

"We're working on it. Don't worry."

"I don't worry. I only think you shouldn't risk losing her. She's so good for you." Peter had become fond of Elizabeth over the years. "She loves you, and you love her, and you have such a lot in common. You are the perfect couple, honestly."

"Yes, I know, she is absolutely wonderful. She's even been talking of marriage."

"Oh, that's fantastic!" Peter was overjoyed. "It would be great to have her as a sister-in-law."

"Hold your horses, little brother. I only said that she's been talking about it."

The brothers drifted into other subjects, and after another hour Peter left. As he was driving away he was thinking of his brother's situation. How good for him to have Elizabeth. She should have been here when they took the pictures of the car. Well, at least Fred and he were on the pictures.

It would be good for Fred to marry. Peter himself, on the other hand, was still drifting. He had the occasional girlfriend but could not think of himself being together with one and the same girl for the rest of his life. He could never be faithful to her. Faithful! What an antiquated concept! He knew he was different from other men. He was not like Fred or Robert. He often suffered under his own sexual urge. This was a subject that he had only ever talked about with Uncle Charles, of all people. He had not really wanted to discuss such a delicate subject but somehow they had slipped into it when he happened to be thrown together with Uncle Charles on one of his recent visits to his parents.

It was an unusual situation. Uncle Charles, whom Peter now called 'Charles', leaving out the 'Uncle' these days, had stayed a few days en route on one of his business trips. He had arrived a little too early, and Peter happened to walk up to the house practically at the same moment. Peter was going to collect his mail that sometimes was still delivered to his parents' address.

"They're not in, but I can let you in. I've got a key." Peter said as he unlocked the door, and they both stepped into the empty house. Peter explained that his parents would probably be back in about two hours. He offered to make some coffee. So the two men sat down and had a good chat. This was unique. Peter had never talked to Charles alone since his childhood. So it felt a little strange at first. Looking at Charles, he noted that he was no longer a young man. He still had his strong voice, his dashing moustache, his easy-going manners and his person was still very upright and impressive. But there was something around his eyes that betrayed his age. He must be in his late fifties, Peter thought.

They chatted about Peter's parents, about his career and about Fred and Elizabeth. Then Charles asked him about his present girlfriend, and Peter prevaricated.

"What's the problem with you?" Charles asked in a very gentle voice, which was rather unusual for him, his voice normally booming like an auctioneer's.

"I don't know. I seem to be attracted by too many girls."

"That's normal for a young man like you."

"Yes, I know. But it's really disturbing. When I walk along and see an attractive woman, I mean a woman who stands out from the masses, a woman who moves in a special way, has a particularly beautiful face or a breathtaking figure, I get aroused and I imagine what she must look like naked, how she would move and moan if I had sex with her and so on. It's really annoying. I don't want that to happen to me."

"But it's the law of Nature. Listen, Peter, Nature makes sure that humanity will not die out. Men have to have this drive, this urge, and naturally it's a lot stronger when you're young."

"It's not funny. I can't even go to the swimming baths. You know, there's this lovely new open-air pool with the new slides and the beautifully landscaped lawn area where you can lie down and relax or get a nice sun-tan. We used to go to the old place when I was a teenager, but now that this new place is there I can't go there. I lie down to relax and straight away some absolutely stunning young girl walks past in her bikini, wriggling her bottom and flaunting her boobs in a way I get hard and have to turn on my stomach. Then I can't relax any more; I can't take my mind off the girl I've seen, I desperately want to take her in my arms and kiss her and stroke her smooth skin and …"

"Oh yes," Charles said in a dreamy voice. "I remember that feeling!"

"How long am I going to be like this?"

"Well, my boy, I can't tell you exactly. A lot will depend on the sort of woman you choose for good. But I can tell you it won't last. At your age you're constantly chased by your sex drive. By the time you get to my age you'll be a lot more relaxed. Your sex drive will be an occasional visitor at best."

"I don't see how I can choose a woman 'for good', as you put it. How can I tie myself down to one woman as a sexual partner if I am aroused by any other hot chick that happens to cross my path?"

"It will happen, you'll see." Charles reassured him. "Everything will fall into place when the time comes. All of a sudden you will know: This is the woman I want to spend my life with."

However, as time passed this didn't happen for Peter. He was glad about the talk he had had with Charles, but the only real consolation he gained from it was the certainty that this state of things would not last all his life. There would be a calmer period.

Peter tried his best to keep away from places where he was in danger of seeing too many attractive women. This was not easy. Even at university there were some female students who dressed in such a way that he had to fight a constant battle within himself between trying to avoid looking at them and wanting to look at them with an erotic flavour. Some had see-through T-shirts or wore low-cut tops without a bra, some moved in a provocative way and others had provocative ways of looking at him...public places with lots of girls became a proper minefield.

He began to avoid going to parties. But he made an exception when Fred and Elizabeth threw an engagement party early in the following year. Fred asked him to bring his camera with the flashlight and to shoot some good pictures.

When he arrived to help with the preparations, Fred and Elizabeth were not dressed for the party yet. Fred was in a pair of old jeans, and Elizabeth wore a loose kimono. This suggested that they had been intimate together a short time before. For the first time Peter saw her as an attractive woman. He could see exactly why Fred had chosen her, although he knew he must have chosen her also for other qualities, not just for her sex-appeal. He himself knew so many of her other qualities, her good sense of humour, her disarming adaptability, her calm nature, everything – so why did he have to take special note of her physical attraction? He cursed himself and his ever-present urges.

Soon they were so busy with the preparations for the party that those unquiet ruminations were forgotten. They got the drinks ready, they arranged the furniture, and when everything was ready Fred and Elizabeth disappeared to get dressed. Peter sat down and had a glass of white wine by himself. Fred was back in ten minutes, and the brothers sat down for a quick chat before the guests arrived. They did not have very much time. Peter only asked about the flying.

"She's set me an ultimatum, but we've come to a fair deal." Fred explained, but he could not continue because the first guests arrived. The party took off, and throughout the evening Peter was very happy for his brother. He never learnt what the fair deal was.

In the spring, Peter saw a young woman standing at the side of the road. Her car had broken down and she was wondering what to do. It was a deserted spot, there was no house and no telephone in the vicinity. There she stood, in the middle of nowhere, her small car immobile with two wheels on the tarmac and two wheels on the grass verge, green fields with black-and-white cows behind her. There was a light drizzle.

Peter was in no hurry so he thought he might as well stop and see if he could help her. He parked his car half-way on the grass verge as well and switched on the hazard lights. As it turned out it was very simple, just a loose wire, which Peter fixed within seconds once he had found it. She was so overjoyed that she wanted to give him some money for his help.

He was horrified. "Don't be silly," he said. "I'd never think of taking money from a person in distress."

"But you've been so very kind. Can I invite you to a cup of coffee? I know a nice place that serves good coffee in the village after the next. Are you heading that way?"

Peter hesitated, then he gave himself a push. "All right, then. I know the place you mean. It's on that corner, next to a baker's shop isn't it?"

They got in their cars and drove the few miles in convoy. They parked their cars opposite the little coffee shop. As they were crossing the street, she said, "By the way, my name is Barbara."

"I'm Peter."

"The car's running fine now. You've done a marvellous job." She had a high sing-song voice that he liked. She walked through the door, which Peter held open for her. They sat down at a table in front of the window overlooking the street and ordered coffee.

Now, for the first time, he had a good look at her. She was not what he would have called a beauty, but she had a lot of charm. Her eyes were fantastic, a sparkling, deep blue. Her hair was light auburn, and her face had a healthy complexion. She radiated energy. To his surprise, he was not embarrassed to talk to her. Within an hour they had agreed to meet again. By the end of the week, Peter had a new girlfriend.

Their relationship developed, and through the months of May and June they not only became more intimate, but Peter also acquired a great deal of self-confidence. They often talked for hours, and Barbara showed a keen interest in his work. He had only started a new job a few months earlier. In July, he got his first fortnight off, so they planned a short trip by car on the first weekend. Driving along through pretty countryside, they talked about everything they could think of.

"So your company sells ideas, really?" she asked.

"Yes, you could put it that way. When a company wants to project a new image of itself but they have no idea what that image could be they come to us. We help them find their new identity."

"And what exactly is your job?"

"Well, many things, really. For one thing, as a historian I am responsible for any research that needs to be done into a company's history, or the history behind the products it deals in." Peter went on and explained the smaller responsibilities and the general working conditions of his job. Barbara listened and asked intelligent questions. After stopping for petrol they were silent for a short while. Then Barbara opened up a new topic.

"That was so nice of Fred and Elizabeth to have us last night."

"Yes, I'm glad you get on so well with them."

"It's not difficult," she said. "They are so natural, so easy-going. If I didn't like them both so much I wouldn't have come last night. After all, I wanted to get all the packing done for this trip. We might have made an earlier start if we hadn't spent last night with them."

"I think we did the right thing. They wanted to have us."

Barbara looked at him out of the corner of her eyes. "You like your brother very much, don't you? You seem very close."

"Yes, we are," he said and began to stare at the road ahead.

After a moment of silence he added, "I tell you, it's the most wonderful thing in the world, having a brother."

"What a lovely thing to say!"

Peter felt very close to his brother at that moment. He was nearly moved to tears, he was so happy to have such a good brother. He knew no other way to communicate this to her than what he had said, so he just remained silent. They drove on.

They spent the night in their small tent on a campground by a lake. Once they had pitched the tent they crawled inside and started to kiss. Kissing her was a true revelation, a momentous experience for him. He had kissed a good number of women, but this was different, this was electrifying. The way her soft lips parted and responded gave him the impression that they were actually communicating millions of messages through their kisses. The evening was very pleasant and the night was a little cooler, but they did not mind. They were so absorbed with each other that they completely forgot the outside world. They did not come out of their tent until late the following morning. It was Sunday, the sixteenth of July nineteen hundred and seventy-eight. Peter stretched his arms over his head in the morning sunshine. Barbara crawled out of the tent and looked at him. He looked strange this morning. She felt that something was wrong.

"What's the matter with you? Didn't you sleep well?" she asked.

"The little time we spent sleeping was fine. I slept like a log."

"But I can see that something's on your mind."

"Yes, you're right. I don't know what it is. I just feel that something's wrong. Let's get packed and drive home."

"Are you sure? We were going to walk up to that mountain valley. You know, those rock formations you were talking about..."

"Yes, but I want to go home."

She did not object. They packed their tent in the boot of the car and collected the few bits and pieces they had taken out the night before. They did not talk very much on their way home, except for a few practical phrases like "Turn left here," or "Take the motorway for this bit, it'll save time." They both felt they were functioning almost automatically. Neither of them could have given a concrete reason, but they felt that they had cause for anxiety. Peter took account of every turn of the road, every house they passed, every traffic sign and even the telephone wires. He found it odd that telephone wires should be installed like that, right across the road. A thing that had never occurred to him before. He took a mental photograph of the phenomenon.

Back at his flat, everything was normal. And yet, everything appeared different. They quickly unpacked their things and had a cup of coffee. For a while, Peter listened to his own heart-beat.

"What's wrong?" Barbara asked.

"I don't know. It's weird. I'm going to call Fred." He took the telephone and dialled his brother's number. He let it ring for a long time. There was no answer.

"Come along," he breathed and led the way out of the flat and back to the car. They drove to the large car-park in front of Fred's apartment block. He rang the bell next to Fred's name on the large panel. There was no answer.

"I know it sounds callous," Barbara said, "but I still don't understand what you are so anxious about. You're making me feel uneasy too."

"I can't explain. It's only a strange feeling that I have. I feel like sleep-walking through reality. Just trust me, please."

They drove back to the flat, where they had something to eat. Peter remained restless and absent-minded, and Barbara did her best to engage him in conversation. She was gentle and understanding with him. To pass the time, they switched on the small black-and-white television-set in the corner. At first there was an empty-headed programme about family conflicts and then there was an old western film with John Wayne. The sound

160

was not very clear, but the hot atmosphere was still as gripping as ever and the clear-cut division between right and wrong was comforting. The vicarious pleasure of accompanying that sturdy fellow with the brass star on his waistcoat lapel on his crusade against evil was so reassuring that it made Peter forget his worries for the duration of the drama. After watching the film he fell asleep on the settee, and Barbara quietly covered his body with a blanket.

"You must be exhausted," she murmured.

He woke up when twilight had already fallen. Immediately his anxiety returned with a stab in his heart. He jumped up and walked to the window, rubbing his eyes.

"Why is it," he demanded, "that we can never see the truth? We are always dependent on our arbitrary perspective. We can only see what things look like, never what they really are."

They went walking along the river for an hour. When they returned he tried Fred's number again. There was still no answer.

"I'm going to call Elizabeth," he said. "Pass me the phonebook, please."

Barbara gave him the phonebook and he scanned it for Elizabeth's name but could not find it. In his disappointment he threw the phonebook on the floor with a loud bang. This seemed to awaken him from his trance of fear, and he heaved a deep sigh.

"You may be right. There's probably nothing to worry about." He stood up and walked over to the window. He looked out at the dark shapes of the tall poplars outlined only very dimly against the blue night sky.

They both jumped up when the telephone rang. Peter picked it up on its second ring.

"Hello, oh I'm glad you're back." It was Elizabeth's voice. It sounded tense and clear-cut. Peter was alarmed.

"What's the matter?" he hurriedly asked.

"It's terrible. Can I come round to your place at once?"

"Of course, but tell me – "

She must have hung up. She must be in a real hurry to see them. Peter could hardly breathe for a few minutes. Barbara did not press him. Eventually he stammered, "She's coming here. Something's happened."

Elizabeth arrived shortly after half past ten. As soon as Peter opened the door and looked at her face he knew that his anxieties had been well-founded.

"Can I sit down and have a drink?" she asked.

They gave her a tumbler of scotch with ice, which they knew she liked occasionally. She took a sip.

"It's about Fred," she began. "As you know he went on one of his longer flights yesterday. I drove to the little airfield at his destination. We had planned to spend the night down there, and he was supposed to fly back today. But when I arrived at the airfield around four o'clock yesterday afternoon, he wasn't there. I inquired at the air traffic control room there, but they wouldn't give me any information. All they told me was that he had not arrived there. But from their worried faces I knew something was wrong. I pressed them for more, but they said I wasn't kin, they couldn't give me any information. I decided to hang around. The police came, but they wouldn't let me in when they had their conference in the control room."

"So what did you do?" Barbara asked.

"I waited the whole evening until they shut down the airfield for the night. I don't know how I got through the night, but first thing this morning I was back hoping at last to get some clear answers."

"And?"

"Nothing. Still the same situation. At eleven one of the younger officials came out. He offered me a cup of coffee and he said that Fred's plane had gone missing. A search helicopter had been sent out."

Peter put his face in his hands.

"I've spent all day," Elizabeth continued, "trying to find out what could have happened. I drove to your parents' place, but they were not in. I think they're on holiday."

"Yes," Peter mumbled, "in Canada."

"There might be a simple explanation for this," Barbara said in a hopeful voice. "Fred may have decided to fly to a different destination."

Elizabeth shook her head. "He would have called me. Oh, if only we could find out what's happened!"

Peter stood up and got his car keys. "We must go to the police. They'll have to give me all the information. I'm kin…I'm his brother! Let's run down to the police station in the town centre."

They took Peter's car. His driving was erratic. At one point he drove straight through a red light. He parked the car in the small car-park opposite the police station. They crossed the street. It was half past eleven.

The officer at the front desk nodded when Peter told him what they wanted. They were shown into a small room with half a dozen chairs grouped round a table that had seen better days.

Peter looked at the photograph on the wall. It showed a group of five smiling policemen standing in front of a patrol car. One of them held a trophy in his hands.

After about five minutes an officer entered. He gave them a serious but friendly greeting and introduced himself. He had a cardboard file which he placed on the table. They all sat down.

"I apologize for this formality, but can I make sure of your identities first?" he asked in his professional tone. Peter produced his driving licence and told the officer who the two women were. This satisfied him.

"I'm afraid I have some bad news," he said. Then he opened his file and told them what he knew. There were two aircraft missing in the area which he indicated to them on a large map.

He pointed at a square of the map grid with his black ballpoint pen. The wrecks had been located earlier that afternoon. The theory was that the two aircraft had collided in mid-air.

"From the information we have it appears that your brother was the only occupant in his 'plane while there were two people in the other. No one could have survived. I'm very sorry."

PART THREE

Cathy

ELEVEN

At last she found her voice. "You can't be serious."

She stared at her mother, who was peeling potatoes in their tiny kitchen, pretending that everything was all right; even when she wiped her hands on her blue apron she did not look back at her. Cathy thought she saw her mother making an effort not to smile. Cathy was well acquainted with this sort of behaviour, and it was her firm plan to break down this barrier set up by her mother in situations of confrontation. She was quite confident that she would succeed in getting her mother to drop that smirk and look at her at last when she wanted her to understand her side of things. Or was it really a smirk? Was it true that she always assumed this air of superiority? Did she really feel superior? Cathy was not one hundred percent sure, but she knew that she hated this attitude of her mother's and that she was going to put an end to it sooner or later.

"There is no more to be said. You're twelve years old and you'll do as I say. End of discussion."

"Everybody else is allowed to go and watch, and they don't have to be home before eight." Even this important comparison, which seemed very convincing to Cathy, could not move her mother. So there was no way she could get to see the arrival of the cycling star along with all the other children of the village.

The cycling star, as he was called by everyone in the village, was a big favourite with all the children. They all knew he was the best cyclist in the world, even though Cathy's parents had tried to explain to her that he was just an occasional participant in provincial cycling events, and yes, he was quite a fast cyclist and he possessed all the glamorous paraphernalia from the flashy bike to the colourful racing clothes and even the right type of sunglasses – but he was far from being a real champion. All the children knew better. They had seen him cycling out of the village and on to the main road at unbelievable speeds, bending down and panting like the cycling champions they knew from television, and some of the boys claimed they had seen his trophies, which he kept in a glass cupboard in his hall.

His name was Hugo Tanner and he was the only person in the village who took the children seriously. When they gathered at his garden gate he would step out of his front door and sit down on a big rock near the children. Then he would listen to their news about their latest achievements, their new games, their parents' strange ideas, and he would tell them stories and explain many details of his cycling experiences. Some children would even tell him about rows that their parents had that day or other details of family life. Cathy thought this too intimate; she would never ever discuss such things with a stranger, not even with the cycling star. But then some of the girls could be so vulgar at times. There was Anna-Maria, for example, who was not satisfied with a merely verbal exchange with Tanner. Whenever he seemed to address the other girls with his stories or his clever responses, Anna-Maria made every effort to stand close to him, to touch him at his elbow and to make big eyes at him in such a wistful manner that she really made a fool of herself. Cathy often wondered how such behaviour must appear to Tanner. Did he not notice Anna-Maria? Or did he only pretend to ignore her so that she would appeal to him in that way?

As for herself, Cathy liked to be part of the crowd of children that usually welcomed him when he returned from one of his longer cycling exploits. She felt that being part of this crowd gave her the necessary scope for her variations of social behaviour patterns. From the stories that her mother had read to her in earlier times and from the few girls' books she had read herself she knew that she could deliberately adopt a whole range of different roles in a crowd or group. She liked to experiment with these different roles and to watch the others' reactions. It was a truly fascinating game, and Cathy did not want to miss such an excellent opportunity as the welcoming crowd for Tanner's return from his three-day cycling tour. As he was said to arrive between seven and eight it was obvious that she couldn't be home by eight.

It was now just after seven. Cathy lay on her bed, staring at the ceiling. From the living-room came the thumping sound of some television show that her parents were watching. She was trying to decide on which course to take. After the evening meal she had quietly retired to her room, giving her mother the impression that she was going to do some reading before changing into her nightdress and going to bed. Sometimes her mother would look in later in the evening just to check or to give her a late-night kiss. But this was not always the case. Cathy observed a slow decline in this near-routine. Was it that her mother was gradually losing her need to kiss her daughter? Or was it part of a plan to make the daughter tougher? This explanation would be in tune with the general tendency towards a stricter style in her upbringing that Cathy was convinced she could detect in the increased orders and prohibitions she had to suffer under. Or was it that her mother found television more and more fascinating and compelling so that she simply forgot the late-night kiss? Would she forget tonight, or would she come?

Cathy sat up and heaved a sigh. This was a difficult decision. Her future course with her mother would depend on it. If she decided to go for an escape through the window she would not be able, in future, to talk to her mother with the same degree of warmth and proximity as she had done for the first twelve years of her life. But then, she admitted to herself, she had already broken that old bond with her mother when she had run away from home three months ago. It had been a proper shambles, a total fiasco, because she had only got as far as the old forester's hut on the other side of the wood, where she remained hidden for several hours until it started to drizzle and she began to feel cold, abandoned and uncomfortable. She had returned, fully expecting a severe scene and punishment, but to her utter amazement her mother hadn't even noticed her absence and the entire episode made Cathy feel extremely embarrassed whenever she remembered it since. What remained a fact for her, however, was the decisive break in the former bond with her mother on that occasion. In a way, this fact now appeared to Cathy as a liberating factor, it had made her free enough to endeavour such a step as she was contemplating now.

She stood up and gazed at herself in her bedroom mirror. Looking at her slim, pale face with that ugly mole just visible behind her left ear and with her dark brown eyes set so asymmetrically rather high up in her face, she appeared quite grown up. This impression was underlined by her height. She was tall enough to pass for an adult, although perhaps a bit too slim, not womanly enough. Cathy hooked a wisp of her dark brown hair and pushed it behind her ears. She blinked her eyes and pouted her lips. Then she pulled ever so slightly at her cheeks. Yes, her face, ugly as it was, would do for the time being. It would change in time.

She looked at her slim figure in her grey skirt and white blouse. On a sudden impulse, she took off her blouse, grabbed two small white socks from her drawer, crumpled them into small balls and stuffed them under her tight body-shirt, then she put her blouse back on and examined the effect. She jammed, shifted and patted all around her chest and executed some swift contortions until the result seemed quite satisfactory. Now she looked more womanly. Perhaps too womanly? The newly acquired breasts suddenly seemed out of proportion, too fully-grown for her slim figure. She patted and flattened them. This was better, more in harmony with the rest of her body.

She listened carefully. The television show was in full swing. She switched off the light. After a short hesitation she put on her shoes and opened her bedroom window. She sat down on the window-sill and dangled her long legs above the bush in the border under her window. The fresh air outside and the approaching dusk were sweet and welcoming, full of promises. Now or never! Looking down at the ground she became aware of the swellings of her blouse that partly obstructed the usual view of the lower part of her body. This couldn't be. She had only looked at herself in the mirror before, not down her front. Quickly, she jumped back into her room, tore off her white blouse and changed into a grey one that would not stand out so much in the evening twilight. After giving her breasts another flattening pat she resumed her sitting position on the window-sill, but this time she looked down only very briefly and only to find her footing as she prepared to jump down.

Leaving her mother's vegetable garden behind her she walked along the back lanes until she reached the crowd of children surrounding the cycling star. Tanner must have arrived only a few moments ago, he still wore his cycling cap. There were about half a dozen children standing around him under the dim street lamp in front of his garden gate. Walking up to the group in the pleasant twilight, Cathy suddenly felt very proud and grown up. She straightened her back into a more upright position. This new consciousness of herself and of her body made her adopt a different role when she joined the crowd, different from her former roles which were marked by her active participation and often her forward manner. Nobody looked at her now. She quickly accepted her present role of near-invisibility. All eyes were on Tanner. The children hung on his every word as he launched into an entertaining account of his adventures, beginning with an episode where he had become lost. Cathy was not really interested in what he had to tell, she was here for the crowd and for her spontaneous experiment.

During the hour-and-a-half which they spent with Tanner before he pleaded exhaustion and went into his house, no one took any notice of Cathy. She played her new role so well that she really was invisible. Even though she was and felt part of the crowd, she was aware of a certain mental distance between herself and the others. She did not utter a single word but just stood there among everybody else. Should she be disappointed? Or should she welcome the fact that no one realized that she was no longer a child like them?

Scrambling over the window-sill back into her room, she scratched and soiled the front of her blouse. She closed the window, drew the curtains and switched on the light. Looking at herself in the mirror she realized her swellings had shifted to a lower and irregular position, probably from pulling the upper half of her body onto the window-sill from the outside. She suddenly felt stupid and childish.

Quickly she changed into her nightdress. As she lay in bed she could still hear the television, a background sound she had not been aware of on her return until now. She had been too shocked and ashamed of herself. Now, in bed, she found she could not go to sleep; she kept thinking about what she had done. Would this experiment, as she liked to call it to herself, have any effect of herself? On her companions, if they noticed? On Tanner, if he noticed? What was the experiment? Cathy was not too sure, but she liked the idea of trying out the effect she would have on other people as an adult woman, or to be a bit more modest, as an older teenager. Also, if she stood back and did not take the initiative with her friends as she was used to do, she might discover new behaviour patterns and get to know the others much better. Of this she was quite confident.

She switched off her bedside-lamp and hoped that, in her sleep, she would gently fall into a dream that might grant her access to the world of the older teenagers and beyond.

This was 1968, an era that made many teenagers aware of

their precarious position between childhood and adolescence. About two weeks later, as she was walking home from school, Cathy saw the cycling star with Anna-Maria. They were sitting side by side in the grass by the footpath leading up to the old forester's hut, his bike lying in the grass a small distance away. Cathy was walking along the pavement of the main road, but they did not notice her. Anna-Maria was eagerly talking to Tanner, making big eyes at him, while he was listening patiently. What a good old soul! Cathy thought. He must be bored to death by Anna-Maria's stupid prattling. No wonder all the children liked him – he had a ready ear for each and every one of them. But something in Anna-Maria's behaviour disgusted Cathy. How could she monopolise the man so persistently? If she went on like that he would probably find ways of avoiding her. It was just too embarrassing. And that would be the exact opposite of what Anna-Maria was after. She was just overdoing it.

Cathy did not stop and join them, which she might have done if she had been in a different mood about Anna-Maria. So she walked on, only a little more slowly. She wondered if Anna-Maria would brag about her private conversation with Tanner when the children met the next time. "Well, let her," she thought.

When Cathy got home she found they had a visitor, and from the coat on the rack in the front hall and its heavy perfume she knew it must be Aunt Gladys. She hurried to her room, took off the flashy belt she had worn with her school dress, arranged her hair in what she believed was a more childish style, and put on her grey slippers.

She was ready to face Aunt Gladys.

"My child! How good to see you!" Aunt Gladys croaked with her deep voice. She stretched out her arms for the compulsory embrace, and Cathy complied. These embraces were like getting squeezed between two soft walls that threatened to choke you. Aunt Gladys kissed her with a loud smack.

Cathy had often wondered about her parents' friendship with Aunt Gladys. She was not a real aunt, she used to be some school friend of Uncle Jonathan's way back before the war, as Mum liked to point out. She had practically adopted the family. They all called her Aunt. Cathy liked her well enough, although she sometimes wondered what made her so loud-mouthed and self-centred. She was what Cathy would call a difficult person to get along with.

Gladys Frossard was indeed a complicated character. Born in the same year as the Queen, she seemed to consider herself some sort of superior human being, at least that was Cathy's interpretation of her aunt's utter disregard of other people's feelings. Gladys had apparently done some wonderful things in her younger years, and from her vast circle of friends and acquaintances – all of whom she usually referred to as 'my little people' – one could assume that she was well liked all round, an assumption that Cathy found hard to believe. After a long celibacy, Gladys had married a French industrialist thirty years her senior, a step that had made her rich overnight and given her not only a French surname but also a set of superior airs. Somehow she had jumped from girl to old woman, leaving out middle age. She must have been a good-looking and lively young woman before her marriage, but now she was much older in her mind, her attitudes, her mannerisms and her social arrogance than her years really warranted.

"*Chez nous*, as my dear François always says," she addressed Cathy with a commanding voice of a sergeant-major, "we consider cycling a thoroughly vulgar and objectionable sport."

Cathy guessed that her mother had told Aunt Gladys about Tanner.

"I've come straight home from school," Cathy blurted out, immediately regretting her urge to justify herself. Although, with Aunt Gladys, she always felt she had to justify herself.

"I've just been communicating with your dear mother,"

Aunt Gladys said. "We agree on all subjects. Indeed, as my dear François says, there is nothing like family. And we are all family, are we not?"

"Can I go to my room? I've got to read a chapter for school."

"Well, my child, if you must you must. But when I was your age and we had an important visitor I had to sit down on the chair assigned to me when I was told to do so, and then I had to participate in polite conversation according to my station in life. There was no question of running to my room. And it did me no harm. Look what I have become today."

Cathy decided not to comment on this matter. She thought it best to wait and let her tiresome aunt get through her snotty speeches.

"Do not sulk, my child. I think young people can learn a great deal from the experiences of the older generations, particularly from those who know the world. If we let them go their own ways without guidance from their betters, just look what comes of it. As you know, my dear Victoria," – she leant over to Cathy's mother, whom everybody else called Vicky – "my François has sent word from the Richelieu, where he is staying for a few days before we can meet up again in Monte, and from what he says Paris is in turmoil. All the low elements are out in the streets, demanding all sorts of wild changes in society and in education. They call themselves students, but if you ask me they are socialist ruffians. Pompidou is a clown, he will never be able to handle the situation as it should be handled. They should all be put in hard-labour camps so they can be taught what is right and wrong."

Cathy did not understand these things, but she felt that Aunt Gladys could not be right. She always misjudged every situation in normal every-day life, so how could she be right about public affairs?

"Can I go to my room now?"

Her mother looked at her opinionated visitor with a frown.

Cathy was convinced that she was in awe of – if not terrified by – Aunt Gladys. She never openly contradicted her, even when the aunt humiliated her in front of other people. While the fake Frenchwoman proclaimed again and again that 'my dear Victoria' and herself were the best of friends, Cathy knew that Mum just went along and played her part in this farce for Dad's sake. Dad would not allow his brother's childhood-sweetheart being criticized. And Aunt Gladys had money. At the tender age of twelve years, Cathy already sensed the power of money.

"Let the child run off if she must."

Over the following few weeks, Cathy heard a lot more about students' protests in Paris. The information that reached her merged with her experiences from various television news items of the past few years or so. Whenever the slightly blurred black-and-white news items from remote countries in Africa or the Caribbean showed marching and running students throwing stones and burning flags, Cathy compiled the information and gradually came to understand that that was what students did. So why worry about the events in Paris? It was what students were there for. She could not see why Aunt Gladys became so upset about such natural events.

The year of the Paris student protests came to an end, and in the first weeks of the new year Cathy felt she was no longer who she had been. In February she started to bleed, an event she tried to hide at first, believing that something must be wrong with her. But her mother found out and sat on the edge of Cathy's bed for over an hour that night, telling her complicated stories about the burden that women had to carry in this world, and about men who could and would never understand. All that Cathy understood in the end was that this bleeding was bad and it obviously had something to do with babies, but it was normal. Her mother said Cathy was now a woman.

This elevated position, as it appeared to Cathy, was confirmed a few months later when she realized that her breasts began to swell and to grow softer almost every day. It was in July, and it was after they had all watched the first landing on the moon. She was drying her body before putting on her night-dress when she found a new softness around her nipples that she had never felt before. She lingered a considerable time, stroking the upper part of her body and looking at herself in the mirror from all angles before she finally covered herself. Going to bed that night she had the impression that a new world had just opened up: men were on the moon and she was starting out in her adult life. She blushed when she remembered her silly impulse with those socks, an episode that now seemed very remote and that she wanted to forget.

Of course she no longer joined the other children in the street. She had more important things to do, being a real teenager, and they were little children after all. The cycling star seemed ridiculous now. If that man liked cycling, fair enough. Why make such a fuss about him? He was no great star, just a simpleton who liked to show off to small children. Cathy found that she walked along the same streets as she had done in her childhood, but now everything looked different. She saw different things while she no longer noticed things that had appeared important to her as a child. As she was walking along the wooden fence of Tanner's back yard one afternoon she realized that the cause of her new perspective must be the fact that she was much taller now, at least she could now look over the fence and spot the cycling champion in conversation with Anna-Maria on the porch. Cathy thought that, whereas she had not been able to see more than the roof of the porch the last time she had walked along this fence she could now see a lot more, even down to where Tanner had his hand on Anna-Maria's shoulder.

At school, too, things were changing. She entered a new school and made new friends. So far she had never connected her school friends with the world around her home, her street, her village. This began to change. They had some interesting boys in her class. One was less noisy than the others. His name was Paul and he sometimes looked at her when he thought she was not looking. He was a year older than she was. His family had moved to the area from somewhere else and the different school systems had resulted in this situation. Cathy thought that a sign of fate. He was special. His hair was longer than most other boys' and he had shy blue eyes. His shyness attracted her, made him more interesting, gave him more depth of character. Cathy found the way he turned his head and the way he walked down the stairs oddly fascinating. His voice had a special resonance because, while most other boys in class still croaked with voices that were neither here nor there and some even kept their little boys' voices, his had already broken. So he was much more like a grown man. And yet he retained his shy glances and his hesitating speech. Perhaps it was this incompatibility that made him so attractive. Beyond that, Cathy did not analyse her attraction to him; she just enjoyed being near him and stealing the odd glance at him.

Another new acquisition in her life was Becky, a small-boned, cheerful girl that Cathy only discovered a few months into the new school. It happened in a very simple way. One day during the mid-morning break the two girls found themselves standing near the school gate together. Afterwards, they could never remember what had brought them there. But that was where they had first met. They began with some small talk about favourite subjects and school rules but soon proceeded to more important topics.

"Do you sometimes feel you don't really belong here, I mean in this part of the world, in this town, in this school?" Becky wanted to know.

"Yes, you're right. It's like looking at everybody from a distance. They all seem so unimportant."

"That's what they are. Unimportant."

"In a way, yes. I'm not one of them. The things I will do when I'm older! When I come to think of it, I'm sure I'll leave them way behind."

"I'm sure you will."

This confirmation, coming from Becky, meant a great deal to Cathy. From that moment, Cathy knew she had a friend for life. Later, she often wondered at her own acquiescence, after all she knew nothing about Becky at the time and yet she believed everything that slip of a girl with those big trusting eyes said to her. Perhaps it was because she said what Cathy secretly hoped she would say. Also the fact that she agreed with her about the provinciality of their place. Was it a large village or a small town? It was one of those places that everybody seems to know but nobody remembers once they've left it. All the houses appeared to look exactly the same, High Street contained the same shops as the high streets in every town. And because the place had neither a theatre, a concert hall nor a museum to speak of, Becky agreed with Cathy that it did not deserve the label of 'town' despite the polished brass plate next to the entrance to that ugly brick building at the top end of High Street which read 'Town Hall'. When, fifteen years later, Cathy read *Main Street*, that great American novel about small-town life by Sinclair Lewis, she clearly recalled her home town and the judgement that Becky and she had passed on it. But the growing relationship of the two girls went far beyond their common opinion about the town and their school. For Cathy, it meant everything. It felt wonderful to have someone she could trust, someone who gave her confidence, someone like Becky.

During that first conversation between the two girls, a bond was tied which was to have a major influence on Cathy's life. And while they were talking in the corner of the school-yard Cathy felt that it just gave her a feeling of warmth to be near Becky, there was something in her soft but firm voice and clear, pale-blue eyes that took hold of Cathy's heart, it was as if this voice and these eyes reached out and grasped her heart, not to suffocate her but to protect and strengthen her. It was almost a physical sensation.

The girls did not have to make arrangements. It was the most natural thing in the world that they got together whenever their other obligations allowed it. In the first phase, Cathy sometimes felt that there existed a sort of rivalry or competition in her mind between her strange and unidentified interest in Paul and her overwhelming attraction for Becky, but that was soon overcome and Becky clearly became her passion and her best friend.

It was not long before she took her home and introduced her to her parents. She had prepared them the night before, making sure that neither her father nor her mother would spoil anything, which they were bound to do if they felt the real dimension of Cathy's passion for the pale girl. So she only added after a conversation about schoolwork:

"By the way, one of the girls is coming tomorrow so we can do our homework together."

"And who would that be?" her father asked, looking up from his newspaper.

"Her name is Becky and she's in my class."

"What's her family name, and what does her father do?"

"It's Winter. Becky Winter. I don't exactly know what her father does, but I think he's something important, something to do with government offices."

"But, darling, what does it matter what her father does?" her mother interrupted. "The girls are just doing some schoolwork together."

"You may be right, Vicky. But one can never be too careful. These days it has become very dangerous for parents to close their eyes and refuse to see their children's friends for what they are. Before we know it we may have a revolutionary cell in this house if we're not careful."

"Now, don't exaggerate. Stephen's friends were a bit wild sometimes, but they weren't revolutionaries."

Stephen was Cathy's elder brother, who had left home to go

to university about eighteen months ago.

"The world has changed," her father said ominously.

"It wasn't all that different at the time he was in his teens."

"There you're wrong, Vicky. Cathy will have to be a lot more careful about choosing her friends. What happened in the streets of Paris last year? It's all those Communist influences. They're all the same – Communists, Socialists, gangsters, crooks, all of them too lazy to work!"

Cathy was about to protest, but she changed her mind. Why oppose her father's paranoia about Communists and terrorists and jeopardize her afternoon with Becky? So she let her parents talk on and on about the dangers of the times, a conversation which eventually lost its steam and faded to nothing in the face of the need to clear the table and get ready for the evening news on television. The result was that there was no parental opposition to Becky's coming.

"This is Becky, and that's my mother," Cathy made the proper introductions as the two girls were taking off their coats in the hall.

Her mother was standing under the old-fashioned lamp that Aunt Gladys had insisted gave the hall an elegant appearance. "I am pleased to meet you, Becky," she said in her sing-song voice, and Cathy knew that everything would be fine. From that moment, Becky became a regular visitor in the house.

Cathy was happy. There was Becky, right here. And there was Paul, out there.

TWELVE

A few months later, Cathy answered the telephone. "Oh, hello, Aunt Gladys. How are you?"

She looked at her watch, wondering if she could get away under half an hour. Once Aunt Gladys had you on the phone she would go on and on almost endlessly. What this verbal waterfall conveyed was hardly worth listening to because everything was repeated at least three times. Moreover, Aunt Gladys tended to circle around the same topics in all her verbal communications. These included the happiness of her marriage to François, the right way of doing things *chez nous*, the proper behaviour for girls of Cathy's age, the sadness over the decline of society and the general setting of rules.

"I would like to speak to your dear mother, if you please. I have to discuss some rather unpleasant business with her. In fact, it is a matter of no small importance. However, I believe it would not be appropriate if I disclosed the nature of my business to you before I have properly consulted the matter with your dear mother. It simply would not do. So you, my dear, will just have to wait until I have spoken to your dear mother before any part of our communication can be passed on to you in due course. *Enfin*, I trust you have been a good girl and a dutiful daughter."

"Of course, Aunt Gladys. No problem, I'll get Mum for you. And don't worry, if it is important I will hear about it from her. Anyway, I'm off to see my friend Becky, so there'll be time to worm things out of Mum later when I'm back."

"Language, child, language! It is not proper for a girl your age to be speaking about her own dear mother in such a flippant manner."

"I am sorry, Aunt, I will mend my ways."

"I should certainly hope so."

Cathy ran to get her mother, then she left the house to meet Becky at the café opposite the church. They were going to discuss a film they had both seen on television. The hero was worth discussing in detail, and with Becky this was always such great fun. The two girls never grew tired of exchanging their views on good-looking boys and men. Their relationship had developed steadily over the past few months. Meanwhile they were familiar with each other's families, with each other's likes and dislikes – Becky liked very hairy men, chocolate ice-cream and American films; she disliked cold weather, spicy dishes and dark green houses – and with each other's strengths and weaknesses.

While Cathy was quite careless about what people thought of her or her family she nevertheless made a habit of complying with most of the unwritten rules of her society, and more specifically with her peers. The majority of her classmates went around with more or less unkempt long hair and rather scruffy clothing. Latin American ponchos and over-large cotton-scarves were very popular. Also, two of the girls regularly wore Palestinian scarves in black and white. Cathy had no strong feelings either for or against these emblems of peer conformity, she merely decided they were not her own style. She went along with the general uniform of blue denim jeans, which were shocking enough for her parents – not to speak of Aunt Gladys – but for the rest she preferred her oversize jumpers with turtle-necks in winter and T-shirts with some silly or provocative caption in summer. On this pleasant spring morning of 1969 she had put on one of her thinner jumpers in dark green, a colour which she knew set off her amber complexion, her brown hair and her dark eyes.

Becky was waiting for her at one of the window tables leafing through a glossy magazine full of film-stars. When she looked up, Cathy could see at once that she had something to tell her. Cathy could read Becky's face like a book. Sometimes when she reflected on this fact she concluded it was due to her friend's extremely pale complexion. All her thoughts and emotions seemed to get written in blue or green ink all across her white face. At other times this explanation appeared nonsensical to Cathy and she told herself it had to be an over-interpretation of some of the light blue veins shining through the skin in Becky's face, for example in the area between her temples and her eyes or down her beautifully long neck. For beautiful her friend certainly was, of that Cathy was convinced.

After a cursory hug the girls sat down and immediately put their heads together in conspiracy.

"So what's the news?" Cathy blurted out.

"Come on, first you're going to place your order."

"Don't play games with me." Cathy's voice had a cutting edge. She didn't like to be kept hanging in mid-air, and she made no compromise when she was impatient, even with her best friends.

"It's about that man, Tanner," Becky readily complied. She just couldn't resist Cathy's urgent plea, especially when it was uttered with that cutting undertone. "They arrested him. Fetched him out of bed in the middle of the night."

"What for?"

"Nobody really knows, but they say Anna-Maria's parents have something to do with it. My Mum made a remark to my Dad over breakfast this morning. I tell you, this is going to be a big scandal, I can feel it. The way it was mentioned and hushed up right away."

Cathy could not find it in herself to be surprised. This news merely confirmed her gut-feeling she had whenever she walked past Tanner's house and saw Anna-Maria making cow's eyes at the man.

In the days that followed, she picked up bits of information, and although her mother tried to keep all the known or alleged details from her she learnt enough to satisfy her own curiosity. It came out that the cycling star had done some dirty things to Anna-Maria, what exactly people did not know but they compensated their lack of confirmed knowledge with an overdose of imagination. Cathy did not care for the details. For her, the entire affair was just another episode to teach her about the enigmatic relationship between the sexes.

At first, the affair boiled for a while beneath the public surface and when, two days after Becky had told her, Cathy confronted her mother, she still tried to avoid the subject. It was in the middle of their evening meal. They were alone, just the two of them. Stephen had wanted to join them but was kept away by some duty to do with his studies, and her father was away on a business trip.

"I hate this secrecy," Cathy blurted out, part of the slice of cold ham still in her mouth. "Why can't people talk openly about what really happened with Tanner?"

"You know, child, this is a very delicate matter."

"Don't call me child!"

"I will call you what I like as long as I like," her mother said in a wavering sing-song that was an expression of something between firmness and sadness, between putting her foot down and beginning to weep.

"So what?" Cathy insisted.

"These are things a young girl like you should not think about. In fact it is nobody's business, really." She said this with a concluding tone as if she considered the subject closed.

"Then why does everybody talk about it?" Cathy insisted.

"We don't talk about it in our house."

"Come on, Mum. I bet you've been on about the whole affair on the phone with Aunt Gladys. I am old enough to know the truth about such rumours. Don't worry, I can handle it, I know more about it than you may expect."

"What is it exactly you know? I'd like to – "

"Don't do that!" Cathy interrupted. "I was asking you, you must know it all."

"It's all very unpleasant, so we'd better not go into any details, if you know what I mean."

It was no use. Her mother would not divulge any more details than Cathy already knew or suspected herself. Cathy wondered whether her mother might reveal more if she asked her again over dinner a few days later, with Dad present? Her father so firmly believed in facing every challenge, telling the truth and being authentic. His presence would force her mother to be more specific.

Cathy did not broach the subject again until two days later, when her father was home from his business trip. They sat down to their evening meal and he questioned his wife and daughter about their activities during his absence. This was the usual routine that Cathy knew. She admired her father for asserting his authority in this way, she admired his bossy air of proprietorship, his acute sense when he detected that his wife's reports were not perfectly accurate, consistent and truthful.

"So what have you been doing?" he asked, munching his steak and glancing sideways at the headlines on the crumpled page of newspaper he kept at the side of his dinner plate.

"We had new people moving in at number sixty-five, a friendly family with two children. Mrs. Jenkins said they must be climbing the social ladder. I think they moved here from – "

"I don't care where they came from. What is he?"

"I don't know. I think he has something to do with psychology or education. Mrs. Jenkins said – "

"A couple of time-wasters. What else? And what about you? What did you do with all that time on your hands?"

"Well, there were a lot of things to do…there was the washing on Tuesday, there was the tidying-up of the attic on Wednesday, and – "

"That's all routine. What else did you do?" He made such

a loud rustling and crackling noise with his newspaper that she could not understand his question.

"Well, there was quite a scandal in town," she ventured. Her nervousness made her take another large mouthful before she continued, "Mrs. Jenkins told me all about it, and ..."

There was a moment of silence, then Cathy saw her father glaring over the top of his newspaper. "Why do you hesitate?"

"Well, I don't know," she looked sideways at Cathy, who pretended not to see. For a moment, there were only the loud munching, slurping and smacking noises of the dinner, noises that were particularly pronounced in Cathy's family.

Cathy saw her chance. "Mum, why don't you tell Dad all about it?"

"Perhaps you'd ...you'd prefer to call Gladys after dinner," she said with a nervous cough. "She might give you the full story a great deal better than I."

Cathy knew this was only to exclude her own participation in the conversation about the Tanner scandal, so she took the initiative.

"It turned out that Tanner tortures girls, and Mum doesn't want to tell because she thinks it's bad for me to know about such things," she blurted out and looked at her father, who put the newspaper down and shifted his reading-glasses down to the tip of his nose.

"Is that so?" he turned to his wife, drilling his eyes into hers.

"It's not exactly torture."

"Then what is it exactly?" he insisted, his voice cutting through the thick air.

"The whole affair is...most unpleasant. Mrs. Jenkins said –"

"I want to hear your version. Never mind Mrs. Jenkins."

"Well, I must say it's all very vague. As it appears – and this, mind you, might be far from the truth – Mr. Tanner from down the road was arrested by the police. Nobody really knows what for, but people will talk."

"Come on, woman. What is it?"

She took another large mouthful before she continued. "They say he…he…abused a local girl."

"And have you any proof for this allegation?"

"Nobody knows any details."

"Then why do you go round disseminating a rumour?"

"I'm not going round –"

Cathy watched her father as he stood up, flung his paper on the table with a violent gesture and walked over to the living-room. She fought between two feelings within herself. On one hand she enjoyed the scene because she thought her mother a silly woman. On the other hand she hated the unpleasant tension in the air whenever Dad pushed her mother into a corner like that. It was only the tension she did not like, whereas her father's bossy way of cross-examining his wife was worthy of great admiration. She took it all in and decided to acquire this art for her own future. It was fantastic to see the power that such a relentless questioning bombardment could give one, especially when one's opponent displayed such weaknesses as trying to avoid the obvious and constantly speaking with a mouth stuffed with food. Her mother was really an easy prey for her father's forceful manners.

"Don't sit there and let me do all the work!" her mother shouted at her.

Cathy realized that she was expected to carry the dishes to the kitchen and help with the washing-up. She also understood that her mother was taking it out on her now. Indeed, the remainder of the evening passed in an extremely tense atmosphere. She couldn't do anything right. Her mother scolded her for this and for that until finally Cathy left the kitchen and slammed the door behind her.

Later in the evening, her father came to her room. This was also a common pattern. After every row between her parents, he would come to her room to put things into perspective. He closed her bedroom-door behind him and sat down on the edge of her bed. She was already in bed, an Enid Blyton book in her hands.

"You know, Cathy my dear, I don't want you to be a bad daughter to your mother. She is your mother and I want you to treat her with respect."

He rearranged his seating position but did not wait for an answer. "About that other story. I don't want you to go round spreading rumours like other people. But you are old enough to know what happened. I had Gladys on the phone for almost an hour, and she gave me all the necessary information. It appears Mr. Tanner has been charged with child abuse. He must have done some awful things to the little Martinelli girl – what's her name?"

"Anna-Maria."

"Yes, Anna-Maria. How far he actually went will be established in court, but her parents found out about the whole affair and told the police and the social office. The girl has been sent away to her grandparents in Italy and the family are trying to hush up the whole story. But there is it. That's as far as we need to know. Now don't you worry about what people say. You know what I told you and you keep quiet about it. I don't want my daughter to gossip. And now you go to sleep. It's half past ten and you've got to go to school tomorrow."

With this, he kissed her on her forehead and quietly left her room. Cathy switched off her bedside lamp. She tried to settle down and fall asleep. But of course she could not go to sleep immediately. Her thoughts were too full of the news she had just heard. While she believed her father's authority unquestioningly, she still wondered about the practical details and about all the aspects that were not talked about.

Obviously, the adults knew what they were talking about when they said 'abused' and didn't have to ask any further questions. She knew 'tortured', but she only had a vague idea of what 'abused' could mean. What exactly was it? It must be very close to torture, and it must be something that the adults didn't like to talk about, a really shameful thing, something that caused Anna-Maria pain, made her suffer in some way or other. But why did they send her away then? If she was hurt physically or psychologically, wouldn't it be a lot better for her to stay with her parents, who could look after her, help her recover, give her comfort?

Cathy imagined in what way Tanner could have caused Anna-Maria any pain. In her mind, she pictured him taking the girl into his house. Did he take her to the kitchen, to the living-room? He could have taken a knife. Yes, he hid the knife behind his back and approached Anna-Maria from behind. No, he didn't need both, either he hid the knife behind his back or he approached her from behind. Then he stabbed her in her back. No, in that case she would be badly hurt and the ambulance would have come for her. They didn't mention an ambulance. So he didn't stab her. He used the knife to threaten her. Threaten to kill her or to cut off one of her hands or to stab her in the stomach. This seemed more likely. But then, logically, if he threatened her with a knife he must have wanted something from her. What could it be? What could Tanner, a cycling star who knew the world and had everything, possibly want from Anna-Maria, a little chip of a girl who had nothing? Cathy felt in her stomach that there was some dark secret, something that she had sensed even on the last occasion she had seen Tanner and Anna-Maria together, something in the man's behaviour that she could not place but that she knew was wrong, something that Anna-Maria obviously could not see, or she wouldn't have made such big eyes at the man. She did not know why, but she found herself suddenly wondering what a boy like Paul would think of the whole affair.

After a while, Cathy switched on her bedside lamp and sat

up. She felt she could think more clearly with the light on. In the dark, her thoughts seemed to go round in circles. She looked at herself in the square mirror on the opposite wall. Would Tanner have tried to approach her if she had let him? What a creepy idea! She sat up more rigidly and decided to order her thoughts and feelings.

One, Tanner had caused the girl pain.

Two, Anna-Maria was packed off, but obviously unhurt, physically.

Three, Tanner must have wanted something from her.

Four, this could be anything, but it was probably something that would have made a normal girl run away. Cathy would have to find out.

She decided to ask her friend Becky. The confidence she had in Becky gave her peace of mind. So she lay down again. After a while she switched off the light and then gradually dropped off to a perturbed sleep.

She dreamt of a big man. He had no face but a stern voice. He had a long kitchen-knife in his right hand and he waved it in the air in front of her nose. His voice grew louder and he stepped up to her, closer and closer. She could smell his bad breath and the sour sweat of his body. He prodded at her stomach with the knife and shouted: "You silly girl, don't you ever disseminate any rumours!"

The next afternoon, she met Becky under the big fir-tree behind Mrs. Jenkins's large garden. It was one of their secret meeting-places. Of late, they had not used it very often, they had shifted most of their important meetings to the café opposite the church, but on this occasion Cathy wanted to meet here. They could not be seen or heard here. She managed to let her friend know in a low whisper during one of the morning breaks at school. After school, she did not have to wait very long, Becky appeared two minutes after her. Whenever they made use of this spot they made a point of arriving separately, it was an adequate measure in view of the atmosphere of secrecy that the spot conveyed. Cathy had to speak first.

"You know, the thing with Tanner and Anna-Maria. I want to know all the details."

"You mean you still don't know?"

"We discussed it at home, but my parents didn't tell me all they know. I'm sure of that. They seemed evasive. They just told me he had tortured her, but not how and what for."

"He abused her, everybody knows that."

"Yes, I know but –"

"You mean you don't know what abuse means?"

"Well, I'm not so sure –"

"It's what dirty men do to little girls. I asked Rachel. She told me all about it."

Rachel was Becky's elder sister. She was eighteen or nineteen, far too old for Cathy to imagine what it must be like to talk to her from sister to sister. Besides, Cathy had no sister of her own, only her brother Stephen, who was ten years older than she was, so she had a very vague idea of sisterly confidence anyway.

"Come on, tell me."

"All right, but don't be horrified. And don't tell your parents or anybody else. Swear on our friendship you won't tell anyone."

"I swear on our friendship," Cathy said solemnly, raised her left hand and placed her right hand over her heart. She looked Becky squarely in the eye.

"There are some men who like to play with little girls. They can't help it, it's just the way they are. They take little girls, they take off their clothes, then they look at them or they embrace them. Sometimes they also take off their own clothes and go to bed with the girls, both of them stark naked."

"Ugh, I wouldn't want to lie in bed naked with Tanner, and him naked, too!"

"Exactly. No normal girl likes it. But there is more to come.

Rachel said some men even put their thing between the girls' legs."

"That's not true. That's impossible! Didn't Rachel tell you that that was how babies were made? When you asked her about …you remember?"

"Yes, of course. That's not impossible. It's no contradiction. It's only when adults do it that there'll be a baby, but with a little girl like Anna-Maria it couldn't happen. It's a case of the man practising with a girl what he plans to do with a woman, sort of thing."

"But doesn't the girl or the woman have to agree, to let him do it?"

"Of course, and that's the whole point here. When the girl doesn't agree they call it abuse. You know, when the man uses, that is 'ab-uses' the girl for his own pleasure without asking her. If he just forces the girl."

"You mean, with a knife or so?"

"For example. But a knife would make it difficult because he needs both his hands to do it to her."

"Then how could Tanner get Anna-Maria to let him do it? I know she always made big eyes at him, she must have liked him very much, but to allow him to do that …!"

Becky shrugged her shoulders. Cathy was impressed. So that was it! No wonder the adults were so stuffed up about it if it was something to do with taking off one's clothes and with making babies. But even if her parents' strange behaviour was now explained, the real details of how Anna-Maria could allow such a thing remained an enigma.

It was easy to imagine how one could get into a situation where one was alone in a house with an adult man. But to let him take off one's clothes! That's utterly impossible without some degree of co-operation. No man could ever get off Cathy's clothes without her consent. She would find ways to defend herself. But what was all that business about nakedness? It was a very private and personal matter to think about one's own body in such a way. Then why did the adults – certainly her parents – make such a fuss about it? Cathy had never ever seen either her mother or her father without their clothes on. When they were in the bathroom they always locked the door, when they had to change into their swimming things on family excursions to a lake or so they always went through complicated procedures involving the most unnatural contortions of the body and rather funny writhing movements with their arms in order to keep towels, shirts or skirts in position. Now that she came to think of it, her parents' entire behaviour pattern concerning their own bodies appeared extremely unnatural. And they were not the only people behaving like that, practically all the adults did it. Somehow it made one even more curious about the true nature of their bodies, which – Cathy thought – must be the opposite effect of what they intended. She wondered if Becky felt the same way.

"Have you ever seen your parents naked?" she asked.

"What makes you ask that now?"

"It just occurred to me, you know, thinking about Anna-Maria and all that."

"Well, no, never," Becky hesitated.

"Would you like to?"

"To see them naked, you mean?"

"Yes. Or how do you feel about it? Don't you think that's a bit unnatural, you know, they're your parents?"

"I never thought about that, but now that you mention it, I must admit it seems rather odd, to say the least. What about you and your parents?"

"The same. I've never seen them. That's what made me ask you. And I was thinking, you know, doesn't that make us wonder and become more curious?"

"You mean, you'd like to see your Mum and Dad naked?"

"I'm not going home tonight planning to spy on them right

away, but yes, I think I have a right, I'm entitled to know what they really look like. Didn't I come out of Mum's tummy as a baby? So, in a way, I'm still part of her body."

"You are right. But it's not her tummy, it's from between her legs."

Cathy decided that their conversation had now drifted in a direction she did not want to pursue any further, even with Becky. She slowly began to stroll along the fence and Becky came along with her. This new movement worked as a signal to change the subject.

"Hey, Cathy," Becky said after a few moments, "are you coming to the party on Saturday? Some boys from school will be there, and they said it's going to be a smashing party."

"I'll think about it. I'll let you know by Thursday. Is that okay?"

They soon reached the footpath between the riverbank and Tanner's back garden, where they parted. Cathy found she was in a strange mood when she walked home, a mood that was altogether new, it was regretful and exciting at the same time. She did not know if it made her happy or sad.

THIRTEEN

The party on Saturday turned into another key experience for Cathy. There were about two dozen teenagers, mostly from her school, but some were a little older and had already left school.

Cathy and Becky came late, when the party was already in full swing. They were greeted by Lisa, who hosted the party. She was at the same school but in a different class. The girls knew each other from their volleyball team, so the two latecomers were not uncomfortable at all. Although they had never been to Lisa's house before, they felt at home immediately. This was due to Lisa's natural and friendly nature. Cathy had brought Lisa a bar of chocolate. And acting on her mother's instructions she also had a small bunch of flowers for Lisa's mother.

"Where's your Mum?" she asked Lisa while she was clumsily unwrapping the bunch of flowers.

"She's not here, you daft creature," Lisa laughed out loud. "Do you think I'm having a party with my old man and woman watching over us?"

"Do you mean they're out? They allow you to have a party on your own? My parents would never do that!"

"Well, I must admit it wasn't easy," Lisa said with a grin. "We had quite an argument, but in the end they agreed. My brother's nearly sixteen, so Mum and Dad decided he's old enough to keep an eye on us. Come and meet everybody."

Lisa threw the flowers on a chair in the corner that was already piled up with coats and jackets and led the two girls to the kitchen. Loud music came from the lounge, Cathy thought she recognized a song by The Rolling Stones.

That was the first of many parties which taught her a great deal about the relationship of the sexes, about boys' behaviour and about her own attitudes towards boys.

The three months that she spent at a language school in Madrid completed her sex education in her opinion, although she returned still a virgin. But she had become a harder person.

After her return from Spain, Cathy's life had entered a new phase. She felt she was really grown up now. And she knew how to handle men, she believed.

Back at school, she felt she could easily handle all the subjects. She could talk and talk and talk. The teachers loved her. If a lesson was in danger of running aground they could depend on her. All they needed to do was to ask an open question, and Cathy would be off, lecturing everybody. Her words erupted like a volcano. Only one of her teachers noticed that she often talked without thinking, her words coming out of her mouth before they could be checked by her brain, but he never said anything about it.

Cathy avoided most other girls except Becky, but she had come to love being with boys. However, she still kept a distance from Paul, she merely observed him from time to time, not quite knowing where to place him in her world. She did not see the boys as equals. She felt her power rising among them. She often found them childish and stupid, but she loved their company. When a boy bragged about something she knew how to take him down a few pegs. She sometimes wondered why the boys seemed to be attracted to her in spite of her harsh treatment of them.

Then, one cold November night in 1971, Cathy was walking home from a school party together with a crowd of boys and girls. She intended to say good-night at her street corner and go home, but to her own surprise she found herself walking on with the others. The group was getting smaller and smaller as, one by one, the young people said good-night and vanished into the darkness. Suddenly Cathy found herself alone with Paul. Her heart stopped. Had she not found him attractive years ago? She must have forgotten her original feelings for him completely in the past three years or so. Of course, Cathy knew he had been in her class all those years, but she had been too self-absorbed and too busy obtaining her leading position in class. She had been satisfied looking at Paul and simply assuming that he would always be there. Now, walking next to him under the street lamps, she rediscovered him as an individual with his own free will who might escape her. A strangely alluring individual. A challenge.

They walked a few paces. Their conversation stopped. They slowed down. They stood still. Paul stepped up to her and put his arms around her. She could see his eyes as she had never seen them before. Even in this dim light of the street lamp she felt that his eyes had an irresistible power. His face approached, and with her full consent he kissed her on her lips. Soon, his tongue probed and she parted her lips while his hands reached inside her anorak and found their way under her thick jumper. She did not even think of why she allowed him to do all these things. Actions she would have rejected, actions which would have made her yell and panic on other occasions suddenly seemed natural and ever so good.

When, three hours later, Cathy reached her bedroom she was a different person. The world was unbelievably beautiful. Her entire body felt anointed, sanctified. New feelings rose in her, feelings she had never known before. They were good feelings. Although the night was rather cold she felt warm. The heat came from her inside. How could that happen? They had kissed and cuddled, Paul had stroked her body under her clothes, and they had both engaged in some kind of rhythmical writhing movement. How could that have such an overwhelming effect? She did not brood, she was far too tired. It was three o'clock in the morning. She went to bed in a state of intoxication and fell into a deep and satisfying sleep.

When she left her home the next morning to go to school

she thought all the other people had to take note of what had happened to her. To her great disappointment, however, the world around her continued to go about its business very much in the same way as usual. Later in her life, looking back, she considered this moment the beginning of her adult life.

Through her last years at school, Paul was her steady boyfriend. Although she believed she loved him she kept him at a certain distance when it came to the business of flirting and petting. She was not ready for what she considered her ultimate surrender to a man. And to tell the truth, Paul was still a boy. Well, she would see...

She became the star of her class in the eyes of her teachers. There was no foundation in her academic work for this exalted position, she rather owed it to her quick tongue, her sharp eyes and her pointed index finger. Most of the teachers were probably a little afraid of her, but they were delighted with her contributions to their lessons. Whenever a teacher asked a question Cathy would be sure to raise her hand first and to start lecturing the whole class before even the teacher had an opportunity to ask her to do so. She had something to say to every topic, in history, in languages, in science lessons and in social studies. She would accompany her statements with non-verbal signals that she had learnt from her father: a fixed look sweeping over her listeners, a look that let everyone know that there was no contradiction tolerated; a raised eyebrow for special effect; the all-present index finger pointing straight at the truth which seemed to hover somewhere in mid-air in front of her. Her paraverbal signals also drew from a rich repertoire: a change of pitch, an effective pause at the right moment, a machine-gun-like rhythm of argumentation especially through the swamps in the land of communication to prevent, or if necessary overrule, any eventual counter-arguments, and of course the all-effective modulation of the voice from a near-whisper to a lion's roar. Cathy really had her rhetoric tools like weapons at her heels.

Particularly in history lessons, everybody in time accepted her interpretations. She told them all what was right and wrong. In literature classes, there remained a few intrepid opponents whom she could not force to accept the obvious fact that Shakespeare was not only a narrow-minded misogynist but also a bad writer. There were even two boys who thought Orwell's *Animal Farm* a highly interesting political parable and who ridiculed Cathy's view of the novel as a silly and boring animal fable. So if she saw herself as the queen of the class, at least a few of her subjects were not altogether loyal, and in mathematics her reign was in serious danger of being overthrown. The truth was that Cathy was a very poor mathematician, but in most situations she managed to throw a veil of verbal abundance over her ignorance and so deceived many of her classmates, especially the girls, and sometimes even the teacher.

What Cathy feared most in life was to appear weak or ignorant. So she convinced herself that she was growing into a person of superior intellectual powers. She considered herself to be a debating champion. The fact that some of her interlocutors in hard-fought debates gave up and merely shrugged their shoulders or cracked a joke she couldn't understand was interpreted by her as a sign of her superior reasoning powers.

Towards the end of her school years, Cathy often found herself brooding. She would sit by her bedroom window and look out across the tall trees opposite. This stance gave her the right mood to reflect on her life. One of the aspects that often occupied her mind was her insecurity about other people, her search for the right treatment of those around her.

"How easy it is for people like Dad," she said to herself, and added: "But then, he is a man."

Despite her firm belief in the relative ease with which men could sail through life, in contrast to the hardships women had to endure, she saw her father as a great hero. He knew how to establish a position of power and how to maintain his supremacy.

She clearly remembered the way he always treated her mother. He was entitled to his supremacy because of his high moral principles. Cathy would emulate him in time.

Then why could her best friend not see that Cathy's purpose was noble? Becky was a darling, but obviously she didn't have the same high moral principles, she was far too emotional for that. She let herself go too often. It would be Cathy's duty to help her friend whenever she was in danger of going astray.

Perhaps, if Cathy reached her father's position of power one day she would be admired by those around her. Admired and respected. The days when everybody was trampling over her feelings and abusing her vulnerability would be over. She would certainly never let a man humiliate her – of this she was convinced.

School ended and Cathy's university education started. She had grown so fond of the world of business that she decided to make this fascinating field the centre of her professional life. As yet, she had no clear notion of where it might take her eventually, but for the time being she was happy to study the details of accounting, to wonder about the differences between micro- and macro-economics, and to learn by heart all those new business models from the 1960s. Although she still had difficulties with her mathematics she managed to get along with most of the statistic facts they taught them as long as she did not have to do her own calculations. The integral symbol still puzzled her, to her it was just a silly worm on the page.

Becky, who continued to be her best friend, chose a different path. For her it was English Literature. The two girls were at the same university, and they regularly met in the large student canteen. In the first few months, they tried to tell each other all the new things they learnt in their respective fields of study. After a while, however, they realized that they were professionally drifting apart. Becky found it more and more difficult to follow Cathy's explanations of the diagrams she was showing her, and

Cathy could no longer summon enough enthusiasm for Becky's interpretations of Lord Byron's early poems. For a time, they still pretended a keen interest, but when Becky tried to make Cathy understand the fascination of Sterne's *Tristram Shandy* and begged her to read the whole novel as well, Cathy gave up.

"You can't ask me to read a novel like that. The hero – no, the narrator – is not even born before page...what were you saying?"

"But that's the whole point! Can't you see the irony, the subtle sense of humour?"

"I've read the first fifty pages, and that's enough for me, thanks!"

When they met the next day after that the two friends discussed their changing relationship. They agreed to disagree on their respective fields of study.

"It's like my brother, Stephen," Cathy said. "We used to be very close one time. Then he left home to go to university and that created a distance between us. When we met up, which was a couple of times a month, it was on a more distant footing. But even so, it was marked by a common understanding. There was a common ground. We shared so many views on the world and such...then one day he tried to make me see the technical aspect of armed conflicts in East Asia and in the Near East, a view I could never adopt." She sipped her coffee. "You know, how certain developments in weaponry brought forth new inventions for the benefit of all humanity. I told him I found it cynical and we had quite a violent argument. Eventually we both came to the conclusion that we could still respect each other as brother and sister, but we had to accept the fact that we were drifting apart in areas that were influenced by his profession. As you know, he is an electronics engineer, and in contrast to his views I could never judge any technical achievement in a scientifically detached light, you know, without its moral or ethical implications. He can. It's daily bread for him." Cathy smiled across the table at Becky. "So what I'm trying to say here is that it may be a similar case with us now. Not that there are serious moral differences between us, but our fields of study clearly take us into different directions. We can no longer share all our interests. But that doesn't mean we can't be friends any more, does it?"

"As long as we respect each other."

"Exactly. But don't we?"

"I think..." Becky hesitated. "I think we will have to work hard at it. It won't always be easy. You see, our chosen professions – or rather our chosen fields of study – matter a great deal. Our souls can't remain untouched. We'll be influenced by our respective views of the world, of reality as we perceive it. And whatever you may say about sharing moral or ethical principles, these will also be influenced in turn..."

Cathy was happy to accept her friend's assessment of their relationship, certainly as far as their professional differences were concerned. When it came to the differences between their temperaments, however, she was not so sure. Yes, of course, she was satisfied with Becky's faithful attitude, her reliability, her never varying friendship...but she would not surrender herself unconditionally to her. Thinking about the entire history of their relationship, she stumbled over several occasions where Becky had annoyed her, annoyed her terribly, unforgivably. Those had been instances of criticism, situations in which Becky had criticized her for being unfair, slovenly, unreliable, unpunctual...

True, Cathy admitted to herself. She didn't take such things as punctuality or museum-like tidiness very seriously. In fact, those were not laudable qualities at all, but rather signs of a narrow-minded character, examples of petit-bourgeois nit-picking. She remembered how her father had told her off as a girl, how she had yearned for her freedom from her father's critical supervision, especially in matters of personal tidiness and so-called orderly behaviour.

At this moment, she resolved to push her convictions through life, no matter what opposition she would meet. She told herself that a strong woman should never allow herself to be run over by what other people wanted her to do. No compromise! If she was going to stand up for herself in the world she would have to dismiss such impediments as politeness and other niceties. Her priority would always be her absolute honesty and authenticity in all her dealings with those around her.

She narrowed her eyes as she looked at Becky, and she said in a slow, questioning manner: "So you expect our friendship to be troubled and perhaps even destroyed eventually just because we have chosen different careers?"

"Yes," Becky answered, "but not necessarily. All I'm saying is that there is this danger."

Becky was to be proved wrong, certainly in view of the period which followed their first steps into the academic world. Over the years that followed, the two friends found that their different careers made them even better friends. There was always common respect and a kind of pleasant and fertile tension between their opinions at times.

And indeed, Becky turned into the more beautiful woman.

FOURTEEN

Cathy was getting ready to go out. She was due to meet up with Becky.

The procedures she went through were routine; they reflected her regular pattern. She rushed to the bathroom to give her hair a quick brushing. She dashed into the kitchen to shove a cheese cracker in her mouth. She stumbled back to her bedroom to look for a shawl she couldn't find, picking up a paper tissue on the run, blowing her nose and dropping the sticky tissue on the floor in the hall, returning to the kitchen to open a drawer and fumble around looking for a small slip of paper – a newspaper cutting she had put away because she wanted to show it to Becky – but without success. Then she remembered something she'd forgotten in the bedroom, jumped out of the kitchen, the drawer left half-open, nearly fell over the vacuum cleaner she had neglected to put away, then forgot that she was heading for the bedroom and stepped into the bathroom instead. She looked around for her wrist-watch, then for her lipstick, then for an extra pack of tissues, ran to the telephone on the table in the living-room to pick up a haphazard shopping-list that she thought she had left there but that couldn't be found now. Well, she would just have to do without it.

Gradually she worked her way to the front door but retracted her steps again and again – this time for a pen to put in her handbag, that time for another look in the hall mirror to check her face, then the erratic and quite virtuoso search for her keys and the other shoe…

At twenty to four, a full twenty minutes later than planned, she arrived where Becky was waiting for her in the rain. Becky had just been starting to walk in the direction of the shoe shop down the street when she saw Cathy running across the street, just dodging and avoiding a collision with a cyclist.

"Hi, Becky! good to see you, let's go." Not a word of apology. Not even a question about how long her friend had been waiting.

Becky just looked at her sideways.

Cathy was full of her own world, she rattled on and on about the latest business figures, about how the oil crisis was affecting international trade, she had her own theories about the future of the oil industry, she even had some juicy story about Sheik Yamani. Cathy believed the smiling minister had a kissable mouth but a very arrogant way of viewing the press reporters surrounding him, especially the women. So her story evolved around Yamani and women. Cathy's verbal waterfall seemed to be passing through her friend. When they reached the shoe shop, at last, Cathy paused to blow her nose. Becky was just going to suggest what types of shoes they were looking for, when Cathy walked to the next shop, obviously attracted by something in the window. She glued her face to the shop-window and pointed with her finger.

"That's a nice tea-cup, isn't it?" Without waiting for Becky's answer she stepped into the shop. It was a trendy shop selling fashionable dishes and kitchen utensils. Becky could only follow her.

Inside the shop, however, Cathy did not go for the tea-cup. She stopped and changed her direction. She took up a sort of bowl or pot. Becky looked puzzled, but Cathy could not be stopped.

"I read about the differences between porcelain and earthenware. What do you think of this? Or do you think that one over there would last longer?"

"I don't know."

"Oh, come on, you always say that when I ask your opinion!"

"I simply don't know anything about these things. How can I decide when I don't even know what the difference is between – " Becky was interrupted by Cathy, throwing up her arms and shaking her head, who had already given her attention to a tea-towel on the opposite wall.

"That's the Sydney Harbour Bridge on that tea-towel," she lectured. "It was based on the Tyne Bridge in Newcastle, you know." But before Becky could answer the two women had reached the door and Cathy was leading the way out.

Cathy could not see herself as selfish or egocentric. She was so full of her own chaotic life that she simply could not take note of those around her. Although she never admitted this to herself, she was convinced that she was an expert in all areas, usually on the basis of a magazine article she had read on the particular subject. If truth be told, she lived at the emotional expense of her friends. In debates or disputes, she always followed the same strategy, when she couldn't convince her opponents with logical reasoning or with facts she raised her voice and became emotional and offensive, only to reproach the others for allegedly raising their voices – a thing nobody dared in her presence. She had adopted the same slave-driving attitude as her father. That showed in the most unpleasant way whenever someone expressed an opposite opinion or – even worse – when someone did not have an opinion on a subject. When she asked your opinion on something you couldn't know or something you didn't care either way she urged you to a decision, and when you said one thing or the other, just to have done with it, she asked you why and you said you didn't care either way, but then you were in real trouble because then she would subject you to a furious inquisition with the full works of her theatrical debating repertoire. She took it for granted that those around her were always at her disposal. She believed she was the only person in the world who worked hard. And she believed herself to be such a good sort. She was also convinced that she was an excellent communicator.

As it turned out, Cathy often refused to accept the truth, she re-shaped episodes from the past to suit her present needs. If a certain event had to be re-arranged in her memory just to fit nicely into a story she was telling, she never hesitated to tell the most grotesque lies even in the presence of the past witnesses of the event in question. Cathy really believed her own lies. From her point of view, they were not really lies but rather credible and acceptable fantasies. Cathy wanted to please people with her stories, she wanted the stories to show up her own character or her intelligence at its best, but only at that moment, because it was only that moment – the moment of her story-telling – that mattered. It was a mystical process, by bending the truth to suit her story she was giving up her own sense of reality and drugged herself to reach a state of mind in which only the effect of her present story mattered, she was giving herself up to her own story. Completely and utterly.

Through her last years at school and her first few months at university, Cathy had stayed with Paul, while at the same time she had tested out a number of alternative boyfriends, but she never let any of them get too close to her. On one hand, she was far too busy building up her reputation as a strong woman, as she saw it herself, and on the other hand she never managed to get the image of Paul from her mind. Paul, who was so steady, so reliable.

During one of their heart-to-heart talks, Becky asked her about her relationship with Paul. For Becky, this required a considerable portion of courage, since she never knew how much Cathy really confided in her. But she was so curious because she was still without any experience in the boyfriend department herself.

"Of course, Paul is number one for me," Cathy answered.

"Have you gone very far with him? I mean, have you ever – "

"You mean, have we ever done it? Yes, we have. It happened after the end-of-school party, you remember when…"

Becky did not want to hear more details despite her curiosity. She was a little offended that she had to ask her friend instead of Cathy telling her of her own accord. Also, because she was slightly embarrassed about her own lack of sexual experience she simply found it offensive to discuss the physical details which Cathy was obviously going to brag about. She decided to give their conversation a different angle.

"So, what next? Are you going to move in with him soon? Are you in love? Are you going to marry him?"

"Marry him?" Cathy screamed out, and the students at the other tables around them all looked at them with raised eyebrows.

"I was only asking."

"That's typical of you with your narrow-minded upbringing. Come on, stupid, let's change the subject. You wouldn't understand anyway if I told you more details. Now, what about this assignment on the poem you showed me last week?"

"It's called *To Autumn* by John Keats. It's an ode to the beauty and the atmosphere of the season. When you read it you are utterly enveloped in this fantastically autumnal mood, it's inevitable, you can't escape the effect."

"Enveloped *by*."

"What, enveloped by?"

"It's 'by', not 'in'. It's a passive construction. You ought to know, you're the language person here," Cathy lectured in her authoritative voice and pointed up in the air with her index finger.

"Whatever you say," Becky said quickly. She knew better than to contradict her friend when she lectured like this.

Eventually, of course, they left the subject of Keats behind them and for the remaining hour and a half they were discussing the World Bank's involvement in the direction that the oil market was taking. It was Cathy who was talking most of the time, and her index finger hardly ever left the air space between them. In spite of what Becky had already learnt about Cathy, she couldn't help admiring her friend. Cathy was so clever in her subject, her knowledge was vast, and what she knew had a connection with what came on the news every day. Becky's knowledge did not have the slightest relevance in the world today, a fact that Cathy was absolutely convinced of. She could not understand how her friend could actually love her subject. One doesn't love one's subject. Knowledge is cold and neutral, matter-of-fact. When Cathy explained things that she had learnt her eyes never sparkled, her face rather assumed an expression of anger. Probably to forestall any contradiction.

Despite Becky's doubts, the two young women remained good friends. Their friendship was not even affected by Becky's occasional critical questions. Cathy herself had no idea of her friend's slightly critical attitude towards her. She was as buoyant as ever and enjoyed every minute in Becky's company. She only wished she could extend the charisma that she believed she had, extend it to be respected by more than just Becky and some of her fellow-students, extend it, for example, to her own family. It was a pity her parents still treated her like a small girl, and she was almost twenty.

"You ought to be more considerate towards your family," was a standing phrase of her mother's. And whenever her mother put on that stern expression of hers, Cathy knew that at least her father shared her opinion that it gave his wife a ridiculous look. That was because he never took her seriously himself. Cathy still admired her father. Her mother was an incapable prattling woman with no real interest in the affairs of the world. And she allowed herself to be humiliated by her husband and by Aunt Gladys again and again.

Aunt Gladys remained an odd fixture in Cathy's life. Three months after telling Becky about her relationship with Paul she decided to test Aunt Gladys by shocking her with the news of her sexual exploits. Gladys invited her to a restaurant near the university. Cathy was pleased to accept the invitation. She knew that Gladys was always very generous when she invited her to a restaurant. So, in a way, she looked forward to an elegant and very tasty meal. They met in the carpeted lobby of the restaurant.

Gladys had been waiting for over twenty minutes when Cathy arrived. "You shouldn't keep people waiting so long. It's extremely bad manners. It doesn't suit a young woman like you," she boomed.

Gladys did not mind the fact that all the other patrons in the lobby felt embarrassed, she was having her say.

"I'm sorry, Aunt Gladys. I had to do some important business."

"There is no business more important than being loyal to one's old relatives."

"Of course, dear Aunt, but what I meant was – "

"Never mind what you meant. Choose your main course now. I have already ordered oysters for our starters and I'm going to have the swordfish as a main. The least you can do when you are so late is to make up your mind and place your order at once." She pointed at the menu with her index finger as if she was going to pierce it with a skewer.

Cathy let her have her way. She ordered *canard à l'orange* with *gratin dauphinois*, vegetables and a side salad.

Gladys lectured the wine waiter on the temperature of the wine that she ordered. "My dear François taught me to refuse any Châteauneuf du Pape which is served warmer than fifteen degrees Celsius."

"Certainly. As you say, madam." The wine waiter was obviously used to difficult customers.

They were led to an elegant table with fresh flowers situated in a cosy alcove of the restaurant. After settling down and placing their napkins over their laps they reached for some bread and butter.

"So how are you getting on with your studies?" Gladys asked.

It was the beginning of an inquisition which lasted until their oysters were served. Cathy endured it with fortitude, she knew there would be a reward in the end if she was just patient enough. At last, she managed to edge in a daring word or two, just to lead her aunt away from the dry topic of her studies. Very carefully she steered the conversation in the direction of her spare-time activities.

They were negotiating who was entitled to the last oyster on the serving dish when she caught her cue. "Oysters are really the crown of all seafood. Paul loves them, too."

"Now, who would that be, my dear?"

"Paul? Oh, didn't I tell you? He's my boyfriend."

"How wonderful. What do your parents say?"

"I don't think they either care or even understand what young love is. They think I'm still a child."

"But you have introduced the young man in question to your dear mother and father, of course?"

"Of course not. Why should I?"

"Now, here I happen to know more about the world." Gladys stuck her index finger up in the air. The space between them was fraught with electric tension.

This was the moment Cathy had been waiting for. "I might consider introducing him at a later stage. When I'm pregnant I'll probably have to, anyway."

"Child, what are you saying? Do you mean..." Gladys searched for words. "Do you mean you...you have fallen into a sinful life-style?"

"If you want to know, am I having sex, then yes, I'm having sex, and it's fantastic. Paul is just great!"

This was the first time in her life that Cathy had ever seen her aunt speechless for a short moment. She felt elated. At last, here she was with Aunt Gladys, they were having lunch in a posh restaurant, and she had given her the shock of her life. Gladys would try to lecture her, but of course she couldn't really make an impact, considering she'd probably never had sex at her age anyway.

Cathy felt she had asserted her own authority, the authority of the new generation. This was the generation that had thrown all the old stuffiness overboard. In fact, she was teaching her old aunt a lesson. She expected some heavy preaching, reproachful words, old-fashioned moralising. She was ready for it. Let the old hag spit out her poisonous words.

"My dear child," were the first words, and the elderly lady smiled. Her eyes took on a truly charming radiance and her voice became soft and benevolent. "This is wonderful news. I am so glad for you."

Cathy was dumbfounded. This reaction was so unexpected.

"You know, my dear," the aunt continued in what was a very low voice for her, "this is such an important experience in a woman's life. Are you truly happy about it? Isn't it an experience which makes one see the world with new eyes?"

"I...I don't know." Cathy was so puzzled she did not know what to answer. And how could she answer these questions in her situation? She still did not know what it was really going to feel like in the long run. She cursed herself. She should have known better. Why did she have to tell her aunt in such a way?

"You see, my dear child, now that you have indeed joined the world of adults I can tell you. There was another man in my life before François. He was my first. I can still remember every detail. Mind you, François doesn't know. I never told him. It happened when I was in Venice in 1947. It was like this – "

"Oh, I'm sorry, Auntie. I'm afraid you will have to postpone your story to our next meeting. I just realized I've got an appointment in half an hour and I have to – "

"What a pity, my dear. Well, in that case I will tell you on another occasion. But why didn't you tell me of your appointment earlier? We could have – "

"Never mind, Auntie. It's all right with me. No problem. I'm sorry, I didn't mean to offend you."

Hastily, Cathy escaped the awkward situation she had brought on herself. She managed a few noncommittal phrases and concocted some complicated arrangement with a non-existing friend which made it at least half-way logical that she had to leave after a few minutes. So the two women made some polite noises and brought their meeting to a close. When Cathy left the restaurant and waved good-bye over her shoulder she heaved a sigh of relief.

She was glad she did not have to answer any more questions about her first sexual experience, and she was equally glad to miss her aunt's story about her first affair in 1947.

FIFTEEN

Cathy could not forget her aunt's reaction to her story. Particularly when her relationship with Paul changed.

At first, Paul seemed to cancel the odd assignation, then he obviously found more and more excuses, and eventually Cathy accepted the fact that their love had evaporated. From other girls she knew that she should be utterly shattered when her love-relationship came to an end; she was supposed to be ill for several weeks. However, she found she was relatively cool about it. She came to admit to herself that Paul had merely remained a sexual fantasy from her puberty. The real Paul was too different, too self-centred. But he had served his purpose.

So she allowed their relationship to fade out just like that. They did not even have a final talk, they merely drifted apart, and after another two months they gave each other up completely. Soon, Paul moved away, and they never saw each other again. Cathy remembered that, according to her aunt, she had 'joined the world of adults' by her sexual experience with Paul. To her, however, the bare fact of the sex she'd had did not constitute joining the adult world. Only a long-lasting relationship could achieve that. She remained without a boyfriend for a while, and about seven months later she did 'join the world of adults' in the true sense.

It was a perfectly simple procedure. Her brother Stephen, from whom she had not heard for quite a while, called her and invited her to a party. It was not really a party as Cathy would have understood it, it was more a ceremony.

Stephen was now working as an engineer. He was employed by

an international company specializing in electronic components for mountain railways, cable-cars and funiculars. He'd spent several months on an assignment in Canada, where he had been responsible for designing the electronic controls of a funicular at Niagara Falls. While over there, he had spent all his free time with the local aeronautic society. After all, he had already become quite an experienced pilot, and the American colleagues had welcomed him very warmly. Among the engineers working with him, there had been a quiet young man called Jim, and as it turned out the two had become such good friends that Jim had joined Stephen in his flying activities.

Now that Stephen was back home his American friend Jim came to see him here with the news that he had also acquired his pilot's licence, so Stephen decided to organize a celebration for his friend at his own Aero Club. Since flying was obviously a hobby that attracted more men than women, they needed some women to shape the event into something that resembled a party. Hence Stephen's invitation. This was the first time ever that Cathy had been invited to a party by her big brother. She felt honoured and was happy to accept.

The event was already in full swing when Cathy arrived. It was a warm evening, and the party took place in one of the smaller hangars at the sports airfield. They had not bothered to wheel out the few light aircraft to make more space, they had only pushed them a little to one side. Cathy was greeted by Stephen and introduced to Jim. She got some nibbles from a buffet which was decorated with model aeroplanes between the plates and looked around. There were considerably more men than women. Several men smiled at her and she did her best to smile back. From time to time, Stephen came up to her to make sure everything was all right with his little sister.

"Are you having a good time, Cathy?"

"Yes, thanks. Who's the guy putting on the records?"

"Oh, that's Jacob, the old bore. I say, why don't you come

over there and listen to Jim's story of how he got the licence? It's fascinating to hear how things are done elsewhere in the world."

Cathy followed him over to the group of men standing around Jim and listening to his exploits, glasses in their hands. But she was not interested. She managed to slip away from the group again. She realized two things. One, flying and pilots' yarns were the most boring things she could imagine. Two, obviously her brother wanted to steer her towards his American friend. Could it be that Stephen was hoping that she might fall for Jim? How absurd!

"A penny for your thoughts." A deep but melodious voice pulled her out of her ruminations. She turned round and faced a tall, slim man with a remarkable sun-tan, short but wavy white hair and light blue eyes. He smiled.

"Oh, I was just thinking. You know, this is not really my world. I'm only here because my brother took me along," Cathy began, but she found it hard to go on talking. This was a novel experience for her. She tried to find appropriate words, but she failed and realized that her knees were feeling a little weak. "Can we sit down somewhere?"

"Of course," he said. He led her to the few seats which had been pushed up to the back wall of the hangar, behind the aeroplanes. They sat down. Over here the music from the wailing record player was more bearable.

"My name is Hanns, with double-N. I'm from Germany. Can I get you another drink?"

"I'm Cathy, I'm local, more or less. Stephen over there is my brother. I don't really belong here. But yes, I'll have another Coke, thanks."

It was with these banal party phrases that she regained a degree of self-confidence. But when he returned with their drinks she realized that this was going to be a new chapter in her life.

Three hours later, Hanns and Cathy left the party. He drove her to his hotel in town. He took her up to his room. He was more than twice her age, but for Cathy it seemed the most natural thing in the world. When she woke up in this strange hotel bed on the following morning she immediately remembered Aunt Gladys and her phrase about joining the adult world. She was not sure about her feelings. She admitted to herself that it was an altogether different experience from the one she'd had with Paul. With Paul it had been more like a biological experiment, or trying to prove something to yourself. This was different. It made one see things from a higher perspective, but it was not something that swept one off one's feet, as some of her friends put it. It was lustful, but why should one lose one's head over it? Cathy knew that she had it in her power to leave it at that and dismiss charming Hanns as a one-off experience or to keep up a daring and probably quite spicy relationship with a middle-aged man over a considerable geographical distance. She weighed the arguments for and against it.

She got out of bed and entered the bathroom. Hanns had got up before her and was already ordering breakfast on the house-telephone. While she was enjoying her morning shower she thought she could postpone her decision about such an affair until later in the day.

As it turned out, she postponed the decision over several months. The better she got to know Hanns the more deeply she loved him. He had businesses in several countries, and even though his base was in Hamburg he managed to come to town and see Cathy almost every fortnight. Occasionally she had to wait for three or four weeks, but mostly it was just two. She learnt a great deal from him. He taught her how to dodge the taxman in Italy and how to open a business branch in France with minimal fees for the avocat, she began to understand the significance of the impending counties reform in Britain and the advantages of having a business address in Liechtenstein.

When she was with Hanns, she felt good.

When they were first together she naturally assumed that he was also into flying since she had met him at the party at the Aero Club. He didn't correct her assumption for over a month. She never asked and Hanns never liked bragging and showing off, so it was only through Stephen that she learnt about Hanns's connection with the flying scene. Stephen's friends told him about Cathy's new relationship some time after the party, when it had become general knowledge, and he couldn't help mentioning it in the course of one of his telephone calls about five weeks after the party. Stephen called because of their parents' wedding anniversary and their father's 60th birthday, two events that were to be celebrated in the near future. After they had settled everything for the planning of the event Cathy expected to terminate the conversation. But Stephen's voice trailed on.

"I say, little sister. Is it true you've started a thing with Hanns?"

"Oh, so the pilots' gossip has reached you at last?"

"Yes, Jacob told me about it. But you know he can't be trusted, so I thought I'd ask you straight out myself. Well then, what's the story?"

"There is no story. I'm just having 'a thing' with Hanns, as you put it. More civilized people would call it a loving relationship."

"But he's an old man, for goodness sake. You could be his daughter."

"He's fifty-two, to be exact."

"You see? Now, come on, Cath, don't throw yourself away like that!"

"You never cared about what I did or even who I was until a few weeks ago. You lived your life and I lived my life. Why all of a sudden do you think you can order me about?"

"All right, all right, little sister. You're absolutely right, it's none of my business. I just thought I could give you some brotherly advice. I just thought you ought to be warned."

"Hanns is not dangerous. He's charming, generous, sensitive and honest. And he has a great sense of humour."

"It's not his character – it's his age! Hanns is a fine man, but he is just too old for you. I don't want you to be unhappy later in your life."

"What do you mean? Do you think it's too dangerous to be connected with two pilots because they might crash with their planes?"

"Hanns is not a pilot."

"Why was he at the party then?"

"It's a rather complicated story. One of his companies sponsored our new training aircraft. The Club wouldn't have been able to acquire a second machine for training if it hadn't been for Hanns. He's financially and emotionally connected with the Club, so he gets invited to all the social functions. But he's not a pilot. In fact, I think he is even afraid of flying."

"Why is he financially and emotionally connected – as you put it – if he doesn't like flying?"

"I think you'd better ask him about that. It wouldn't be right if I told you." Stephen's tone of voice indicated that he was bringing the conversation to a close.

After this news, Cathy tried to call Hanns, but his secretary at the Hamburg office said he was engaged in an important business meeting in Vienna. Cathy left a message for him. He called back in the evening. She asked him about his connection with her brother's Club, but he was evasive about it. He said he'd rather tell her when they were together the next time, so she had to wait for over a week. Eventually, they did get together in his hotel suite facing the market square in town. After they had made love they relaxed on the huge double-bed. He stroked her head and kissed her hair. She had not asked him again since their telephone conversation over a week before, and now he began to give her the explanation she had asked for. He was lying on his back, propped up against the head-board and he gently pulled her head down so she could relax with her head on his right shoulder.

"You asked me about my connection with the local Aero Club," he began, "and I didn't want to tell you over the telephone because it's not a happy story. In fact, it is rather painful. For a start, I was never interested in flying an aeroplane. But my younger brother, Christian, he was very keen on planes, gliders, helicopters, anything that could fly."

"I didn't know you had a younger brother," Cathy murmured.

"Indeed, I never told you about him. Well, he was so keen on learning to fly. He became quite an able pilot, as his fellow-pilots told me. He devoted all his spare time to his great hobby. One day he took me with him on a short flight. While I was desperately hoping for the flight to end because I was so scared, I began to understand some of the fascination that flying exercised over him."

"You mean, you began to like it?"

"No, it was just that I suddenly saw how wonderful it really was to see the landscape from up there even though I couldn't enjoy it because of my terrible fear."

"And what happened then?"

"Nothing happened then. But about a year later he crashed with his plane. They never found out why."

"And what about Christian?"

"He was killed, of course. It was terrible. We used to be so close, and all of a sudden he was no longer there. In the weeks following his accident he was constantly on my mind. Somehow, I thought I ought to have prevented him from taking up flying, because he had always been the type that attracted calamities. Already at school, when a group of boys did a naughty thing he was sure to be the one who was caught and punished. Then, when he had his first car – a VW Beetle – all sorts of silly little accidents happened to him. You know, the sorts of accidents that can't really happen. Looking back at his life after his death, I was reminded of that other Christian in *Buddenbrooks*…you know the one who is also unfit for this life. Have you ever read any Thomas Mann?"

"Is he a German author?"

"Yes, and he was one of the best in his time. But that's beside the point I was going to make. Christian always tried to achieve extraordinary things and he was always caught up in the complexities of normality."

"Did he have a family?"

"He was married, but they had no children. After his death I offered to help his wife, not only emotionally but also financially. While she was glad about the emotional support – I think we were both glad, we helped each other – she refused any financial support. She said she had enough money and could make a good living with her work. She's a dentist. But I felt I had to do something, something positive, something that somebody could benefit from, some kind of atonement. I knew that he had a very strong interest in training aspiring young pilots and he was a member of your local Aero Club."

"Didn't he live in Hamburg?"

"No, he left when he was in his early twenties. And it was here that he originally learnt to fly and where he made most of his friends. He always felt grateful about the support he had got here when he was in training and didn't have a lot of money. At the time of his death he was engaged in a campaign to raise money for a second training plane. So I decided to make sure the Club got what Christian had wanted to achieve."

They were silent for a long time. Cathy wondered how anybody could love his brother so much to do a thing like that. Or was it an act of general magnanimity? Hanns certainly didn't do it to make himself important. She wondered how many people knew about this.

Why do people act? What makes them do certain things,

take certain decisions, accept certain situations and avoid others? Where she was now, where she stood now in her life, depended on thousands and thousands of decisions taken by herself, by other people around her, by her parents, her grandparents, her great-grandparents and so on. What did people mean when they called a situation a coincidence? They probably used the term whenever they could not explain a situation they believed they ought to be able to explain. But Cathy thought it was an admission of defeat. The real question was not whether or not one could explain a situation, but rather whether one should allow oneself to be tempted by the urge to find an explanation at all. "We shouldn't think we're so important," she decided.

Cathy's ruminations did not leave her alone for several days. She judged every event under the angle of her new perspective. She was very grateful to Hanns. Their relationship became more intense. There were times when she could hardly believe how much of her independence she had sacrificed. And gradually her friends accepted the fact that she was in love with a man so much older than herself.

Of course, Becky had been the first friend to be informed, but she took quite a while to come to terms with it.

"Such a relationship is bound to fail," was her prime objection. "Your worlds are too much apart. You don't sing the same songs, you know what I mean? Just imagine, he had already left university when you were born. His opinions, his world-view, his political notions et cetera…How can you be so naïve to think you will get along over the years?"

"You silly. I'm not planning ahead like that. You're only talking such rubbish because you see the world through the eyes of Jane Austen and other literary dinosaurs that are really just unfit for real life."

"No, Cathy. I honestly believe you are going to make yourself unhappy after a short while, and as your friend I like to warn you."

"Don't patronise me. Are you jealous because you have no boyfriend?" Cathy hissed and took another mouthful of wine. "Come on, old chick. You're always so stuck up. Do you want to know what it's like with a man? I mean a real man. An experienced man."

Becky could feel the drift that their conversation was taking. She knew that Cathy would try to cross-examine her and get more and more aggressive if she tried to tone down the whole thing or to find a way out to a different topic. She had to be very careful, she did not want an unpleasant scene in the quaint little candle-light bar where they were seated at a table in a corner. So she decided to ignore the last question.

Cathy wasn't accepting her silence, however. "Hey you! I'm talking to you, you moron. Tell me, what's wrong with me if I have sex with a more experienced man?"

"I didn't say there was anything wrong with you."

"You did. You don't even know what you're saying. Are you too drunk? Of course, you're too drunk to see how utterly ridiculous you are!" Cathy raised her voice.

Becky was familiar with this. Whenever Cathy couldn't convince someone with logical argumentation she tried the steam-roller technique of illogical accusation. And if that didn't work she resorted to the alcohol solution, which was very simple. Just accuse your opponent of being drunk. Since such situations normally arose in the context of a discussion over a glass of wine in the company of other people or in a bar or restaurant, Cathy could be sure of general consent all around. Everybody in the bar could see that Becky must have had too much to drink, she still had a half-full glass of wine in front of her. Nobody suspected the contrary, nobody suspected Cathy. At least, that was the assumption on which Cathy's strategy was based.

This time it seemed to work. The other patrons in the bar looked at Becky and there was pity in their eyes. They felt sorry for a young woman like her, how could she let herself go and get drunk like that?

Even though it was a grotesque situation, Becky accepted it on the surface, because it stopped Cathy's verbal attack. At least there was some sort of peace and quiet now. They could change the subject and soon afterwards they left the bar.

The next time they met, Becky did not oppose Cathy's picture of her relationship with Hanns. Two weeks after that she actually met Hanns in person. Cathy had told him about her best friend Becky, so he invited both of them to dinner. Becky was impressed. She liked him immediately. Becky could clearly see the attraction he had for her friend. He was slim, suntanned, well-mannered, so experienced in many ways, a man of the world, and he had charisma. It was more than the usual old-world charm that other men of his age had in the eyes of younger women, it was something that was very immediate. He had presence.

As it turned out over the following months, Hanns and Cathy were a definite item. All their friends had accepted them as a fixture. Over Christmas and New Year Hanns rented a chalet in the French Alps and that was where the love-birds spent more than an entire week together. For New Year's Eve, Hanns paid for a group of friends to join them there for a party. There were three of his friends – a middle-aged couple from Berlin and a single man with a slight lisp from Hannover – plus Stephen and Becky. Why he invited Stephen was not quite clear, since neither he nor Cathy were very close to him. He probably did it because they owed their acquaintance to him in the first place. Of course, Stephen flew to Grenoble, steering the Pilatus Porter of his Club that Hanns had helped to buy. Hanns had a rented car, an extremely comfortable orange Citroen CX, so he fetched Stephen from Grenoble airport while the others were driven up from Geneva airport by the man with the lisp.

When they all arrived Cathy had a pleasant evening meal ready. She had always been interested in cooking and her relationship with Hanns had added a more sophisticated taste in good food. Becky was particularly delighted to see her friend and registered her happiness with relief.

The evening turned into a success for Cathy. All the guests praised her cooking skills, and there was general merriment as the evening proceeded. After the meal they made themselves comfortable in the wood-panelled living-room. Fritz and Helene Obermann from Berlin were especially taken by Hanns's charming young lady-friend. They were sitting on the cosy sofa and Cathy sat down in one of the armchairs opposite them.

"A wonderful meal." Helene smiled. "Thank you very much, Cathy. Of course, Hanns has told us a great deal about you."

"We understand you are about to complete your studies in economics," Fritz noted with satisfaction. "A very useful line of study, I must say."

At this point Hanns stepped up behind Cathy's chair. "I say, Fritz, don't corrupt my little Cathy."

"We have just been doing our very best to do just that. How did you guess?"

They all had a good laugh. Then Hanns bent down and spoke to Cathy in a gentle tone while he placed his glass on the little coffee-table between them. "Why don't you ask Fritz for advice? You know, about your job search. He might have some good ideas."

"I don't know if this is the right time or place…" Cathy faltered.

"You see," Hanns turned to Fritz, "Cathy has been looking for a part-time job to make some money because she'd like to move out from her parents' and get some degree of independence. And of course she's looking for a job that won't look too bad on her CV later."

"That's very interesting," Fritz beamed at Cathy.

"Hanns thinks you might have some good ideas because of your varied business connections," Cathy said. "I'm not looking for anything grand, and I'm quite flexible about the working hours since I have rather a free programme in my last year at university."

"Are you good at book-keeping, accounting and facing customers?"

"I'm quite good at book-keeping and accounting, but I haven't got a lot of experience with facing customers."

"Would you mind working on weekends occasionally?"

"I don't think that should be a problem. Only, on some weekends Hanns and I can meet and then it would be a bit awkward if – "

"I understand." Fritz took out his little notebook and noted down a few things. "Let's sit down together tomorrow morning. I need to know a few more things about you. I might have something in mind."

The subject was closed. Helene wanted to know how Cathy had managed to keep the vegetable so crunchy and the beef so juicy, so they got talking about cooking. The men drifted over to where the wine-bottles stood and helped themselves to some more of the Châteauneuf du Pape. Cathy noted it out of the corner of her eyes and had to smile to herself, thinking of Aunt Gladys and her craze about the right temperature for this wine.

"How much more of a gentleman Hanns is," she thought. "Gladys's François must have been a narrow-minded social upstart to make such a fuss about his wine. A real man of the world doesn't need that."

The evening proceeded and the atmosphere of carefree joy prevailed. The wine, in spite of the wrong temperature, made everybody happy and relaxed. It even loosened the lisping man's tongue. It appeared that he was responsible for one of Hanns's business branches in Northern Germany. Becky talked to him for the greater part of the evening, and she was deeply impressed by his knowledge not only of his immediate field but also in other areas, particularly in ancient history and archaeology. Naturally, they also drifted into a discussion of literary topics. They were just arguing over the relative merits of Samuel Johnson and Henry Fielding when they were interrupted by Hanns who announced in a booming voice: "All take up your champagne glasses, which are ready over here, and come out to the patio with me. It's just three minutes to midnight!"

They all took hold of their glasses and stepped outside. They listened to the church bells from the village in the valley below. On the twelfth stroke they raised their glasses and shouted: "Happy New Year! Happy nineteen hundred and seventy-eight!" Then they clinked their glasses and sipped from the mellow liquid that Veuve Cliquot had provided.

They stood around for a while, chatting and talking about their resolutions for the new year. Hanns came out with a fresh bottle with the orange label to top up those of the glasses that badly needed it. Cathy was standing next to Becky when the first guests got cold and lurched back into the warm chalet. Becky gave her friend a long hug.

"It's so good of you to have me here. Thank you very much. Your Hanns is really a very generous host. You don't know how lucky you are."

"I don't know," Cathy answered. The wine and the champagne had made her a little moody if not melancholy. "It was all right till midnight, but now I have this strange feeling."

"Aren't you feeling well?" Becky was concerned for her friend.

"I don't think it's physical. It's – well – it's an odd feeling I've never had before. I can't exactly say what it is. It's a sort of fear."

"Let's get our coats and go for a walk through the snow," Becky suggested. "That should do you a lot of good."

The two friends grabbed their coats from the rack in the hall. Nobody noticed them leave. They walked rather briskly for the first ten minutes or so, then they slowed down and fell into a leisurely stroll that allowed them to look up at the stars in the night sky from time to time. Becky did not press Cathy for any more explanations. They were silent for a long time.

"All this merriment," Cathy began, "and all this bragging get on my nerves. I can't help it. I feel there is calamity in the air."

"You are probably tired from all the work, you know, getting everything ready for us and all that, and then the wine and the champagne…"

"Maybe. But there's something else. I feel as if this was an immoral festivity at the court of Louis XVI shortly before the French Revolution."

"You mean, you are living a life-style that is above your reasonable expectations?"

"Not really. I just feel something really terrible is going to happen in the near future – a revolution, a natural disaster, a bad accident, a death – I don't know."

"How long have you had this bad feeling?"

"I'm not sure, it sort of started when we were getting ready to wish each other a Happy New Year."

"People often have strange feelings on birthdays, at Christmas and so on. Important anniversaries can make them realize the finality of life." Becky put a soothing hand on Cathy's shoulder.

"I'm not 'people'!" Cathy snarled, flashing angry eyes at her friend. "When I say something terrible is going to happen then I say it because I feel it."

This tone poisoned the atmosphere between them and Becky walked back into the warmth of the chalet to join the others. Cathy followed after two or three minutes. Everybody was shouting for a last drink, and Hanns was already getting the brandy bottles out of the drinks cabinet. Cathy and Becky did not exchange another word, and shortly after one o'clock they all turned in.

In the months following this episode in the French Alps, Becky often remembered what Cathy had said to her. But she never let on in any way.

The immediate result of the New Year outing was a job offer for Cathy. Fritz Obermann had liked her immediately and pulled a few strings, so that she got the perfect part-time job for her particular situation. She worked at the reception desk in one of his subsidiaries on three days a week, this left her enough time to study for her exams, which were coming up in the autumn of the same year.

Cathy and Hanns continued in their routine of meeting on a fortnightly basis, initially at the same hotel in town because Cathy still lived with her parents, but in April she got herself a small flat. In fact, it was hardly more than a room. There was a very primitive kitchenette in one corner, and the only other room was a tiny bathroom. But it was her first flat. The rent was very low, so Cathy could afford it with the money she made. Of course, Hanns had offered to pay for the flat, but this was a point on which she remained resolute: she wanted to stand on her own two feet.

She had lived there for three or four days when she invited Becky to a modest evening meal. It was only spaghetti Bolognese and green salad, but it was Cathy's first dinner invitation as a hostess. The two friends had a very happy evening together, and Becky was pleased that Cathy didn't lapse into one of her abusive moods. She was bubbly and pleasant throughout the whole evening. She even managed to listen with interest when Becky told her about her progress in her studies.

"But what I can't really get," she asked with genuine concern, "is why you chose such a dry subject. Literature! What a bore! And besides, you'll never be able to make your own living. Look at this flat. How will you ever be able to pay for such a place yourself? You still live at your parents' place. That must be awful. I could never stand it. Don't you have quarrels every day?"

"But you lived with your parents until very recently, and you survived."

"Honestly, I can't understand how I survived it for so long.

My Mum got so silly that we often had rows. My Dad is not too bad, perhaps a bit too overbearing at times, but I always respect his high moral principles. Because my Mum knows she's so far beneath him intellectually she invents these silly stories. Whenever he catches her out on something he doesn't approve of he questions her, and that's when she gets so cornered she invents such utterly stupid explanations. They usually play the same game over breakfast or dinner, and you can tell how nervous Mum gets by the amount of food she has in her mouth when she speaks."

"That must be difficult," Becky sympathized. "My parents are different, as I am sure you must have seen for yourself every time you met them."

"Yes, that's true. But still, you must want to move out as soon as you can afford it."

"I don't see why this should be such an urgent business. The present arrangement suits me fine."

"But what about when you have a boyfriend?"

"I'll tell you when the time comes. Never mind."

Becky had always been very quiet about her love life. Although the two friends exchanged a great deal of general information about boys and men, about their friends' love affairs, about sex and relationships, Cathy never managed to get any closer to Becky's intimate desires. She did not even know if Becky had ever had a love affair.

A few weeks later Becky happened to be in Cathy's flat when Hanns arrived. He came in and beamed at them, but Becky could see he was exhausted. He must have had a hard day. He kissed Cathy and shook hands with Becky, then he sat down with them.

"*Phewww*, what a day! I say, darling, have you got a sip of whisky for me?"

"In that yellow cupboard over there. Get it yourself. I'm not your servant."

Hanns stood up and walked over to the cupboard, but he looked at Cathy with a puzzled expression. This was the first indication for Becky that Cathy was beginning to treat him as she treated her.

He found the ice cubes and the bottle. He mixed his whisky and came back to the settee. He was very satisfied with himself.

"Isn't it wonderful what Cathy has made of this flat?" he asked Becky, and his beaming face clearly betrayed his pride. He was proud of his capable girlfriend.

"This flat means a great deal to me," Cathy said. "And to know I can pay for it with the money I make! You know, this job is just perfect. It suits me to a T. What a piece of good luck, and what a good idea I had when I asked old Fritz for a job when we were up there in that chalet!"

"Well, darling," Hanns put in, "actually it was my idea that you could ask him."

"No, it was all my idea," Cathy insisted.

"I don't think it was, but never mind. What about tonight? Is Becky staying for dinner?"

"Don't change the subject," she hissed. "You always do that when you realize you can't bend the truth to your needs and whims. I know it was my idea to ask old Fritz."

"Let's just forget about it."

"No. I want you to see how awful that is when you constantly re-interpret the past. You just twist the facts. You always do that."

"I am sorry," Hanns turned to Becky. "We shouldn't quarrel when we have you here, should we?"

Their conversation moved away from the painful disagreement, and they spent a reasonably pleasant evening together. Cathy did not realize that she was eroding her relationship with Hanns from the inside, like rust eating away a metal sheet.

Becky began to feel sorry for her friend – why was it so

impossible to make her see her own flaws? Were her difficulties rooted in her upbringing...her early childhood? Why could she not be more critical about her own ways?

How long could her relationship with Hanns last? How long?

PART FOUR

Cathy

SIXTEEN

Cathy had no idea of how other people experienced her. She had become a prisoner of her egocentricity.

Hanns was extremely sensitive and understanding when Cathy became more and more nervous over the summer months. She was studying for her exams, which were due later in the year. By the end of June she had already become quite unbearable for those very close to her. When Hanns visited her she spent most of the precious time they had together telling him how stressful everything was and reproaching him for not trying to understand her difficult situation. When Becky telephoned her she did not really listen to what her friend said, her mind was absent from their conversation and her heart was not in it.

One day in early July Hanns came to see her in her flat. She had not let him have a key so she opened the door for him. He noted the half-open drawers with socks and T-shirts hanging over the edge, the half-open kitchenette cupboards and the ruffled carpet under the dining table. There were scattered sections of newspapers and used tissues crumpled up in various corners of the room, a half-empty tea-mug standing on the window-sill and teaspoons, pens and pencils spread out all over the flat. "Obviously," he thought, "she must feel quite comfortable in such an environment."

He walked over to the kitchenette, closed one of the cupboards and bent down to pick up a stray teaspoon and a tape cassette of Chopin's first piano concerto.

"Why do you have to torture me with your crazy sense of order?" Cathy snapped. "Leave things as they are. Don't come and rearrange my flat!"

"I'm sorry. I thought I could make myself useful and help you get things tidied up a bit."

"You're a pain in the neck! I would have cleared up everything in time. No need for you to barge in and lecture me on how I have to live."

"I didn't lecture you. I don't think I ever – "

"Just leave me alone. You're getting on my nerves." She flashed her sharp eyes at him as if she could kill him.

Hanns sat down in the green armchair and picked up a section of a newspaper lying next to the chair. He began to browse through the paper hoping she would give up studying for a short time so they could see if they could do something together. After all, he had taken the day off especially for her. She did not look at him for over an hour and a half. At length he remarked in a gentle voice, "Cathy, dear – can we have a few words?"

"What do you want? Can't you see I'm busy?"

"I'm sorry, but I thought you knew I was waiting for you to come to a point in your studies that would allow you to take a short break."

She gave no answer. She bent down over her books again and ignored his presence in the room. Eventually, after another half-hour, Hanns said good-bye and quietly left the flat.

When he called her two days later she accused him of leaving her in the lurch. "You just sneaked out without telling me, and when I wanted to talk to you, you were gone."

He did not comment on that. But on the following weekend the crisis between them escalated even further. They had agreed to attend a function at the Aero Club. It was an official celebration of a new partnership with an American flying association, brought about by Stephen and some of his Canadian friends. The event was scheduled to start with a brunch at eleven o'clock on Sunday morning. Hanns and Cathy had said they were both looking forward to this event because there was going to be a good jazz band. But on Sunday morning when Hanns called at her flat to take her in his car, she opened the door with a sour face and squinted at him through a pair of small slits of eyes.

"You go alone," she said. "You know I hate events like that. How can you expect to drag me to such stupid male chauvinist parties?"

"I thought you were looking forward to it. And from what I know there are going to be men and women. It's a social thing, promising to be quite good fun."

"You go alone. Do you hear me? I've got a splitting headache." And she banged her door shut in front of his nose.

Hanns heaved a sigh of disappointment and descended the narrow stairs. With a heavy heart he got in his car and drove to the hangars of the local airfield. When he arrived there he realized that things were not what they should be. The band was not playing. He couldn't even see a band. Instead of people sitting round the wooden picnic tables and enjoying a pleasant Sunday brunch, there were scattered groups of men and women standing around and discussing nervously in undertones. The general nervousness in the air gripped his throat and he swallowed. He walked up to the circle of people standing nearest to him.

"What's the matter?" he asked a man he thought he knew well enough from earlier functions. His name was Thomas Brenner.

"You mean you don't know? You haven't heard?"

"No. Please, tell me."

"Stephen's plane is missing. He started for this flight yesterday about lunchtime, together with Jim, but they never arrived. Some of us came here last night when we heard about it, and we spent the whole night waiting for any news. The police arrived at the control room late last night, and they are here again this morning. We're expecting an announcement any minute now."

Just then two senior members of the Club and two officials

239

of the airfield stepped out of the control room and looked down at the silent crowd waiting in the space below. When Hanns saw their faces he knew what their message was going to be. He fell into a trance-like state and could not understand the words they used, but he grasped the fullness of the terrible truth.

"I must go and tell Cathy," he thought, and he returned to his car like a sleep-walker.

Brenner came after him. "Where do you think you're going?"

"I must tell his sister."

"They said they had to inform his family before telling the public. So there's no need to bother them with our vulgar curiosity."

Hanns was too dazed to note the insult implied in Brenner's remark. "I don't think she knows. I saw her only a quarter of an hour ago. They probably told the parents, assuming they would inform the rest of the family. That's standard procedure in such cases. I think the painful duty falls on me." He slumped down in the driver's seat and started the engine.

When Cathy opened her door she was the same as on his previous visit, still in her nightgown. This time she let him in. "Make yourself a cup of coffee while I'm having my shower," she grunted and walked in the direction of her bathroom.

He put his hand on her shoulder and gently asked her to sit down and listen to him first. She gathered from the tone of his voice that there was something terribly important. Was he going to leave her? Was he going to end their relationship now that she needed him most of all, in the middle of her exam preparations? He couldn't be so cruel. And yet, there must be an extremely unpleasant message that he was about to convey to her. What could it be?

"What I have come here to tell you is not easy. I'm afraid I have very bad news for you. You must be very strong now..."

Then he calmly told her in plain words that her brother

Stephen had been killed in an air crash. "His friend Jim was with him in his plane, and they were both killed. Apparently they collided with another machine in mid-air. I'm very sorry to be the bearer of such bad news, but I thought the sooner you know the truth the better."

Cathy stared at him with big empty eyes. For what appeared like an eternity to him she did not utter a word. Then she jumped up and began to scream. He stood up and tried to comfort her as best he could, but she ran away across the room and disappeared in the bathroom, where she continued to scream.

She did not reappear for two hours. He tried to get through to her with comforting words through the door several times, but without success. When she emerged at last her screams had stopped and her face looked worn and exhausted.

"That's typical of you," she growled. "You have to torture me whenever you can."

"I'm so sorry."

"Don't always say you're sorry. You're always sorry. Sorry, sorry, sorry, sorry, sorry! I can't bear it." She was working herself up, and he expected her to end in one of her especially violent fits.

"Can I be of any help? Or would you prefer me to leave you alone?"

"Go – just go!" she yelled.

She walked over to her small record player, put on a record with Tchaikovsky's sixth symphony and turned up the volume to drown any possibility of conversation.

Hanns hesitated for a moment, and then left.

The new situation changed Cathy's life. She spent the following days buried in her flat. She did not answer any telephone calls, and she did not open her door to anybody. The first person who managed to see her and talk to her was Becky, who had heard the bad news from Hanns. It was on Thursday when Cathy opened her door and received Becky for the first time. Becky took her in her arms and held her there for a long time. She felt deeply sorry for her friend and hoped she could comfort her a little by offering her warmest friendship. At length, the two women sat down.

"Is there anything I can do for you?" Becky began.

"I don't think so. I've got to get through this on my own."

"No, Cathy. This is a time when you need a good friend. And I am your best friend."

"You can't bring him back to life."

"No, I can't. You are right."

"What's the use of talking then?"

"A bereavement is always a difficult test. It always takes time. And sharing your pains with a friend can help, make it easier, more bearable."

"How naïve you are, Becky. This is going to be like hell in our family. You don't know how fond my parents were of Stephen. This is going to crush them. He was their pride and joy, while I was just a silly burden. An accident. A freak. I'm sure this is going to turn into a mourning contest. I can already hear them, reproaching me for not mourning my brother thoroughly enough!"

"Don't be too hard on them. This is a very difficult time for them."

"I know bloody well how they're going to take advantage of this." Cathy looked out of the window and shook her head.

Becky did her best to give her friend the moral support she could. But it was not easy. "They didn't give me that impression. Their grief is genuine."

"How do you know? Have you seen them?"

"Yes. Hanns and I went to see them right on Sunday afternoon, to offer our condolences and to see if we could be of any help."

"That was none of your business. How could you position yourself between us like that? And with Hanns? Are you trying to lure him away from me? Did you go to bed with him afterwards?"

"Don't be silly. You know that's not true. It was just that we felt we wanted to do something useful. And in this situation it was obvious that we thought of your parents first. They lost their only son."

"And I lost a brother!" Cathy shouted. "Have you taken their side now?"

Becky merely shook her head. She sat down in the green armchair and remained silent. Cathy walked over to the kitchenette and put the kettle on. But before it came to the boil she collapsed on the floor and started to cry again, but this time more silently.

Becky stood up and knelt by her friend. She put her hand on Cathy's back and stroked her with gentle movements. When the kettle sang she stood up again and prepared the tea. Then she led the bent and shaking wreck over to the settee and sat her down.

She placed a hot fresh cup of tea before her. "Here you are. A nice cup of tea will do you good now."

Cathy waited a few moments. Gradually, her weeping softened and gave way to intermittent sobs and periods of quiet self-pity. Then she began to sip from the cup. Her world had collapsed. Only now did she realize how she had felt about her brother. How could she go on living if Stephen was no longer around? Why had she never told him that she loved him? Why had she neglected him all these years? Why couldn't they be closer when she was a child, a teenager? She knew it was due to their age difference, but she did not want to know now. It must have been her own fault.

And why was everybody turning against her now? Hanns, the old sod, jumping at the opportunity to ingratiate himself with her parents. And now Becky! Why was she taking her parents' side in this?

Cathy came to the conclusion that she would have to harden

herself, to become a tough person. One's best friends could not be relied on in cases of emergency. The world did not give one any presents. No favours from fate!

There was a period of two weeks between the accident and the funeral. The unusually long period of two weeks was due to the investigations into the accident which had to be carried out before the bodies were released and the families could bury them. Cathy never once spoke to her parents. She remained buried in her flat, smoking lots of cheap cigarettes and drinking large quantities of cheap Italian white wine.

At the funeral there was a small crowd of Stephen's flying colleagues, there were some other old friends of his, his boss from work, very few relatives, and then of course his parents, and Cathy, Becky and Hanns. It was the first time that Cathy was face to face with her parents again. She did not say a word to them. They were silent, too, and the father was holding the mother, whose face looked at least ten years older. There were even some people who – according to Hanns – were from the family of the pilot of the other plane involved in the accident. Their attendance at Stephen's funeral appeared rather odd to Cathy. But she admired their courage.

About two months after the funeral, Cathy emerged from her hibernation and contacted Becky by postcard. The two friends had not seen each other during the whole period. Becky had tried to call several times, but Cathy was not in and did not answer the telephone. Now all of a sudden this postcard from Florence: "Hi, old Pal! Sent Hanns packing. Chilling out in Poggibonsi. Back in a couple of weeks. Cathy."

That the relationship with Hanns would come to an end sooner or later had been one of Becky's fears for a long time. Probably he could no longer put up with Cathy's tantrums, her aggressive moods and her abusive treatment of him. So he'd left her. But Becky was disappointed that Cathy could not be honest with her and admit that he had sent her packing, not the other way round. And what was she doing in Italy? Cathy had never been particularly fond of the country, she had always preferred Spain. She had always insisted that Spanish was a more beautiful language than Italian. She said Spanish was authentic and 'puro', whereas Italian was exaggeratedly sentimental and hypocritical. She said she just couldn't stand the Italian sing-song discourse. And now here she was in Florence, or near Florence, 'chilling out', whatever that could mean.

It was late October when the two friends met again. The leaves had all turned brown, yellow and dark red. Half of them had fallen to the ground. The weather still behaved rather decently, and the air was still full of autumnal smells and 'mellow fruitfulness'. Becky was expecting violent storms any day, but they seemed to hold back, she felt, just to allow her to resume her friendship with Cathy on a new basis. The colourful atmosphere, particularly the autumnal hues of yellow in the late afternoon sunlight invested their reunion with a degree of significance and confidence. They met on the garden patio of a restaurant by the river. The afternoon sun was reflected by the flat surface hosting a myriad tiny insects celebrating life and witnessing the reunion of the two women.

"I didn't want to come back," Cathy began when they had settled down with their cups of tea and their scones. "I seriously considered settling in the hills between Florence and Siena. But I needed an income, and I didn't stand a chance down there."

"Of course not, you'd have to learn Italian first."

"Oh, I picked up quite a smattering. I think I can get by in most every-day situations. It's not all that hard after Spanish, you know." Cathy's lecturing finger was in the air and told Becky to accept the statement as a fact.

"Have you got a job now? I didn't think it was a good idea to throw away your good part-time job, particularly when you flunked your exams. Will you go back to it?"

"I'll see about all that when the time comes. I think I might get another job – I've got my ideas, but it's too early to pass it on to the town-crier. I think I'll earn some money for two or three years and then take up my studies again. We'll see. What about you?"

"I'm still immersed in my literary studies. I'm working hard for my Ph.D."

"Will I have to call you 'Dr. Winter' then?"

"Don't be silly."

They laughed. It was the first laugh they had shared for many months. Becky could not remember when they had been so merry and carefree together. It was too long ago.

"Any boyfriends, at long last?" Cathy inquired.

"There is someone."

"Hey, that's great! Come on, tell me all about him."

Becky hesitated. "It's a delicate matter. I don't want to tell you more for the time being. I'll let you know when things are in less troubled waters. But what about you? Have you had enough time to get over Hanns?"

"He's history."

"Is there a successor?"

"Of course, stupid. Why do you think I wanted to stay in Poggibonsi? Why do you think I went to Italy in the first place? When Antonio said he'd go back to Italy I saw my chance – "

" – are you telling me you knew your *gigolo* when you were still *with* Hanns?"

"I was never with Hanns, as you put it."

"You cheated on him? While Hanns was still in love with you and supporting you in every possible way, you were already carrying on a sleazy affair with your sunny Italian *paparazzo*?"

"Come on, you prudish little creature. For one thing, Antonio is neither a *gigolo* nor a *paparazzo*, he's a professor of chemistry. And then I won't have our beautiful relationship pulled through the mud of your antiquated moral standards."

"Of course, you would see it that way." Becky shrugged her shoulders.

"Let me tell you," Cathy breathed and shifted closer to her friend, almost upsetting their tea cups. "He's absolutely fantastic in bed. The Italians really know how to please a woman. Our old stumbling-blocks around here could learn a great deal from the Italians."

"So it's the sex that attracted you. That's what you left Hanns for?"

"I'm a young woman, and I mean to have my fun. I am entitled to a little bit of fun now and then. Life is hard enough as it is. No, Aunt Becky, you're not going to throw your narrow-minded mud over the most beautiful experience in my life."

"I'm glad it makes you happy. I only hope it will last. Has Antonio come back with you?"

"No, he had to resume his duties at Florence University. We're going to meet up over Christmas and New Year. I'll introduce you."

The friends continued to discuss the fashions of the day, and eventually they drifted into current affairs. Cathy had a great deal to say about the rivalry between Italy and Germany in their fights against terrorism. She said one German magazine carried a front picture showing a plateful of spaghetti with a hand-grenade lying on top instead of tomato sauce, and the following week an Italian magazine sported a front picture showing a plateful of sauerkraut with a pistol on top instead of German sausages.

After this initial meeting, Cathy and Becky met again on a regular basis. And after a very short time Cathy had secured another job. This job was with an international company, and apparently they did not mind the fact that she had not taken her final exams. According to Cathy, they took her because they were impressed with the reports they had from the firm she had left a few months before, her old boss having written an excellent reference for her, 'for whom it may concern'.

As the days were getting shorter and the violent storms were stripping the trees of their last remnants of foliage, Cathy had recovered enough from the shock of her brother's death that she could begin to talk about it. One night she told Becky that she had not spoken to her parents since the funeral.

"As far as I can remember," Becky remarked, "you didn't speak to them even then. I always wondered why."

"I didn't want it to turn into a mourning contest. Mourning is a very private affair, very personal. My mother reproaches me for not mourning enough. The rules of the game are awfully easy: the more theatrically you mourn the more genuine your love for the deceased must have been. I simply refuse to enter into such a contest."

"But how do you know? You haven't spoken to her."

"My father sent me several letters, moaning about how hard it was for them, what an ungrateful daughter I was to leave them alone in such a difficult time, and didn't I have more decency in me than that. It's pathetic! They go on and on about having lost a son, and they refuse to acknowledge that I have lost a brother."

"But aren't you exactly joining that contest with an attitude like this?"

"You don't understand. They have got all their friends and relatives on their side. And I am all alone."

"If I were you, I'd end this childish game as soon as possible. Is it really such a shattering experience, I mean losing your brother? I never knew you were so close. Stephen was a lot older than you."

"You're right, he was older. We weren't very close in the beginning. But when the thing with Hanns started we saw quite a lot of each other."

"That was how long? And for your parents it meant losing a person they had loved and admired for something like thirty years or so?"

"These things cannot be assessed mathematically. Anyway,

I miss him. You know, one day I went with Antonio to Florence Airport to meet his best friend Claudio, and when I saw a plane I had never seen before my first impulse was: I must tell Stephen. Only after a split second did I realize that I could no longer tell him. It only occurred to me that he was dead after I had thought of him as a living person. Isn't that crazy?"

"I don't think that's crazy. I think that's quite normal. Death is something we humans can never fully accept. If we did accept the reality of death we would, by implication, accept our own mortality. And that's something that we can't do without doubting our existence, it causes an identity crisis. Or perhaps I should say that the task of learning to accept the reality of death is a life-long task. Literature is full of it."

"But Stephen died so young."

"Yes, this is an additional difficulty. The death of an old person, say someone over eighty, we can soon come to terms with. But when a young person dies it is a reversal of the law of Nature, particularly for the parents. The natural order of things is that one generation is born after another, and one generation dies after another. When that order is broken it's more than a personal crisis, it's an ontological enigma."

"How clever you are," Cathy said. "But I think you've certainly given me an eye-opener in one respect. You see, I feared I would have these crazy moments again and again, and I would be unable to avoid thinking of him alive first, even ten or twenty years after his death."

"This might very well turn out to be the case. But I wouldn't worry if I were you. Learn to live with it. It's part of our greater task, the task of learning to live with the world's inconsistencies and incompatibilities."

"Whatever you say." Cathy nodded and looked away. "I think we should order another drink now."

SEVENTEEN

The friendship between Cathy and Becky drifted into calmer waters in the year after Stephen's accident. Cathy had become a more balanced person, probably mainly because of her job, which gave her a great deal of satisfaction. And the fact that she had taken Becky's advice and resumed what could be called a working relationship with her parents also helped. After a while she even began to acknowledge the fact that her parents' suffering was one of the most painful and fundamental sufferings that humans can probably experience. The older generation mourning the loss of a member of the younger generation. The brutal destruction of a couple's link with the treacherous illusion of immortality. However, Cathy was more concerned with her love life than with her parents' worries.

Becky had been introduced to Antonio, and again she thought her friend had been extremely lucky to win the love of such a charming man. If anything, he was perhaps a little too charming. But Becky had witnessed so many strange shifts in Cathy's life that she decided to go with the flow and just accept her old friend with all her moods and her choice of partners.

As for herself, she had started a careful clandestine relationship with a married man. That was the reason why she did not talk about it so openly. She only hinted to Cathy that there was somebody, but she did not go into more details. Sometimes Cathy was almost offended because she did not tell her more, but most of the time she was too fully absorbed by her own relationship with Antonio to care for her friend's amorous details.

But Antonio disappeared from her life as suddenly as he had appeared.

They had arranged for him to join her for Easter 1979, and she went to the airport to meet him. She had put on her new mauve dress to please him, knowing that mauve was his favourite colour. Also, the dress was cut very low and presented a great portion of her cleavage to the world, something that would turn him on. She waited in front of the arrivals' hall…but he didn't come through. He wasn't on the plane.

She inquired about the next flight from Florence. There was one at eight thirty in the evening. So she was at the airport again for this arrival. Again no Antonio! She went home disappointed and tried to get through to him on the telephone. It was the beginning of another crisis in her life, for she could not get hold of him for days. When she managed to have him on the line eventually he was evasive and formal. She sensed that that was the end. She tried again several times, but when a young woman's voice answered his phone about three weeks later she accepted the fact that her Antonio was history.

In this period of her life – as in earlier times of crisis – Cathy found that her love for music provided the best opportunities of consolation. She returned to her old love of Chopin, Berlioz, Brahms, Tchaikovsky, Antonin Dvorak and César Franck. In particularly difficult moments she even found solace in Mahler and Bruckner. To get over her loss of Antonio, she spent hours listening to Dvorak's sixth symphony.

After this fiasco she reverted to her old teenage slogan about all men being dirty pigs. It was a slogan she knew Becky didn't like, although it had originally come from her, too. Becky thought they had moved beyond that stage of black-and-white painting of the world. On the other hand, she had become accustomed to Cathy's inconsistencies. You never knew with her. She could always surprise you. Becky remembered the suddenness with which Cathy had begun to treat her with such apparent disdain when they were teenagers. So she knew that Cathy did not really mean it when she spoke of men in such vulgar terms. It was her way of coping with her disappointment. Sometimes she shifted her complaint from the low quality of all men's characters to her own inadequacy.

"I didn't deserve him," she said to Becky. "He was such a dream of a man."

"In the realm of Love, deserving is not an issue. Who decides about who deserves whom?"

"My God, you are an academic through and through. *Whom* are you talking about?"

"I was merely trying to make you understand that the notion of deserving implies some sort of absolute value judgement, which is an oxymoron, a contradiction. No authority in the world can decide which woman deserves which man and vice versa. It's a matter that lies entirely between the two individuals concerned."

Cathy grunted. "If that's what it is I can make my peace. But men are dirty pigs, whatever you may say."

While Cathy's love life went through a series of calamities after Antonio, her job continued to keep her very busy and to fascinate her. The company was Australian-owned, and they were very supportive and generous in every respect. Cathy stayed with them longer than she had anticipated, but she told her bosses that she was still planning on completing her studies. This state of things lasted for more than two years. Then, one day in the spring of 1981, her boss called her to his office.

"Well, Cathy, how long have you been with us now?" he asked. "It must be nigh on three years soon. Am I right?"

"Two and a half...although it feels like ten years," Cathy joked. She felt very comfortable with Ron. He was the best boss anyone could have.

"I have been studying your performance with us. In your file I've come across your initial plan of completing your studies."

"Yes, that's what I've always wanted."

"As it happens, there might be an opportunity to have your cake and eat it. Our company – as you may know – has a few links with Australian universities. And we have a special travelling scholarship for younger members of our staff. I'd like to propose that you could complete your studies in one of our Australian partner universities on this scholarship on condition that you agree to stay with our company for at least another five years after obtaining your degree. How does this sound to you?"

"That's absolutely marvellous. What would I have to do to get this scholarship?"

"There's your snag. It is competitive. I can't promise you anything. All I can do is draw your attention to this opportunity. There are usually about half a dozen applicants from our various branches in Europe."

"You mean for one position? One scholarship?"

"Indeed."

Cathy thought for a few moments. This was really a great opportunity. She decided on the spot that she would do everything to get this scholarship. It was the chance of a lifetime. So she went ahead with her application. In the weeks following the deadline for submissions she was invited to several preliminary interviews, then she had to sit a written exam, followed by a final interview.

On the Wednesday of the last week in June Cathy was informed that she had won the scholarship which would allow her to complete her studies and obtain her degree at the University of Queensland in Australia. She jumped with joy when she opened the letter. After reading it twice to make sure she had not misunderstood anything, she called Becky and told her. In the evening Becky came round to her flat, and the two friends discussed all the possible implications of this new situation.

"You must come to see me in Australia," Cathy insisted.

"Of course, I'd love to. I'll have to see about the money.

Flights to Australia are not cheap. What about your flights?"

"They are paid for as part of the scholarship. It's a travelling scholarship."

"And how long do you have to stay down there?"

"Until I get my degree. Probably about two years or so."

The summer months were filled with preparations for the big trip. Cathy organized her life to suit the new perspective. Once she knew how much money they would pay her she made a financial plan for her time in Australia. She would probably have enough money to rent her own flat and perhaps get her own car, if she was lucky enough to find a cheap one.

When she thought of the new phase in her life she tried to imagine what Australia would be like. How would the Australians treat her? Would she understand their sense of humour? From what she had heard, they appeared to be people who had a very unfair sense of humour and who could be aggressively individualistic. And what would the men be like? Athletic, perhaps. Would she have any affairs in Australia? It was hard to imagine two years of celibacy. In all probability there would be new sexual encounters in store for her.

She left Europe in October, flying via Singapore, where she had a two-day stop-over, because she had to pay a courtesy visit to their Singapore branch in Bukit Timah Road. She was overwhelmed by the tropical atmosphere, the sweet smells in the air, the constant heat and humidity, and by the dense but orderly traffic in the city.

The vice-chairman of the branch, a Mr. Lee Kok Wang, took her out for lunch.

"Now that you are here," he remarked in his clipped way of speaking as soon as they had settled down in the luxurious-looking restaurant, "you will no doubt register a great many differences between Europe and Asia."

"Well, I don't know. Two days might be a bit short for such insight." She smiled.

"Sure, sure." His smile was broader than hers.

"Perhaps, if you or one of your employees had the time and could show me a few things…?"

"Sure can."

Right after lunch a young woman who introduced herself as Shirley took hold of Cathy's elbow and steered her to a company car. Through the rest of the afternoon, Shirley showed her many interesting spots. They saw the zoo and the botanical gardens and the new airport at Changi. When Shirley proudly showed her a placard with an artist's rendering of the airport in its final stages, Cathy asked if they were going to retain the name.

"What name?" Shirley wanted to know.

"Changi. Are you going to keep calling the new airport Changi?"

"Of course, it's the name of this place."

"But won't that be a bit awkward?"

"Why should it be awkward?"

"Well, I mean because of the English and Australian memories of this place and particularly its name, Changi. It used to be a very inhuman military prison of the Japanese in World War Two, Changi Prison, a deep wound especially in the Australian historical psyche."

Cathy had done her homework on Australian culture. She wanted to enter this new continent well prepared. She knew about the 'cultural cringe' in Australia and the urgent need of the Australians to establish their cultural identity. She had read a lot of books which deal with Australian history and the Australian consciousness. Her favourite authors were Geoffrey Blainey and Donald Horne, although she knew that their theories were not without contradictions. She thought it was rather inconsiderate of the Singapore government to stick to the name of Changi for their new airport.

She thought it wise to change the subject and followed her guide to the next sight, a seafood place in Jurong. But she considered this confrontation with Australian history an official beginning of her Australian existence.

Her short stay in Singapore came to an end, and she boarded the Qantas 747 bound for Sydney. While boarding she remembered that the name of the airline, Qantas – as far as she knew the only word with a Q but without the U – was an acronym meaning Queensland and Northern Territory Air Services. She settled in her window seat and relaxed for the long flight ahead.

When the new morning dawned she looked out of the window and was shocked. She had read about the barrenness of the Outback, but what she saw from her altitude was worse than barrenness – it was nothingness.

After a while, however, her eyes grew accustomed to the emerging light and to the strange new colours of the landscape below and she began to identify certain lines and patterns running criss-cross over the barren emptiness. As if a giant had played marbles on top of this toy landscape and left those traces behind. She was reminded of that funny best-selling author from Switzerland who claimed he could interpret such natural phenomena in terms of extraterrestrial visits to our earth, and she wondered what he'd make out of the type of country she saw beneath her now, on this beautifully crisp morning.

She imagined the land would turn green a long time before their descent towards Sydney. However, it appeared to her that the Outback was so vast it almost reached the outskirts of the city. Of course, she knew that that couldn't be the case, but it was her honest impression, nevertheless.

In Sydney she had to catch a connection to Brisbane. After a tedious change of terminals and a very long waiting period at last she got on the plane for Brisbane. And when she was met by a representative from their company at Brisbane airport she was utterly exhausted. The man took her to a hotel, where she spent the first three days sleeping off her terrible jet-lag. Then, and only then, she was ready to make a new start in Australia.

Cathy embarked on a very happy time in Australia. For the first few months she was extremely busy coming to terms with her study programme, which was rather tough. She spent most of the time in the library. But gradually she began to expand her activities. She joined a squash club and became more active in the social life which was always waiting for her on her doorstep in true Australian fashion. She had a small flat in St. Lucia within walking distance from the campus. She spent a lot of time in her flat listening to music on her cassette player. She was glad she had brought some of her romantic favourites with her. However, since her neighbours persisted in inviting her to parties and Aussie barbies she gave in and found she quite liked most Australians.

In time she discovered that Aussie barbies always followed the same strict social rules. Everything was fixed: what you had to bring along (a bottle of cheap wine from the bottle shop behind the Regatta Hotel), where the men were allowed to position themselves (standing in a circle round the actual barbecue) and what they were allowed to hold in their hands (a can or a stubby of beer in your right hand, keeping your left in your pocket), where the women were allowed to wait for the men to bring in the burnt chunks of meat (in the kitchen) and what they were allowed to talk about (cooking, kids, men). Also, she thought it was a pity that the meat you got on these occasions was usually not grilled *à la minute*, as Aunt Gladys used to call it – which meant rosy, tender and juicy – but horribly overdone, grey, tough and dry. Cathy was convinced that was something she could never get used to.

She could come to terms with other negative aspects of Australian leisure culture, for example with the permanent loud noise everybody produced regularly on Friday and Saturday nights. She accepted the fact that in Australian suburbs – where more than ninety percent of the population lived – it was a matter of sheer impossibility to go to sleep before three o'clock in the morning on weekends because there was always one of your neighbours producing such a loud hullabaloo and forcing hundreds of neighbours to put up with it. To her, this was the practical expression of the typically Australian aggressive individualism. For a European, this was not individualism but arrogance, thoughtlessness and sheer violence. Especially the bad habit of sounding your horn when you left a party and drove away at three in the morning. But Cathy learnt to come to terms with it.

The city of Brisbane spread out over a vast area, it was an endless village. The city centre was the most boring accumulation of business buildings Cathy had ever seen. In spite of the beautiful climate which reminded her of the Mediterranean, there were no street cafés or acceptable outdoor parks with the types of facilities you got in Italy or Spain. After five o'clock everybody fled from the city, and what remained was an urban desert of no significance, an accumulation of archaeological ruins of a forgotten era of rampant capitalism. There wasn't even a decent concert she could go to, except those few occasions on campus, but nothing to attract her in the city. So Cathy decided to direct her interest to the surrounding countryside. She bought an old Toyota Corolla for two thousand dollars, which was still too much for the wreck it really was, but it suited her. She began to explore the Pacific coast north and south of Brisbane, the Darling Downs and other attractive regions.

In the love department, Cathy held back for the first few months. She was too insecure with Australian males. When she got into closer contact with men she did so with European men at first, but she never got intimate with any of them. There was always an influx of visitors from Europe at the parties she attended. Mostly English, but also a fair portion of Americans, Germans, Italians, Greeks and even the occasional Scandinavian. An Australian, Alan Petworth, a lecturer from her department at university, tried very hard to intensify their friendship. One night he gave her a lift home, and when she said thank you and good-bye he took her in his arms and kissed her on her lips.

She let it happen for a short moment before she pulled away. "I'm sorry. I'm not ready for this. It's not your fault. Really sorry. Good night."

In the short break in the middle of the academic semester, she was invited to attend a conference in Newcastle, a coastal city in New South Wales. She inquired about air fares to Newcastle, which proved to be far too expensive for her budget. So she had to go by car. She was not too sure if she could trust the old car to take her there and back without a break-down, but she liked the idea and she had grown to like the car. On her trip down she was in a very special mood. Perhaps it was the music of Tchaikovsky that she was playing on her cassette deck as she was driving along. While she was concentrating on the rather aggressive traffic, she reviewed the recent experience with Alan and realized she had not been intimate with a man for too long. Suddenly she yearned for it. It was not a matter of logical volition. It originated from somewhere deep down inside her body. She located the source of her yearning in the region of her stomach, which made her laugh at herself. It couldn't be the stomach. She decided to give up searching for the source and just let herself drift into an erotic mood, which she found appropriate at this moment in her complicated life. She entered some strange sexual fantasies while her eyes were fixed on the narrow, winding tarmac of the Pacific Highway ahead of her little car.

She checked into a hotel in Nambucca Heads. She settled down in her room, then she went to the bathroom to freshen up a little. She was just stroking her wavy auburn hair with her thick hairbrush when she glanced sideways from the mirror and discovered two huge cockroaches in the bath-tub. The insects were scuttling frantically around the bottom of the tub, trying to climb up the slippery sides. They must have been at least four inches long, it seemed to Cathy. With a shriek she ran out of the bathroom, grabbed her room-key and left her room, slamming the door behind her.

Down in the reception area, which was really at the buffet area of the hotel's own restaurant, she lodged a complaint. She was furious. How could a decent hotel allow such a thing?

The sneering man behind the counter didn't appear to take her seriously. Cathy felt she needed the moral support of the rest of the world, or at least somebody else in the restaurant. Turning round, she discovered someone sitting at a table right behind her.

"You'd think a hotel of this category should be interested in complaints like that, wouldn't you?" she asked.

It was a question directed at the world in general. But the young man at the table answered, "Well, yes."

His voice immediately attracted her attention. While she stepped closer to his table she felt drawn in by an invisible force. The present moment merged with her previous mood in the car, her sense of sexual frustration. It was the most natural thing in the world to accept when, after a few more words, the young man offered her a drink. He called it 'a night-cap', which she considered very cute. Their conversation was drawn out while her desire for this good-looking man grew until she could hardly keep it back.

He said his name was Ivan. He was an Englishman working down in Sydney for a stint, and he was on his way up to Queensland. He had a clean-shaven, regular face, thick dark hair combed straight back and he wore thin, gold-rimmed glasses. His voice had a resonance which grabbed her heart. It was mellifluous, suave, extremely interesting. Cathy realized that this man had appeared in the right place at the right moment for her. Was this fate?

Later, when they were in bed together, Cathy felt that she had never been with a man who could give her exactly what she needed. This was why she gave herself to him utterly and completely. For her, there were no restrictions or inhibitions during this memorable night. She did not care what would follow. Everything else was forgotten during the intoxicating hours she spent with this man, Ivan. It was like a sleep-walking experience for her. Certainly, looking back at this experience later, that was how she stowed it away in her imaginary memory-closet. He was probably a bit younger than her, but that did not matter. Their sex was truly fantastic, earth-rocking. If she was honest towards herself she had to admit that she had really fallen in love with that young man.

In the morning, she felt so close to Ivan that she had to tell him about the loss of Stephen. Together, they listened to some Tchaikovsky on her tape-deck. She found Ivan's fascination with this music very charming. She told him so over breakfast, which they had downstairs in the same area where she had met him on the evening before. But they did not talk a great deal over breakfast. The meal had an aura of a farewell ceremony because they both knew they would drive in opposite directions, and they didn't know when they would see each other again. Afterwards they returned to her room for another session of love-making, but soon they found themselves on the car-park, saying good-bye. When Ivan drove off in his yellow car her eyes followed him with a sad tear.

But somehow, the wider the geographical distance between them grew, the less important he became, and when she was back in Brisbane ten days later she had already forgotten his name. They had exchanged names and addresses, even telephone numbers, but she must have thrown away his small slip of paper along with her superfluous conference pamphlets in Newcastle. Thinking of that beautiful night with the young man became a sort of private treasure which gave her new mental energies. She resumed her studies feeling more satisfied, more fulfilled. Looking back, she concluded that the one-night-stand in Nambucca Heads had been a good thing, a drug she had been in urgent need of.

Young Ivan from the hotel in Nambucca Heads never contacted her.

When she attended another Aussie barbie a few weeks later she felt unwell. Also, she found she no longer liked all that meat, those huge steaks, mealy sausages and greasy hamburgers. The thought of having to eat such food suddenly disgusted her. She ate nothing but a small plate of salad and made sure to go home before midnight. She felt exhausted.

Another few weeks later she realized she had missed her period and was sick every morning. It suddenly dawned on her that she could be pregnant. After a few days of ignoring this possibility she went to a pharmacy for a pregnancy test. When she got the result she jumped into her car and drove to the Pacific coast. She parked the Toyota in the Esplanade at Wellington Point and sat down on the grass in the small park at the tip of the little peninsula. Looking out towards North Stradbroke Island and the open space of the Pacific Ocean, she tried to cope with her feelings. One moment she soared high on a pink cloud of sheer bliss. The next moment she fell into a black hole of utter despondence. Pregnant! How to feel about it? The world was not going to help her in this. She knew she had to manage this all by herself. "I don't even know if Becky could help me if she was here," she shouted towards the low waves lapping at the boat ramp near-by.

Would she be able to complete her studies if she had this child? How would it influence her every-day life? How would it limit her? Would she still be able to write the thesis for her degree? Obviously, her social life would be changed radically. It was really not easy to imagine all the changes she would have to cope with and the challenges she would have to meet if she had this child. She fixed her stare on the ocean for a while, hoping to get some good answers from the vast space out there. She imagined she could see the coastline of Chili but she knew that was impossible. Of course, you can't combine your fantasies and the hard facts of Nature, they are incompatible.

When her glance travelled right and came to rest on the green vegetation of North Stradbroke Island she knew that she was going to have the baby. It was the ocean and the island that told her. It was no question. It was a clear blue certainty, as clear and blue as the vast expanse of water and the infinity of the crisp sky.

The next day Cathy went to the social services bureau of the university. She was invited to take a seat in a pleasant interview-room and a middle-aged woman sat down opposite. She introduced herself as Pam. One-syllabic, like all Australians, Cathy thought. After a few preliminaries, Pam asked her if she intended to have the child. Then she asked a strange question. "Do you know who the father is?"

Cathy hesitated. "Why is that relevant?"

"Well, Cath, you'll find that raising a kid's going to cost you. Nothing comes for free in this world, I'm afraid."

"Of course. Yes, I see."

"So, do you know the father?"

Cathy did not know if she ought to feel ashamed. "I'm afraid I don't."

" Okay. I see." Pam was not impressed.

"I mean, I know who must be the father, but I don't know him. Not personally, by name. Do you know what I mean?"

"I see. Well then, have you seen a doctor?"

"Not yet."

"You'd better see one. You want to know when to expect your confinement. You see, it's going to change your life completely. So we better get down to some planning. Tell me about your studies, the assignments you have to write, your thesis, your exams et cetera. I'm going to take some notes so we can draw up a plan."

Cathy had a long session with Pam. It was very good for her.

Pam was a wonderful social adviser. She had a very agreeable way of striking a balance between empathy for your predicament and a clear sense of reality needed in this situation. She went through every detail of Cathy's study plan, she was very understanding about the difficulty of some of the assignments and exams that lay ahead, and she had a very realistic idea of all the domestic arrangements that Cathy would have to make for her new life with a child. The entire interview lasted over two hours, and when she came out of the bureau she felt a lot better than before the interview. She felt stronger, more confident.

One thing had come out of the talk with Pam: it was imperative for Cathy to work as hard as possible and do her utmost in her academic studies. The important criterion was to get to a point where it would be realistically possible for her to complete the remaining tasks for her degree after the birth of her child. This meant longer working hours and a drastic reduction of her social life.

She took it seriously and immersed herself in work over the following months. She did not attend a single social event for more than four months. When, eventually, she agreed to come to the fiftieth birthday party of the head of department, charming Cecil Gray, whom everybody loved, it was her first reappearance in a social context after her long hibernation. She decided to let them see her condition. Whereas she had dressed in such a way as to hide the moderate but unmistakable swelling of her belly whenever she showed herself in seminars or otherwise around the department, she now chose a light party dress that would leave no onlooker in doubt. She thought this an ideal opportunity to make her statement.

When she entered the room and the first eyes took her in she felt a little nervous. But as soon as she realized that everybody smiled and when some of the women congratulated her she was more relaxed. Her best fellow-student and friend Paula Jamieson came over and offered her a glass of white wine.

"I'm sorry. I'm off alcoholic drinks. You know," Cathy said and glanced down the front of her gently bulging dress.

Paula looked down and nearly spilled her wine. "Wow! You sly customer, you!"

Cathy beamed with pride because she registered her friend's sincere joy and admiration behind the artificial shock.

"You must tell me all about it. How far are you gone?"

Cathy was pleased with Paula's genuine interest and with the fact that her first question had not been: Who's the father? She sighed with relief. "Nearly six months."

"And how are you going to cope with it? But wait, we'll have a proper talk about it later. Let's not talk about such personal things with all these people around. Let's mix and mingle and have a good time, even with orange juice in your case. Hey, but I'm really very happy for you, and what I really admire in you is your courage. I mean, other women in your situation might have considered an abortion, but not you. It's a true acknowledgement of Life with a capital L."

Cathy smiled. Just at this moment one of the male lecturers joined them. He looked down her front and smirked. "Eh, Cath, so you've discovered the reproductive potential of the Australian male, after all?"

"You male chauvinist pig," Paula snarled.

Cathy was going to say something more humiliating to him, but Paula steered her away to another part of the room, where they enjoyed a pleasant conversation with a few post-graduate students who were discussing the Falklands War. Everybody in academic circles hated Maggie Thatcher, and this group was no exception. It was good for Cathy to join in the general mood of ridiculing the Iron Lady's outdated notions of a British Empire.

The remaining months of Cathy's pregnancy went very quickly. She managed to write two more assignments in the last three months, which gave her a great sense of achievement.

Then the time for her confinement drew near. It was a fine, autumnal afternoon when her first pains started. Cathy was in the library. She stood up from where she had been reading an article about the social background of the Paraguay Experiment which had originated in Australia, left through the glass doors and intended to walk to her car at the bottom of the car-park. On her way, another contracting pain made her bend over like a jack-knife. Fortunately, another student whom she knew only slightly, came up and recognized her from a lecture they had attended together a few months back.

"Are you all right?"

Cathy tried to answer but could not find the air in her lungs. The other student realized what was going on. She took charge. Helping Cathy along, she steered her to her own car and placed her in the passenger seat. Then she asked Cathy about the hospital and drove off as fast as she dared. Cathy held on to the dashboard when she felt another contraction coming up. At the hospital, the student passed her on into the competent hands of a nurse, whose trained eyes told her enough about the state of Cathy's condition.

Cathy's labour lasted only two more hours, a fact that the nurse, the midwife and the doctor all found extraordinary for a first confinement. They called her a very lucky woman. Cathy found it hard to consider herself lucky while the pains lasted. Several times she wished she had never allowed this to happen to her. Why had she given in to that man? But then her thoughts were swallowed up again by the next earthquake of pain. At last, her contractions caused the baby girl to be pushed out into this world, its tiny head all crumply and her hair sticking to her head. Everybody smiled, the midwife said what a wonderful girl it was, the doctor congratulated her, and Cathy – despite her exhaustion – felt an enormous sense of achievement.

Hardly cut off from her, the little girl was placed on her breast, the tiny head touching her chin. Cathy held her very carefully, she didn't want to break anything, the little thing looked to fragile. But the midwife said she could give her a good cuddle, the baby looked so healthy and strong. So Cathy took courage and gave her a proper cuddle. The baby heaved a sigh and issued a pleasant moan.

"You wonderful little girl. Aren't you the most beautiful little human being I have ever seen?" Cathy found herself croon.

"What are you going to call her?" one of the nurses asked.

"Emma," was all that Cathy managed to say to what was the outside world at this moment. She wanted to be alone with her girl, with Emma, and together with her she wanted to fall asleep, forgetting the rest of the world.

"No middle name?" the nurse asked.

"Does she have to have a middle name?"

"Well, no, but most people do – "

Cathy hesitated, then she said, "Ivana," and added, "It means Joan in Russian." But after a few seconds, she sighed, "No – no middle name!"

Cathy found that the love that she felt for this tiny creature was greater than any serious emotion she had ever felt in her life before. It was truly overwhelming. She knew she would do everything in her power to protect this human being.

EIGHTEEN

Becky stood in the large hall of the airport and studied the black information board with the arrival times. Cathy's plane was obviously going to be delayed.

"Well, it's only one hour," the tall man standing next to her remarked in a soothing voice. "Let's get a paper and go for a cup of coffee over there. It's not very long."

She did not particularly like restaurants and coffee-bars at railway stations and airports, but she knew he liked to sit in a cosy café and read a paper, so why not grant him this small pleasure here at the airport? Mel was so good to her in every possible way.

"And a good thing I've got my book." She smiled at him.

They walked over to the newsagent's where Mel bought a *Daily Telegraph*. They found a vacant table in the café inside the terminal. He ordered a cappuccino, Becky decided on a glass of fresh orange juice. He gave her a warm kiss on her cheek and settled down to his paper and the ugly facts of the world.

Becky took her book from her bag. It was *The French Lieutenant's Woman* by John Fowles. Everybody had been talking about it when it appeared a few years back, but somehow she had never managed to read it until now. She knew there was already a film with Jeremy Irons, one of her favourite young actors. But then films could never convey the same flavour as the books they were based on. Of course, films and photography were the true art forms of the twentieth century. Remembering how the invention of photography had made realism in painting obsolete in the nineteenth century, she wondered whether either of these forms were ever able to reveal the truth of things. What does a photograph convey? Does a film tell us the truth? It was all make-believe, and it was treacherous because it pretended to reveal the true nature of things. It was merely truth hidden behind a veil of images of the truth, one perspective of the truth, never truth *per se*. In this light, she thought, a book could probably be nearer the truth than a photograph or a film. It was certainly the case with the book she was reading now. She was now just seventy-four pages into it. She opened it, flipped back a few pages to remember what had happened most recently, and she quickly grasped the narrative thread which enabled her to continue with the plot and enjoy it. Yes, this was an extremely pleasant moment. Becky bathed in her happiness.

After reading a few pages she realized that her mind was not fully immersed in the story. She could not help thinking of Cathy and of their relationship. What would it be like to see each other again after all this time? More than two years! True, they had written many letters, and four times they had even spoken to each other on the telephone, which had been a financial extravagance. But Becky had never made it to Australia. She knew Cathy could not forgive her for that, she had really insisted, pleaded with her, urged her, and she just couldn't understand that she didn't have the money. Well, she simply had to accept the fact.

And then the baby! Becky wondered what the little girl would be like. She must be what? just about a year old? It was very courageous of Cathy to have this baby. She was to be admired for it. Becky was looking forward to seeing the little darling in person. Would she look as charming as on the photos Cathy had sent? Could motherhood have changed Cathy? Would she be a softer person? Would she be more considerate? Would she allow other people to express different opinions? And what about her ever changing moods and her violent tantrums? Becky hoped that little Emma would have a positive influence on her friend. She'd seen from her other friends that motherhood did wonderful things to women.

Her thoughts shifted to the opposite perspective. How would Cathy react to Mel? She was quite confident that Mel wouldn't have a problem with her, he liked everybody, he was so positive, so optimistic. But what if Cathy didn't like him?

"That must be her," Mel said in his quiet voice when, two hours later, they scanned the stream of passengers emerging from the sliding doors of the customs area. Some passengers looked exhausted, some sun-tanned, some were obviously very bored, and some were eagerly looking around for their reception party.

"How can you know? You've never seen her before in your life."

"It's the photograph with the kangaroos. Lone Pine, or what was it called? She had the same strained expression."

"Oh, you…"

Then Becky recognized her, too. Cathy had put on some weight and her hair was a bit shorter, but she was definitely her old self. Becky ran up to her and hugged her. The shaky stroller with the child in it and the various plastic bags attached to it was nearly thrown over in the process. It was a very long and very warm embrace, a truly great moment of happiness for the two women.

After the introductions were made and Cathy had sized up Mel, it was little Emma who became the focus of attention. Becky picked her out of her stroller. While she was kissing the little girl Mel picked up some of the heavier bags and they started to walk in the direction of the exit to the car-park. Emma gurgled with delight.

"She likes me," Becky smiled.

"Yes, she's very good with people."

"Can I carry her to the car?"

"Of course, take her off my hands for as long as you like."

They arrived at the car-park. The wind was howling through the building. Mel took the ticket out of his pocket and walked to the paying machine while Cathy and Becky made sure all the luggage was in the boot and Emma was safely settled in the back of the car. There was no baby-seat in Mel's car, but they had placed a sort of cushioned box on one of the rear seats that allowed the child to sit in a position that she could be buckled up with the normal safety belt. Emma beamed with pleasure and babbled something that was obviously meant for her new Auntie Becky.

Cathy's return from Australia meant a new chapter in her life and in the relationship between her and Becky. During the first few days and weeks it seemed that they were getting to know each other all over again, like new friends. Becky was very fond of Emma, a feeling which was reciprocated by the child, and it came to a point where she realized she had to be a little more careful in her loving attention towards her friend's little daughter. She did not want to risk too much, Cathy might suddenly become jealous and turn nasty on her. At least that was what Becky could reasonably fear on the basis of her familiarity with her friend's unpredictable temperament.

Over the months, the two women established a routine which suited both of them. Cathy, who worked for the London branch of her old company, took a flat in a quiet street in Croydon so that she lived near enough to Reigate, where Becky had only recently moved in with Mel. They saw each other at least twice a week, usually in the early evening. Becky would drop in on her way back from work and help with the evening routine of preparing food, supervising Emma's meal and then playing with the child until bed-time. When the two women had finally closed the door on sleeping Emma they sat down to a quiet glass of wine and enjoyed a relaxed chat about their days, their jobs, about Mel, about Mrs. Thatcher and Mr. Reagan, and about all the little news items of the period. Sometimes they had a good laugh when they lost themselves in reminiscences about their childhood days.

"I wish my parents had taken more photos of me when I was a small girl," Becky said. "I'm already beginning to forget some of the things that were important to me when I was a child. What will it feel like when I'm older? I won't even be able to remember all the books I've ever read."

"And that wouldn't even be the worst thing that could happen to you," Cathy smiled. "What about all the men you loved? What if you can't remember them one day?"

"Oh, there aren't as many as in your life."

"You never know."

In their conversations, they often circled around topics like these. They were drawn to the strangely alluring mystery of the passage of time. They realized that maybe it was because they were both approaching their thirtieth birthdays. They were now definitely leaving the days of their youth. Middle age was waiting for them round the corner.

Soon it became clear that neither Australia nor motherhood had been able to improve Cathy's bad side. She was as slovenly in her own flat as she had always been. She obviously felt comfortable with half-open drawers and cupboards, ruffled carpets, bits and pieces strewn over the floor, an array of used and crumpled-up paper tissues spread out over kitchen, bathroom and bedroom, half-empty tea-mugs left standing on sideboard, table and desk, sometimes staining the polished surfaces with their wet rings of spilt tea, old socks and sections of newspapers under the dining-table, the odd pencil or teaspoon in the most unexpected places, and sometimes pieces of stained underwear on the hall floor. The only things that were always tidied up and stowed away with perfection were the things connected with Emma.

Her behaviour was as unpredictable as ever. After the initial phase of newly getting to know each other, Cathy dropped her mask of politeness and kindness towards Becky. This became clear one afternoon when they were out shopping. They could leave Emma with Janet, a friendly neighbour of Cathy's. Becky had Mel's car. They wanted to get some clothes for Emma from Marks and Spencer's and they both had to do their food shopping at Sainsbury's.

"Where shall we go first?" Becky asked when Cathy had made herself comfortable in the passenger seat.

"It doesn't really matter."

"Then let's go to Marks and Sparks first." Becky turned left at the traffic-lights.

"That's fine with me," Cathy mumbled and scanned through her shopping list.

Traffic being quite bad on this particular afternoon, they drove for a quarter of an hour without speaking. They were both absorbed by their thoughts of what they had to get from the shops and Becky had to concentrate on her driving. When she indicated to turn right into the car-park of Marks and Spencer's Cathy looked up and jerked her head round.

"Why are you going here first? You stupid bitch! You could've told me you were going here first, you bloody idiot!" Cathy shouted.

"But we were..."

"You're such a selfish brute. Why didn't you tell me you'd changed your mind?"

Becky immediately realized that there was no point in arguing with her. She was so worked up that she could hardly breathe.

"All right, all right," she said as she was turning the wheel to rejoin the main road. "I'll drive to Sainsbury's first, if that's what you want."

"No, don't just do what you think I want," Cathy snarled. "If you want to come here first then let's do this, but tell me: why didn't you want to go to Sainsbury's in the first place?" Cathy drilled these words into her friend's face.

"Never mind, just let's go there now."

"No, don't do that. Don't evade my question. Why didn't

you want to go there in the first place?"

Becky decided to remain silent, which had the effect she already knew from their younger days. For a while Cathy went on calling her bad names and lecturing her on how unfair of her it was to do things without giving her reasons.

"You know, I like to call a spade a spade, but I'm always fair and honest. My father taught me that. It was his principle." After this final display of her distorted self-image she fell silent. They spent the remaining afternoon doing their shopping in relative silence, merely talking when it was practical or necessary. On their way back Cathy warmed up again and slipped back into her role of a caring friend, chatting away about all sorts of small things, daily events, Emma's new words and her plans for the weekend. As if nothing had ever been amiss between them.

For their thirtieth birthdays, which were only two months apart, good old Mel announced he would organise a party. He booked a function-room in a beautiful country pub somewhere between Dorking and Crawley and had the two women draw up lists of people they wanted to have invited. He said he would also bring along a few friends.

It was a hot summer evening. Cathy drove to the pub in her new car. After she had obtained her degree she had been promoted and could afford a better life-style. So she had only just bought this new car a few weeks before her thirtieth birthday. She considered it her own birthday present for herself. It was a dark-green Austin Allegro. She parked it in the large car-park. Walking from her car to the pub she saw a tall man walking in the same direction, and when their paths nearly merged she stumbled over a dry branch lying on the ground. She was falling when the man jumped forward and caught her in mid-air. He took a firm grip of her shoulders and elbows and set her upright again. In the process of this mishap her low-cut summer dress was pulled awry in such a way to reveal altogether too much of her breasts to this stranger. She quickly re-arranged her dress.

"I'm terribly sorry," she mumbled, blushing.

"Are you all right?" the man inquired. His voice had a warm resonance.

Cathy wondered how much of her breasts he had seen. Typical, she thought, men would take any opportunity to catch a glimpse of a woman's cleavage. She was torn between two feelings. On one hand she felt slightly embarrassed because this man might have seen more of her than was considered decent. On the other hand she felt touched by his kindness. After all, she might have injured herself if he had not saved her.

"My name's Don, Don Richardson," he said, offering his large right hand, as they were entering the back door of the pub together.

Cathy politely introduced herself and noticed the gentle glow of his blue eyes and the small wrinkles on their edges giving his face a smiling aspect.

When they reached the function-room Cathy realized that this tall man with the smiling face was one of Mel's friends. Mel wanted to introduce him to her, but Don said they had already met. The way he said it gripped her at her heart. From this moment she knew she had to get to know this man better. She had to connect herself with him in some way. She suddenly became aware of the fact that she had not been close to a man since her return from Australia, a period of more than four years. She had been so full of her child, her beautiful daughter who had taken up all her energy. This was a pleasant awakening from her hibernation. But she was not going to lose her head and fall in love, she told herself.

The party was one of the happiest events in Cathy's life. The people were all wonderful, she felt loved by everyone, the food was fantastic, and the music was heavenly. At half-past eleven she found herself clinging to Don. Around them, people were dancing to a slow tune, but they were only pretending to dance.

275

They were standing together, moving only slightly, rhythmically. His arms enveloped her entire body, while she had her bare arms round his firm neck. What mattered to them was the close touch of their bodies. There were only two thin layers between them, his summer shirt and her summer dress. She had the illusion that their skins were touching. She hoped he could feel the soft pressure of her breasts now and remember how beautiful they were when he had spotted them on the car-park.

The outcome was obvious.

Everything went very fast from then on.

Don was a man of many talents. He had made some money from a business venture in the early days of the personal computer, and now he had his hands in a whole range of businesses. One of his companies worked as a liaison between large printing factories and their bulk customers. Another company ran a chain of restaurants in the western suburbs of London. And the company that interested Cathy's friend Becky most of all was his publishing firm. However, he was much more than a businessman. He was cultured, he read a great deal, particularly nineteenth-century authors, and he played the violin. From the start of their relationship he absolutely worshipped her. He was ready to turn a blind eye on all the negative sides of her character. Always the true gentleman, he considered it his duty to forgive any petty flaws in the woman he loved.

Within six months after Cathy's birthday party, they joined their households and moved to a country house in Surrey, planning their common future. When, in the last week of November 1987, they got married it was a relatively quiet affair. Mel and Becky were their witnesses, and there were only a few other guests. Immediately after marrying Cathy, Don adopted Emma and gave her his name. So they were a proper family now. Cathy continued working for the same company. She refused all offers of Don's to find a suitable posting in one of his companies. She cherished her portion of relative freedom.

Becky found it a bit more difficult to keep in touch with her friend now that she lived in rural Surrey. For the first few months after their marriage she saw very little of either of them, but about ten months later she had a manuscript ready for publication. She phoned Cathy and asked her if she should approach Don's publishing house. Cathy thought it an excellent idea and told Don. He phoned Becky on the following evening.

"Hi, Becky, it's Don."

"Don, it's so good to hear from you. How are you?"

"Terrific! Married life really agrees with me. Then there's Emma, of course. She's an absolute darling."

"I know she is. Give her my love."

"Will do. Listen, Cathy told me about your manuscript. About some unknown author from the early nineteenth century, is it?"

"Yes, it's rather a comprehensive study about James Justinian Morier, you know, the man who wrote the Hajji Baba books, and a lot more." Becky would have liked to tell him more about the subject, but she sensed that he was trying to say something else to her.

"Well, I'm sure you've dug it all up. We've got to have a good talk about it. But I say, why don't you send it to my publishing house? Send it to a Mrs. Alice Pemberton and mention my recommendation in your cover letter."

"I'm glad to send it to Mrs. Pemberton, but I won't mention your recommendation. I think the manuscript ought to speak for itself."

"There you're wrong," Don laughed. "Academic publishing is not a very lucrative business, so unless you have some sort of recommendation or other credentials most publishers won't even bother to look at your manuscript."

"What about my other books then? This is going to be my third."

"Yes, but they appeared as volumes within a series and were

subsidised. This time I'd like to give you the opportunity of a commercial publication if your text deserves it. And I'm quite confident that it is a good manuscript."

"Well, I'll sleep on it and decide tomorrow."

Becky sent the manuscript with the cover letter referring to Don's recommendation. The result was that she was invited to have lunch with Alice Pemberton to discuss the publication of her third book. The lunch took place at the Copper Chimney, a very nice Indian restaurant in a little side street off Regent Street. Alice Pemberton turned out to be an extremely charming and efficient woman. They had a good discussion, and Alice arranged for her to come to her office two weeks later to discuss more details. When she called at the office on the day they had arranged, Becky was shown round and introduced to several men and women in the firm as 'our new author, Dr. Rebecca Winter'. Then they had a long business meeting in which they discussed many details of the proposed publication, and as it turned out they argued for quite some time over the title of the new book. *From Ispahan to London*, which Becky had suggested, was considered too banal, too plain, even boring. Alice suggested a better title, *The English Godfather of the Persian Novel*, but they both found that too long. At last, they agreed on yet another title, *The English Hajji*. This was it. At the end of the afternoon Becky had her contract.

The book was published in spring 1989, and Don himself made a very witty and intelligent speech at the book launch. He managed to link the book's bridge function between England and the world of Islam with the prevailing interest in such cultural connections in the wake of the Rushdie affair. As it turned out, this link resulted in extremely high sales figures for Becky's book, which would have been considered a much more obscure contribution to the literary discourse of the time under normal circumstances. However, now that even the most illiterate British subject – of Christian or Muslim background

– had been made painfully aware of a cultural clash involving Western intellectuals on one side and fundamentalist Muslims who had no cognizance of post-modernism on the other side, the reading public had a keen interest in all other books throwing some light on this cultural clash. Becky's book did not satisfy such expectations, of course, but it was an example of a cultural connection between England and Islam in an earlier period. As such, it could be said to contribute a minute side aspect from a literary and historical perspective to the current main-stream debate about the alleged blasphemies in Rushdie's latest novel.

As Cathy found out from Becky in the course of their conversations, Becky found the accusations levelled at Salman Rushdie extremely unfair. The reason for this was not only her admiration for his style, for the intricate artistry of his literary discourse, it was also her conviction that the very people for whom he had written his book were now attacking him: the displaced poor Muslims from the Diaspora of Northern India living in the poorer quarters of English cities. Moreover, she realized that the controversial chapters about early Islamic history were protected by several layers of literary filters: a drunken actor dreaming the entire episode. Cathy was impressed with this explanation.

At first, Becky found it unmerited that her own book was so successful because of the Rushdie affair, particularly since that author suffered very severe consequences. But gradually she accepted Don's arguments about the well-deserved success.

Don and Becky were often thrown together in the months and even years after the publication of Becky's book. They met at literary gatherings, at publisher's lunches and sometimes even in bookshops when she was signing copies of *The English Hajji*.

Initially, Cathy was very happy about the fact that her best friend and her husband were on such good terms. But one day about two weeks after the book launch Don happened to mention Becky in the wrong context. Cathy had been arguing with Don about the colour of their new awnings. They had looked at samples in a catalogue and Cathy had found she liked a material that was striped blue and white. Don was horrified at the idea, but he remained calm and sensible.

"My dear," he carefully began, "I don't mind the colours so much, though blue seems too cold to me, but I don't think it would look very nice if we chose striped awnings. Striped awnings look like an Italian ice cream parlour."

"That's nonsense, it would look very chic," Cathy retorted.

"Besides, I have lived in various houses and flats with awnings. And in my experience the pattern and the colour define the kind of shade you will enjoy when you sit under the awnings on a hot summer afternoon. If we choose the type that you suggest we will feel rather uncomfortable in a striped atmosphere alternating between a blue and a white hue."

"How do you know?"

"Well, only the other day, Becky and I happened to discuss something along these lines. A neighbour of hers had got new awnings, and she was very unhappy about them, so we exchanged our views on the matter."

"So it's Becky now," Cathy hissed in a sly tone. Don knew straightaway that it had been a mistake to mention Becky. The atmosphere grew tense.

"You seem to be very fond of Becky," she said, pretending a common concern.

"What are you trying to insinuate?" he asked calmly.

"What is it she has that I haven't got?" Her voice had a cutting edge now.

"Please, my dear, don't talk like that. You know perfectly well that my relationship with your friend Becky is a business connection first, then a respectable friendship. So don't ask such awful questions."

Cathy looked at Don sideways from the corner of her eyes. This was a method she had acquired only recently, a trick with which she tried to give an impression that meant, "Don't fool me, my little boy, I have caught you out and you know it." Without realizing it she was quite proud of herself as a very acute observer whose perspicacity nobody could escape.

"Do you have sex with her?" she blurted out.

"Of course not, don't be silly."

They were silent for the rest of the evening. Don realized it was the first indication of Cathy's jealousy, and he found it hard to swallow that she was jealous of her best friend.

In the morning she announced that he was right about the awnings. Stripes were out, she agreed to plain ones in light brown, a warm colour.

NINETEEN

Cathy and Don lived through a reasonably happy marriage. They were both very busy in their jobs, and Emma continued to give them a great deal of joy. The girl was not only beautiful but also very sensible. Don proved to be a very good father for her. In spite of his various professional commitments which gave him only limited time for his private life, he spent a lot of time with Emma when she was small. He took her to many of the London museums, occasionally to a concert in the Royal Festival Hall or a West-End theatre performance, he took her to Chessington several times, he went on moderate walking tours with her – they did parts of the South Downs Way – and he was present at most of her garden parties on birthdays and other festive occasions. At such parties he made sure there was enough sensible entertainment for all the children invited. He organized games with an intellectual flavour that appealed to the children, quizzes and musical activities. He engaged a magician with lovely tricks for children and a puppeteer with a puppet show that even the adults thoroughly enjoyed, and once he disguised himself as a clown and gave the children a performance they would probably never forget. By the time Emma reached the age of ten Cathy had become accustomed to the fact that every party had a fresh surprise for her in terms of her husband's unsuspected talents.

If the marriage was reasonably happy it was primarily due to Don's generous and forgiving nature. Cathy treated him as she had always treated those close to her. Emotionally she lived at his expense. All their friends – except Becky – had no idea that Cathy could be such a slave-driver within the family. They considered her entertaining and witty and they liked her party stories. Only Don and Becky knew how cruel and abusive her sense of humour really was and how she always re-shaped the past in her stories, humiliating others in the process.

One evening some time around the early nineties, they had two other couples for dinner. Things went very well throughout the meal, but they all enjoyed the jolly spirit so much that they lingered on for another two hours over their cheese board and the full-bodied Ribera del Duero. Cathy, either because of her considerable intake of wine or because of her deep-rooted wish to shine as the queen of party-stories, launched into her version of how difficult relationships can sometimes become. She began to dish up more and more examples of instances where she and Don had disagreed on minor intimate details.

"And you know what? Sometimes you discover that your partner disagrees with you on something you never even suspected one could disagree about," she beamed at the jolly faces round the table and took another sip from her glass.

"Indeed, that's quite a common experience," their friend Ben murmured and his wife nodded her head in agreement. "Every couple has a story to tell."

"Listen to what happened to us," Cathy dictated and pointed her didactic index finger in the air. "We were choosing new awnings, and you know how things are. You go to the shop or browse through the catalogue and select the colour and the pattern."

"Please, my dear," Don gently suggested, "I don't think that's of any interest to our guests, Why don't we – "

"Be quiet," she snarled at him, then she turned a smiling face to their guests and continued. "What surprised me was the fact that one can discover different opinions one never suspected. In the case of the awnings I had assumed as a matter of course that if I suggested a vertically-striped pattern Don would agree, but he wanted a horizontally-striped one. Ha ha! So we came to a compromise and got plain awnings."

"I'm sorry, my dear, but as far as I can remember it was not quite like that."

"Oh, you're drunk, you don't know what you're saying," she said and smiled at their guests in a suggestive way which expressed something like, "That's what you get when your husband has had too much to drink, he tends to embarrass your guests, but please just ignore him, he's really a good sort."

Don apologised and stood up from the table. Very discreetly he began to tidy up the kitchen. For a brief moment he wondered why he was doing this. He came to the conclusion that she actually left him no choice. If they wanted to live in relative happiness and didn't want a row every day it was the only course of action open to him.

Their lives continued very much along the same lines over the following years. Cathy believed she loved Don very much, and she was convinced that they were the model couple for all their friends. She never read the small hints and signs that Don gave her from time to time, indicating that he would like to talk to her about their relationship but couldn't because she would always cut him short from the outset.

It was in 1995, when Don happened to run into Becky in front of a pub in the Covent Garden area. He invited her in for a drink.

"How's Cathy these days?" Becky began after a few minutes.

"Oh, she's all right. You know, since Emma left for school she has become more nervous than ever. I only hope she will find back to her old self, her spiritual centre, as it were. To me she seems to function at odds with her own convictions. She's beside herself with her fits of sadness and her tantrums."

"Yes, I know what you mean. Poor Cathy! There's nothing we can do about it. You know I often tried to help her."

"When I came home last night it was the usual mess," Don

confessed. He knew Becky was the only person he could tell such things.

"You mean around your house?"

"Yes. Stepping through the front door I nearly fell over a pair of her shoes lying in the middle of the hall floor. I placed them on the shoe rack when I discovered a dirty sock of hers on the banister. The doors of the hall cupboard were half open, and so were half a dozen drawers and doors in the kitchen. A few pages of Monday's *Independent* lay in disarray under the dining table. When I went to the toilet I found the seat cover open and the bowl containing a fine brown turd and a bunch of hair. I flushed the toilet when I saw her lipstick and a five-pound-note under the wash-basin. Of course, the carpets in the living-room were not where they should have been and in our bed-room the beds were still unmade. What I saw when I went to the – "

"Don't go on," she interrupted. "I know it all. That's our Cathy. I hoped you might have a good influence on her, you know, making her realize how difficult it is to live with her and…and, well I don't know."

"I don't think she has the mental capacity for such insight. She's so full of herself. She always boasts about how altruistic she is. She says she always thinks of others first and neglects her own wishes. Her image of herself is the complete opposite of how we perceive her. Mind you, it's only you and me. Others seem to believe her when she goes on about her own modesty."

"How do you manage to live with her then?"

"Oh, you know," Don sighed, "it may come as a surprise, but the fact is I love her. That must be my source of energy to put up with her day after day."

"I admire you."

"Please don't. I don't deserve your admiration. It's not such a grand thing. In fact it's rather humiliating."

They finished their drinks and left the pub. Don offered to give her a lift, but she thanked him and said she had to see someone before meeting Mel at the Barbican for a fine concert. They smiled in a knowing way when they touched each other's cheeks and said good-bye.

When he reached home he found Cathy in a cheerful mood. They sat down and had a chat before going to the kitchen to prepare the evening meal together.

"How was your day?" she asked.

"Good. I had lunch with Annie O'Connor, the new woman I appointed for that Oxford job, you know, the long-term vacancy I told you about the other day. She's the sort of person we had been looking for, so I gave her the Oxford job."

"Is she good-looking?"

"Well, not in the general sense. She has power and charisma. Of course, she was well-groomed, perfect business suit with stylish scarf and, oh yes, her hands are really beautiful, very slim. And she has a good sun-tan and a pleasant face."

"Not your type, then?"

"That's not the point. I wasn't looking for a mistress, I needed a person with strong leadership qualities. By the way, she's not really Irish. She was married to an Irishman, but he died. She's originally Italian, I believe, at least her maiden name was Italian."

Cathy was impressed that a woman could appear so competent, but she was quite satisfied about the situation. No danger from that new woman in Don's life. They went to the kitchen and got the meat and vegetables out of the fridge. While Don was peeling the carrots Cathy was seasoning the meat. She had already forgotten the Irish-Italian woman.

Two weeks later, Don came home and told Cathy about the success the new woman had in her new job right from the word go. This made her curious about her again.

"Tell me more about her."

"Well, what do you want to know?"

"Is she really Italian? Is she hot-blooded?"

"Not hot-blooded, but efficient and rather on the cool side. About her Italian background, well, her maiden name was Martinelli, but she grew up over here."

Cathy looked up from her paper. "What did you say her maiden name was?"

"Martinelli."

"And her first name?"

"She calls herself Annie, but it's really Anna-Maria."

"Not Anna-Maria Martinelli!" Cathy cried. "It can't be!"

"Yes. Why not? Do you know her?"

"There used to be a girl of that name in our village when I was small. She was such a little chit of a girl, and she was such a simpleton. Easily fooled. It can't be her. Impossible. You say she's a strong personality and she has all those degrees?"

"Yes. Why can't it be the person you used to know so many years ago? People change, people develop."

They argued over the identity of the new manageress of Don's Oxford branch for the whole evening. At last they came to the conclusion that it would be best if Cathy met the woman in question. That ought to settle the question.

Lying in bed at night, Cathy listened to Don breathing quietly at her side. They had had sex in their accustomed way, Don waiting for her to reach her climax before releasing his own urge. They both felt good afterwards, Don staying on top of her for a while before slowly dropping off to sleep and snuggling comfortably along her side. Though she felt fulfilled and relaxed she could not go to sleep immediately. She was puzzled. She had to direct her thoughts to the enigma of Anna-Maria. Could it really be the same person? Hadn't there been a scandal? How could she develop into an able and impressive woman? It couldn't be her!

Cathy tried to sleep but had to revert to the image of Anna-Maria as a small girl. She remembered looking down her nose at her, thinking that such a stupid nobody of a girl would never amount to anything. She would probably end up at the check-out of some supermarket or become a prostitute. Cathy realized that her assessment of little Anna-Maria had been a product of her own snobbery. What right had she to predict such a bleak future for the poor girl? Even if she had ended up at the Tesco check-out, at least that would have been an honourable job, no need for her to despise people who had jobs like that.

When she eventually drifted off into the land of dreams she found herself sitting at an elegant dinner table and an adult version of Anna-Maria was sitting opposite, smiling uncertainly at her. She looked almost exactly the same as thirty years ago, only larger. Still very slim, almost anorexic, no breasts to speak of, as pale as ever and with deep-set eyes staring hollowly at the great world. Cathy felt extremely uncomfortable. She wanted to stand up and get away from their table, but every time she tried that she found herself back in her chair, facing the accusing features of Anna-Maria. Every time she stood up she heard Anna-Maria's voice – her piping small girl's voice – accusing her of snobbery.

"You're a snob, a snob, a useless bloody snob!"

Then Anna-Maria's face suddenly changed and adopted the features of Cathy's father. His stern eyes drilled into her deepest soul and his mouth carefully formulated a sentence. "You will never measure up. You will never amount to anything."

Sweating, Cathy tried to hit her father's face, but she was pulled back and suddenly found herself thrown into a deep well. The light faded away and everything turned a dark red. She tried to cry for help, the red faces of her father and of Anna-Maria flashed through the haze again and again…then she was awake.

She climbed out of bed and tried to put on her night-dress, but it was not easy. It clung to her wet skin. She entered the bathroom, closed the door and stepped into the shower cubicle. She waited a few moments, breathing heavily, before she turned on the water.

The shower was good for her. After carefully drying herself she looked at the reflection of her naked self in the large mirror. She had to wait for a few seconds for the steam to clear before she saw enough of herself, her long auburn hair, her well-rounded shoulders, her slightly sagging breasts with the large and dark nipples Don liked so much, the swell of her belly, too much fat round her midriff – didn't they call these love-handles? – yes, too much fat there, also her thighs, too much fat there. She discovered that her pubic hair was beginning to turn grey. She rubbed herself all over a second time before putting on a new night-dress which she took from a drawer that she left half-open. She stepped up to the mirror again and addressed the image of herself.

"You will never amount to anything."

Then she quietly returned to the bed-room and slipped in without waking up Don, who merely changed his breathing rhythm and turned over.

TWENTY

The Gravetye Manor Hotel was situated in a truly magnificent spot in the middle of a wooded area of particular beauty in the country, only a few miles from East Grinstead. It was a bright afternoon in June. There had been signs of a shower earlier, but it had blown away, and now the light green foliage of the tall trees was bathed in sunrays that gave the forest a translucent quality. The air gave off an atmosphere that made one aware of one's lightness of being.

Cathy was driving her new Renault Clio through the green transparency. She found the abundance of speed-humps on the long driveway to the hotel utterly superfluous, a real nuisance. They were so massive that she nearly bumped her head against the roof of her little car every time she negotiated such a hump.

At last she reached the grey walls of the ancient Tudor building of the hotel. She climbed out of her car, locked the door and entered the hotel.

"Good afternoon," she said in a business-like tone to the receptionist who greeted her. "My name is Mrs. Richardson. My husband has booked a table for dinner in your restaurant."

"Yes, of course, madam. A table for three, isn't it?"

"Yes."

"Your husband hasn't arrived yet. Would you like to take a seat in our lounge over there or would you prefer to sit outside? We can serve you a drink in our beautiful garden if you like."

"I'll do that. Can you get me a glass of Chardonnay? Very cold, if you please," Cathy said as she walked to the French windows connecting the lounge to the garden. It was more than a garden, it was a proper park, sparkling in a rich variety of colours, with flowers galore. A paradise of a spot.

She sat down in a comfortable garden chair and looked at the ancient façade of the building. Yes, original Tudor.

Who would the woman turn out to be? Her Anna-Maria from the old days or some other woman who happened to have the same name? It had been an excellent idea of Don's to have dinner together, and in such a nice place as this.

Her Chardonnay arrived. She took a sip.

"Please, can't you get one a bit colder than this?" she asked the waiter.

"I will see what I can do, madam," he replied discreetly and disappeared.

A few moments later he returned with another glass. This time it was cold enough for her. She sipped and enjoyed the spicy coolness of the Australian wine that always reminded her of the pineapples of Queensland. She squinted towards the late afternoon sun, then she looked at her watch. "Twenty-five past six, so I am a bit early," she admitted to herself. Another thirty-five minutes to go. Don was bound to be on time, he always was, he was so pedantic. If he managed to fetch the Annie woman from King's Cross in time and if the traffic out of London was not worse than anticipated.

If she turned out to be the Anna-Maria, how would Cathy find the right words? What would they say to each other? Would Anna-Maria remember her? Would she remember her arrogance and her criticism? It was no use getting nervous in vain. She was certainly a different Anna-Maria. It was quite a common Italian name, wasn't it? Looking at the abundance of colours around her, she suddenly regretted she had come here. Why should she meet that woman just because she happened to have the same name as a nobody of a girl from her childhood days?

Don stepped through the French windows, followed by a very elegant woman in a dark blue business suit with a very stylish Hermès scarf draped around her shoulders. The two briskly walked over to where Cathy was rising from her garden chair to greet them.

It was her!

She was so different in every possible way from the girl Cathy had known thirty years earlier. She was impressive, charming and – yes, one had to admit – breathtakingly beautiful. But it was her. It was the fine swan that the ugly duckling had grown into. Cathy held her breath and placed her left hand over her heart.

"How wonderful to meet you again after all these years," Annie beamed, and Cathy took note of the perfect shape of her mouth and the fine, spotless teeth. So the recognition was mutual. "Don told me so much about you, but he didn't tell me who you really are, and it occurred to me that it could be you. And it is you, Cathy."

Annie's warm friendliness and the charm she exuded immediately created an atmosphere of relaxed cheerfulness. Cathy's premonitions were blown away, and her uncertainty gave way to a feeling of relief and unmitigated joy. She realized she was happy to meet this gorgeous woman who had once been part of her small world of childhood.

They sat down and enjoyed their pre-dinner drinks. They were handed the menu and slowly made their choices. Don's face showed how pleased he was. He was very proud of what he had achieved. It was so good for these two women to get together and to exchange their different views of their common phase in their lives. What a fantastic opportunity to re-assess one's past from such a perspective!

When their table was ready, the waiter took up their glasses and placed them on a small silver tray, leading the way to the restaurant inside. Throughout the elegant meal they never ceased to talk in a lively way about their present situations in life and gradually drifted to the topic of the old days.

"Oh, Cathy," Annie said at one point, and she placed her

knife and fork on the rim of her plate for emphasis, "I admired you so much. You were my idol. I worshipped the ground you walked on. You seemed to have everything that I lacked – beauty, charm, intelligence."

Cathy was shocked and touched. "I don't believe you. You're making this up."

"No, no, I am serious. I even remember one night when we were all out in the street and I saw you in a new light…it seemed to me you had become a grown-up woman all of a sudden. Your whole figure seemed so much more mature and sophisticated. I wanted to step up to you and give you a big hug. But of course, I didn't dare. You were so far above me."

Cathy was dumbfounded. There was nothing she could say to that. So she changed the subject and began to talk about their common companions of those days. And as the meal and their conversation proceeded Cathy became aware of her own inhibitions. She knew that she wanted to ask Annie about that scandal, the one with the cyclist of the village, but she did not manage to summon the courage. She carefully avoided the very topic that burned the hottest in the steam-engine of her curious mind.

Don had a long discussion with the waiter over the temperature of the wine. They had a bottle of Aloxe-Corton 1985, truly magnificent wine, but unfortunately it was served far too warm.

"I do apologize, sir," the waiter begged, "but our patrons normally ask for room temperature."

"You must be joking," Don politely replied, "on a day like this the temperature in here must be something like 28 degrees Celsius, and the wine simply loses its richness at such a temperature."

Cathy did not concentrate on what else was said about this problem by the waiter or by her husband, because her mind drifted back to Aunt Gladys, her dear François and her stories about unsuitable wine temperatures. She tried to remember. When was it that she had died? Was it 1988 or 1989? Poor old Gladys and her old-fashioned views of the world!

"And do you remember the shambles with Tanner?" Annie cut into Cathy's ruminations with what seemed like brutal suddenness. So here they were. The brazen woman had actually opened the delicate subject herself. Annie really had character, Cathy had to give her that.

"Yes," she said and stowed Aunt Gladys away in the bottom of her mind. "It was quite a scandal."

"You can say that again."

"But I can hardly remember what it was all about," Cathy lied. She thought it was probably better to let Annie come out with her version rather than making things more difficult for her by dishing up the immoral aspect of the affair.

"I remember every detail, I tell you. Don't you remember? I was part of it."

"Yes, now I remember. You must have suffered a great deal."

"I did. It was terrible, I nearly killed myself."

"Was it so bad? I mean…well, the bad things he did to you? Did he make you suffer a lot, the bloody pig? Pardon my language."

"No, not what he did." Annie looked straight into Cathy's eyes. "So you still don't know?"

"What do you mean?"

"You called him a bad name, so you don't know what really happened."

"I'm sorry, Annie, I didn't mean to offend you. But then I really don't understand."

"What I suffered most dreadfully about was the mendacity of the whole thing. The way they treated Tanner, all for nothing, and I was to be blamed."

"Hey, listen. There must be a terrible misunderstanding.

From what I understood he must have abused you and – "

" – and that's where you were wrong! Like everybody else. He never did anything to me. He was always kind and understanding, all above board. He was my best friend through a difficult period in my life, you know, when my parents were having rows every day and I was glad to get out of my home and have someone to talk to, someone who took time to listen to my problems, someone who cared."

"Then how could it all blow up as it did?" Cathy inquired with genuine interest.

"It was all because of Mr. Newman, the school inspector. He saw me sitting with Tanner on his porch one day, and he ran up to me and pulled me away, out of Tanner's place and to the police station. He told them a lot of stories about Tanner's bad character, how he was a bad influence on all the children, and then he fabricated this story about me and Tanner – a story I didn't understand at the time, I only knew it was not true – and when the police and that big woman from the social service office questioned me I got more and more confused. They talked and talked and insisted on things that they said must have happened. In the end I didn't know when to say yes or no, I just wanted to get out of it."

"Are you saying that Tanner was innocent?"

"Of course he was! He was such a good soul, he just wasn't clever enough to defend himself. They told him I had told them what he had done to me. His word counted for nothing against Mr. Newman's. They simply ignored what he had to say."

Cathy heaved a deep sigh and remained silent for a few moments. This was something she had to learn to digest first. A fake scandal, fabricated by old Newman! And Tanner's reputation ruined. The question was now whether to continue with this delicate and shocking topic or to change the subject to spare Annie's feelings.

"Cathy, I'm so glad I have this opportunity to talk to you

about it." Annie said as she finished her main course and placed her cutlery diagonally across her plate. "It's good to clear up that mess. Especially if you didn't know the truth."

"I don't think anybody knows the truth."

"Oh, many people in the old village know. It all came out about ten years later. But we had both left by then. I had won my scholarship and didn't want to go back to the village, and you had also turned your back on those things. It was after your parents had moved to Southampton. I only found out when I returned from Harvard. I happened to run into Paul – you know, Paul Linley, who liked you when we were children. I ran into him at Heathrow one day and he filled me in on all the scandal as it had blown up."

"What happened?"

"Well, about ten years after the fabricated scandal about Tanner – in fact I believe Tanner was out of prison by that time – they found out that Newman had been the bad man, after all. Someone made a statement to the police, he told them what Newman had done to him as a boy, and they took Newman. It turned out he was a paedophile who liked to take pictures of naked children. Apparently he was afraid Tanner could have found out because he had such a good relationship with the children of the village, so he fabricated this story about Tanner. To get him out of the way. In the end Newman went to prison – he died there a year later."

"Have you any idea what became of Tanner after he had served his prison sentence?"

"Once I was old enough to understand the full meaning of what had happened I was so tortured by my bad conscience over my role in the affair that I couldn't rest until I had found Tanner and apologized to him. It took me a long time and I did a lot of detective work, but eventually I traced him. He had emigrated to Canada. When I was in Calgary in eighty-three I drove out to his small farm near the foot of the Rockies. He was so glad

I called, and we had a long heart-to-heart talk. He had never blamed me, and he was forgiving towards everyone else. He said he had learned a great deal through that affair...he said he thought he had acquired more wisdom in prison than ever before in his life. He's still alive, and we still send each other Christmas cards every year."

This was a revelation indeed. Cathy was so relieved that there wouldn't be anything standing between Annie and her. She saw Annie in a completely new light. She felt she was beginning to admire this competent woman who had fought for what she was now. What an achievement! Such a long way from little Anna-Maria! How was it possible that she had interpreted things so wrongly?

After dessert and coffee in the other lounge of the hotel, they walked out to their cars. Don was to take Annie to Gatwick, from where she would take a train back to London. Meanwhile Cathy would drive her car back and wait for Don. Standing between their cars in the car-park the two women hesitated for a split second, then they embraced.

"Good-bye, let's meet again soon."

"Good-bye and thank you for opening my eyes to the truth."

Cathy drove back through the night and in her mind she went through a re-play of the entire conversation with Annie. How humiliating and how elevating at the same time, to find one has misinterpreted the world over such a long time! From where she had been placed by fate, however, she had no choice. She could only try to understand the Tanner scandal from her own perspective. But now the angle had been widened. She had to think of a wide-angle lens of a camera. This was how she felt now.

Don reached their home about three quarters of an hour after her. They took out a bottle of cognac and went over the entire revelation again. They spoke about Annie with admiration. At two o'clock in the morning they were too tired to go on talking. Don rose from his armchair and slowly moved in the direction of their bedroom.

"Don't bother to get up in the morning," he said. "I've got to make an early start, you know. I'm driving up to see Hunter in Liverpool. I'll see you when I get back late tomorrow night. Are you going to be in tomorrow night?"

"Yes, I'll have to go up to Cricklewood in the afternoon, but I should be back by six or seven."

"All right. Good night."

"Good night, Don."

Cathy's sleep was troubled. She was thrown from one dream into another, her dreams constantly merged. All the people who meant anything to her appeared somewhere within this mélange of dreams: girls and boys from her childhood, most prominently little Anna-Maria of course, but also pale and slim Becky as a girl and Paul as a dashing young lad; they were thrown together with fellow-students from university and people she had known in Australia. Again and again people like Aunt Gladys, Hugo Tanner and even Hanns loomed up somewhere in the background and always gave her a fright by their threatening faces. On one occasion Gladys and Hanns had a violent argument about the right temperature of a wine served at Changi Airport. Their row escalated and was suddenly interrupted by Don who warned them that many more lives would be lost at Changi Airport if they couldn't get things right. Then there was Stephen, waving from the cockpit of his aeroplane and smiling happily, but as Cathy was trying to take her eyes away from him the face was no longer his but the young man's from that hotel in Australia, the father of her child. His face came closer and closer, and when he was close enough to kiss her and she pouted her lips in readiness for his kiss she was suddenly sucked away into a dark hole that had opened beneath her feet. She felt herself falling, falling and getting colder...

She awoke with a shock. Her heart drummed like mad and her night-dress clung to her body bathed in cold sweat.

She got up and lurched to the kitchen where she poured herself a glass of water. She swallowed about half of the water. As she was putting the glass down on the kitchen table she missed and let the glass slip from her hand. It landed on the floor with a hard and loud crash, the fragments jumping all over the kitchen floor.

"Oh, shit," she yelled at the top of her voice. She hesitated for a few moments, undecided if she ought to clean up the mess. Then she came to the conclusion that she needed her sleep now. So she walked back, not without cutting her left foot with one of the small glass splints near the door. She swore and pulled it out of her foot, noticing that there was only very little blood. Back in her bed, she was surprised that Don was sleeping peacefully on his side. He hadn't heard a thing.

It took her an eternity to get to sleep, but eventually exhaustion overwhelmed her and she drifted off.

When she opened her eyes in the morning she saw that Don had already left. She checked the alarm-clock. Half-past eight. He must be on the other side of London by now, perhaps approaching Birmingham. Cathy yawned and got out of bed. She dropped her night-dress on the floor and stepped into the shower-cubicle. After her shower she dressed and had a large breakfast. She couldn't give any reasons, but she felt that she had deserved a proper breakfast, something she rarely craved and almost never indulged in.

She left her plate on the table. It was adorned with traces of yellow egg-yolk, a spoonful of baked beans and half a sausage. She went to the bathroom and brushed her teeth, leaving the open tube lying on the edge of the washbasin with some toothpaste oozing out at the top. Then she got ready to go out, but she couldn't find her keys. She rummaged for them in various drawers and cupboards, leaving them all open. At last she found them. With brisk movements she left the house.

She drove her Clio to Gatwick and parked it in the multi-storey car-park. The Gatwick Express took her to Victoria Station, from where she took the underground to Oxford Circus. She really hated shopping, but there were a few things she needed to get from some of the larger stores in Oxford Street, John Lewis, Selfridges, and also from some smaller shops. Oxford Street was packed with people, tourists, shoppers, teen-age pick-pockets and lazy bums. Cathy was glad of this. Somehow, because she hated shopping, she felt that she could not be observed as she was engaged in this tiresome occupation in such dense crowds of people. That is, if someone tried to follow her and observe her, which was utter nonsense, of course, but she often had this feeling of someone looking at her, criticizing her, checking on her actions from some higher vantage point. So she felt more relaxed in a crowd like this. This was the good side of shopping in Oxford Street.

At ten to twelve she looked up at the sky. A large aeroplane was passing on its way into Heathrow. "How glad the passengers up there must be," Cathy thought. "Their flight would soon be over." Then she was reminded of Mrs. Dalloway, the woman in that Woolf novel Becky had tried to get her interested in. Wasn't she going through her various errands in London in a similar way? And there was that plane in the sky...

Her morning passed very quickly. After a perfunctory lunch, she took the bus for Cricklewood. She had this agreement with Becky. They shared a charitable duty towards Becky's old aunt, who lived in a small flat in Cricklewood. Aunt Eadie ought to be in an old people's home, but she absolutely insisted on staying in her flat. But she had considerable health problems. For one thing, her walking was quite handicapped. If she wanted to walk down her street to the shops and the bank in Finchley Road it took her almost an hour just to get there and back. So, whenever either Becky or Cathy happened to be near this part of London they

300

made a point of calling on the old lady and doing some shopping for her. Today, Cathy knew that Becky had not been there for at least three days because she and Mel were on holiday in Spain, so she expected Eadie to need a few things, probably food mostly.

Cathy was glad to find Eadie in good shape and in a cheerful mood. It was their routine that they only exchanged a few words and Cathy got the shopping list that Eadie had prepared. Then she had a quick look in the fridge to check if there wasn't anything else that might be needed and that Eadie had forgotten to put on her list. Then she left the flat to do the shopping. They usually had a cup of tea and a longer chat after her return.

"Don't forget to take the cheque to the bank for me," Eadie croaked after Cathy as the younger woman was about to close the front door behind her.

It was only a five-minute walk down to Finchley Road. Cathy decided to go to the bank first. The Barclays branch was quite busy. She had to queue for almost five minutes before she reached the cashier counter. As she was walking away from the counter she looked up and her eyes fell on a good-looking man at the end of the queue.

Her heart missed a beat.

She knew that man. She had met him before, but long ago. Who was he? His face was so distant and yet so familiar. When the man brushed his right arm across his forehead, she began to understand. Australia. Nambucca Heads. The hotel with the cockroaches.

Suddenly, the world fell apart. Men were shouting, there were yells and shrieks, shots were fired. Cathy did not know what happened, she felt a strange heat burning right through her chest before she collapsed on the floor. She did not even have time to realize that this was the end of her life. What followed had nothing to do with her. She was no longer part of it.

PART FIVE

Peter

TWENTY-ONE

As he crossed the busy street in North London, Peter looked at the people and their faces, their preoccupied expressions. Some men gave him the impression that they were walking through their lives without ever looking back or sideways.

It was a grey day, which intensified his pensive mood, especially now, in the late afternoon. He reached a wrought-iron gate leading into one of those small parks that seemed to serve no purpose because you hardly ever saw anyone sitting in them. People only ever crossed parks like this, they were never tempted to linger inside. And yet, there were three empty benches in the park. One of the benches was full of pigeons' droppings.

He sat down on the one facing it. Breathing deeply, he tried to set his mind in order. What he had witnessed this afternoon had shaken him. Things had to be put in their proper places in the museum of his mind. He imagined somebody sitting on one of the old oak trees to his right and taking a picture of him sitting here, not knowing how to feel. It was one of those photographic moments which he used to have more often in his childhood, but which had also accompanied him through most of his adult life so far.

He had never seen a person dying before. The moment he had bent over that woman with the fine auburn hair lying on the cold floor of the bank, that was a moment he would never be able to forget. He still did not know what had given him the certainty that she was dying. And when her breathing had actually stopped and the paramedic pushed him aside...Peter thought he had been very lucky to be thrown together with that friendly young man –

well, younger than himself, certainly – that man who had spoken to him and then they had gone for a drink together. The alcohol had at least stopped the trembling of his hands.

He still had the young man's handkerchief in his trouser pocket. Trying to remember the exact order of events, he took it out and looked at it. It was full of blood, his own blood. Very carefully he dabbed at his forehead to check if the bleeding had stopped for good. Maybe he ought to have had one of those paramedics examine his head. Hardly had this question been born in his mind when he dismissed it with a feeling of shame. How could he think of his own little scratch, which was really nothing, in the face of other people losing their lives? That fine woman. He wondered who she was, what her life had been like.

This confrontation with the undeniable power of death took him back to a difficult time in his life, more than a quarter of a century before. He admitted to himself that he had never really allowed himself to mourn the loss of his brother Fred. He remembered that he had refused to let that awful event influence his life, his career, his desperate search for happiness. What had followed was a period of full immersion in his work, a period, he now admitted, which had lasted through all those years, right up to now. In the ditch along this high-speed track of his life over the past two or three decades there lay the craggy rocks of many disappointments, mossy tufts of various humiliations, and a number of black holes of deaths that ought to have touched him. Deaths occurring within the circle of human beings in his emotional vicinity. He tried to remember what he had felt when his parents died, more than ten years ago, first his father then his mother. Impossible. His mind was blank, there was no distinct memory of his feelings, only a memory of what his father had looked like in his coffin, beaked nose, shrunken hollow cheeks and the neck of a vulture. Then there had been the shock of Bordeaux.

* * *

306

Peter was on his way back from a pleasant trip around the wineries of the Médoc. At the railway station he picked up a copy of *Le Matin*, which had the fall of the Berlin wall on the front page. After studying the TGV connections to Paris-Montparnasse, he was turning away from the large notice-board when he bumped into a woman pushing a wheel-chair.

"Oh, pardon," he mumbled, as he picked up the book which the woman in the wheel-chair had dropped in the collision with his legs. When he handed it back to her he looked into her eyes. He felt a pang in his heart. He knew these eyes. But he could not recognize the poor woman. She was an elderly woman with a shrunken grey face and her eyes were set in deep hollows.

"She looks like living death," he said to himself.

He could not tell whether the woman also knew him or not, so he tore his eyes away from her and faced the younger woman who was pushing the wheel-chair.

"*De rien, monsieur,*" she said and gave him a polite smile.

They stood still for a few moments. A high-pitched gong rang from the loudspeakers and announced a train from Carcassonne.

"I'm sorry," he said in English and felt very foolish.

"Don't apologize," the young woman said. "It was our fault."

Peter scanned his mind for the right thing to say. Then he surprised himself when he came out with, "Can I get you a cup of coffee, perhaps?"

The woman smiled again. "Actually, we were just going to have one."

They walked over to the café in the large hall. When they reached a vacant table in front of the café the woman turned the wheel-chair round so that the old woman in it could see the busy hall with all the people. The handicapped woman had still not uttered a single word.

Peter ordered coffee for three, but the young woman

corrected him. It was no use trying to get her patient to drink from a cup in a public place like this. She opened one of the bags and took out a yellow Tupperware container with a drinking nipple at the top. Very carefully, she held it to the old woman's lips. Peter admired her patience. The old woman only accepted a few sips before she began to moan in an eerie voice.

"She's never very thirsty," the young woman explained.

Their coffees arrived. After they had both tasted the strong beverage and introduced each other, Peter summoned his courage and decided to ask her about her patient.

"Her name is Mrs. Morales," the young woman, whose name was Sandra Flick, began to explain. "She can't understand you. She can sometimes understand me when I talk to her very slowly and place my mouth right over her left ear. Her mind's quite gone, poor soul, after her third stroke. She's also had multiple sclerosis for many years now, and even before her first stroke she had to take to the wheel-chair."

"Are you a friend or a relative of hers?"

"No, they pay me. It's my job. Her family – what's left of them, anyway – could not care less about her, poor old soul."

He felt strange discussing a person sitting opposite as if she was not there. How insensitive! And yet, Sandra did not give him the impression of a callous person. It was probably just a sign of her professional attitude. This was just a job for her.

"Are they paying you well?"

"Yes, very well. But I can tell you, it's not an easy job. Do you know why we're here in Bordeaux? I'll tell you. I had to take her to Lourdes. I had orders from one of her daughters who happens to be very religious and extremely superstitious. We're on our way back now. Of course, it was all for nothing. But you should have seen those people at Lourdes, hoping for miracles to happen..."

"So her children do care, after all, in their own way, don't they?"

"Well, in a way, if you like to put it that way. They're all in Argentina, two daughters and a son. Her husband left her ages ago. But she wanted to come back to her old home in Europe, where she originally grew up."

At that moment, the old woman belched, and the orange juice that Sandra had given her before gushed out of her mouth and ran down the front of her coat. Sandra jumped up and grabbed a tissue from her bag.

"Oops, Vita, that was a bit too much," she crooned in a friendly sing-song voice, while she expertly cleaned the front of her patient's coat.

"What did you just call her?" Peter quickly asked.

"Vita. It's her first name."

Suddenly it dawned on him. With a terrible shock he knew why he had recognized a look in her eyes. It was the girl he had known in his childhood. The girl who had dreamed of going to live in Buenos Aires when she grew up. He could still remember her freckles and the smell of her young hair.

"So she's not as old as she looks," was all he managed to say.

"Yes, she's only in her forties, but her disease has caused her to age prematurely."

Peter could not recover immediately. This woman was a wreck. How was it possible for a girl like Vita to turn into such a wreck? He was sure that Sandra could tell him a lot more about her patient, but he did not want to know any more. He made a few polite remarks, called the waiter to pay for their coffees and rose to leave.

"I'm afraid, I've got to leave you now. My train, you know."

"Thank you for the coffee and the company," Sandra cheerfully answered.

"I say," he suddenly remembered, "if I give you my card, will you send me word when Vita dies?" He took a business-card from his purse and placed it in front of her on the coffee-table, while he grabbed his small suitcase.

She was going to say something, but he had already turned abruptly and walked briskly away across the hall to the trains.

Later, looking out of the window of the TGV racing through the open country of the Charente, Peter tried to set his mind in order. Why had he made that request in the end? Vita was even a year younger than himself, so why should she die sooner? But what a shock! She had seemed so reduced, so utterly miserable, a mere vegetable. He decided to develop more respect for handicapped people in wheel-chairs. Many of them could have been blooming young men and women like Vita.

He now remembered, sitting on this bench across from the pigeon droppings, the curt note he had received from Sandra only about three months after their meeting in Bordeaux telling him that Vita had died. No sender's address. Chapter closed.

He stood up and walked to the bus-stop near the little park. When the bus came he was too absent-minded and lost in thought to remember that he had intended to take the bus. The bus-driver shook his head and drove off.

For the remainder of the day, Peter walked through the darkening streets of London. He just continued walking, preferring the side streets to the busy thoroughfares. He found that walking was good for him, for his peace of mind. As he was crossing several quarters north of Marble Arch he was reviewing his situation in life. His earlier memories of Vita and her sad, short life had somehow thrown him back on old days. He tried to recall all those mental photographs he had taken in his childhood, his adolescence and his young adult life. He remembered that he used to worry about the passage of time when he was younger. Now, nearly fifty, he was more careless. There was nothing he could do. Time just happened.

This took his mind back to his old school-friend Robert, who had told him one day when they had been exchanging their views on the nature of time that there were certain phenomena in physics which could only be explained in physical terms if you allowed time to run backwards. That had been a shock. But then Robert, who was studying nuclear physics at the time, had also told him, "If you want to see real ghosts I advise you to study physics."

What had become of Robert? Peter tried to remember when he had seen him the last time. It must have been some time in the early eighties. Oh yes, now he remembered.

Peter reached his flat in South Kensington after ten at night. This was one of those nights, he thought. Normally he did not mind living alone, but tonight he would have been glad of some company. He took a few slices of rye bread, a mature Camembert and a bottle of Montepulciano and made himself comfortable in front of the television. The programme was not very riveting. So, with a few glasses of wine and some good bread and cheese in his stomach, he dropped off to sleep on his settee. His body reacted to his mental stress with complete exhaustion.

In the morning he dialled the number for directory enquiries and got Robert's telephone number. When, later in the day, he dialled the number a boy's voice answered his call. Peter asked him if he could speak to his father.

"I'm sorry. My dad's out," the boy answered in a very competent manner.

"Will he be in later?"

"Yes, he said he would be home by three. Or would you like me to take a message?"

"That would be very kind of you. Tell him his old friend Peter Hoffmann called, and give him my regards."

Making sure to find him at home, he called again at four. Robert answered the telephone on the second ring. He was prepared for Peter's call. His voice was friendly but a little flat, betraying no emotions. After a few friendly noises between them, Peter suggested they could meet for a drink.

"Just the two of us?" Robert asked.

"Yes, just the two of us."

They met two days later in a pub near the British Museum. It was full of students and there was an assortment of younger tourists. Peter realized he was probably the oldest person in the pub, except perhaps the publican. He did not have long to wait.

"Hi there, Pete," Robert said in a tone of old camaraderie. Peter sensed that it was not one hundred percent genuine.

They sat down with their pints and took a few sips before Robert shot his first arrow.

"So what's this? Just a social get-together, or have you got something on your mind? I mean – it's thirteen years or more, isn't it?"

"Yes, as you say. But to tell you the truth, I don't even know myself. I have just been shaken a bit lately, and I felt I wanted to see you again. Take up our good old friendship where we left off, sort of thing, you know…"

"Aren't you forgetting something?"

Peter knew what Robert was referring to. Years before, in the early eighties, when Robert was courting his wife, there had been a period of estrangement between the two friends because Peter had tried to attract the same woman and had actually made a pass at her when she was already engaged to Robert. The old friendship between the two men had never been the same ever since. They had still seen each other two or three times and pretended nothing had happened between them, but gradually their lives had drifted apart.

"I hope you aren't holding that old story against me after all these years, are you?"

"She has been a very good wife to me, so why should I harbour any ill feelings? She told me nothing had happened between you, and I believe her."

Peter was going to ask him if he would have believed him, too, if he had told him the same thing. But he did not want to sound provocative or even just ironical at this moment. He was too happy to have Robert's company now.

The two men took a second pint and caught up with each other's lives. While Peter had been going through his protracted and unresolved relationship with Barbara, which just faded out in the end, Robert and his wife had been enjoying a smooth and happy time together, and they were still married today. They had two children, who were now eight and ten years old and doing fine. Robert worked as a nuclear physicist for some secret branch of the Ministry of Defence. Peter had less to show. He had remained childless, and after his two long-term relationships with Barbara and an Italian woman, he had never managed to trust another woman to the point where he would have wanted to share his life with her. But at least he had a successful business. He dealt in American real estate and owned half a travel agency. As they were unfolding their personal histories and their professional careers, at least some part of their old ease with each other slowly returned. When they left the pub and parted they agreed to stay in touch.

"Yes," Robert said, "let's do that. Where can I reach you? Do you live in town?"

"Well, yes, I still do. But I'm thinking of moving into the country. What I experienced the other day has had a frightening effect on me. I'm scared of the city and of its anonymity. But I'll let you know when I've found the right place in the country."

They exchanged business-cards and said good-bye when they reached Tottenham Court Road.

What Peter had mentioned as a vague plan became a fixed idea of his. Starting the following day, he drove out into Surrey and Sussex every other day and checked out all the estate agents that he could find. He had the advantage that he already had some business connections with some of them through his own dealings in real estate. So it was no wonder that it did not take him very long to find what he was looking for. He found a beautiful country house in a secluded spot in the middle of East

Sussex, an absolute gem of a place, not too large for him – after all, he still lived alone – and in very good condition. House prices had been very low over the past few years, but they were already beginning to pick up again. He paid more than two hundred thousand for this small paradise, but he considered it was worth every penny of it.

It took him more than two months to get settled in his new home. Not only did he have to decide on the decoration of the rooms but also on the proper and practical position of the furniture. This was not so easy, since he found he would probably have to develop new routines for his every-day procedures. Where would he do this, where would he do that? It started with getting up in the morning. Would he get dressed right after his shower in the bathroom, or would he walk back to the bedroom and get dressed there? Would he have his scanty breakfast in the kitchen standing in front of the worktop while reading a paper, or would he go to the trouble of laying a breakfast table for himself and have a sit-down breakfast? Where would he keep his briefcase? Would he want to grab it quickly as he was leaving the house, or would he leave it in his study so that he could always do a last-minute check before leaving? In which room would he want to be most of the time when he had no specific duties or practical jobs that required his presence in a particular room of the house? He found it more difficult to find solutions to all these questions and to related domestic problems now that he was alone. He remembered that on all other occasions when he moved into a new flat or house there had always been a woman at his side to assist him, sometimes to direct him. It was not easy to go through all this on your own, without advice, without the possibility to consult somebody who cared.

On some days he was just too exhausted to worry about the arrangements in his new home, especially coming home from a long day's work in the City. On such days he would just drop into his armchair in front of the television and stare into the gogglebox without taking in anything. The six o'clock news passed him like the twitter of birds. He would fall asleep in his armchair and only wake up some time between eight and nine o'clock. That would be the moment to lurch to the kitchen and get something out of the fridge. He knew that such a routine was not good for his health and ruinous for his spiritual well-being. It made him feel even more lonely than he was.

One night he was just about to drop off in his armchair when his attention was aroused by something on television. It was something about that bank robbery in Finchley Road a few months before, so he sat up and was all eyes and ears. Apparently, they had captured the criminals who were now shown on television as they were led out of the magistrate's building and herded into a prison van with barred windows. Then the anchorman appeared again and reminded the viewers of the fact that a woman had been killed in that bank robbery.

"And how does the man who lost his wife on that day feel about these criminals now that they are caught? We have asked him." Then the scene changed from the studio to a street in London. A tall and elegant man in his fifties was shown and a microphone was thrust into his face. The man had an oval face with a thin moustache and was nearly bald. He had a pair of stylish thin glasses and his whole appearance and personality reminded Peter of Charles Dance in the role of Mr. de Winter, in a drama on the BBC. The husband answered the reporter's questions in a calm and well-mannered voice, and his rising intonation gave you the impression that he was asking a question.

"I know this man," Peter thought. He could not place him exactly, but he knew that he had seen him before, and more often than once. He listened attentively.

"Mr. Richardson, what sentence have these criminals deserved in your opinion?"

"I am not a lawyer and at this time it seems very early to pass sentence on these men. It will be the task of the prosecution to prove their guilt. But naturally, if you ask me I hope that once they are found guilty of having committed robbery and manslaughter they will be given the maximum penalty whatever that may be." He nodded his head at the camera and enforced his balanced answer with a meaningful stare.

"But," the reporter insisted, "it must be a nightmare for you to lay eyes on the men who murdered your wife. No wild rage surging inside your heart of hearts?"

"As I said, it will be for the court to ascertain whether or not they intended to kill."

Peter admired the man. Morally, he appeared to be so far above the idiotic reporter. Wonderful how he obviously refused to give the press the sort of emotions they craved for. Blood, murder, wild rage and public tears: he would have none of it.

Then, just as this Mr. Richardson turned to move away from the camera, Peter discovered him in his photographic memory. Yes, he was the man who often travelled on the same train between Gatwick and Victoria, the morning train that Peter often took from Haywards Heath. He often sat in the same carriage reading either the *Daily Telegraph* or *The Independent*, making a loud crackling noise as he turned the pages. So his name was Richardson and the woman who had died on the cold floor in that bank had been his wife. Small world, he thought.

Over the next few days, Peter was too busy to remember a great deal about that television appearance of the woman's widower. But when, about ten days later, he actually saw the man getting on the train at Gatwick it all came back to him immediately. The man sat down on the other side of the narrow aisle, took a copy of the *Daily Telegraph* from his briefcase and opened it with the usual noises. Peter looked at him sideways. Should he talk to him? He decided not to address him now, but he was determined to do so when he saw him again on the same train on another day.

On the following Thursday the man again got on at Gatwick,

but this time he sat down right opposite Peter. Now or never, Peter said to himself.

"Excuse me," he began in a very polite tone, "but aren't you Mr. Richardson?"

"Yes, that's me. Should I know you?"

"No, no. My name is Hoffmann, Peter Hoffmann. There is a very particular reason why I am addressing you like this."

"Pleased to meet you, Mr. Hoffmann. And what is this reason? Are you trying to sell something?"

"Oh, no, not at all. It is rather a delicate affair. I even wonder if we should have this conversation on the train, you know, with all these other people around…"

"Then just give me an indication of what you're on about. You've made me uneasy."

"It's about your late wife."

Mr. Richardson stiffened and looked worried. "What about her? Did you know her? Or are you from the press?"

"I was sitting next to her on that cold floor when she died."

Richardson looked startled. "I'm sorry – I don't know how to take this. This comes as a shock. What can I say?"

"No need to say anything. And I'm really sorry if I have upset you. I'm sorry. I just thought I had to let you know, that's all."

Richardson was silent for a few moments, then he changed the subject. "You're on this train quite regularly? I've seen you before."

"So have I. Yes, this is my usual morning train to Victoria."

"So let's say we leave it to chance. When we happen to be on the same train again on another day we will see if we want to reopen the topic of my wife."

Peter agreed, and they took up their newspapers. For the rest of the journey they remained silent. When they got off at Victoria they said good-bye and parted. Peter saw the man cross the large station hall at a brisk pace, never looking back.

TWENTY-TWO

Peter steered his dark blue car out of the roundabout and into the car-park of the Copthorne Hotel. He parked the car between two black SUVs and shook his head.

"Useless monsters, these SUVs," he said to himself.

He got out of his car, locked it and walked into the building. When he reached the restaurant he found Don Richardson sitting at one of the tables near the wall. He had obviously arrived earlier and was already studying the menu.

"Hello, Don. I'm not late, am I?" Peter asked as the two men shook hands over the beautifully laid table.

"Good to see you, Peter. No, not at all. I got here a bit too early. Sit down and have some white wine. I ordered a nice Pinot Grigio. I hope that's all right with you."

Peter had no objections and sat down. It was good to be with Don. Over the past few months, the two men had become friends. Both of them were going through a phase of relative loneliness in their lives, so they both welcomed each other's company. It had started when, after meeting on the train again, Don had invited him for a drink in the City in order to listen to his version of the Finchley Road bank robbery. Don was very grateful to be allowed to share Peter's perspective of the terrible event. The fact that Peter had actually been present when Cathy had drawn her last breath connected them.

Over the months, they had seen each other on a regular basis, and Peter had learnt a great deal about the fine woman with the auburn hair whose life had expired on that cold floor. He had been impressed to discover how deeply Don had loved his wife.

His terrible loss must have been almost unbearable.

The men were naturally drawn to each other. Peter happened to be without female companionship, Don was a widower with a daughter who was away at school, the two men lived only about twenty miles apart from each other in the green country, they shared a range of interests – private and professional – and they both felt comfortable in each other's company. And they liked to talk about Cathy.

"I put some fresh flowers on her grave," Peter said.

"That's very thoughtful. Thanks."

"And how are you getting on these days? Are you still missing her in every room of your house?"

"Yes, the emptiness is still there. And I still can't get rid of my habit of saying something to her only to discover that she's no longer around. For example I still shout a cheerful 'hello' through the house when I step through the front door coming home in the evening."

"Just give yourself time, Don. In my opinion there's nothing wrong with shouting a friendly greeting into an empty home. It's probably a good way of coping with such a loss. You really loved her. I can see that." Peter turned round to face the waiter, and they placed their food orders. Then they were silent for a minute or so.

"It wasn't only love. It was more than that." Don sighed.

"What can be more than love?"

"I was dependent on her. Utterly dependent. I was her slave."

Peter understood that love can turn you into a slave. You want to fulfil every little wish and whim of the person you love. He did not comment on this. They drifted into other topics, and when their meals arrived they directed their conversation into the realm of good food, one of their common passions. After the main course, they both felt that it would do them a power of good if they allowed themselves a selection of tasty cheeses and a bottle of Amarone to round off a perfect meal.

"There's hardly a more enjoyable pleasure than a bite of Gorgonzola dolce or a spoonful of Vacherin Mont d'Or accompanied by a glass of Amarone," Don remarked with a big smile.

"I wouldn't object if it was a mature Reblochon or a nice Chaumes," Peter added.

"Not bad either. Though I'd prefer a nice Ribera del Duero with that, a Gran Reserva, to be sure."

They laughed. And as they plunged into the pleasures of wine and cheese, their minds were eased and their tongues loosened by the strong Italian wine.

"I was her slave," Don suddenly returned to their old subject. Peter wondered if the tear that ran down his new friend's left cheek had its origin in the high percentage of the Amarone or the painful loss of a beloved wife. He said nothing and waited for Don to decide if he wanted to expand on that cryptic remark.

"Yes, she had me in her firm grip. She was so relentless."

"What do you mean?"

"You see, life with her was anything but easy. She chased me, she hunted me, she haunted me. She was my thought police."

"But you were happy with her, you loved her."

"That was my tragedy. When she trampled on my feelings and treated me like dirt I felt awful, but I always forgave her because I loved her."

"Couldn't you discuss that with her?"

"Oh, she was so convinced of herself as a clear-minded, intelligent, intellectual person who would always argue with plain facts, but in reality she was a temperamental, moody, spiteful woman who lost her good sense and went over the top in every argument. All her decisions and arguments were purely emotional. Her treacherous moods reigned her life. And then there was her constant self-inflicted stress, her mismanagement in her daily routines. At first she always dawdled and lingered over her jobs, only to find in the end that she didn't have the time to finish them. Often she would just lose her head, and then she would keep everybody else waiting. She was never in time for an appointment, and when we had arranged to go out she always kept me waiting and then we had to rush to get there in time. I was going to give up taking her out. It was just no fun, getting late all the time, you know. Concerts, the theatre, parties…"

"That must have been difficult." Peter murmured.

"For example, she would not tolerate any weaknesses or mistakes on my part, while she herself was the slave of her numerous shortcomings. She liked to criticize other people if they committed a social blunder in her eyes or if they had what she considered bad manners. But she often treated other people in a way that left them wondering. And as to good manners, well, certainly her table manners were anything but acceptable. They left a great deal to be desired. She ate like a pig, loading her mouth with large portions, chewing with her mouth open and constantly talking with her full mouth. It was extremely unpleasant. Sometimes I observed other people having a meal with us as they were exchanging discreet but meaningful glances while she was rattling on and spitting out food particles with her words. In this respect she was as bad as her mother. They both had that bad habit of beginning a sentence and taking a mouthful of food before continuing, instead of taking their bites between sentences. When I tried to tell her she only yelled at me and called me names. And yet she criticized me wherever she could. Let me tell you. The last two things she turned into a terrible row in the last week of her life concerned a minor computer problem and a silly detail in kitchen routine. I was working on my computer, fiddling with the new version of Microsoft Word when she came to my study and looked over my shoulder. She reproached me for being too slow with one of the tricks. She shouted at me and accused me of missing the boat in modern technology, of becoming a premature old idiot. Why didn't I want to go along with the new challenges? Why did I constantly refuse to accept what she was trying to teach me all the time? And so on and so on."

"And the kitchen thing?" Peter asked.

"Oh, that. We were preparing dinner in the kitchen. I began to clean the mushrooms. Hardly had I turned on the cold water tap when she yelled at me. How many times had she told me that mushrooms were not washed under running water, why was I doing things like that on purpose just to annoy her! She called me a stupid idiot, and why couldn't I learn to do things the right way! I had always washed my mushrooms, otherwise I could never get them clean enough. But of course, I have always been ready to learn and accept new rules. Oh, the things that I've had to learn over the years! When I tried to discuss the subject in a detached, matter-of-fact way because it genuinely interested me she flared at me. 'Are you trying to pick a quarrel with me or what?' That was her trick in all such situations. It was so humiliating. "

"But was she so flexible and adaptable herself?"

"Not at all. For example, her driving skills were really atrocious, often dangerous. She cut bends, hardly ever indicated when she turned left or right or when she changed lanes, and her speed was erratic, to say the least. She was usually too lazy to change gears, so she often found herself wanting to make a quick start at a set of traffic lights and couldn't because she was still in fourth gear. The interior of her car was always a mess, used tissues strewn over the seats and the floor, old parking tickets, empty plastic bottles and crumpled sweet wrappings all over the place. And when I occasionally got into her car I usually banged my nose and brow on the sun-visor which she had forgotten to push back up again. I told her many times in a friendly and supportive way that it would be a good thing for her to improve her life around her car, but she only reacted by telling me off to mind my own business."

"So she preached lessons that she had never learnt for herself?"

"That just about sums it up. She called herself a Christian woman, but the Christian principle that you should not do unto others what you would not have others do unto you was completely alien to her."

"How could you bear such a life? How could you summon the energy to forgive her again and again?"

"I loved her."

Peter was impressed. He wondered how Don could be intimate, could have sex with a woman who treated him like that. Perhaps they had given up sex ages ago. He did not dare to ask such a delicate question, but he could not help wondering. He thought it was time to change the subject.

"I say, Don, do you realize how property has begun to pick up? In the Greater London area property prices are reported to have risen by five percent over the last twelve months."

"Not a bad thing. But we should be careful about the threat of rising inflation in this country. What's going to happen if Labour wins the next election? This Blair chap is said to be a real wizard."

Once they were off into lengthy discussions of politics, Peter felt relieved. He still felt connected with Cathy because he had witnessed her death, but what Don had told him about her had pulled her down from the pedestal on which he had originally placed her in his mind. It was amazing how human relationships could become so difficult and how often it was the seemingly banal and small things of daily life that really gnawed at the foundations of mutual understanding. It's strange, he thought, how different things can sometimes appear to be, depending on your own perspective. Would he have recognized the tyrant in Cathy if he had met her socially? Perhaps not. Probably not. From what Don had told him he gathered that she must have been quite popular in a social way. Her friends and colleagues saw her as a witty, humorous and entertaining woman who was also clever and efficient.

Then, Labour did win the election. Don and Peter carefully watched the new developments in Britain. When they had a discussion about current affairs with some other men that they were playing snooker with, in the spring of 1998, Don made a daring remark.

"Inflation is getting worse almost day by day, and meanwhile the general public is being drugged with ever new versions of Lady Di's tragic accident last August. So nobody has the energy to be critical about the downfall of the economy. I mean, just look at the galloping rate of increasing Americanisation in our society. Everybody is getting hysterical about safety from terrorists. That's all imported from the other side of the Atlantic. People worry about the wrong issues." He paused to see how the others were taking this.

"Come on," a man called Bertie said. "You're not saying Blair is selling us to the Yanks, are you?"

"In a way he is. Everybody is too blind to see it."

Peter said, "I think you're exaggerating. Yes, you're right about inflation, but I won't go along with your theory of Americanisation."

Another man, Jack, said, "I read in the paper the other day that we've had practically no inflation over the past three years, at least that's what the government's statistics seem to show."

"There you go," said Don. "That's exactly what I mean. They tell the man in the street that there is no such thing as inflation and feed him with faked statistics and a poisonous cloud of unimportant news items. People are being drugged on sex and crime by the media so they're not interested in the real issues, I mean the genuine problems of our times."

"If people can't see that we're in the firm grip of steep inflation in this country," Peter added, "just let them have a look at the quick changes in the ownership of shops and restaurants down that street. Property gallops high, landlords put up their rents, tenants go bust. Let them check out the number of bankruptcies in small businesses."

"You may have a point there," Bertie admitted.

"But why are you saying that we're being Americanized?" Peter asked Don.

"Just look at your ordinary high-street shops. It's all chains, chains, chains. Hardly any individual shops of character. And then the products you get, and then the shopping malls, and then the hamburger places…Oh, I could go on almost endlessly." Don took a sip from his pint glass, and then continued. "And what about our media? Our TV programmes are mostly cheap imitations or even blunt copies of American shows. Just look at the talk-show format. Our newspapers are fooling their readers following the pattern of their American models. Even our speech has been influenced by American expressions."

"All right, all right," Peter admitted, "I'll give you all that about the shops and the media. But I don't think you're right about our language. The increasing slurs in most people's speech are not an American influence. They are a sign of middle-class English taking precedence over what used to be called RP – wasn't it called that? Received Pronunciation? – especially in London and the home counties, I think they call it Estuary English."

"I think you're right," Bertie said. "These days, when I hear a chap speak as my parents used to speak I suspect him of being a foreigner. And he often turns out to be one. Only the other day it was. I picked up a conversation with a young couple in a pub in Crawley. Their English was absolutely perfect. You just couldn't find fault with anything. And yet, to me it sounded altogether too perfect. So I asked them, and it turned out they were from Denmark."

The men continued talking on the same subject for a while. Though they did not come to an agreement about the current use of English, Don eventually convinced them about the

Americanisation of British society.

A few months later Peter took up the subject of the English language again when he met Don for a meal at the Ganges Restaurant in Nutley. They had placed their orders when Don made a remark about the excellent English accent of their Indian waiter, and this prompted Peter to refer to what Bertie had said.

"Bertie was right. Do you remember what he said about foreigners often talking better English?"

"Yes, of course I remember," Don replied, smiling. "It's a never-ending topic. I don't think there's another language group in the world that worries about their language as much as the English do. I can't imagine the French or the Germans constantly discussing the way their language was being pronounced by the rest of the world."

"Yes, but then neither French nor German is a world-language."

"You're right, but still..." Don looked into the middle distance, and Peter could tell his friend was reminded of something that he was not sure about, something he wanted to discuss with him but could not make up his mind about. He wondered if it was something to do with his dead wife.

They talked about some unimportant business news and about the unusually warm weather until their food arrived. When they were eating Don suddenly returned to the former topic.

"This thing about language," he said and placed his fork on the table-cloth. "I don't think I have told you about our daughter, have I? Her name's Emma. She's a bright young girl, just turned sixteen. And she told me an interesting bit about our language that she had picked up from an Austrian. You know how they have these school exchanges...her school had a girl from a place called Klagenfurt, somewhere in Austria. Now, Emma told me she'd been saying something in conversation when the Austrian girl actually corrected her. Emma had said something with 'I',

I mean 'I' the personal pronoun first person singular, but the Austrian girl told her it wasn't 'I' but 'me'. So Emma explained to her how we consider 'me' less educated, you know, lower-class sort of thing. That was when the Austrian girl gave her a lecture on the subject which Emma relayed to me. Peter, did you know it was wrong to say something like, 'He gave Cathy and I ten pounds'? It's not 'Cathy and I', it's 'Cathy and *me*'. And that's because it's in the accusative case. The Austrian girl was right. Now, that's something that impressed me."

"Of course she was right," Peter answered. "But people don't care about all that Latin grammar stuff in this country. What did your daughter say?"

"She said she'd learnt to be more careful about her use of 'I' and 'me' in future. You know, she's really into languages. She's very good at writing texts. She wants to become a journalist."

"Why haven't you mentioned her before?"

"I don't really know. It's probably because she was so close to her mother. In fact, I'm quite a bit worried about her. You know, the loss of her mother has been an awful shock for her. I only hope she's not going to crack up…you know, drift into the drug scene or some other escape thing. She's such a sensitive girl."

Peter did not press Don for more information about his daughter. But over the following months he gradually got to know her through the filter of Don's reports. When Don told him, towards the end of the following year, that Emma wanted him to come out of his mourning period with a party Peter found himself taking her side.

"Of course she's right," he argued. "We all know you loved her, but your life moves on. You still have a bright and promising future ahead of you."

"Hardly promising, I'd say, at my age." Don shook his head, smiling.

"Come on, just give yourself a push."

"All right, what can I say when my best friend and my only

daughter are in league against me? After all, everybody is giving parties now with all this millennium craze."

"Even though they're all wrong. They can't count from one to ten. The new millennium won't start until the end of 2000. The last day of the twentieth century will be the thirty-first of December 2000, not this end of December."

"Yes, mathematically you are perfectly right," Don smiled at his friend. "But people don't care about the scientific aspect of such things. It's the every-day perspective that matters, and that shows a change from one to two in the date. I say, Peter, don't be so bloody pedantic."

"I'm not being pedantic. Not more than you or Emma when you worry about Latin grammar in English anyway. It's just one of these things with me. I hate it when people go crazy about the wrong things."

Don slapped him on the shoulder and said, "So I probably ought to give this party."

"Of course you should," Peter answered.

"Even if it's just to annoy you, I'll give a millennium party like everybody else."

The two men laughed. They had this unique relationship that allowed them to take different positions, and even though they argued from their different perspectives they still respected each other. They often just ended such friendly arguments with a good laugh.

The party was scheduled for the last day of the year, the premature fake end of the millennium. Don was extremely generous. He consulted with his daughter and together they drew up a list of guests to be invited. One day in the middle of November, Don called Peter in the evening.

"I just thought you could help," he said to his friend after their routine greetings.

"I'd be delighted. How can I help?" Peter asked.

"There's a number of things. Why don't you come over

328

tomorrow night, then we can go over all the details?"

"Fine, what time?"

Don consulted Emma, who was sitting next to him, and Peter heard her voice over the telephone. He had never met her. He liked her voice immediately.

"Emma says why don't you have dinner with us. Say seven-thirty?"

"Thank you very much. Anything you want me to bring along?"

"Nothing, just your common sense. You know the way?"

Peter had never been to Don's place before, so he had to check the itinerary in his mental map for a few seconds before he answered, "Yes, it must be left after the Red Lion? Then down that narrow lane on your right?"

"That's it. Give us a call on your mobile in case you get lost."

" Okay. I'm looking forward. See you tomorrow then."

"See you."

Peter put the phone down. He wondered what Emma would be like. He had lost touch with the younger generation, particularly with young women. Well, she was not a woman, only a girl, a teenager, wasn't she? He would have to be careful not to say the wrong things. Young girls were very critical these days. He would be extra polite to her. He hoped she would not be dressed in rags like so many girls her age. He believed himself to be rather old-fashioned. He preferred a woman to look like a woman. A nice dress did so much more for a woman than a pair of dirty denim jeans.

It was Emma who opened the door for him on the following evening.

"So you are Dad's mysterious friend," she smiled as she gave him her hand. He liked her appearance even better than he had liked her distant voice over the telephone. She wore a rather elegant combination of a chestnut-coloured woollen jumper and a pair of comfortable-looking dark pants. Though the jumper enveloped her body in a loose fashion he could see that she had a fine figure with firm breasts. Her movements were bouncing and athletic. She took his coat and threw it over a chair in the hall. Then she led him to the living-room where Don was just filling their glasses with white wine.

"Mr. Hoffmann, may I introduce you to Mr. Richardson, the best dad in this part of the country and the best connoisseur of Italian wine?" she said in a theatrical sing-song voice. They all laughed. Peter was so glad she had such a good sense of humour. He almost envied Don. How wonderful it must be to have such a delightful daughter! His own lack of children gave him a stab in his heart. But he recovered within seconds.

"Cheers!" Don cried.

They clinked their glasses and took a sip. The cool wine cleared Peter's head.

"Can I give you a hand in the kitchen?" he politely asked.

"No, thanks. Everything's in good hands." Don proudly glanced at Emma and gently placed a hand on her wrist.

Through the evening, Peter came to understand that Don was very fond of his daughter. He could see that there was an invisible bond between them. He was glad for his friend. They prepared the party in a relaxed atmosphere. Peter managed to throw in some good ideas, and Emma fascinated him by the ease with which she combined hard facts with friendly bantering. She made fun of his suggestions and took them seriously at the same time.

The party turned out a real success. There were more than thirty people. Peter, Don and Emma managed everything together in the background, communicating with brief glances. Food, drinks, a few special effects, and a funny quiz about the twentieth century. When, at four o'clock in the morning of the first of January, their last guests had left they stood in the hall and looked at each other. They had made it. The three of them felt like one family. Peter was genuinely satisfied.

"So what about the clearing-up?" he inquired.

"Let's do that in the morning," Don suggested. They agreed, and after a few happy remarks about the success of the party they all turned in. Peter was offered the guest-room. He dropped into the soft bed like a log and was asleep in no time.

Peter's acquaintance with his friend's daughter was a new dimension in his life. He saw her again from time to time over the following months. In June, Don informed him that Emma was going to take up journalism and media studies after her A-levels. In September, Don told him to join them for Emma's eighteenth birthday. Peter was happy to accept. After they had enjoyed a good meal at the Plough Inn, Don suggested a night-cap at home. So Peter found himself in Don's house again. The two men sat down in the living-room and Don opened a bottle of Château Margaux. Emma was getting ready to go out for a late-night stint with a group of her friends.

Peter observed his friend. While Don was going through the procedure of decanting the dark red liquid he was taking in the scene and adding it to his photographic memory. How lucky he was to have such friends. He was grateful that his life had developed like this, and he realized that he had come a very long way from the mediocrity that had imprisoned him in his childhood.

"It must feel very good to see your own daughter turn eighteen," he remarked when they had taken their first sip of wine. "Your own flesh and blood stepping out into the world."

Don was silent. Peter could tell that his words had caused a certain tension, a slight uneasiness he could hardly pin down.

"There's something I have to tell you," Don said at last. "It's about Emma. I meant to tell you before."

"Is there a problem with her?" Peter asked and he felt concerned.

"Not really a problem. Just a fact." Don looked at him with

a serious expression and put his glass down on the table with emphasis. "She's not my daughter."

TWENTY-THREE

This was a shock. What was coming now? Peter tried to remain calm while he waited for his friend to explain.

"She's Cathy's daughter all right," Don said.

"Was Cathy married to someone else before you met her, then?"

"No, she was a single parent. When we got married I adopted the child and gave her my name. It was the only right thing to do, and I've never regretted it. Emma is a wonderful daughter. I couldn't love her better if she was my own flesh and blood. That's a myth, anyway, this thing about your own flesh and blood. And I have good reasons to believe that she loves me just as much."

"Does she know you're not her real father?"

"Of course she does, but she never seemed to make a big fuss about it."

"Does she know her real father?" Peter felt he could ask such personal questions since Don had originally opened the door to this intimacy. Don obviously wanted him to know these facts about his family.

"No, how could she? Not even Cathy knew him."

"Are you sure?"

"Yes, I am. But of course I can only tell you what I know about the whole affair based on what she told me. And I can't see why I shouldn't believe her." Don poured another glass of wine while he paused and hesitated for a brief moment.

"I may as well tell you all I know about it," he continued with a sigh. "You see, Cathy was in Australia when she got pregnant. When the time of her confinement came she secretly travelled back to England to have the baby in this country. Emma was born in Newcastle-on-Tyne, where Cathy had some family. As soon as the baby could travel she took her back to Australia. Nobody ever knew, not even her best friend Becky."

"That's interesting. However, it doesn't explain how it happened."

"Yes, but it goes to show that Cathy was a very determined woman and that she tried to mystify everybody. When the question of adoption came up I made it a condition that she should tell me everything she knew about the child's origin. She told me it was an accident, the result of a one-night stand. She solemnly swore she had never met the child's father again. In fact she positively stated she had even forgotten his name and would not recognize him if she ever met him again in her life, a very unlikely thing anyway. So you see, Emma could never know her real father, and I am the only man she will ever call her father."

After this lengthy revelation, the two friends' conversation drifted in a different direction. They exchanged their views on the apparent housing boom in Britain. Property prices were climbing constantly and nobody knew what consequences this development could have.

"It's all on loan," Peter said. "I tell you, this can't go on for ever. This whole thing of living to the full on borrowed money is really an American thing, and it's bound to collapse like a house of cards one of these days."

"Don't be so gloomy, my friend," Don crooned. "I never knew you to be such a pessimist. Come on, have some more wine."

Over the following months, Peter often remembered what Don had told him about Emma. It must be strange not to know your own father, he thought. And then there was Cathy, secretive and enigmatic Cathy, who had died on that cold floor next to him. What secrets had she taken to her grave?

One day Don asked Peter to meet him in the City. They

met in Don's office from where they proceeded to a near-by pub. It was obvious from the start that Don had something of importance to tell his friend.

"I want you to do something for me," he began when they had settled down with their pints.

"Tell me more," Peter replied.

"It's this. I'm going away. I've decided to build up a new branch in Canada. I've been over to Toronto twice, and things are ready to take off pretty soon now."

"How long will you be away for?" Peter asked.

"That's the whole point I'm trying to make. I don't think I'll be coming back. You know, Emma is quite grown-up and she can look after herself. I've even made provisions for her to get her own flat. I'm selling the house. You know I still miss Cathy. Ever since her death the house has never been the same to me. It's so empty without her. So at last I've decided to draw a line and make a new beginning. A new beginning in a new country, a new environment, a new challenge."

"You have quite made up your mind then?"

"I have."

"So what can I do? You said you wanted me to do something for you," Peter reminded him.

"Oh yes. I am coming to that now. You know Emma is barely nineteen. There are a few things she's not ready for. As I said, I've made ample provisions for her. She will have enough to take her through her education. But there will be more to come when she reaches twenty-one. Also, if anything should happen to me…"

"You are a very generous father. I mean, considering."

"Listen, Peter," Don said and moved his chair closer. "I want you to act as my representative here in England. I've instructed my lawyer accordingly. In particular, I want to hand over all responsibilities concerning Emma's inheritance to you. I've also made you the sole executor of my will."

Peter looked at Don's staring eyes and saw that he was serious about all this. He only hesitated for a few seconds.

"I hope I'll be able to honour the trust you put in me. What do I have to do?"

"So you accept the responsibility?"

"Yes, I do," Peter said and the two men shook hands.

Don explained that he wanted him to see his solicitor, a certain Mr. Cruikshank, who would put him in the picture. And when Peter saw that paragon of the legal profession a few days later he was quite surprised to learn the extent of the assets that Don had set aside for his adopted daughter to take possession on her twenty-first birthday. It was all done properly, with signatures on legal documents and the customary paraphernalia.

The time of Don's departure approached very quickly. Peter helped him to sell some of his furniture and to put some of his possessions into storage, either for his eventual return or for Emma if she was interested. And then the day of his departure was there. It was the third of April 2001. Peter drove him to Heathrow. Emma was with them. Their good-byes were short and manly, whereas Emma had a few tears. Don's flight was on time.

On their way back to town, Peter invited Emma for lunch. Their conversation was a little awkward at first. Of course they knew each other well enough, they felt. And especially over the past three weeks they had seen quite a bit of each other in the course of helping with the arrangements for Don's departure. But still Peter had to get used to his new role in view of this beautiful young woman sitting opposite and munching her macaroni cheese. She warmed up to his friendly manner and smiled at him.

"So from what Dad has told me you're now some sort of an uncle to me. Or are you my guardian? Like Mr. Jarndyce. Are you going to turn into a Dickensian character now?"

"Ha ha," Peter laughed. "I don't think I ever could, even if I tried."

"But at any rate you're not going to fall in love with your Esther Summerson, are you? You're far too old, you know."

They laughed. The awkwardness between them was gone, and they established a relationship based on common trust and friendly bantering. Their conversation turned to current affairs, and Peter gradually slipped into his role of guardian. More guardian angel than prison guard, he told himself. He drifted off into his vast store of memories. While he was keeping up the conversation with Emma he managed to live a second life in his mind. He remembered other occasions when he had been close to young women. Strange, all the other times that he had been close to a young woman the atmosphere had been fraught with erotic tension. Was that a typical memory for a middle-aged man? Was it a typically male experience? Or was it only his view? There had been women in his life who had told him that men had a basically dirty mind, all they could ever think of was sex. But then, wasn't that the human instinct to preserve the species? There would be no procreation without it.

He thought of those precious moments when he had first realized that a woman reciprocated his feelings. Feelings? What was it that he had felt, for example, when it hit him that Barbara was equally interested in him as he was in her? Love or lust? Yes, strange how they could ever drift apart as they had…he remembered how she had stayed with him and supported him emotionally after Fred's death, but then they'd gradually lost their hold on each other. Just like that.

"Can I give you a lift to wherever you're going?" he asked Emma when they left the restaurant.

"That would be nice," she answered. "Can you drop me somewhere near the South Bank Arts Centre? I've got to meet a friend at three-thirty."

"That's no problem," he smiled.

They got in his car and drove east along Cromwell Road. At one of the traffic lights a black Audi squeezed in between the car

337

in front and Peter's old Ford. Peter had to slam his foot on the brake pedal.

"That was close," he sighed.

"You never know these days," Emma remarked and shook her head. "Some of these drivers think the road belongs to them."

"I wonder what the world looks like from their perspective," Peter murmured.

"I'm sure they don't care. I can't imagine them ever trying to see what their selfish behaviour means for other people."

"Look at him now! It's only just jumped to amber and there he is, speeding off like a rocket. If he goes on at this rate he'll cause an accident sooner or later."

"Don't say that. It makes me afraid of driving."

"All right. But you've got to admit that that was an aggressive driver."

"Yes, sure."

"And the snarling front of his black Audi seemed to announce the fact even before he overtook us. I saw him in my mirror and expected such a thing."

"I only hope he'll never come my way when I'm on the road." Emma took a paper tissue and blew her nose.

They continued their journey through the West End and approached Kensington Gardens. At Hyde Park Corner, Peter looked left at the treetops which were visible even from their lane in the middle of the heavy traffic.

"Amazing, isn't it? There's this huge park in the middle of this urban desert. Do you sometimes go to Hyde Park? I think it can be very relaxing, that is when the weather's right. You can walk quite a distance within the park."

"Yes," she replied with a smile. "As a matter of fact, I often go for walks in the park. I don't even need a dog, I do it for myself."

"That's good."

"Yes, it is, for me anyway. But the other day I had a strange encounter. I mean in the park."

"Were you harassed by a dirty man?"

"No, not that. It wasn't so bad. It was really nothing. I don't know if it was good or bad. It was just one of these things…"

"What happened?"

"Well, I had just entered the park from the Bayswater Road side. I was walking across the grass, not keeping to the footpath. Suddenly I came across this group of women. There were four women dancing in a circle, without music, silently, holding hands, and a fifth woman – she was a lot older than the other four – was kneeling on the grass about five or six yards away from them. At first I thought she was praying. Then I discovered she was holding a camera in her hands and she was taking pictures of the dancing women. You know, she had one of those box cameras where you look in from the top – "

" – a Hasselblad," Peter suggested.

"I don't know what they're called. Anyway, there she was, seriously absorbed by what she was doing, as if the camera was some holy relic. It even flashed through my mind that she could be holding a baby. And the dancers also had an eerie look about them. They were smiling, but their faces expressed a ceremonial seriousness at the same time. There was almost a religious atmosphere."

"Did you talk to them?"

"At first I only watched. Their dance was well-measured, it was like some of the dances you see in TV documentaries about temples in Bali and such places in the Far East. When they stopped I waited. There was a phase of transition and they became ordinary women. They took their bags and slowly began to walk away in different directions. The photographer woman turned her head and smiled at me. I said hello and stepped up to her. She was a wonderful woman. She must have been at least sixty-five or seventy, but she had such a breathtaking beauty about her. She had true dignity. 'The right shot will catch the bottom of their soul,' she said. I was going to ask her what she meant, but the way she bent down to put her camera in her bag struck me silent. She turned round and walked towards Bayswater Road. When she was about twenty yards away she looked back over her left shoulder and said, 'You will see, young woman'. Then she was hidden by the bushes."

"Why are you telling me about this?" Peter asked.

"I don't know. I only just remembered when you mentioned the park. It's not important. It's nothing, really. I'm sorry, I shouldn't have told you. I must look very stupid in your eyes."

"No, no! I believe you. A thing like that could have happened to me. I sometimes see people do things out of the ordinary. I think these are really important moments."

"I don't know. They're probably not important. But they are memorable."

"Who or what decides on whether something is important or not, anyway?"

At this point they reached the corner where he was going to drop her. So he stopped his car at the kerb and switched off the engine. He got out and walked round the car to open the door for her, but she was already halfway out of the car when he reached her side, so he closed the door behind her and offered her his hand.

"You've got my address and telephone number. Here's my e-mail address. So you can contact me any time." He handed her a small business-card. "Let's meet up sometime next week. I'll let you know when I've got news from Don, anyway."

"Thanks for everything," she said as she shook his hand. Then she walked away in the direction of the Royal Festival Hall.

Peter got back in his car and drove off. He crossed Waterloo Bridge and wondered if it was still worth while to go back to his office or if he should call it a day and just head for home. He continued travelling north, and when he was in Southampton Row the cars in front all came to a sudden stop. There was an accident further ahead. All the engines were switched off and the drivers got out of their cars, trying to find out what was the matter and how long they would have to wait. He walked past a few cars in front until he could see the accident. It was difficult to ascertain what had happened. There were several cars involved, three or four? But as it appeared, nobody seemed to be hurt. It was just a matter of hard metal interlocked with hard metal. One of the cars was black. Immediately, he remembered the black Audi with the aggressive driver. Could it be the same car? Impossible, with all this traffic in a city like London! He saw that the black car was not an Audi but a Peugeot. He felt relieved. Then he checked himself. Why should he feel relieved? What was that stupid idiot in that Audi to him?

He walked back to his car and sat down in the driver's seat. After waiting in silence for about five minutes he pressed the button of the radio. Classic FM came on. Some sentimental piece from the nineteenth century. He had heard it many times before, but he did not know what it was. And when it was over they did not say what it had been.

"Well, then," he said to himself, "as soon as the road is clear I'll probably head straight for home."

He placed his hands in his lap and was quite happy.

TWENTY-FOUR

A crisp and clear September morning. Peter was walking down Shaftesbury Avenue to meet his old friend Robert in the lobby of the Regent Hotel. They had recently become more relaxed with each other and returned to the good friendship of their younger days.

The brakes of a lorry screeched. Peter turned his head and looked if anything had happened. But nothing had happened. No accident. Nothing to worry about.

"It's only right and proper," he said to himself. "No bad accidents should happen on such a perfect day."

He crossed the street. As he looked up he saw a huge placard announcing a popular comedy that was being shown in one of the theatres. One of the actors in the picture had a dashing moustache which reminded him of his old Uncle Charles. Strange old man, Charles was. Peter tried to remember his age. He had to be in his late seventies by now. He had not heard from him for a long time, except for the yearly arrival of cheap Christmas cards.

Peter remembered how he had admired Charles. But then, he had begun to see through him. Then there had been the realisation that Charles must have cared for him, as he had told him last time in the retirement home. Yes, small Peter left alone in the world with the task of looking for worms for fish bait, and Charles speeding through the landscape in his blue Ford fearing he had lost the boy in his care. Peter's photographic memory showed him the sad farm houses around the deserted manure heap. Even though he had all those photographic memories that remained unchanged and unchangeable, he was impressed by his own experience through the past fifty years or so, the experience of shifting perspectives.

First, a long time ago, there had been the different perspectives one could take in view of Fred's fatal accident. Surely, the family of the other pilot had seen the accident from their perspective. They had lost a son, a brother, a member of their clan. Not to speak of his friends, who had lost someone they had loved. Expectations thwarted, half a life thrown away. And his own family? Had they ever really understood or accepted Fred's death? It was a strange thing how accidents could shift everybody's perspectives within a split second. Nothing was permanent, everything could change any moment.

And then this whole story about Don and Cathy. In one of his early e-mail messages from Canada, Don had told him even more details about Cathy's difficulties in dealing with those around her in a fair and respectable manner. Peter still admired Don's persistent love for his dead wife, but he found it hard to understand how anyone could have lived with such a woman. She had been so egocentric as to pick a quarrel almost every day of her life. Don had told him how she had seemed to manage the really big conflicts in her life. For example, she had lost a brother in an accident quite early, and that had obviously not been such a big problem for her. On the other hand, all those small exigencies of every-day life had appeared to be a huge problem for her. Whenever she had been under stress about minor household matters she had apparently created an inescapable atmosphere of terror. Sometimes, Don confessed to him over a drink very late one night, he had suspected her neurotic fits to be a mere strategy to prevent any possible contradiction from those around her. In one of his latest e-mail messages, Don had told him some examples of her frequent accusations in their small household routines.

There was one episode where, after they had been cooking dinner together, Don tried to help her put the meat and the vegetables on the plates in the kitchen. He approached her from the right while she was weighing her portion of beefsteak – because she happened to be on one of her numerous diets at the moment – and carefully took hold of the spoon to scoop the vegetables out of the pan onto their plates. In such manoeuvres he knew he had to be extra careful because he had to get past her to do his job and she never budged an inch, she always stood where she was. She never ever sensed when other people would find it convenient if she made room, even if it was just a minute shift of one leg. She flared at him and told him to get out of her way. Stupid idiot, didn't he know that she had to weigh her vegetables as well before they could be served? So he thought he'd better make himself useful if he walked over to their dining-room and made sure everything was in place, to check on their drinks and the cruet on the tablecloth. Hardly had he reached the dining table when she yelled at him from the kitchen that he was torturing her. She reproached him for putting pressure on her by waiting impatiently for her at the table. And why was he letting her do all the work alone? Why was he making life so difficult for her all the time? Why was he such a selfish brute?

Peter saw such extreme misjudgements as examples of a person's imprisonment in his or her own perspective. Really, Cathy had been a very desperate woman. Obviously, she had expected a larger share of happiness than life had allotted her. And poor Don had represented the shield on which all her arrows of frustration bounced off. She had probably hoped to reach personal fulfilment by aggression towards all those close to her because she had seen them as the major obstacles between her unhappy position and the distant aim of complete happiness. A dangerous fallacy. Nevertheless, Peter remembered how impressed he had been with the dignity that she radiated in the last few moments of her life. The proximity of death must have invested her with this special quality. With her last breath she seemed to give up her struggle within some huge, superhuman task.

Don had also written about his success in the Toronto business world. He was actually expanding his business activities. He had already opened a second office in Montreal, and these days he was down in New York, negotiating an even more promising expansion. Peter was planning to go over to see him some time in the near future. He would like to see his friend again and admire his success. Well, perhaps he could get away in October or November. Yes, that would be a splendid idea. Why not fly over for a week in November when the property market in England might allow him a week off?

When Peter reached the hotel lobby he saw Robert at once. He was studying a newspaper, which he folded up when he saw him. The two friends shook hands and walked over to the tea lounge.

"I say," Robert began when they were seated at a table near the window, "you must be very busy these days. I mean, with property prices rising almost day by day."

"You can say that again," was Peter's answer. "But I don't think it's a healthy development at all. Take my own house down in Sussex, for example. Five years ago I paid two hundred thousand. I could easily get four hundred today. It's absolutely ridiculous. There's nothing our business can do about it…it's something that's beyond our control. And what is the worst thing about it is its effect on first-time buyers, they simply can't get into the property market. This will have further repercussions on the social behaviour of young people in this country, believe me."

Their tea arrived. They spoke about their jobs, the Enron scandal in the States, the Prime Minister's admiration for the American President and about London's traffic congestion, which was still getting worse every year. Then they happened to mention a new film which was on at the Odeon in Leicester Square.

"Why don't we treat ourselves to something like that?" Robert suggested. "You used to like to go to the pictures. Do you remember that time when we saw *Ben Hur* together when we were…how old were we?"

"Of course, those were the days…But let me see. I've got a business lunch at one, then there's that appointment at half-past three." Peter took out his pocket diary. "Yes, we could meet at four. Why don't we meet again right here? We can have a quick drink and walk over to the Odeon."

They agreed to meet at four. It was soon time for both of them to leave and look after their respective professional interests. They were both looking forward to go to the cinema together later in the afternoon.

When Peter entered the same place again at five to four in the afternoon, he sensed that something was wrong. There was a mysterious atmosphere in the hotel lobby, and there was hardly anybody around. When he approached the glass doors leading to the tea lounge and the bar, he saw that there was a large crowd of people trying to get into the bar area. He pushed his way through to where he had spotted Robert. When he reached his side he realized that everybody was staring at the television screen in the corner.

"It's terrible," Robert said. "A catastrophe!"

Peter looked at the screen and tried to understand the commentary. The picture showed the twin towers of the World Trade Centre in New York, and one of the towers had a huge cloud of black smoke emerging from its midriff. Just at that moment an aeroplane appeared from the left and flew right into the second tower. A fantastic fireball and more black smoke! The people in the room screamed. Everyone was absolutely horrified. For a period of about five minutes, which felt more like five years, everyone was so dumbfounded that the crowded room remained as silent as a church. Gradually, though, individuals began to whisper, but what was happening in New York at this moment was too incomprehensible.

"They're going to collapse," Robert suggested.

"What do you mean?" Peter did not understand what his friend was referring to.

"The twin towers. Their structure consists of steel girders, and that steel is going to melt now that the kerosene has exploded and created astronomical temperatures inside the buildings. And once a small section has melted there'll be a chain reaction. It's simple physics. They're done for. Anybody within the towers will perish. It's only to be hoped that as many as possible may get out before the whole shebang is going to collapse like a house of cards. Just wait, this is going to be an even more horrifying sight than the two plane crashes. Just wait and see."

The men standing near Robert had started to listen to him. Some were shaking their heads, others stared at him with gaping mouths.

"It's physics, you see?" was all he could say, shrugging his shoulders.

The world stood still. For how long exactly nobody could say. One hour? Two hours? Five hours? Then the towers collapsed, exactly as Robert had predicted. What followed on the television screen was absolute pandemonium in the streets of New York. The grey dust clouds ate up the whole city it seemed, swallowing houses, cars, people.

It was impossible to leave the television screen and return to any form of normality. Every man and woman in the hotel bar – and as Peter realized, every man and woman in the Western World – knew that the world was no longer what it had been. What they witnessed on television was certainly going to change the world. Could it be the beginning of a Third World War? Who could be behind such actions? How was the American President going to react, hysterical as he had already been about terrorism even before this?

"I don't think the Americans will ever be able to understand this," Peter said. "Their world-view is altogether too simplified, their thought structures imprisoned in a black-and-white perspective. Good versus evil, just look at your typical Hollywood movie."

"Let's wait and see what Bush is going to do about it," Robert suggested.

Peter watched television with everyone else in the room and nearly forgot an appointment later in the afternoon, which he had come here to tell his friend about, since it prevented them from going to the pictures together. But then he told himself that all those events in the States would be covered abundantly in all the news programmes over the next few days anyway, so he decided to go about his own business for the time being.

He was right. The terrorist attacks on American symbols of power dominated the public discourse in the Western World over the following weeks. About one week after the attacks, Peter found himself sitting comfortably in his living-room, watching television and enjoying a glass of red wine. It was a programme with a panel discussion. There were specialists on American politics, on international relations, on Islam, on east-west relations and a few journalists from various corners of the world. Peter was particularly impressed by what a woman on the panel had to say about the perspective of the Muslim world, their view of the Western World and American arrogance.

"Isn't it clear," one of the journalists asked, "that the majority of the population in countries like Iran, Iraq and Afghanistan is really in agreement with those terrorists?"

"I wouldn't put it like that," the woman answered.

"How would you put it then?" another journalist insisted.

"Well," she began while she was obviously arranging her arguments in her mind, "the entire matter is much more complex than some people in the West would like to present it. If we want to understand how the mind of certain Muslims operates in view of the West we have to see how western dominance in world politics, in trade and commerce, in technology, even in morals…how all this must appear from the perspective of these underprivileged people in the Muslim world."

Peter read at the bottom of the screen that her name was Dr. Rebecca Winter.

"But surely," the presenter threw in, "all that inferiority complex doesn't justify terrorism. Are you saying that we ought to accept all the evil dictators of the world? Isn't it a noble and highly moral undertaking if we – that is, the West – are trying to bring democracy to some of those dictatorial and potentially dangerous countries?"

"I'm sorry if I appear to be rude," she answered, "but your question…I mean the way you ask this question…that is already an expression of western arrogance."

A murmur of protest came from the other members of the panel.

"Yes, I mean exactly what I'm saying. Who are we? How can we justify our role of world police? Who can guarantee that the western version of democracy – or even just the American variant of it – that this version is suitable for all the different cultures of the entire world in every way?"

"Are you opposed to the idea of democracy, then?" asked an energetic young journalist on the panel.

"Of course not," was her quick reply. "But where some of the cultures stand at this stage in their development they're simply not ready for our western version of democracy. They might even develop their own versions. What I'm trying to say is that we are as blind in our own perspective as the blindness some politicians attribute to cultures of the Middle East. Look at our glorification of the nation state stemming from Romanticism in the nineteenth century and causing such nationalistic arrogance that led us into two world wars in the twentieth century alone. We even exported nationalism to the Third World through our system of colonialism, and now we pretend to be horrified at the way some African dictators imitate the behaviour of the European rulers of earlier periods. In a few hundred years the history books might present not only Caesar and Napoleon as great and heroic rulers but also figures like Hitler and Idi Amin."

"Aren't you going too far here?"

"Not at all. The point is…" she interrupted herself for a moment to clear her throat, then continued, "the point is that our perspective of what is right and wrong in the world changes over longer periods of time. Today we know that the concept of the nation state has to be modified and adapted in order to save the planet. Take the UN or the EU. Rulers of only one or two hundred years back could never have envisaged such a thing. Just as some of the extreme leaders of countries like Iran, Iraq or Afghanistan can't understand certain concepts of western democracy. And then there's the social aspect…"

The telephone rang. Reluctantly, Peter heaved himself out of his armchair and walked over to where he kept his telephone.

"Hello," a deep voice said. "It's Morgan Bloomfield."

It took Peter a fraction of a second to remember who Morgan Bloomfield was. He was the lawyer who looked after Don Richardson's legal issues here in London, and it was quite a while since Peter had had anything to do with him in his capacity of Don's business representative, simply because there had been no business and no legal issue to be looked after. He wondered if there was going to be some business activity now. He had not heard from Don for over a week, so he did not expect any big business to be looked after. Probably some minor legal thing.

"I say, can you come round to my office some time tomorrow. It's rather urgent."

"Yes. As it happens I'm free tomorrow afternoon, say after two-thirty. What is it about? Do you want me to bring along any of Don's documents?"

"No, just come empty-handed. It's about Don himself. He's gone missing, so we'll have to decide on what to do, you know, how to act, sort of thing."

"What do you mean? Gone missing?" Peter was shocked. Suddenly he cared for his friend in a way he had never cared before. "How serious is it?"

"I think we'll wait till tomorrow. There may be a new development until then. Just come to my office at three."

They rang off, and Peter walked back to his armchair. He took the remote control and switched off the programme which had interested him so much before. It was of no more significance now. His friend Don was much more important at this moment. What could have happened to him?

Later, he dialled Don's number in Canada, but there was no answer. Then he tried to put all the puzzle pieces together in his mind, the pieces of information about Don. He must be back in Montreal after his stint in New York. It suddenly occurred to him that he ought to have had some communication from him these days, but nothing. Don had not phoned for over a week. Was it on the day he had left Montreal for New York?

He went to bed, but he hardly slept through the night. Images of Don appeared in his wakeful dreams, Don's face laughing at him, Don waving good-bye at Heathrow, Don sitting in the train and crumpling his newspaper...

It was exactly three o'clock when he entered Morgan's office. The two men shook hands, and Peter sensed the tense atmosphere.

"This is serious," Morgan began when they were seated on opposite sides of his large mahogany desk.

"Please, tell me what you know." Peter was impatient to learn the truth.

"As I told you last night. Don has gone missing." He picked up a red pencil on his desk and turned it round between his fingers. "I've been in touch with colleagues in Montreal and New York. So what we know now is that Don checked in at the Doral Inn in Lexington Avenue on September the tenth. He left for some business appointment early on the following morning, and he has not been seen since."

"Are you saying he might have been near the World Trade Centre on that day?"

"We don't know. One of my American colleagues is trying to find out together with the police. But you can imagine how many cases of missing persons they have to deal with in New York these days. As far as I know, they're trying to find out the addresses of his business contacts in Manhattan, but that's not so easy either."

"My God." It suddenly dawned on Peter that Don might have been killed in the terrorist attack on the World Trade Centre.

"I'm afraid we may have to face some really bad news," Morgan breathed as he placed the red pencil on the smooth surface of his desk. This gesture appeared to Peter like a final abandonment of his friend. By giving that pencil out of his hand Morgan had thrown Don overboard, had dismissed him, cut both of them off from any hope of a possible life-line with Don.

"What do you suggest? What can we do?" he asked.

"Not much, I'm afraid. We'll just have to wait for more news from New York. It's chaos over there, so things might take some time."

"I can't wait and do nothing," Peter said in a firm voice and slapped his right palm on the desk between them.

After a few more words and a friendly but formal goodbye he left Morgan's office. From his own office he inquired about flight connections to New York. It was easy to find a seat on the morning flight the following day, since nobody wanted to travel to the stricken metropolis after what had happened.

In the evening he packed his suitcase. Then he sat down and wrote a note for Emma. He had wanted to phone her but then changed his mind. It was easier to put things in the right perspective in writing. On one hand he did not wish to alarm her unduly, on the other hand he felt he had to prepare her for the worst. He told her he was going over to New York himself to see what could be done and to find out what had happened to Don. He did not use the computer, he thought a hand-written letter was more personal and more appropriate in this case. After three abortive drafts he managed to compose the right sentences. He posted the letter from Heathrow in the morning.

Peter stayed in New York for three days, then he returned with the certainty of the bad news. It was Inspector Kuczinsky from the New York Police Department who had come up with the decisive clue. He had found out the address of one of Don's business partners in Manhattan, and it was in the World Trade Centre, on the eighty-third floor. That decided it. Don must have perished in the great catastrophe. Peter felt a bitter sickness in his stomach when he realized that he had been watching his friend's death on television with Robert that afternoon. Why did he not feel that his friend was being killed there and then? What could have been Don's last feelings, his last thoughts, his last words? Had he been in conversation with his business partner or had he been walking along the corridor or had he been sitting on the toilet? Silly idea, Peter told himself.

After his return to London he went straight to see Emma. They spent the rest of the day together, talking about Don, the things they remembered about him, asserting to each other what a good man he had been, wondering if he had suffered any pain in the last moments when the building collapsed. Peter felt that his role of guardian, which they had originally joked about, was now a serious fact. He contacted Morgan on the following morning and told him everything he knew. Morgan said he would settle all the legal aspects of the situation. He said they would have to wait for confirmation from his Montreal colleagues before the will could be read here in London. Of course, as Emma's guardian he would have to be present as well. Peter understood. He asked him to let him know as soon as things were ready for the reading of the will.

It was more than two months later that the will was read

to Emma and Peter in Morgan's office. Peter had brought along Harry Browning, his own lawyer, just in case. It turned out that Don had made a will on his arrival in Montreal, and in that will he announced the equal splitting of all his worldly assets between Peter and Emma. When it came to the actual figures things became rather complicated. At first it seemed that there were considerable riches, but with the slump of the New York Stock Exchange these had dwindled dramatically between the time the will had been written and now.

As they walked out of Morgan's office, Peter said good-bye to Harry and took Emma by her elbow.

"Let's walk through the park," he suggested.

They walked to the Serpentine and sat down on a deserted bench. The park was without colour at this time of the year, and there were very few people about. A middle-aged woman walked past with a lively Labrador on a leash. She did not turn her head at the two people sitting on the bench.

"So, Don has really connected us now," Peter said.

Emma blew her nose and nodded.

"I promise I'll try to do my best," he croaked with emotion and placed his hand on her shoulder. "Really, I do."

TWENTY-FIVE

He was sitting in a quaint French restaurant, waiting for Emma to join him. He had just been reading some of the depressing news in the *Daily Telegraph*. The awful verbal battle between Ahmadinejad and Bush. He was reminded of the arguments he had heard on television that evening, the evening Morgan had first called him. He could not remember the name of the woman on the panel, but her clear voice and some of her arguments came back to him now. Of course he did not condone the way they treated the human rights in Iran, but after all it was a different culture, wasn't it?

"Hi, have you been waiting long?" Emma smiled as she breezed into the restaurant and rushed to his table.

"Not at all," was his reply.

"I'm sorry. You see, I don't come to town so often these days. Most of my activities take place in Surrey or elsewhere, so I clearly underestimated the time needed to make it to this place."

"That's quite all right."

They ordered their food and exchanged their latest news. She had a great deal to tell him about her job. For two years she had now been engaged in fashion-journalism and lately she had tried to get into the world of script-writing, both areas that he was not very familiar with. So he was often very glad to learn about a world which was so different from his.

"I've been studying the photo series Andy brought back from Milan. I think I got the right angle now. I'm going to tell the girls in this country what's coming up in the next season, and I'm going to use the emotional approach, you know, a bit of romance and such stuff…"

"How's Andy?"

"He's all right," she answered a little too quickly and went on about the upcoming colours and the female business-look. He sensed that there was something wrong about Andy, her cheerful boyfriend from Betchworth, the young fashion-photographer who had a permanent smile on his lips and whose charming ways were even evident to a middle-aged man like Peter. He knew they had been to the Milan fashion show together, but something she had said to him before their departure had already given him the impression that things between the two lovers were not exactly what they should have been. He had no right to question her about her love-life, after all he was not her father, neither her uncle, no longer even her guardian. But he still took a fatherly interest in her welfare and her happiness. He knew she would tell him eventually if things were awry, so there was no need to press her, she would come out with it anyway sooner or later.

When their main course arrived her tales about the fashion world gradually petered out and her speech became hesitant. She looked at the steak on her plate, took a salad leaf to taste it and then, quite suddenly and energetically, carved a mouthful of juicy meat with a decisive and jerking movement. He knew it was her physical announcement of a more personal turn in their conversation.

"The Granada people rejected my script, you know, the one about the Moss Side Soap we'd been planning. I knew it was wrong to take his advice." She took another mouthful of steak and glanced into the middle distance, not exactly knowing what else to say.

"Whose advice are you talking about?"

"Andy's, of course. He told me to change the relationships between some of the characters, and of course I knew it wouldn't wash."

"Have you talked it over with him?"

Emma abruptly changed the subject. "They do know how to do a good steak in this place."

As if to underline her statement she took another mouthful. Peter knew that this indicated an extreme emotional stress, since she normally enjoyed her salad much more than her meat. Ever since she had joined that health club she had seemed to consider meat as a pleasant but not necessary adjunct to the centre-piece of a meal, which was the salad.

They continued their meal in silence for two or three minutes. Then she suddenly threw down her fork and broke out in tears.

"I'm sorry, oh, I'm so sorry. Please, I don't know. Oh, Peter, I don't know what to do, it's such an awful mess…"

"Just relax, my dear," he said and looked round the restaurant to check if they were a disturbance for the other patrons. Nobody heeded them, they were all engaged in animated conversations. "Let's just finish this meal, then you can tell me everything you wish over coffee."

And she told him over coffee what he had been expecting. She had had a huge row with her charming boyfriend and they had split up. It had been brewing for some weeks before, but his interference with her script-writing work and then some of her observations of his behaviour with other women during their stay in Milan had led to the final row after their return.

Peter gave her what consolation he could. While he was giving his avuncular advice he had a few moments in which he felt rather pompous. But she obviously did not feel this, she was clearly very grateful for his advice. When they left the restaurant she seemed relatively composed. She gave him a calm smile.

"It's so good of you, Peter."

"You know you can always come and talk to me."

"Yes, I know. And I know you do this for the memory of my dad."

"Not only."

"Of course. All the more gratitude from me, *Uncle* Peter."

They laughed. It was good to see her laughing face again, after the worried looks and the tears and the angry scowls. He knew she would get over it. He walked her to Covent Garden tube station, then directed his steps to Soho. He was planning a modest little Chinese dinner with Robert and his wife, so he wanted to get some Chinese food items from the Loon Foon supermarket. As he was crossing Charing Cross Road he saw a group of young women or girls walking in the opposite direction. His male ego was disturbed by the see-through tops that two of the girls were wearing, their breasts wobbling in rhythm with their steps and their nipples showing clearly through the thin material of their tops.

"Unbelievable," Peter told himself. This would have been utterly impossible in his young days. He remembered some of the episodes from the restricted days of his childhood, when he had first discovered girls. All of a sudden, he remembered the first time he had seen a girl's private parts, that day so long ago, his friend Thomas, that big tree, Vita…Had that been so different from what disturbed him today? Could it be that today's treatment of sexuality was more natural, more healthy perhaps? In his days, women had always gone to extreme troubles to cover their bodies. The more interesting parts had been kept hidden at all times. He remembered the complicated contortions of some of the women he had seen changing into their bathing costumes; to hide, hide, hide at all costs had seemed to be the most important thing under the sun. And what had been the effect? Well, the game was called hide-and-seek, so the effect was that the boys became crazy even for a quick glance at something more, something that had been kept hidden from them. And today? Did the constant exposure of the female body in films, magazines and even in daily reality – like the glimpse he had just had himself – lead to a more relaxed attitude? Were the young men of the twenty-first century less eagerly interested in the attractions of the female body?

Two weeks later he saw Emma again. They ran into each other at Victoria Station.

"Have you got time for a cup of coffee?" he asked.

"Why not? My train leaves in half an hour."

"What are you up to, these days?" he began as they were sitting down on two flimsy stools with their hot paper cups of cappuccino.

"Nothing much. First I've got to pick up my Nissan from the garage. It's got a new MoT. Then I'll have to drive over to a small place called Crowhurst. It's a village near Lingfield. I'm going to meet an upcoming young fashion designer who agreed to give me an interview. Then I'll have to drive back to Reigate to have a look at a new flat. So, as you can see, my day is quite full."

"Are you planning to move? Aren't you happy with your place as it is?"

"Oh, I'm just looking," she laughed.

"Seems a waste of time to me, if you're not thinking of moving," he grumbled.

"Oh no! You see, if and when I'm really planning to move I'll have all this pre-knowledge, I'll know exactly what I can get for what sort of money. I am well-acquainted with the market, if you know what I mean. Yes, I do enjoy looking at houses and flats. Besides informing me about the market – something you ought to appreciate since you work in the industry – it gives me lots of good ideas about how to arrange things in my own place. It's educational."

"All right then. I hereby give you permission to inspect one desirable property in the town of Reigate this afternoon," he announced in a mock-military voice. They laughed.

"All this fuss about something that might not even happen."

"What do you mean? Aren't you going to see that flat after all then?"

"I only said I was planning, that is, if I've got the time after my interview in Crowhurst. If the young designer has a great deal to tell me I might run a bit late. I'll probably have to rush to make it to Reigate in time." She sighed and looked at her watch.

"I see. But don't put yourself under stress. And above all, drive carefully!"

They parted, and she ran to catch her train. Peter walked out of the station. He had a strange feeling about her. He wondered when he would see her again and what would become of their friendship.

He took a taxi to his office. Once inside his own professional sphere he forgot everything about Emma. His working day was very full, today in was laden with negotiations about several larger projects in the Docklands area. When it was five o'clock he was genuinely tired and very glad to leave his office. He had a drink at the pub across the street. Then he took the underground to Hammersmith, where he knew his friend Robert was expecting him.

He was glad they had invited him for an early dinner tonight. It was the final touch of the paintbrush that completed the picture of their friendship. How long it had taken them to return to their old warmth and trust! Several years. But then he had worked at it, too. Robert's good opinion was very important to him, so he had done his very best to prove to him that he could be trusted in every way. It was really good of Robert to allow their old friendship to return to its former quality.

He walked the short distance between the underground station and their house. He had the address written on a small piece of paper. He was sure he would find their house in no time at all.

He had just given up thinking of his hosts and was turning a street corner when he was accosted by a woman of indeterminate age. She was about four inches shorter than he was, and she was extremely dirty. Her brown jumper was full of holes and had stains of various colours down her front. She wore a whole array of skirts and scarves, and her wrists sported a jingling collection of cheap bracelets and bangles which could not quite hide the clearly visible marks made by drug injections. Her hair-style resembled a wild bird's nest rather than human hair. In the cradle formed by her left arm she was carrying a rat. A live rat. His first reaction was one of disgust.

"I beg your pardon," he said and tried to edge past her.

"No hoity-toity with me, you old buffer," she said, and he detected a slight northern accent. Yorkshire? He was not sure. "Why, can't you have a decent word for a respectable woman like me?"

He noted the deep blue of her eyes while he could not prevent an amused smile at her pronunciation of 'respectable', obviously a hard word for her. He decided to humour her. "All right then. I'm pleased to make your acquaintance," he said, hoping to be allowed to continue on his way.

"Oops, here we go again. Why can't you just say hello, good to see you, sort of thing?"

"Hello, good to see you," he complied.

"And would you have some change for me?" she pleaded and held out the open palm of her right hand. The rat's tail moved, but the rat stayed where it was.

"You see, young woman – " he began.

"Not young no more, but hungry."

"Well then – "

"You like my Thatcher then?" She must have noted his glance at the unusual rodent on her left arm.

"You mean your rat?"

"That's him. He's my pet. I call him Thatcher, you know, after that woman who ruined our country. He helps me to make my peace with my history."

"That's an excellent idea," he said, just to humour her.

There was a moment of silence between them. He saw that she had some sort of skin problem along her neck and up to her left ear, some of which she was trying to hide with one of her scarves.

"What about that change then?" she pulled him out of his inertness.

"You said you were hungry."

"What else do you expect me to do with the change?"

"Oh, there are endless possibilities." He was thinking of drugs. "But if you're really hungry I'll take you to MacDonald's."

"They wouldn't allow me in. Not people like me."

"All right then. What do you say if I go over there and get you a nice and juicy hamburger?"

"You'd just run away," she laughed in a derisive tone.

"Just wait and see," he said and walked away in the direction of the hamburger restaurant. Five minutes later he returned with a pack of junk food for her: a hamburger, chips and a large coke. She was still standing on the same spot. Obviously she had been waiting, half trusting him to come back with food.

"Here you are," he said as he handed her the pack.

"Thank you, you're a real gen'lm'n," she said and beamed at his face with her blue eyes. Then she sat down right there on the pavement and began to eat. He saw that she must have been really hungry, she devoured the food with such urge.

"You probably wonder what brings a woman down like this," she said between two bites. He noted that she had good manners, she did not speak with a full mouth.

"You don't have to feel obliged," he said and made a calming movement with both hands, palms down.

"You seem like a decent sort, after all. So I'm telling you."

"Not if you don't want to."

"I used to be on the right side of things. I had a job, I had money, I had kids. I even had some edication, like."

Peter wondered how long he ought to stay and listen to her. At the same time he wondered whether this was time wasted or time well-spent. What could this woman tell him? Perhaps it was not so much for his intellectual profit that he ought to stay on, but rather for her comfort. She was obviously enjoying his company.

"When I was left alone with my kids my friend Sally told me I'd do fine. 'Lucy,' she said – Lucy, that's me, you know – 'Lucy,' she said, 'you're such an able girl, you'll manage, you'll do fine'. And she was right, Sally was." She nodded her head to underline her proud statement.

"I'm sure you're doing fine," was all he managed to say.

"Sure enough, never on the wrong side of the law." And she took another bite of her hamburger.

Lucy went on about the good opinion everybody had of her, but it was impossible to get her to divulge any real information about her moving career. Moving it must have been, he thought. How different the world must have looked from her perspective! She was certain to store a huge memory of very significant events in her life. What if one tried to write down her biography? Why were only people who thought highly of themselves writing their autobiographies? Politicians, actresses, public figures, even footballers! What was going on in the mind of a person who came to the conclusion that his or her life story might be of significant interest to the public at large?

Then there was this almost hysterical urge to convince him that other people thought well of her. Had her self-respect been shattered so terribly that the good opinion of others mattered so much – not only her peers, but figures of relative authority like the postman, the policeman, her children's school teachers and even the old man who ran the newsagent's at Hammersmith tube station – that their opinion counted for so much in Lucy's life? She could be a sort of prototype of modern man. Wasn't our craze of consumerism really a way of craving for recognition? And wasn't her life-style in agreement with today's galloping neo-capitalism? Take what you can, and rely on the moral merits of your past?

Lucy had finished her meal and began to sing. He did not recognise her song, but he heard that she had a good voice. She must have had some professional training at one time in her life. Her intonation was perfect, the range of her alto voice considerable and her vibrato – or was it called tremolo? – betrayed a high standard of artistry.

"Thanks for the food, like," she said after her first song.

"And thank you for your song," he replied. "I think I've got to be pushing on now. Anyway, it was good to meet you. I wish you all the best."

"You never know, you never know," were Lucy's last words before she turned abruptly and crossed the street. Peter saw that she was steering towards a new victim, an elderly woman with a shopping-bag who was hesitating at the kerb.

Her turned in the direction of his friends' house. At the next corner he nearly stumbled over a stray dog that was crossing his path, but he managed to balance himself and walked on unharmed. As he was putting more and more distance between himself and Lucy he was gradually dismissing his former ruminations. He even felt a little ashamed of himself. How could he have been so gullible? Lucy was just a tramp, nothing more.

He decided to divert his thoughts away from Lucy and think of more pleasant and more important things. What would the evening be like? Then he thought of Emma. What an energetic young woman she was! She had set herself quite a steep programme for today. Rushing from place to place in her little Nissan. Thank God she was a good driver. Well, sometimes she went a little too fast, and sometimes she was a little too absent-minded while she was driving, thinking of her latest fashion-show or drafting her next article in her mind. He decided to talk to her about her car when he saw her next time. With all her rushing about, the speed she was going at and the distances she was covering she really needed a larger car. A safer car. That nippy little Nissan was all right for getting around town, for short-distance shopping trips and the like. What car should he recommend her then? Perhaps it would be a good idea to collect some brochures from the different agents and then let her decide.

When he arrived at Robert's house he had to ring twice before the door was opened. Robert looked strange, different, haggard. Something must have happened.

"What's the matter?" Peter asked.

Peter stepped into the hall. It was a very modern, elegantly appointed hall. Tiled floor, glass doors, bare metal frames and fixtures, indirect lighting, African art on the walls and a huge Inuit sculpture of the transformation type on a pedestal in one corner.

"I'm sorry, something's happened," Robert sighed.

"What is it?"

"She has left."

"Who?"

"My wife has left me."

PART SIX

Ivan

TWENTY-SIX

It is a grey and cool day when Ivan takes delivery of his new Toyota. He does not mind the weather, when it is time to take possession of a new car there is bright sunshine in his heart.

He arrives at the Toyota garage half an hour before the appointed time. He parks the Vauxhall in front of the customer service department, and as he locks it he is glad to get rid of it, it has not given him a great deal of joy.

The salesman is as suave as ever. Ivan tries to get rid of him as soon as possible. They have a quick look at the sales contract, which they both sign on the dotted line at the bottom, then the salesman gets up and dusts his creased trousers. Ivan notices that this dandy smells of a very heavy after-shave lotion.

"Let's step up to your new vehicle, Mr. MacGregor, and I'm going to explain all the controls and the functioning of the GPS to you."

"That's very kind of you," Ivan boldly counters, "but that won't be necessary, thank you very much."

"But Mr. MacGregor! This must be a great moment in your life. To take delivery of a new car. That's not exactly an every day event."

"I know, but I have to be off, I'm afraid I've got an important appointment. If that was all the paper work we had to go through just give me the keys and I'll manage all right."

After hesitating for a brief moment the man nervously dusts his lapel with the back of his left hand and stretches his right arm, intending to pat Ivan on his back. Very discreetly Ivan manages to avoid the man's clumsy attempt at false familiarity. For a split second he wonders if the man's behaviour could possibly be a sign of homosexuality, but he dismisses this notion immediately. At last the man hands him the new keys. Ivan mumbles a polite thank you and gets behind the wheel of his new car.

As he is driving out onto the main road he congratulates himself for the way he just managed to escape from the clutches of the sweet-smelling salesman. He grunts with pleasure as he accelerates. The torque at low revs is really quite stunning with these new diesel engines, he notes with satisfaction. He drives onto the M23, then the M25, hoping to get into the pleasant mood of his accustomed driving style. However, somehow the right feeling does not click in. He leaves the motorway at exit number 11, turns around and rejoins the motorway, this time driving east. He finds that driving has somehow lost its former attraction for him. It can no longer invest him with that feeling of satisfaction and superiority. He realizes that he is not even disappointed over this loss.

He decides to leave the motorway and drive over to Emma's flat. He knows she is normally at home on a Friday afternoon. At least he will have a certain pleasure in showing his new car to her.

She opens her door with a big smile and leads him into her flat. As they step into the living-room he realizes that she already has a visitor. An elderly man with an almost bald head, dark-rimmed glasses and a dashing moustache is sitting in one of the armchairs. He stands up and extends his right hand with a polite smile on his lips.

"I'm so pleased to make your acquaintance at last, Mr. MacGregor. Or may I call you Ivan? My name's Peter Hoffmann."

Ivan notices that the man has a small paunch. He wonders if he ought to give in to his impulse of immediate dislike.

"Yeah, Ivan will be okay with me," he answers, giving the man a quick smile, then turning to Emma. With raised eyebrows and a slight jerk of his head he indicates to her that he is somewhat puzzled about the presence of such a man in her flat. Particularly a man with such an air of familiarity. The old codger seems to feel quite at home in this flat.

"I can see how surprised you are to find me here," the man says in a friendly voice. "I'm a very old friend of Emma's. I knew her father and for a short time I was her guardian."

The two men sit down while Emma disappears to get a cup of coffee for Ivan from the kitchen. For a long period of thirty seconds the men stare at each other, the older man making every effort to keep his polite smile and Ivan narrowing his eyes. Then Ivan jerks his athletic body out of the armchair and walks to the kitchen.

"Why didn't you tell me you had an old friend like this?" he urgently whispers in Emma's ear.

"Come on, Ivan, hold your horses. I told you about my former guardian, you remember? That time in the hospital? He's just an old friend. Now go back and behave like a good boy."

Ivan is hurt. The tone of her 'good boy' is particularly irksome. But he walks back to the living-room and sits down.

"I say, Ivan," the man makes a fresh start, "Emma has told me a great deal about you. How you were ever so concerned when she was in a bad way after her accident, how you helped her ...oh yes, and how you even got her a new car. Very generous indeed, I must say. You're a very generous man, Ivan."

Ivan wonders how she could have told this man so much about him, but hardly so much about the man to himself. He looks down and spots a small breadcrumb on his left trouser-leg. He makes a small gesture to sweep it off.

"Oh, I felt I had to do it, I mean, after the accident."

He looks down at his trouser-leg again. The crumb is still there. He quickly wipes it off again.

"No no, not at all. Despite your involvement in the same accident there was no responsibility on your part, was there?"

Why can't he get rid of the crumb? It makes him nervous. This crumb is going to stick to him. He will be unable to discard it to his dying day, he fears.

"Listen, Mr. Hoffmann – "

"Call me Peter."

"I say, I'm at a loss to understand your attitude. What I consider to be my duty is certainly none of your business."

"Please, Ivan, don't be offended. I didn't mean to – "

"It's okay. I'm sorry."

Emma enters with Ivan's cup of coffee. They launch into some small talk and she makes every effort to improve the atmosphere, which remains tense in spite of her efforts. Ivan drains his cup, then takes his leave.

Emma walks him to the door. As they say good-bye she whispers, "That wasn't very friendly. Peter is really a very good old friend. He means a great deal to me."

Driving away, Ivan realizes he has forgotten to show her his new car. It doesn't seem important now. The new Toyota has lost its significance, the glamour of its new ownership has been overshadowed by his anger over this intruder in her flat.

Why has she never told him that her former guardian is really a very close friend? He means a great deal to her, so she says. It's hard to believe that a charming young woman like Emma can throw herself away like that. How can she? He is far too old for her. And then his bald head, his paunch, his quiet avuncular ways...

Ivan changes gears with energy. He punishes the Toyota's gearbox for Emma's apparent blindness.

Suddenly he imagines her having sex with the old chap. Tender and slim Emma with a smelly old man on top of her, a man with a flabby paunch and a bald head. The mere idea is too revolting, he dismisses the vision after a few seconds. Looking down on his lap he sees the breadcrumb still clinging to the material of his trousers, only a few inches further down his left leg.

In the evening he cannot stay in, he has to go out and get a few drinks. At the pub he tries to strike up a meaningless conversation with the girl behind the bar, but he soon gives up. He is on his second pint of London Pride when he sees the old man's face in his mind. For the first time he studies the memory of Peter's face. Now it strikes him that the face looks familiar. Has he seen the chap before? Certainly not in connection with Emma. But the more he reconstructs the image of the man in his mind the more he convinces himself that he has seen him somewhere before.

"Silly, I'm just imagining things," he mumbles to himself.

"What?" a voice on his right asks.

"Oh nothing, I was just talking to myself."

"Talk to me if it makes you feel better," the young man on his right offers.

"Thanks."

But Ivan is not interested in the young man. He drains his glass and leaves the pub. This thing about contact between human individuals, he thinks, is a very complex affair. Why can't he dismiss his worries about Emma and her relationship to this older man?

He drives into his garage when it suddenly strikes him that he could be jealous. Why jealous? Jealousy means he has designs on Emma for himself. Has he? Not really. He likes her, yes, he likes her company, her cheerful sense of humour…but he has never thought of her as a possible girlfriend. She is far too young for him. But why being jealous then? Is it because that man is even older than himself? Is it some archaic form of natural jealousy among males? The sort of thing that used to cause cavemen to slay other cavemen if they appeared more attractive? But then, is the man really more attractive than he is? No, but relatively speaking it is quite remarkable that he should be more successful with young Emma than he. But then he never tried, up to now the idea has never entered his head.

Sitting down in front of his computer in his flat, Ivan wants to check his e-mail inbox. But his heart is not in it. He wonders why he has never had an affair with a woman since the accident with Emma. He comes to the conclusion that it is not because he is in love with Emma, but because his mind has been too preoccupied with the business of looking after her. Strange. For the first time in so many months he realizes that he has to find his way back to his former interest in good-looking women. It might be a good idea to get himself a girlfriend again, then he could be more relaxed about Emma.

He starts a Google search, and within a surprisingly short time he has found an internet dating service which appeals to him. He enters his nickname. He chooses 'Tchaikovsky', but that is already taken, and besides it is too long. So he tries 'Navi58' – his name spelt backwards and his year – and this is accepted by the system. After entering his personal identification number he can fill in his own profile – age, height, weight, level of education, interests and a few more details plus what sort of woman he is looking for, then he can browse through a list of seventy different women who fit the profile. He takes a long time looking at their photos – he has not uploaded a picture of himself, he wants to see first – and their descriptions of themselves. There is a broad variety, 'young, energetic, fun-loving'; 'excellent cook'; 'just recovered from a broken heart'; 'only serious enquiries'; 'looking for a spicy adventure'; 'more on the quiet side'. Endless descriptions.

He finds a friendly face that appeals to him. She has a smiling round face and wavy fair hair. In her picture she is sitting on a sofa, leaning forward towards the camera. She calls herself Frances and gives her age as forty-five. There are several options that the system offers him. He can send her a virtual kiss – what a crazy oddity of today's digital age! – or a text message on her mobile phone, or an e-mail, or he can add her to his virtual 'list of friends'. He chooses to send her a text message. *Hello Frances,* he types, *my name is Ivan, I am 49y, good-looking, wld like to get to know you.* He clicks 'send'. Then he tries to write an e-mail message for her, but when he clicks 'send e-mail' the system tells him that this option is only for premium members, which means he will have to pay the system £100 to obtain this status for a period of three months.

"What a dirty trick," he says to himself, and he decides to send her a virtual kiss instead.

This works. Hardly has the system told him that his kiss was sent off when his mobile phone, which he has left in his jacket pocket, signals the arrival of a text message. He gets up from the computer and reaches for his mobile phone.

Dear Ivan, thank you for making this contact. Your profile appeals to me. I would like to know more about you. Where do you live? Are you free, or do you live with a partner? Looking forward to your answer, Frances. And there is a postscript: *£2,00 per message.*

"Now, that was quick," he thinks, "she must be online at this very moment, and she must be a very deft user of the keypad." He is not so quick himself, so it takes him some time to type in his answer. But even before he has completed his short message, the phone beeps again. *He reads: I am really very keen. Why don't you answer. Have you got cold feet? Waiting for you, Frances.*

This is really strange. Can a woman be so eager? He becomes suspicious. Could this be a fake message? He decides to put it to the test. He types: *Dear Frances, I am as keen as you. If you are real, please contact me from your real number, no longer through this expensive system.* He gives her his own number, then punches on 'send'.

Within the next hour he receives three further text messages from 'Frances', reminding him to text her back, pleading with him, enticing him, but never divulging either her own real phone number or any further revealing information about herself. She only talks about how much she would like to meet him and what an interesting man he is.

He knows he has been fooled. How disgusting to operate such a dating system! And how typical of this day and age! People are so lonely, they are prepared to walk into such traps every day. Imagine someone believing these messages and sending in his own answers again and again…and then the huge phone bill!

But he does not give up. Very carefully he goes through several other virtual dating agencies. Eventually he finds one where he can exchange messages and e-mails with potential partners, they are only limited to five messages before he will have to pay his 'premium membership', which will allow him more contacts. He decides to try it again with this system. After going through a similar procedure as the one in the previous system he finally reaches a stage where he can actually exchange some information with a real woman. She answers with concrete information about herself, and since they have five messages before they will have to make up their minds for a costly membership they can really get to know quite a lot about each other. Her name is Samantha, she is forty-two years old, lives in Swindon and works as a secretary in a large law firm. They just manage to exchange their real phone numbers before the deadline.

"Success, at last," he cries, and when he looks at his watch he sees that he has spent more than five hours at the computer. He has a good feeling about Samantha. At the back of his mind he wonders whether Frances was really a fake profile. Or was she just too shy? No, it could not be, because no woman would pursue an unknown man with repeated messages like that, and then there was the speed of her initial replies. Impossible. Yes, he will build his hopes on Samantha.

During breakfast on the following day his landline telephone rings.

"Hello, Ivan, it's Peter Hoffmann. How are you today?"

"Oh, hello."

Silence for three seconds. Ivan wonders how to communicate with him.

"Ivan, I'd like to meet you. I think we should talk. What do you think?"

"What is there to talk about?"

"Emma."

"I see. Well, what do you suggest?"

Peter gives him the address of a café near Trafalgar Square. "Can you be there at four? Or would you prefer a bit later?"

"Four is fine," Ivan agrees and quickly terminates their conversation. He feels strangely nervous. "What can he have to say to me?" he asks the blank wall in front of his nose.

When he enters the café he sees Peter sitting at a table in the corner, reading a book by Rohinton Mistry. They shake hands and exchange a few friendly remarks. Ivan orders a large cup of cappuccino.

"So, about Emma," Peter opens the sensitive subject. "I don't know exactly how you feel about her, and I don't know what your intentions are with regard to her. But I would like to talk to you in order to avoid any disappointments, and just to make a few things clear."

Ivan wipes across his forehead with the back of his left hand. "Well…yes…go on."

"Ivan, you are a generous and intelligent man."

"Never mind about my qualities."

"Please, don't take offence. I just want to be friendly. What I mean is, well, you seem to be the sort of man who can appreciate a person's merits and who can understand complex situations. And I would like you to understand Emma's situation for what it is. As I told you before, she means a lot to me. So I don't want her to get involved in situations that she can't handle in the end."

"Come to the point," Ivan urges.

"There is no point, really. What I want you to understand is the fact that Emma is a very important person. She is the daughter of a very dear friend of mine who passed away a few years ago. He asked me to look after her, as her guardian, until she came of age, and I have become very attached to her."

"But she no longer needs a guardian now, does she?"

"Of course not. But I still feel responsible for her, in a way."

"That makes two of us." Ivan realizes he has been smiling. He does not want to smile at this man. All right, he has agreed to call him Peter and to accept the fact that he is connected with Emma, but he still doesn't have to like him particularly. Probably he wants her for himself, so he is warning off any potential rival.

Peter goes on talking about Emma's merits, her fine character, her hopes for a good career in script-writing, and finally he manages to convince Ivan that, as friends of hers, they should be friends, too. They part shaking hands, and they agree to meet again a few days later. When Ivan walks away from the café he admits to himself that Peter does not seem to be such a bad guy, after all. Besides, Ivan knows he has no amorous intentions with her, she's just not that sort of woman for him, and she's far too young.

Sitting down in his armchair in the evening he reviews his situation. For the first time in months he allows himself to examine his relationship with Emma in a critical light. He sees that his interest in her has been a little exaggerated, a little uncalled for, a little cryptic if judged from the outside. He remembers several extremely memorable moments in his life. There was that dying woman in Finchley Road, there was the mystic experience of the solar eclipse in France, there was that old man with the dog in Brighton. What have all those experiences been able to teach him? Or is it wrong to think that we can learn from certain memorable experiences, from events that have touched us in a special way?

He decides to abandon his former plan of opposing Peter. He intended to devise some intricate plot to estrange Emma from him, but now he has arrived at the conclusion that he should not interfere. If Emma and Peter are good friends he must accept it. She is a grown woman who knows what she is doing. Peter could even be honest. Ivan admits to himself that the vision of Peter as her lover has probably emerged from his own secret wishes, because he has not been intimate with a woman for such a long time. But even without the possible existence of Samantha he knows that he never ever looked at Emma as a potential lover. He still cannot explain his interest in her, but he knows it is there. They are still connected by the accident.

Now that he has allowed himself to be tolerant about Peter's interest in her he finds it a lot easier to meet with him again. It is a cloudy but friendly day when they meet at a pub near Dorking. They sit down at one of the rickety wooden tables, Peter orders a plate of garlic mushrooms and Ivan decides for the soup of the day with a bread-roll.

Peter detects the slight improvement in their relationship at once. He beams at Ivan through his glasses and shows him his best smile. "I'm glad you feel more relaxed today," he remarks.

"Yes, I was under a great stress the last time."

Their food arrives. They take a few bites in silence, then Peter raises his glass.

"Here's to our common friend, Emma," he pronounces in a ceremonial manner.

"Yes, here's to her, and a good girl she is," says Ivan.

"Indeed she is."

This ceremony has made things clear. Peter understands that Ivan has abandoned his critical attitude. They can become friends.

"I really thought you wanted her for yourself," Ivan says.

Peter is so surprised he spits out a mushroom. "Now, that's a thing that's never occurred to me! How could you? I'm old enough to be her father, nearly her grandfather."

"Yes, I can see that. But then, so could I, couldn't I?"

They laugh.

"You see, Ivan, I was there when her mother died, and – "

Suddenly it hits Ivan like a bombshell. Of course! That's why the man looked slightly familiar. "Don't you remember me then?" he asks.

"What do you mean?"

"Finchley Road, the bank robbery, do you remember? I think I gave you my handkerchief."

"You are – ?"

"Yes, we were both there."

"Well, I never! Yes, indeed, now that I look at your face again. But you have changed."

"So have you."

"This calls for another pint," Peter says and makes a sign at the barman over his left shoulder.

While they wait for their pints they look at each other in silence, trying to recognise each other again after all those years. Then Ivan takes a bite from his roll. Instinctively he looks down at his lap, expecting to have to wipe off a breadcrumb from his trouser-leg. But his lap is as clean as new. If there ever was a breadcrumb it's gone now.

The two men continue with their meal, and Peter tells Ivan a great deal about Emma and about her father. When they leave the pub two hours later, Ivan is impressed by Peter's knowledge, about what he would call his sense of history. Peter has told him about his photographic moments, about how things changed over the years and about how his experiences shaped his life, his viewpoint, the way he now approaches the world.

"I have experienced mediocrity, I have experienced extreme pain and pleasure, and I have experienced the cruelty of death. There is still a great deal that I don't know. For example, I am still struggling to understand the female psyche, and of course I have still not discovered the secret of love."

Ivan is impressed. His own life seems so void and futile

besides Peter's. He will endeavour to live with a higher intensity of consciousness. Of that he is convinced.

EPILOGUE

Peter and Ivan get out of the car first, then Peter opens the door for Emma. The air is crisp, birdsong in the distance, a tired breeze in the poplars along the car-park. Ivan expects to smell the typical odour of graveyards, a somewhat romantic expectation, he admits, but he has to accept that there is no such thing as a typical odour about a place like this.

The black wrought-iron gate to the large cemetery is open. They slowly walk between the two stone pillars, the pebbles in the footpath crunching beneath their feet. Ivan carries a large bouquet of chrysanthemums in his right hand.

"It's a good thing you could make it," Ivan says to Emma.

"Yes, I nearly missed you. There was that colleague of mine from the magazine, Aysha, who just wouldn't stop entreating me to come to some fashion-show with her. She wanted me to see how fashion worked as a channel to more social mobility among Muslim women. I said I would come with her some other time. Only, she was so persistent."

"But you got rid of her," Peter says.

"Yes. But as I said, I will deal with her view of things some other time. I won't forget, she deserves it, she's such a good sort."

They walk on in silence.

When they reach the grave, Ivan bends down and places the bouquet on the bare ground between the headstone and the evergreens.

"Hi, Mum," Emma says in an even but cheerful voice. "We've come here to tell you that everything is fine. Don't worry about me. These two men have both seen you leave this earth, so they are your friends, too."

The men smile.

They remain standing in silence for a while. Then they slowly walk away.

"I wonder what secrets she took to her grave with her," Emma whispers. "There is so much that the older generation knows but never tells. What will my life teach me, I wonder?"

The path crunches, a dog barks in the distance.